Praise For

Genevieve Graham

"Genevieve Graham has produced another winner in this nostalgic sojourn to the 1960s. *On Isabella Street* is a deeply thought-provoking novel set against the backdrop of the deinstitutionalization of mental health care in the twentieth century (the ripple effects of which are still felt to this day). Through evident in-depth research, Graham highlights Canada's complex role in the Vietnam War, as well as the experiences of women fighting to forge unconventional paths for themselves in an era still struggling to accept women's liberation. A snapshot of a city teetering on the precipice of massive socio-cultural change, Graham's latest work explores themes of freedom and choice, and reminds us that there are lessons to be learned from those who see the world through a different lens than ourselves."

HEATHER MARSHALL, #1 bestselling author of *Looking for Jane* and *The Secret History of Audrey James*

"*On Isabella Street* is vivid and remarkable, a profound story rich in historical detail that brings the vibrant unrest of the late sixties alive, sweeping the reader from the coffee houses of Yorkville, Toronto, to the jungles of Vietnam. An uplifting novel on the impact of war on families and relationships and the power of love to transcend all. Genevieve Graham has a rare gift—immersing the reader in a time and place in the past and making it all so immediate. I couldn't take my eyes off this incredibly moving story."

MAIA CARON, bestselling author of *The Last Secret*

"*On Isabella Street* unearths Canada's entanglement in the Vietnam War, set against the backdrop of a Toronto caught in the throes of post-war transformation. Genevieve Graham's remarkable gift for uncovering Canada's unsung histories is matched by an immersive, deeply sincere storytelling style that uniquely captures the female experience."

ELLEN KEITH, bestselling author of *The Dutch Orphan*

"The incomparable Genevieve Graham has done it again, weaving two disparate chapters in Canadian history—our unrecognized involvement in the Vietnam War, and the mid-century movement to discharge patients from mental hospitals—into another captivating work of fact-based fiction. Not only did I enjoy the engaging characters and the strong storyline, but after finishing the book I could not stop thinking about it."

ELINOR FLORENCE, bestselling author of *Finding Flora*

ON ISABELLA STREET

ALSO BY GENEVIEVE GRAHAM

The Secret Keeper

Bluebird

Letters Across the Sea

The Forgotten Home Child

At the Mountain's Edge

Come from Away

Promises to Keep

Tides of Honour

Somewhere to Dream

Sound of the Heart

Under the Same Sky

ON ISABELLA STREET

GENEVIEVE GRAHAM

Published by Simon & Schuster

New York   Amsterdam/Antwerp   London
Toronto   Sydney/Melbourne   New Delhi

SIMON &
SCHUSTER
CANADA

A Division of Simon & Schuster, LLC
166 King Street East, Suite 300
Toronto, Ontario M5A 1J3

This book is a work of fiction. Any references to historical events, real people, or real places are used fictitiously. Other names, characters, places, and events are products of the author's imagination, and any resemblance to actual events or places or persons, living or dead, is entirely coincidental.

This Simon & Schuster Canada edition April 2025

SIMON & SCHUSTER CANADA and colophon are trademarks of Simon & Schuster, LLC

Simon & Schuster strongly believes in freedom of expression and stands against censorship in all its forms. For more information, visit BooksBelong.com.

For information about special discounts for bulk purchases, please contact Simon & Schuster Special Sales at 1-800-268-3216 or CustomerService@simonandschuster.ca.

Interior design by Erika R. Genova

Manufactured in the United States of America

1 3 5 7 9 10 8 6 4 2

Library and Archives Canada Cataloguing in Publication:
Title: On Isabella Street / by Genevieve Graham.
Names: Graham, Genevieve, author
Description: Simon & Schuster Canada edition.
Identifiers: Canadiana (print) 20240460820 | Canadiana (ebook) 20240460839 | ISBN 9781982197018 (softcover) | ISBN 9781982197025 (EPUB)
Subjects: LCGFT: Novels.
Classification: LCC PS8613.R3434 O52 2025 | DDC C813/.6—dc23
ISBN 978-19821-9701-8
ISBN 978-19821-9702-5 (ebook)

To the "Unknown Veterans," and to everyone in need of a home.
And always, to Dwayne.

In Vietnam, you didn't have to be related by blood to be family. The guys I served with were my brothers, and we always had each other's backs.

—MICHAEL THOMPSON, VIETNAM VETERAN

PART ONE

There is no touchstone . . . which reveals the true character of a social philosophy more clearly than the spirit in which it regards the misfortunes of those of its members who fall by the way.

—R. H. Tawney, *Religion and the Rise of Capitalism*

one

MARION

❧

— May 1967 —

Marion Hart glanced up from the thick old textbook, distracted by voices beyond the window of the Sigmund Samuel Library. An hour before, she'd noticed four or five students hanging around out there, wrapped in a rainbow of ponchos and patched jean jackets, accessorized by sunglasses, cigarettes, and signs. Now there were about a dozen of them, and their volume had risen with their numbers.

She rubbed her burning eyes, worn out by tiny print, then set her pen aside. Leaning back in her chair, she scanned the familiar placards outside. Dotted by peace signs, hearts, and flowers, their slogans demanded, END THE WAR! GET OUT OF VIETNAM! CANADA WANTS PEACE! She spotted a large LOVE sign painted in luminous orange, outlined in red, and framed by a scattering of cheery daisies. A young man, his crown of brown curls only partially restrained by a bright yellow headband, had taken control with a bullhorn. He was bellowing something Marion couldn't make out, but the crowd evidently heard. They raised their arms and cheered joyfully in response.

The 1960s were all about change, and that was even more noticeable this year. For someone like Marion, quietly studying within the walls of the university, there was so much to observe. All over the world, eager young fists grasped at fresh ideas and opportunities while shaking with disapproval at The Man. *All will be solved*, those young people swore, *through peace, harmony, and free love*. If only they didn't have to make a living.

Marion was quietly envious of the kids outside her window and their enthusiastic approach to the world. Throughout her youth, including the past few years she'd studied at the University of Toronto Medical School, she had not once stood up to the status quo, though her presence there had challenged it. She had accepted early in her education that, as a woman, her questions and arguments would rarely be addressed by her male professors or fellow students. As a result, she had spent most of her time with her head in books, shutting out the rest of the class. What mattered was attaining her degree and becoming a practicing physician, not drawing attention to herself, and certainly not pointing out the shortcomings of her colleagues.

It wasn't until fourth year, when Dr. Reginald Perkins came to teach medical ethics and economics, that she dared to lift her gaze from the page. Marion had been awestruck by Dr. Perkins's eye-opening approach to medicine. He taught the practical topics, like medical economics and the pitfalls of running a practice, but he also led them beyond the textbooks, discussing the bond of a physician to his patients, other doctors, and society as a whole. One of her favourite lectures addressed how doctors should communicate with patients during difficult times, such as discussing a terminal diagnosis. At present, a woman received news of her own condition and prognosis secondhand, *after* her husband had been told. Dr. Perkins had startled the class by suggesting that approach should change. Either the woman should learn about her own illness first, he said, or the couple should be told at the same time. That had roused quite a discussion. They also deliberated over contentious issues like organ transplants, birth control, abortion, and euthanasia. The lessons were vital, she believed, because society was undergoing massive shifts and the health-care system had to as well. She was disappointed that Dr. Perkins's four one-hour sessions were "recommended" but not mandatory, and that they weren't graded. They deserved more weight than that.

Marion graduated with a degree in medicine in 1965, one of a handful of female doctors in a class that was 90 per cent men. After graduation, she earned a position at the Ontario Hospital, formerly the Hospital for the Insane, becoming the only woman doctor in the building. She was proud of that accomplishment, but without female classmates, she got a little lonely sometimes.

Then again, Marion was used to solitude. She and her sister had always been disconnected, with Pat preferring a social life to the classroom. Their father carried mental scars from his time in the war, and though he was perfectly able to speak of other things, any mention of his service made him close up like a clam. Their mother was also private. Though she was a loving woman, she rarely expressed her feelings in words. Marion was used to her parents' companionable silences, and she was comfortable with that volume most of the time. Once in a while, though, it would be nice to have someone to talk with outside of lecture halls and hospital corridors.

Beyond the library window, a young woman in the little group shook a tambourine over her head like a gypsy dancing, bringing a jangly cheer to the afternoon. She was tiny, a little slip of a thing with long blond hair like Marion's, but hers was twisted into two loose braids interlaced with red ribbons then folded back on top of themselves like puppy ears. It was such a carefree, feminine touch. Marion couldn't imagine herself having the nerve to wear her own hair like that. Fun, but not her style.

Except sometimes she wished it was.

Who was the girl? she wondered, feeling a familiar twinge of envy. How had she met the others in the group? How had they introduced themselves in the beginning? She understood how it worked with group therapy. In those situations, she sat with patients and carefully drew out their thoughts, helping them get to know each other. Real life was different. And so much more muddled. What did these kids do when they weren't wandering around with signs and placards? Who were they as individuals, and how had they achieved such natural confidence in themselves, the women painting their faces with peace signs, the men growing their hair past their shoulders? This generation had leapt into the surging waters of revolution and protest, while Marion stood on the shoreline in her sensible shoes, studying them as they sailed past. What gave some people that kind of courage but left others, like her, without?

She guessed she was about ten years older than the kids in the group. She'd grown up just ahead of the colourful activists, one ear listening to their protests and the other hearing the criticism of the older generation. "Hippies," they called them, or "scum." To the establishment, this generation was no longer a troublesome group of rabble-rousing children; they were adults who refused to grow up. They made a lot of noise but no money. And their numbers were swelling now that they included tens of thousands of American draft dodgers, hiding anonymously within Canada.

The older generation called them "parasites," but Marion disagreed with that term. The flower children might make life a little more challenging for those who did not like or want change, but she didn't agree with the name-calling. She peered out the window and read their handwritten signs again. There was nothing parasitic about love and peace.

The May sun blazed invitingly through the library window, and she reminded herself that today was a holiday. She had planned to do something unrelated to work, but she hadn't figured out what yet. With a sigh, she closed her books and slid them into her black briefcase, resigned to the fact that she wasn't going to get any more work done today.

It was cooler outside than it looked, but it was such a nice day, she decided to walk home instead of taking the bus. She wrapped her grey wool cardigan tight around her body as she crossed the campus, hearing the clatter of the tambourine up ahead. She spotted the happy little parade strolling toward Queen's Park. That was Marion's direction as well, so she caught up and followed in its wake.

The row of cars parked at the side of the busy street was an unusual sight. Some passengers had even gotten out and were leaning against their vehicles, their attention drawn by something in the park.

"What is it?" she asked the first man she came upon.

"Those long-haired freaks. Dancing and singing. Do they call that music? Look." He pointed. "Does that one there even have a shirt on?"

Marion squeezed past him and lifted onto her toes so she could see. The girl in question was in the middle of a small gathering a few feet away, whirling to music Marion couldn't hear.

"She's wearing a dress," she told him. "It's beige, so it appears as if she's naked, see?"

"She's on LSD or something," he grumbled. "Spinning like a lunatic."

Marion pursed her lips in disapproval, stopping short of correcting the old-fashioned term. It was her personal mission to remove the words *insane* and *lunacy* from the public's vocabulary, but this man had already turned to talk with someone else.

"Maybe she's just having a good time," she said anyway.

To Marion's left, the brightly coloured troop from the university continued into Queen's Park. The curly-headed youth with the bullhorn cheered the group on, past the gawking audience by the cars.

"Bunch of reprobates!" someone shouted.

"Go home!"

"Get a job!"

"I love you!" the tambourine girl sang back, blowing a kiss to the crowd.

Curious about their destination, Marion tagged onto the end of the procession, but when they reached the huge stretch of grass in front of the Ontario Legislative Building, she forgot all about them. The park was teeming with people like the group she'd followed, sitting, standing, and dancing, using placards for shade. There had to be thousands of them. She had suspected something was going on due to the skunky odour hovering over the grounds, but she'd never imagined anything this big.

Feedback squawked from a microphone, briefly overwhelming the throng, and she noted a large stage set up at the end of the park. A man introduced someone, but his mouth was so close to the microphone Marion couldn't understand what he said. Then he stepped back, and a woman took his place, her long black hair spilling over the guitar in her arms. The crowd rose as one, applauding and cheering, then growing quiet with anticipation.

"Thank you," the performer purred, gentle as a breeze. "Thank you, everyone. My name is Buffy Sainte-Marie, and I'd like to sing you something I wrote called 'Universal Soldier.'"

A cheer exploded from the crowd, and Marion set down her bag to listen to the words. She didn't know the song, but Miss Sainte-Marie's voice was clear, and Marion liked hearing the probing questions and the message of personal responsibility. She'd heard a lot of angry lyrics lately, and there were plenty in this song. Every generation wanted to be heard, and this one was especially demanding. She wished Miss Sainte-Marie would play something more cheerful or contemplative, like "Blowin' in the Wind." That's the kind of melody Marion preferred. One could always find a reason to be angry, but it was important to be grateful and hopeful as well.

Marion scanned the crowd, thinking her sister would fit in well. Marion didn't think Pat smoked pot, but she did enjoy the music, the fashion, and the rebellious momentum behind the protests. It made sense that this was her world, since Pat had always been the hip sister, the younger and more beautiful of the two, and the life of every party. A cheerleader who, straight out of high school ten years ago, had married the quarterback of the football team and become the envy of every girl in her graduating class. When he inherited a small fortune, Pat had become—in her own words—"the expensive candy" on her wealthy husband's arm. The kind of woman who sunbathed on the front lawn of her large brick house without a care in the world. She'd recently cut her golden hair into the latest style: a bob with heavy bangs that tickled her false eyelashes. She tucked it behind her ears so everyone could see her diamond earrings glitter in the sunlight.

All of that was fine, Marion thought. Good for her. But she didn't like how Pat continued to preach to her, and to anyone who would listen, about the importance of women's independence. Marion wasn't sure if her sister saw the irony.

"Everything a man can do, a woman can do better," Pat liked to say. "Think about it. We don't even need men anymore, now that artificial insemination is available."

"Well, artificial *semen* is not," Marion replied flatly. "Women cannot live without men. We might want to sometimes, but men take care of a lot of things we can't do."

"That's silly, Marion. We can do anything a man can do. Name one job I can't do."

"You've never had a job in your life."

Pat rolled her eyes. "We're not talking about that. Name one job I couldn't do that a man can."

"Just one?" Marion started counting on her fingers: "Build a bridge, dig tunnels for the subway, install plumbing, fix a car, carry a piano . . . Want me to go on?"

"Those don't count."

"Why not? Are those jobs not vital? Maybe not the piano carrying, but the rest are."

Pat thought it through. "Well, if we were *trained*, we could do those things, but they wouldn't pay as us much. And women should be paid equally for doing them."

"I agree," Marion said, "as long as the women are accomplishing the same."

Pat scowled. "How would we know if that's possible? Women aren't even given the opportunity to accomplish things. Male chauvinism exists, Marion. Men don't want to work with us, so they put up barricades. They think the workplace is their territory alone, and we belong barefoot in the kitchen."

"I'll give you that," Marion said reluctantly. "But chauvinism and bigotry are manageable. It all depends on if you let it get to you or not."

"Manageable? We shouldn't have to deal with it at all!"

"Of course not. But look at all the progress women have made over the past fifty years."

"We don't beat our laundry against rocks in the river anymore, if that's what you mean. And sure, we can vote, but this is still a man's world. I mean, look at you. How many women were even admitted to that medical school? If we can't get the degrees, we can't get hired, and we can't do the work."

Marion knew that all too well, but she wasn't ready to concede the argument to Pat, since she had never had a job or gone to college. Her sister was right, of course. All her life, Marion had encountered chauvinism at every turn. Throughout medical school, most of her professors had dismissed or discouraged her, and male students either kept their distance or suggested doing a different kind of "homework" with her. The prejudice against Marion and every other woman in those classrooms, then in the Ontario Hospital itself, was exhausting. It didn't seem to matter how well she did something; it wasn't enough. So many mornings she'd gone to work, done everything she was supposed to do and more, then had her pride squashed by a random catcall in the hallway or a discouraging, narrow-minded remark from her prehistoric boss, Dr. Bernstein. Their message was the same: she did not belong in their hallowed halls. What was a woman doing, they scoffed, working elbow-deep in blood and bone, when she should be cleaning her house or preparing dinner for her husband?

The truth was, Marion could probably bake a soufflé better than any of their mothers or wives, and her apartment was spotless. She assumed a husband and family would come eventually, but that had never been her priority.

"Like you said," she replied, "look at me. I am where I am because I wanted it too much to give up. The only way to achieve acceptance in the workplace, and therefore equal pay, is to work harder than the men."

Pat turned her face to the sky and made a sound of frustration. "News flash, Marion. Working harder than men for equal pay is not equality. And not everyone has the kind of determination you had. You've always wanted to be a doctor. Most women aren't like you. A lot of them just want to work without being treated harshly. Why should we have to fight every step of the way?"

"Because that's what it takes. Things are changing, though."

"Way too slowly."

"One step at a time. It will get better. In the meantime, women have to toughen up. We need to be better than the men, like I said. Every day, I remind myself of that."

Pat's nostrils flared with disdain. "Well, aren't you special?"

"I do what I have to do in order to get what I want. Not such a difficult concept."

"You are too intense, Marion. Lighten up. You know what else? You work hard so you barely know what's going on in the rest of the world. Being a doctor is all you know now."

Marion blinked. "That's rude."

"No, it's true. Sorry, but you have blinders on. Look up from your text-books and take a look around. Life is to be lived."

Pat and her perfect family were in Montreal now, celebrating Canada's centennial at Expo 67. The postcards she sent were fascinating, and a part of Marion was sorry she'd turned down Pat's invitation to go. She'd put on those blinders again, choosing responsibility over adventure.

But what Marion did was important, too. People needed their doctors to be focused and effective. Other people were Marion's priority. She picked up her bag and turned toward home.

"Maybe you can live that way," she murmured to her absent sister, "but I can't."

She envied the hippies their freedom, and she envied her sister her com-fortable life, but not enough to change her own. Marion had been a healer since childhood, supplying Band-Aids, pulling splinters from her friends' fingers, and providing a shoulder to lean on whenever required. All Marion had ever wanted was to be a doctor. She'd never really thought about what that might entail until she was starting high school and she overheard one of the boys talking about his brother, who was one year away from enrolling at the University of Toronto in medicine.

"Four thousand dollars?" she gasped. There was no way her parents could afford that kind of tuition. Her father was a busy plumber, but there wasn't nearly enough money coming in to pay for that.

"What's it to you?" one of the boys asked. "It's not like you gotta pay for it. You won't be going to med school."

"It just seems like a lot. What about scholarships? Government grants?"

He lifted a lip in a sneer. "Not that it's any of your business, but my par-ents are looking into it."

After school that day, Marion marched to the local grocer's and asked for a job. They started her in the back room, but it wasn't long before her intelligence and organizational skills became obvious to the owner and she was moved up to cashier, where she was paid $1.50 per hour. Every payday, she dropped her money into a coffee tin that she placed under her bed.

On the last day of school, she carried almost $300 into the kitchen and set it on the table for her parents to see. Their eyebrows had shot up at the sight, then she told them she wanted it all to go toward university so that she could be a real doctor one day. Her parents exchanged a look.

"You should be very proud of yourself, Marion," her mother said.

"Oh, I am," she replied. "And I will do this every year."

"My dear girl," her father said, beaming. "We'll put this in your bank account, where it'll make a little interest."

"But Marion," her mother continued, "keep your options open. You just completed grade nine, which means you have four years ahead of you. While you learn, consider other options for a career. Becoming a doctor is a great deal of work, and because of all its demands, it might be difficult to have a family of your own one day."

"I don't want a family of my own," Marion told her. "I want to be a doctor."

"Think about nursing."

Marion crossed her arms, annoyed by her mother's apparent lack of faith.

Her father observed the conversation with a gentle smile. "Your mother's right. Becoming a doctor is very difficult. But if, at the end of high school, you still want to go to medical school, we will support your decision."

When Marion presented her final coffee jar at the end of grade thirteen, her parents congratulated her on her hard work, as well as the scholarship she had won. Then they told her that they had been planning for her tuition for years.

"We've always known you would want to go to university. It has already been paid for," her mother said, pleased.

At first, Marion had been upset. "All that work, and you never needed any of the money? Why didn't you stop me?"

Her father grinned. "How many of the other girls at school already have more than fifteen hundred dollars in their bank accounts?"

She didn't touch the bank account until the fall, when she was to start at the University of Toronto. She realized early on that the daily bus ride to and from school would be exhausting, so she decided to spend her money on renting an apartment. When they realized she was determined, her father told her he had a friend who owned an apartment building downtown. She never met the man in person, but he gave her an amazing deal on the rent, which meant she was able to spend all her time studying, not working at another grocery store.

Marion's favourite place to be was in the hospital emergency room on a busy day, which she supposed was a little ironic. She wasn't generally comfortable in hectic situations; however, she was very good at what she did, and being in almost total control in the middle of a storm—as she always was at the operating table—was the opposite of chaos. It was power.

It turned out that life had different plans for her. When it was time for Marion to choose her specialty—emergency surgery—she had fallen ill with double pneumonia that evolved into septicemia, which kept her in hospital for two months. As a result of missing so much practical training, she had not qualified for a position in emergency medicine.

Once she moved past that setback, it dawned on Marion that she wasn't entirely locked out of the medical field. With this disappoinment another door had opened. For a long time, she'd been considering another specialty. One that was a bit closer to home.

But her focus shifted from the body to the brain. More specifically, to psychiatry and the spectrum of mental, emotional, and behavioural disorders.

Marion's father had seen action overseas in the last war. Once, as a child, she had asked him for stories about his experiences, but he firmly refused to talk about that time. Later that afternoon, she'd discovered him curled up on the floor behind the furnace, violently shaking and not making sense when he spoke. He hadn't remembered where he was until she called her mother for help. After that, Marion observed her father retreating to the basement more and more, withdrawing to a place so remote even his wife couldn't find him sometimes.

As a child, she'd been frustrated by his strange behaviour. And embarrassed for him.

As Marion got older, she noticed other veterans around the city, many of whom were on crutches or in wheelchairs. But there were others, more difficult to discern, like her father, who either stood like statues or wandered aimlessly, shouting at shadows. Even now, more than twenty years later, her father sometimes went days without speaking to anyone. It was obvious to Marion that the war might be over, but her father still fought the enemy.

As a daughter, Marion was concerned but reluctantly accepting of his strange ways.

As a psychiatrist, she was intrigued. She wanted to know more. Her body might have failed her when it came to working in the emergency room, but her brain never gave up. As soon as her fever broke in her hospital bed and she was able to think clearly, she dove into her psychiatry textbooks and graduated at the top of her class.

In the end, she'd surprised herself by how much she enjoyed studying psychiatry. The field had undergone so much change over the past twenty years, moving from drastic, often violent "treatments" to very interesting talk- and medicine-based care. There were many new, effective therapies and drugs available now, and she was fascinated by it all.

Marion spent whatever spare time she could find studying surgical procedures and attending classes as an auditor, keeping on top of everything she would need to know if the opportunity to get her hand on a scalpel ever arose again. Near the corner of Jarvis and Isabella, Marion arrived at the white-brick apartment building she called home, its lawn brightened by two forsythia bushes in full bloom. Blossoms of all kinds had awakened throughout the city, like the daffodils and crocuses popping up in greening yards. She stepped past a cheerful cluster of candy-apple-red tulips along the front walkway then reached for the door. The hinges groaned as she pulled it open, a sound so familiar it had almost come to feel like a greeting. Inside the entry on her right was the mail room, but she walked past without looking. It was Victoria Day—Queen Victoria's birthday—so no delivery today. At the bank of three elevators, she pressed the button. When the one on the left arrived with a rattle and a clunk, she pressed 5 then leaned against the back wall, riding the familiar rocking motion of the box as it climbed.

Marion had never been entirely comfortable with the elevator, or with heights themselves. Originally, she had asked the building manager if he had any apartments available on a lower floor. He didn't, but at least she wasn't up top, on the eleventh storey. Over time she adjusted to the altitude, even come to enjoy the decadent solitude the balcony provided. From her apartment halfway up 105 Isabella Street, she could hear the honking of cars and the occasional shout bouncing off walls, but they were distant. Especially at night.

At the fifth floor the elevator lurched to a stop, and Marion felt the oddly pleasant sensation of her stomach rolling with it. She stepped into the hallway and turned toward her apartment.

The door to her left clicked open then closed.

"Good afternoon," she said to 509's door. As usual, there was no response. Marion had never met the mysterious man within, but she had put together a mental image of him: older, solitary, and tight with nerves. Almost every time the elevator arrived, his door opened a couple of inches, then shut. Mr. Snoop—a nickname Marion had given him—either considered himself to be the watchdog of the floor, or he was just plain nosy.

She followed the hallway's burgundy-coloured carpet and ivory striped wallpaper, somewhat yellowed by the effects of time and cigarette smoke. As she dug her key from her purse, she passed two apartments on either side. At 512, she turned right and unlocked the door, still humming.

"Hi, Chester." She crouched to greet the black and white cat winding around her ankles. "Did you miss me?"

His response rumbled through his chest, warming her inside.

"You won't believe what I saw in the park," she told him, passing the coat closet on her right. "I've never seen so many people. They were having a great time."

Chester gazed up at her, the tip of his tail flicking with interest.

She tossed her purse and briefcase onto the olive-coloured living room couch then walked barefoot across the parquet floor toward the galley kitchen. The apartment was awash in late-day sunlight, bringing to life the tiny dust motes and cat hair disturbed by her arrival. She considered closing the floor-to-ceiling drapes, which matched the couch perfectly, but she decided against it. The sun felt good.

She filled Chester's bowl with cat food then placed it on the floor and stepped back so he could enjoy his meal, and she could pour herself a little wine. She carried the glass to her balcony and sat in one of the two chairs she had bought specifically for out there, admiring the lovely day. Across from her was the neighbouring apartment building. It was similar to this one, but a good distance away, so it didn't affect her limited view of the city. Between the buildings stretched a park area carpeted by spring grass, edged here and there by bursts of tulips and patches of wilting daffodils. Best of all were the two magnificent cherry trees growing almost directly beneath her, a cloud of white-pink blossoms, offering Marion and her neighbours a soft perfume of lilac with a pinch of vanilla.

Her balcony faced northwest, and the air was warm. She knew the heat would be practically unbearable in the summer, but for now it was perfect. She glanced to her left, admiring the big potted geranium in the far corner, with its mounds of red petals. A gift from her neighbour, Mr. Levin, two weeks before. He'd informed her very seriously that her balcony would be perfect for it. Mr. Levin was very serious about plants in general. He and his wife were lovely people, but she was aware her quiet lifestyle was a topic of conversation between them. On his way out the last time, he muttered something about "If a woman has to live alone, she should at least have plants to talk to."

Now she took a sip of wine then closed her eyes and turned her face to the sun. She didn't usually indulge on weekdays, but today was a holiday, and she felt a little inspired by the party in the park.

"Besides, I'm not really alone, am I?" she asked Chester as he strolled outside to join her. He seemed inclined to jump on her lap, but then he spotted an unsuspecting fluff discarded by a poplar tree nearby and chose to pounce on it instead.

She might come out here again tonight around ten, hoping to see fireworks. The Queen's Park party would probably have moved on before then. She pictured the attendees huddling together in blankets, sound asleep after the excitement of the day. Or maybe they were sitting outside the Yorkville coffeehouses, enjoying cigarettes and conversation. It had been a beautiful day. It would be a lovely evening.

In a few hours, her sister would be tucking Marion's nieces into their beds in the hotel in Montreal, then she and her husband would probably sneak to the bar for a drink.

"Life is to be lived," Pat had said.

Marion took another sip and gazed over the quiet grounds below. A dog barked in the distance, but she didn't see any movement. For a heartbeat, she felt like the only person in the city. The only person anywhere, even, and her pulse sped up at the thought. She took a moment to consider her brief reaction, then she asked herself what she asked her patients most days.

How does that feel?

Was she lonely? Was that what she was feeling? Should she be somewhere else with a crowd, having a different sort of fun? Was she missing out?

Or was she just fine on her own?

Chester made a little sound, and she met his hypnotic green stare. The seriousness of his expression made her smile, and he took that as an invitation to spring onto her lap.

"I'm not alone, am I?" she asked him, stroking his velvety back. "I have you."

two
SASSY

ॐ

Sassy Rankin hugged her arms around herself, trying to stay warm despite the May chill. Forty-six degrees, someone had said. Nowhere near the seventy it had been only four days ago. It had been so warm then, she had loaned out her poncho, and she hadn't seen it since, which was too bad. She really could have used it right now. She glanced up, wondering where her friends had gone, and hoping they'd bring back snacks. Whatever Sassy had just smoked was making her crave peanuts. The buzz was fading fast, and her stomach was demanding attention.

Today was an awesome day: the biggest love-in the country had ever seen. After weeks of planning, the organizers filled Queen's Park with people like her, providing entertainment through singers and poets and speakers. The day was all about peace, and about proving to the public that she and the other hippies were not the monsters they were made out to be. Most were nonviolent and loving and offered no threat at all. They were happy just to *be*.

She couldn't tell if their message was getting out, though. The waves of people dancing and singing around her blocked her view of everything else. It didn't matter. She was here for a good time. She'd worn the mod dress she'd sewn, which covered her in big flowers but left her goose bump–rippled arms bare. She lamented her missing poncho again, but she had no idea who she had loaned it to.

She and her friends had arrived at the park early enough that they'd found a spot on the grass in the midst of hundreds of warm bodies, as close to the stage as they could get.

The blond girl sitting on her left leaned toward her. "I think I should paint a flower on your cheek."

Sassy took in the girl's crown of daisies and her peaceful, glazed expression, and she offered her face.

"Wiiild," the girl said, long and drawn out. She reached into an overstuffed bag at her other side, embroidered with all the colours of the rainbow. "Here you go."

Sassy closed her eyes, enjoying the caress of the stranger's paintbrush skimming over her cheek.

"You need two," the artist declared critically, dipping her brush into a bright orange pot. When she was done, she handed Sassy a compact. "How's that?"

Sassy angled her face toward the little mirror, appreciating the simple, childlike flowers that took up her entire left cheek, as if she grew a garden from the corner of her lip to just under her eye. One was yellow, the other orange, and their centres were switched.

"Groovy," she said with a wide grin.

"Yeah," the artist agreed. "I'm Sagittarius."

"I can tell. It's in your smile. I'm Libra."

"The keeper of peace." The girl sighed, soaking in the meaning. "Cool."

Joey is Sagittarius, Sassy thought vaguely. Her brother would have loved this scene. When she glanced up at the stage, a random memory came to her of sitting on the school's gymnasium floor, watching the grade threes put on a play. *Three Little Pigs*, she remembered. Joey was supposed to be sitting with the grade twos, but he'd snuck back to the grade fours to sit with Sassy. The two of them had nearly split their sides laughing at the girl playing the wolf. She had worn a ridiculously huge wolfskin coat, probably provided by her mother, and its hood kept falling off her head. Doing her best to appear big and bad, the diminutive actress kept yanking the hood over her blond curls. Joey laughed so hard at her frustration that the teacher dragged him back to the place of discipline, at her feet. Even then, he'd glanced over his shoulder at Sassy, still grinning.

He hadn't been afraid of that teacher or anyone else. Not that Sassy knew of, anyway. Joey lived in his own world, and she'd often felt lucky that he brought her into it. He was always doing unexpected things, and he did them with commitment. Like that toothpick house he'd glued together one time. The teacher had asked the students to assemble four simple walls and a roof, but Joey added a second floor and only quit building walls when he realized the stairs he'd built didn't fit.

When she was ten and he was eight, the two of them had constructed a playhouse within the trees around their large home by bending saplings together and piling branches for walls. They'd rolled in stones and a short log to serve as stools. Joey lost interest in the playhouse after a couple of days, but Sassy loved the little shelter. She carried books out and read them there in private.

She preferred the playhouse to their home, a mansion that echoed with empty rooms and hiding spots. Her father had inherited the big house from her grandfather, and to Sassy, it always felt too big and too quiet. One night in her playhouse, the soothing sounds of the woods lulled her enough that she forgot to go home once it began to get dark. She'd glanced up from the pages and found herself in dusky shadows, a place she'd never been before. With wide eyes, she'd stepped out from between the branches and surveyed an unfamiliar night that suddenly screeched with scary-sounding crickets. Somehow she'd gotten turned around and had no idea how to get to the house. Her father's estate had extensive grounds, but with so many tall shade trees, she couldn't see any lights from the house between the boughs.

Then Joey was there, like a puppy with a wagging tail, waiting for her to follow him. He didn't tease her for the tears on her face that night, never made fun of her for getting lost in her own backyard.

"I can't," she said.

"Come on. It's easy. Just two little steps."

Then he just took her hand and chattered the whole way back. The following afternoon, he'd suggested they go out to the secret spot together, but she'd refused. No way she was going to get stuck like that again. He persisted, so she reluctantly agreed, but only for a short while. She even wore a watch to make sure she didn't overstay. When they reached the spot, Joey was beaming, looking like a cat who'd swallowed a canary. Confused, she ducked inside to find a bouquet of flowers he'd plucked just for her and stuck in a bottle of water. He'd even built a wobbly little bookshelf, where he'd stacked her favourites along with a flashlight.

"See?" he said. "You never have to be scared, because I'll never let anything happen to you. You and me, Sass. We're like peanut butter and jelly, remember?"

That was something their nanny, Minnie, had said, shaking her head at the song they'd performed at her birthday party years ago. "Peanut butter and jelly, you two. Good on your own, but better together."

Sassy's stomach growled. Now she was craving a peanut butter and jelly sandwich. She sighed and leaned back on the grass, determined to appreciate the gorgeous day. The only thing that could have made today better was if Joey was here.

"Ladies and gentlemen, we have a surprise guest artist coming onto the stage now."

Sassy held her breath and crossed all her fingers. There had been rumours, but she'd hardly dared to believe. Could this be . . .

"Please welcome Vanguard recording artist Buffy Sainte-Marie."

With a cry of joy, Sassy jumped to her feet and threw her hands into the air. She'd listened to Buffy's records so many times, doggedly attempting to mimic the singer on her own guitar, that the record player's needle needed to be replaced. Now she stared up at the stage, holding her breath as the legendary woman walked to the microphone and stopped only a few feet away. Her long black hair flowed like water over her shoulders, and she wore a deceptively shy smile as she began to strum. When she belted out "Universal Soldier," Sassy felt torn between closing her eyes and watching every little thing that Buffy did. The next song was "Until It's Time for You to Go," and Sassy's fingers itched to play along. Every woman in the crowd must know this song, she thought. This was the anthem they all needed, reminding them they did not need to wear shackles because of a man's set of rules. Women were powerful, mothers and daughters sprung from the maternal spirit of the earth, and they needed their freedom. Sassy sang along, rocking from side to side and watching Buffy's shining black eyes, feeling one with her as they shared the words.

After Buffy left the stage, Sassy sank back onto the grass, still buzzing with adrenaline. Her makeup artist lay dazed beside her, blinking at the sky.

"Buffy's righteous," a young man said, sliding in on Sassy's right. He was medium height with brown hair almost to his shoulders, and a flop of it fell over one side of his brow. Without hesitation, he gave her a shining smile. He held out a thin, tightly rolled joint, already lit.

"You knew all the words."

Sassy observed him as she inhaled, letting his face blur a little as the high entered her brain. She liked the look of him. Soft, but strong. Casually intelligent. She also liked that he'd been watching her. She held her breath a moment then released the smoke.

"I know everything she sings," she said, passing the marijuana to the girl lying beside her. "She speaks to me, you know?"

"Far out. You sing like a bird," he said.

A plume of smoke rose on Sassy's left, then the artist returned the joint. Sassy took another puff and passed it back to the young man. She wrapped her arms around herself again, keeping warm, relishing the sense of mellow as it spread through her.

"You couldn't hear me."

"Sure, I could. I was listening. I can't sing a note."

"Bet you can," she said, taking to him.

His gaze dropped briefly to the goose bumps on her arms. Without a word, he slipped out of his brown sweater and handed it to her. The soft polyester fibres still held his heat, and she was instantly warm once she'd dropped it over her head.

She went back to what she was saying. "Anyone can sing."

The young man finished the joint, and his eyes drifted closed. "I don't know about that," he said tightly, holding in his breath while he spoke, "but right now I'm feeling so good I might jump on the stage and give it a try."

She leaned back on her elbows. "You're funny."

"Funny enough to take you out sometime?"

"Fast, too," she noted, catching a glimpse of lion-gold eyes under long lashes.

"Toronto's a busy place. I might never see you again. I gotta act quick."

He might have been fast, but his laid-back accent was nice and slow. It charmed her. "Where are you from? I like the way you talk."

He reclined on his side beside her. "South Carolina. I like the way you talk, too."

Another performer approached the microphone, and the announcer introduced her as Cathy Young. Sassy had never heard of her, but she liked her voice. Lulled by cannabis and music, she closed her eyes and drifted, letting herself forget where she was, who she was, why she was . . . Eventually, she glanced back at the boy and wondered how much time had passed since he'd spoken. Time was a funny thing in all this smoke.

"What's your name?"

"Davey."

"Why are you here? In Canada, I mean."

He held her gaze, as if he was daring her. "I came here because I ain't gonna fight another country's war."

She had no argument with that. "Davey," she mused, curling a lock of her long chestnut hair around one finger and regarding him through soft eyes. "Davey the Dodger. Interesting. My brother's fighting over there."

"So was mine."

Past tense. The finality of his words silenced her.

You had better be all right, Joey.

"But your brother's Canadian," Davey said, sounding keen to continue the conversation. "Why's he there?"

"I guess he's the opposite of you." She shook her head, jostling Joey from her thoughts. She didn't want to wreck the day by being sad or angry. "I've never met a draft dodger before."

"I prefer 'war resister.'"

"Far out. Whatever you call it. We should be loving, not fighting. Why are we sending our sons and brothers to kill another country's sons and brothers? In the end, no one wins except big corporations and government. It's all about money to The Man."

"I think I'm falling in love with you," Davey breathed.

She laughed. "Cool. This is a love-in."

He chuckled and produced another joint from his pocket. He raised an eyebrow at her.

"Why not?" she said.

The face painter had fallen asleep and was quietly snoring. A girl in a beige, lacy dress danced behind her, not noticing or caring that the music had stopped. She spun so fast her feet barely touched the ground, and the sun took advantage of the angle, making it appear as if she was naked. It was a beautiful illusion. What was the girl seeing? Sassy wondered. What did she hear?

"You know who's coming on soon, don't you?" Davey asked. He squinted as he lit the joint and drew in the smoke, then he slowly let his breath out through his teeth so it hissed on the exhale. "Leonard Cohen."

"I saw him once at the Riverboat. His poetry was out of this world, but in my opinion, he has a terrible voice."

"Ah, so you're more than a nightingale. You're a critic."

"I'm a singer. Someday I'll be famous."

Davey brought back that slow smile, and she felt her cheeks warm. "Out of sight. Now you gotta tell me your name so I'll know who to watch for."

"I'm Sassy."

"Sassy. Very cool," he said.

Over the course of the afternoon, between loud music sets that drowned out attempts at conversation, they talked. To her delight, she rediscovered a package of Starburst candies in her pocket, and they feasted on those. Eventually, he asked more about Joey, wanting to know why he'd chosen to go to Vietnam. She wished he hadn't asked. Almost a year later, it hurt to think of her brother over there. When she let herself remember, what she saw was the apology in his expression. She hadn't accepted that apology, and he'd gone anyway. Off to war. Off to die. God, she had hated him and his selfishness in that moment. When had he gotten so cruel? When had fighting another country's war become more important to him than his sister?

She didn't hate Joey anymore. She'd changed. She still missed him constantly, but now instead of anger, she mourned for him. She'd never admit it out loud, but she knew what happened to men who went to war. Even if he came back physically unharmed, he'd never be the same. War broke people.

Davey didn't seem to understand that Sassy was trying to sidestep thinking about her brother, so she gave him a different sort of answer. She told him their father was a bigwig in the city, and a rich man, so she figured Joey's move was rebellion.

"I'm not about to rebel," she admitted, feeling smug. "Dad made me a deal. If I hold down a full-time job, he'll pay all my bills for three years, including rent."

"Sweet," he said, awe in his voice.

"Yeah. Joey couldn't have gotten that deal. He doesn't do anything that people tell him to do." She scowled. "Like stay home."

She'd gotten occasional letters from her brother, grimy and stained, telling her Vietnam was a terrible place and that men over there were either dying or going crazy, but when she wrote back and begged him to come home, he said he couldn't. He and his "brothers" had a job to do down there. *Try to understand, Sass.*

She couldn't. Never would.

"I don't want to talk about Joey anymore," she said. "It's bringing me down. Tell me about you, Davey the Dodger."

His family had a small farm. He had three older sisters, a mom, and a dad, who would probably never speak to him again. The only thing he missed about his home was his dog, a good old hunting hound named Bowzer. When she asked him what he liked to do, Davey said he liked to paint, but he wasn't any good at it.

Sassy leaned in closer, increasingly attracted to him. She studied the lines on his face and the light scruff around his jaw. She wanted to touch his cheek.

"So you can't sing and you can't paint. What are you good at?"

"Cooking. It's like art, only you can eat it after." He grinned. "I'm real good at cooking. And I'm starting to get active in, like, the movement, you know? Like, with organizing protests and stuff like that. Somebody asked me to set up a sit-in last week, and I didn't think it'd be my thing, but pulling all the details together was cool. Went off without a hitch."

"So, like, you could have run today's show?"

He smiled languidly. "Yeah. Someday I'll run something like this. Gotta start slow."

After the music and the poetry and the speeches ended, men began disassembling the speakers and clearing the equipment. Members of the audience reluctantly wrapped blankets around themselves and wandered off the field, leaving a trail of cups, cigarette butts, and various plastic wrappers behind them.

When Sassy looked at Davey, he was watching her.

"I guess it's over."

He gazed back, smiling. "Guess so."

"I'm hungry," she declared coyly, wondering if he'd take the bait.

"I have an idea," he said, reading her mind. "How about I make you dinner at your place?"

three
MARION

◈

Tuesday morning, bright and early as always, Marion rose and dressed for work. She'd laid out her clothes the night before, and it took no time to brush her long blond hair and roll it into a tight bun. She never rushed if she could avoid it, didn't like the sense of urgency that stuck out like a hurdle in the path of her deliberate equilibrium. By rising early, she was able to make her routine comfortable then arrive at work fully awake and ready to be productive.

Humming to herself, she popped a couple of pieces of bread into the toaster, pulled a jar of her mother's strawberry jam from the refrigerator, then plugged in the kettle. With her mind on her Tuesday schedule, she poured a spoonful of Nescafé into a cup and waited for the water to boil.

This was the perfect apartment for Marion. She'd learned all about it before she'd moved in two years ago. She appreciated knowing details before she agreed to anything. Being prepared led to fewer mistakes.

When she was considering 105 Isabella Street as a home, Marion's first step was to figure out its location in relation to everything else. The apartment building was on a quiet street between Jarvis and Church, a short two blocks north of Wellesley. It was about a half-hour walk to work or campus, and the buses were conveniently regular, though they didn't stop on her street. It was also a half-hour walk in the other direction to Yorkville, which interested her. Marion had strolled through the popular spot, and on occasion she had played with the idea of "hanging around," as people called it, but so far, she hadn't. She didn't feel she was ready for that kind of scene, whatever that meant.

The apartment building was just under ten years old, built in 1959, and she'd liked the look of it right away. It stood out from the street's redbrick, Victorian-style homes and low-rise apartment buildings. In comparison, the pale white bricks of 105 made the building look almost elegant. Every floor had twenty-four apartments, either one-bedroom or bachelor, divided into three hallways in a T, and almost every apartment had a huge balcony. The laundry room was on the first floor, where noisy machines chugged all day long, and Jack's Variety Store was nearby for her groceries. And if she ever bought a car, the building had its own underground parking garage, tucked neatly beneath a grassy yard. But why buy a car when she never went anywhere? Walking suited her just fine.

"'Goodbye, Ruby Tuesday,'" Marion sang without thinking, then she bent and stroked Chester's head. "See you later."

After throwing back her coffee then cleaning her cup and saucer, Marion collected her bag and stepped into the hallway, locking the door behind her. The heavy aroma of sweating onions immediately clouded around her, and she thought it was coming from 517, where Mrs. Moore would be making cabbage soup again. The poor woman always looked tired. Her husband was a veteran of the last war and had been badly wounded in battle. Mrs. Moore was a tiny little thing, so they hired a girl to bring groceries up to 517 as well as to clean. She rarely saw any sign of Mr. Moore.

The Levins lived in 503. They told Marion they had a nonnegotiable clause in their lease guaranteeing them a southern exposure and balcony to contain their massive garden.

Like Mrs. Moore, the Romanos in 505 were always cooking. Especially when their large family came to visit, which was fairly often. Every year near the end of summer, Marion came home to the heady aroma of Mrs. Romano canning tomatoes. Last year, she'd been invited to help, and that had been an experience in itself. Marion had returned to her apartment afterward with an entire pot of pasta and two cans of homemade sauce. It had taken her three days to eat all that pasta. Just thinking of it made her mouth water.

Outside her apartment door, she paused, hearing a dozen tentative notes being plucked on a guitar in the next apartment. The melody almost sounded like a foreign scale, and she remembered enough from her childhood piano lessons to know they were in a minor key. The tune was vaguely familiar, though she couldn't quite place it. A sad song, she thought, setting her bag on the floor. Something about painting things black to match the singer's unhappy life. His voice came to her—the Rolling Stones, she recalled, pleased with herself. The notes stopped, then they began again, more confident this time. Marion preferred this tender, slower performance; the original sounded hostile. Then a girl began to sing, and Marion closed her eyes, soaking in the gentle melody.

"'I see a red door, and I want it painted black . . . '"

Halfway through the song, the guitar gave a percussive twang, as if the musician had smacked the strings with her palm. She heard a woman's muffled voice in conversation, so she collected her bag and proceeded briskly down the hall to the elevator. She had stopped to listen, not to be seen.

She pushed the button and heard a click behind her. "Good morning," she said to Mr. Snoop. "Have a nice day."

The door closed.

The song had embedded itself in her mind, and her steps matched the lyrics as she strolled down Jarvis to Wellesley then waited for the bus to Wellesley Station. It was a nice walk; the air was a little warmer today, and she'd worn her cheerful yellow cardigan.

"Good morning," the bus driver said, nodding as she dropped her quarter into the fare box.

"It is, isn't it?" she replied. "Transfer, please."

She took a seat then watched the familiar press of rush hour from her window. Marion's destination this morning, as it was three mornings every week, was the massive old Queen Street Mental Health Centre, popularly known as 999 Queen Street West. The original building had been constructed more than a hundred years before, in 1850, and had been named the Provincial Lunatic Asylum. It was the oldest public mental health hospital in all of English-speaking Canada. When the doors had first opened, the place had filled with every sort of society's rejects: hysterics, depressives, psychotics, schizophrenics, idiots. Over the next hundred years, patients were admitted then treated within their walls, outside of the public eye. Out of sight, out of mind.

After its first twenty-one years, the building became the Asylum for the Insane, then the more dignified-sounding *Hospital* for the Insane. After being inundated by a huge influx of veterans following World War I, the name was whittled down to the Ontario Hospital.

So much had been learned since those early years, so many improvements made, that a seismic shift in psychiatric treatment was underway. Deinstitutionalization, defined as the safe release of psychiatric patients into the community, had been made possible through astonishing developments in psychiatric drugs. The media and the general public supported the idea, declaring that people with psychiatric illnesses should no longer be hidden away. The provincial government hoped to promote community integration by transferring patient care to newly setup community mental health centres. By shutting down the institutions, they also hoped to save a great deal of money. The Ontario Hospital was about to become redundant.

Marion did not support deinstitutionalization in the least. For the past two years, she had burned internally over the dangerous plan. Closing down the hospitals and entrusting patients' care to community centres could only do harm to both the patients and the public at large. At one point, she had mentioned her concerns to Paul McKenny, another doctor at the hospital, but their conversation had gone no further than that. To her shame, even though Marion believed very strongly that the plan was a bad one, she hadn't worked up the nerve to speak with her boss, Dr. Bernstein, to voice her objections. As she had always done, Marion kept her head down, unwilling to rock the boat. She knew how easily a woman could get swept overboard by the men pulling the oars.

But there was a storm coming. She could feel it.

The bus pulled into Wellesley Station and descended underground. From there, Marion took the subway to Queen Street, then the 501 streetcar to Ossington. As they rumbled past 999 Queen Street West, she became uncomfortably aware of the local myth manifesting: some of her fellow passengers were holding their breath, wanting to avoid catching whatever contagion was within the walls of "the nuthouse."

When the streetcar reached her stop, Marion exited on Queen Street then walked through the centre's entrance, which was part of the institution's new Administration Building. It had been constructed ten years ago, directly in front of the old structure, and since the two were the same width, the asylum was completely blocked from view for anyone passing by. Again, out of sight, out of mind. In a few years, the original building would be demolished, along with the old system of care.

"Good morning, Dr. Hart," chirped the secretary by the entrance. A vase of fresh tulips stood in a sunbeam on the corner of her desk, their bright red petals curving toward the source.

Marion inhaled the nutty aroma of coffee with pleasure. "Good morning, Miss Prentice." She paused by the folders affixed to the walls, checking for anything that might have come in for her, then pulled out the week's schedule, a listing of two new patients, a memo about a staff meeting—the usual.

"I hope you enjoyed your weekend."

"Oh yes. We went to my grandparents' house, and my father was in charge of the barbecue. He claims he's never burned a hot dog in his life, but his perfect record ended yesterday. Afterward, we shot off fireworks. Did you get to see any?"

"A little," Marion replied, scanning a file. "I watched from my balcony, so I saw what I could over top of the other buildings. Better than nothing. Is Dr. Bernstein in yet?"

It was a silly question. Her boss was always there early.

"About an hour ago."

"That man never sleeps," Marion muttered. "I thought I was the early bird."

Miss Prentice brightened. "That's all right. There are plenty of worms to go around."

With her paperwork clutched to her chest, Marion headed down the hallway and peeked into Dr. Bernstein's office on the way by. He was there, of course, bending over a pile of paper and squinting through thick glasses. Almost ten years past retirement age, he was slowly losing his sight, but he was as stubborn as he was old. Dr. Bernstein was polite enough, but he clearly disliked her. She was confident that was due to her sex, since she had never knowingly offended him.

There were 136 beds in this new building, ten more than what the builders had planned for. Of those, Marion was responsible for twenty-six women. She checked her notes then knocked on the door of the first patient room on her left.

"Good morning, Barbara. It's Dr. Hart. May I come in?"

A muffled groan came from within, which Marion took as an invitation. Barbara Voss was twenty-eight years old with neurotic depression. She and her husband had admitted her a few months ago, after she suffered multiple miscarriages and plunged into despair, becoming emotionally unstable. She'd lost her job, stayed in bed for days without eating, and terrified her husband by entertaining suicidal thoughts. After an admittance interview, Marion had given Barbara a room at the hospital. It was exactly what she wanted and needed, but even then, her anxiety had fought her on it.

"How much is this going to cost? I don't have any money. My husband is worked to the bone. I can't—"

"Barbara, do you remember what Prime Minister Pearson introduced last year? The Medical Care Act? All your expenses here are covered by Medicare."

The relief that had come over the woman's face was a beautiful thing to see.

Marion understood that question, though. She was doing relatively well these days when it came to finances, but she was still a penny-pincher. Her parents had raised their daughters in a small house, and while they had never gone hungry, they certainly didn't splurge. It was a mystery to Marion that her parents, on their very limited income, had been able to send her to university, let alone medical school. Many times, seeing them in obvious need, she had threatened to quit school, feeling sick with guilt, but her father had not permitted her to consider it.

"We have the money," he had assured her, over and over. "It's been put away so you can be what you always wanted to be. Do your best and make us proud. That's all we ask."

So she had done exactly that.

At a recent meeting, the general consensus between the doctors was that Barbara's dosage of 75 mg/day of Tofranil should be increased. Marion believed 150 would be too high in this case, so she upped it to 100 mg instead. She wanted to observe and be certain. Barbara was also undergoing counselling, including group therapy. She'd improved tremendously under that course of treatment, to the point that she was now labelled "domiciliary." That meant she required a safe place to live, three meals a day, and some treatment, but for the most part she was able to administer self-care. That was a relief to Marion, considering the future plans for the hospital.

Marion's next patient, Alice Sumner, was twenty-two. She was a diagnosed schizophrenic who had lived there for six years, and, as Marion had discovered firsthand, she was sometimes dangerous. The second time Marion had met with her, she had taken a seat at her bedside, and Alice had punched her in the face. Marion fled the room and rushed toward the washroom with a hand cupped over her bleeding nose. On her way to cleaning herself up, she'd accidentally bumped into Dr. Bernstein.

"What happened?" he asked flatly, squinting at the mess on Marion's face. "Did you fall? Did your patient hit you?"

"The latter, but I'm not sure why," Marion replied. "We were having a pleasant conversation about how she was feeling, and she punched me."

He folded his arms. "Do you have unresolved disagreements with the patient?"

"I've only met her once before, Dr. Bernstein. That meeting was uneventful and cordial."

"The Stanton-Schwartz phenomenon suggests otherwise."

Marion had read Stanton-Schwartz and did not agree with it, but she was in no position to argue with her boss. Besides, she didn't have time. She needed to get past him, wash her face, and see if the bleeding had stopped.

"Are you familiar with the phenomenon?"

"Yes, sir."

"Then you know that it is likely Miss Sumner punched you because the two of you disagreed on the planned treatment. That bothered you, and when the patient struck you, she was acting on an impulse that you, yourself, felt."

"I'm sorry?"

"She punched you because, unconsciously, you felt the urge to punch her."

The urge to roll her eyes almost won, but she kept that in check.

This morning, Alice was quiet and on guard, squeezed into a ball at the end of her bed with her back against the wall. Occasionally, her right hand rose, and she pointed at something unseen on the ceiling. Marion followed her finger. Nothing was there but a light fixture.

"Good morning, Alice," Marion said gently. "How are you feeling today?"

The patient shook her head violently, then she pressed a finger to her lips. "Shh! He's listening."

"Who is listening?"

"I don't know. I don't know, I don't know, I don't know," she whispered, eyes bulging. She stretched her legs out in front, and her ankles rotated so that her feet drew circles in the air. "Can you hear that?"

All this quick chatter and movement told Marion that Alice was more worked up than usual. A quick check of her medications, then Marion made a notation on her chart, raising Alice's daily dosage of chlorpromazine to 500 mg. Recent studies had proved that effectiveness of the antipsychotic improved noticeably once that threshold was reached.

Marion kept her expression open. "Can you tell me what I am listening for?"

Alice dropped her chin and flung her arms out to either side. "It's very loud in here," she murmured. "I have tickets for the opera in my purse, you know."

Some appointments went more smoothly than others, and Marion clung to the good ones. In particular, she liked to remember a young woman named Deborah. Deborah had lived at the hospital for four years, suffering from acute anxiety and never speaking a word. By the time Marion had graduated, Deborah was attending daily art therapy classes at the hospital. As she expressed herself through art, she began to verbalize words, one at a time. The last time Marion had seen Deborah, she was smiling and pointing out two of her paintings displayed on the wall of the Administrative Building. Deborah's was the kind of success story for which they all strove.

This morning, after Marion finished seeing her last patient in the new building, she sat in on a short meeting with some of the other doctors on their rounds and two of the senior nurses, comparing notes. Then it was time to visit the last fourteen of her assigned patients. Those were all men, and they lived in the original building.

To Marion, stepping into the old asylum was like entering a different world. It was one of the saddest places on earth; she could feel it in the walls. Layers of misery and neglect had seeped in then hardened into the brick and mortar. Some of the treatments and abuse that had happened in the original hospital—even as recently as five years ago—were shameful and often inhumane. Even today, the building was over capacity by two hundred inmates. That meant less personal care, more overworked nurses and staff. A recipe for disaster.

When it came to deinstitutionalization, the building made a good case against itself. Demolition and delegating psychiatric services to community centres certainly seemed like common sense.

But how could it be rational or practical if a good percentage of these patients could barely feed themselves, let alone live independently? The most severe cases would have extended in-hospital treatment, but what about those on the cusp?

Marion visited with three patients in the old building, all of whom seemed content, then she squinted through the window of Ward 6B, where the "incurables" lived. Most were gathered in their common room for now, and she spotted her patient, Big John, in one corner, playing checkers with another man named Ian.

Marion took a final breath of fresh air then stepped through the door and was instantly assaulted by the reek of the place. The nurses and staff tried to stay on top of the problem, but it was a Sisyphean task. Most of the men in 6B were incontinent, and they didn't use utensils when they ate. This area was as close to medieval times as Marion ever wanted to get.

"Good afternoon, Dr. Hart," a stout, bald man called loudly, giving her a toothless grin. "I know it's afternoon because we had lunch."

"Hello, Burt. Good for you for remembering." He had given her the same sort of update almost every day for six months now. It had been sweet at first. "How are you feeling today?"

"Today's a happy day," he reported.

"I am delighted to hear that," she replied, still walking toward the checker match. "Can you think of another word to describe how you feel?"

She saw in his expression that he'd anticipated the challenge. "Cheerful."

"Excellent, Burt." She shared her smile with the room, purposefully meeting each man's vacant expression, always hoping for some kind of recognition or acknowledgement that she was there. Not for her own gratification, but as a sign of a patient's improvement. "Hello, Francis. Hello, George."

"Hello, Dr. Hart. Dr. Hart. Dr. Hart."

"Hello, Mr. Thicke," she said to the stooped man by the window. Mr. Thicke had been brought here by his family ten years before, when they could no longer deal with his senility. He had a sweet, uncomplicated face, and the messy white wisps of his hair looked as confused as he was. On some days, the old gentleman turned with a vague smile to greet her. Today, he did not recognize his own name.

"Good morning, Bruce," she said, watching a redheaded fellow with akathisia pace up and down the edge of the room, twitching and talking to himself. She knew he wouldn't respond, but she said it just in case.

"Good morning, John," she said, reaching her patient. "Are you having a good day?"

As usual, Big John did not register her presence. He was thirty-one, but he looked much older. As his nickname suggested, John was a large, lumbering man. He had the size, the strength, and the sense of a bull, but a gentle one. Marion recalled the tale *Ferdinand the Bull* every time she saw him. Then again, John's gentle nature had a lot to do with the medications he was on. Without them, he could be dangerous. Ferdinand had been a natural pacifist.

"How about you, Ian? Who's winning the game?"

Both men stared at the board. She wondered if either had moved the pieces at all or if someone else had just left them in place. Neither knew the answer, but she could tell from a slight shift in their expressions that they had heard her.

John's empty gaze gradually rose, shifting in small, jerky movements due to his nystagmus. The motion left him dizzy and with a kind of double vision, trapped in a sliding world of vertigo. He could see, but everything was blurry. Besides that, he had catatonic schizophrenia with both negatism and mutism, meaning John rarely acknowledged stimuli, nor did he speak. His checkers partner looked equally lost. Neither of them was aware that anything was wrong with them.

"Looks like you both are winning," Marion said, leaning over the board. "Who is red and who is black?"

After a couple of long breaths, Ian gingerly picked up a black piece and gripped it to his chest.

Big John's eyes widened, but he said nothing. Other than his eyes, he did not move.

"My mistake," Marion intervened gently. "I should not have asked. May I have the piece, please? There, that's it. It was right here before I interrupted."

Once everyone was calm again, and Marion had finished her examination of Big John's status, she signed his chart, left it with the weary nurse, then left the ward. Her happy mood from the morning had dissolved, and she blamed herself. If she could manage to switch her schedule around, she could get past this most discouraging ward first, then move onto brighter, more manageable cases. But Marion was a creature of habit, like many of the patients. And like them, she might never change.

As she headed toward the exit, a man's slurred voice travelled down the corridor. "Help. Help, please."

Marion was done for the day. She picked up her pace and strode past his door, certain that whatever it was, a nurse would take care of him.

"Doctor. Help!"

She hesitated then backed up to regard the man in his room. Not too many people immediately identified her as a doctor. Most assumed she was a nurse.

The patient was unfamiliar to her. She frowned slightly, wondering at the restraints binding the young man's wrists and ankles to the bed. Nothing to cause bruises, just soft sheets tied tight, but it was enough to hold him down. Every part of him was contained except for his head, and he'd lifted that off his pillow to watch her. She tried not to react when she saw the disaster on his face. He'd obviously been in some kind of brawl or accident, because it was terribly cut and swollen. She noticed with a clinical interest that he wore a black eye patch over the place where his right eye should have been. The left side was purple with bruising.

"What do you need?" she asked, remaining in the doorway at a safe distance. The restraints were on him for a reason.

"Let me loose." His voice was thick, like cold syrup. "I don't need to be locked up."

"Somebody thinks you do."

His file hung on the door, so she lifted it off and read through. Daniel Neumann. Born in 1945, so twenty-two years old. His eye was gone due to trauma, she read, and the left side of his face, chest, and shoulder were badly burned from an explosion. The initial surgery had been done long before, but the site had gotten infected. As a result, he'd spent a day at the Toronto Western Hospital getting antibiotics, then he'd checked himself out. Two days later, the police picked him up from a fight outside a bar. That's where he'd gotten all the bruises, she surmised. They didn't charge him with anything, because according to witnesses, he had been the victim, not the instigator. Nevertheless, he'd hospitalized two men and left three others injured. He refused to return to the hospital, but he was still behaving wildly—shouting profanities, swinging fists—so the police had brought him here. Two nurses stated they felt threatened, and the decision was made to restrain him. Only the most senior nurse, Thelma Goodwin, had been able to medicate him when he arrived.

No one messed with Thelma.

"Daniel Neumann," Marion said. "My name is Dr. Hart. I'm reading your history here. It appears you don't like hospitals. You left the last one against your doctor's advice."

"I didn't need to be there."

From this distance, she sensed intelligence, though he was clearly heavily medicated. "You seem to know a lot about what you need and don't need."

"You can come in." He jerked his wrists up an inch, yanking the sheets against the bed frame, then he dropped his head back onto the pillow. "I'll behave."

She stepped inside the room, intrigued despite common sense. Most of the patients in this building were doubled up in a room, with a small bed on either wall and a window and nightstand in between. Or else they were in group rooms, which held eight or more beds. This patient was on his own. His room was tiny, made even more so by his large size.

"Were you drunk last night, Mr. Neumann?"

"Major."

"I see."

"No. Major Neumann." He had to turn his head slightly farther when he faced her to compensate for his missing eye. "And no. I was not drunk."

"Why did the police bring you here, then?"

"They got the wrong guy," he said lamely.

"Oh?"

"I don't want to talk about it."

"Why did you call me in here, then? I can't untie the bindings because I'm not your doctor."

She approached the bed, inspecting him. A deep cut across his swollen lip seemed to be healing on its own, but it threatened to open again when he spoke. His brown hair was swept loosely over the right side of his brow in an attempt to conceal his eye patch, and he wore what she guessed was a scruffy four-day-old beard.

"What are you staring at?"

"I'm looking at the damage on your face. I'm a doctor. It's what I do. What happened to you?"

The scar darkened along with the rest of his face. "Untie me."

"No. What happened?"

He turned away, so she lowered her gaze to his chart and flipped through more pages. The notes on his chart said he was aggressive. Delusional. Violent. Volatile. She turned back further into his history, seeking more details. When she found the answer, she tried not to change her expression, but her interest was piqued. He'd been fighting in Vietnam.

The subject of wartime trauma had intrigued her for years because of her father. Twenty years after the end of the last war, he still suffered from "battle fatigue," which some textbooks referred to as "combat stress reaction." She didn't know if either of her grandfathers had been affected, but she had her suspicions. They had both served in the Great War. Her maternal grandfather had died over there. Her father's father was more of a mystery. The story was that he got sick and died, but after grilling her parents for more answers, Marion speculated that his life had ended in suicide, as it did with so many veterans. After the Great War, medical professionals labelled similar symptoms as "shell shock" or "war neurosis," and the exponentially growing number of affected men returning from battle demanded more research be done. Over the past thirty years, doctors had studied survivors from World War II and the Korean War, including veterans who had been taken as prisoners of the Japanese, and some who had survived Nazi persecution.

And yet, despite Marion's searches, she had found little solid literature explaining either the phenomenon or any definitive treatment.

Based on the knowledge that Daniel Neumann had fought in Vietnam and suffered a terrible, life-changing injury, followed by his recent violence and his refusal to discuss the reasons, Marion strongly suspected he suffered from the disorder. She wasn't surprised. She'd seen photographs and watched footage of what was happening over there. She couldn't imagine what he had survived.

"Water?" His voice was gruff. His face was still turned away.

"I will send in a nurse."

"No nurse. No more needles. Untie me."

"It's for your own good. For your pain, for your mental stability, and for other people's safety."

"No more." He took a shuddering breath. "I can't think."

"I'm afraid the treatment isn't up to you. Your doctors will discuss your case on Wednesday morning."

"When's that?"

"Tomorrow."

"How can they talk about me when I'm stoned like this? They don't know me."

It was a valid question. "They have your hospital records and police statements."

Nurse Thelma, on her rounds through the ward, entered behind her. "Beg your pardon, Doctor. I'm a little behind. How are we today, Mr. Neumann? Calmer than last night, I hope?"

Marion stepped out of the woman's way. He was secured so tightly to the bed he could hardly move, but as the nurse approached with a syringe, Marion saw him try to evade her. His sleeves pulled taut against his biceps as he struggled against the restraints, then his face tightened as the needle penetrated his vein.

"There we are, Mr. Neumann. Right as rain again. Dr. McKenny is your doctor. He will come see you in a few hours, and he'll decide what to do with you. In the meantime, you have a nice sleep." She smiled tightly at Marion, who was clearly overstepping, and held out her hand for the clipboard. On her way out, she hung it on the door where it belonged and wished Marion a good evening.

Daniel was silent. He closed his eye, and Marion wondered if the drugs had put him to sleep already.

"Mr. Neumann?" she said softly. "Major?"

"Go away." His voice dropped to a heavy whisper. "Just leave me alone."

four
SASSY

❧

Swathed in an itchy wool tweed suit, her blazer tight around her upper arms and buttoned snugly around her waist, Sassy checked the clock on the wall. This was quite possibly the longest day of her life. To ease her frustration, she practiced her own private form of meditation. Davey called his cooking "art," so she tried to think of her typing as music. She was a good typist, so her work had a rhythm. She just had to make up the melody.

Every morning at Jamieson, Baines, and Brown Law Firm, lists and letters appeared in the basket on her desk. Some were written in forceful capital letters, some in rushed handwriting that leaned excessively to the right, and some were printed in such light pencil strokes she had to squint to make out the words. Those pale scribblings came from Miss Drummond. When Sassy suggested the woman put a little more pressure on her pencil lead, she had been met with such a scowl of disbelief she'd given up and gone back to squinting. It wasn't her fault if the writing was illegible and she got some of it wrong.

Her mind wandered. Davey had still been in the apartment when she'd left, his bare chest golden as he basked in the sunlight flooding through her living room windows, sipping his coffee and munching on Pop-Tarts. On her way out, she'd said to help himself to whatever he wanted to eat. Not that she had much in her kitchen, but after the love-in, they'd stopped on their way back from the park and bought the ingredients he needed so he could cook for her. Chicken, vegetables, rice . . . it was a bigger feast than she'd had in months. She hoped there were leftovers when she got home. She hoped he'd still be there, too.

Davey was groovy. He had a confident, contagious laugh, and he had lied about his musical abilities. Turned out he could sing, even manage a little harmony. She played for him that night, and he sang along. He told her she was really good, and she knew he was saying it for real because they'd already done what they'd come to her place to do, so there was no need for flattery. He told her she belonged onstage at the Riverboat, which made her laugh.

"Not quite," she said.

"Maybe not, but soon," he assured her, pressing a cool strawberry to her lips.

Davey hadn't passed the "husband test," though. Not that she was ever going to marry—she wasn't—but she'd read somewhere that most girls "married their father." Davey looked nothing like hers. Jim Rankin was tall and slim, whereas Davey was only a couple inches taller than she was. He wasn't fat, but she could tell that he preferred food to exercise. She didn't mind. A person's physical body wasn't important, after all. It was about their life force. Their aura. Their capacity for love.

But it didn't hurt that Davey was the sexiest man she'd ever laid eyes—or hands—on.

Mostly what people saw when they looked at Jim Rankin was that he was wealthy. Sure, he was tall and darkly handsome, with sad brown eyes that held deep thoughts, but mostly he looked like money. A lot of it. He had come home from the war with shrapnel scars all over his body, jagged, violent marks that Sassy rarely saw, and he had inherited his father's real estate practice. He got married, had two kids, then his wife had died. After he lost her, Jim Rankin had put all he had into expanding his company in preparation for his only son to inherit it. But Joey didn't want it. He never had any interest in the family business. Sassy hadn't been surprised by that. She'd never been able to imagine him in a suit and tie.

"Wild oats, Dad," Joey said, shaking his dark curls and wearing the smile of a romantic. "So many wild oats to sow."

Her father had been quietly devastated by the news, she could tell. He had raised both children after their mother died of brain cancer when Sassy was six and Joey was four. Neither of them remembered her very well, and their father didn't talk about her. He never dated after she died, or if he had, he never brought a woman home. From that, Sassy came to believe that her mother had been something special and her parents' love unique. Even though Sassy had only ever known one parent, she based her marital goals on that lofty example.

Sassy was positive she would never find anyone like that, who filled her in every way. She doubted it so much that she had decided never to get married. Besides, marriage was such an outdated tradition. She had no interest in living monogamously, when everything happening these days was so much more liberating. The sixties suited her perfectly. Being single was much less complicated.

Her father hadn't been completely on his own, raising them. Minnie, short for Minerva, was a fortysomething, wiry woman, just a little older than Sassy's father. Minnie was a housekeeper, but she was also their nanny most of the time. Sassy loved her dearly. Monday to Friday, Minnie lived in a small room on the first floor of Sassy's father's house, then she was gone until the next Monday. Sassy remembered asking Minnie why she disappeared on weekends, and Minnie said she had two little boys at home who needed her. She'd had a little girl as well, but the baby had died. When Sassy was about ten, Minnie grew a belly then took a short time away from work to take care of her third son, who she cheerfully declared was "quite a surprise." When she came back, Sassy asked if she would please bring the baby sometime. There was more than enough room in their house, after all. Minnie had shaken her head. Too much work, she told her.

"The two of you are more than enough," she said.

Sassy's father oversaw their childhood, but Minnie managed it. She stayed with them until Joey turned sixteen.

All her life, the only thing Sassy ever wanted to do was sing, and since her father gave her such a generous allowance, that's all she really did. She sang, she read, she played guitar and sometimes the piano, and every day, she dreamed. Joey's heart was set on playing pro baseball. He was very good, Sassy knew, since she'd seen him play at school and at the park with his friends.

Last January, Sassy had performed for her dad and Joey in their living room. She would never forget that night. It changed everything. When she finished playing, her father smiled and clapped, but she could tell he was doing it out of obligation more than anything else. He didn't know anything about music. Joey, on the other hand, leaned back in his armchair the whole time, ball cap tugged low over his forehead, listening with his eyes closed. When she finished, he let out a whoop.

"Far out! My sister's going to be a star!" He grinned. "I'll be your roadie, Sass."

Her father regarded Joey. "You already have a job lined up."

"Come on, Dad," Joey scowled. "She's great. You know she is. Tell her."

"Of course you're good," her father said. "Very good, Susan. You have your mother's gift." He turned back to Joey. "And you're going to be very good in the real estate business. It's time, you know. You're old enough to hold down a real job."

Joey chuckled and mentioned the wild oats again, then he hesitated, which was unusual for him. Joey wasn't the kind of guy to think about things before he said or did them. The unfamiliar tension in his brow made her nervous.

"I ain't taking your job, Dad. I got other plans."

"I hope not as a roadie or a ballplayer," her father said wryly. "Neither of those will cover groceries when you're out on your own."

She set her guitar down, recognizing the moment the spotlight moved from her to her brother. Joey didn't look fazed on the outside, but Sassy felt a twinge of alarm when she saw a tightening at the side of his mouth. He was nervous about something, and it was something big. She hadn't thought Joey was afraid of anything.

"I won't be buying groceries where I'm going," he said. "Won't be cooking for a while, either."

"No? You have a girlfriend I don't know about?" Her father glanced between them with frustration. "I hate to break it to you two, but thousands of other kids want what you want. You're not the only ones who dream of being rich and famous. The fact is, neither of you is going to get that coveted dream career. But," he said, taking a breath, "even if I'm wrong and it does happen, I want you to have something else to fall back on. Something practical. Real jobs. And Joey, when it's time, I want you to come work with me."

"Not gonna happen, Dad. I have other plans."

"So you said. Like what?"

"I wasn't gonna tell you like this, but why not?" His casual smile looked forced. "I'm going to Vietnam."

The words dropped like a bomb in their quiet living room, blowing their world apart. Sassy felt its impact like a shock wave slamming her chest. She couldn't breathe.

"No, you aren't," her father replied quietly, his voice like steel.

Sassy continued to stare, mute with shock.

Joey dropped his gaze to his lap. "Sorry, Dad. Already done, paperwork complete, aced my physical exam. I'm on a bus to Buffalo next week. Already got my ticket."

Her father was red-faced. "That is the most ridiculous thing you've ever said. You'd better get yourself out of this before it's too late."

"Can't."

Fear and fury blended together in her father's expression. A wide-eyed, livid glower. Sassy felt the same emotions deep inside herself, but her face was frozen.

"You think you are going to do anything to stop the communists by going over there? You, Joe?" he spat. "Get over yourself."

Joey met his father's eyes. "Better dead than red, Dad. Somebody's gotta protect the world. Might as well be me."

Sassy finally found her voice, though it sounded high-pitched to her own ears. "Don't be stupid. What the world needs is peace. You don't belong over there."

Her little brother faced her, his brown eyes pleading for understanding. "We gotta *make* that peace, Sass. The war will keep on blowing people apart until we go over there and put a stop to it. I'm doing the right thing. You gotta believe me."

But she hadn't. She never would. "Don't you dare," she whispered.

"I'm going, Sass. That's how it is."

And that's how it was.

About a month after Joey left for Vietnam, the house echoed with emptiness. Her father was rarely home, and when he was, he barely spoke. One night, she told him she wanted to move out.

He glanced up from his desk and studied her. Dark half circles underlined his eyes, and she wondered if he was sleeping. She hated how her father had aged in only four weeks, and she would never forgive Joey for what he'd done to the two of them. She didn't care that he refused to sell real estate. She'd never thought he would. Like her, he regarded that line of work as a prime example of capitalism, with the wealthy getting wealthier and the poor losing every time. Joey might never make it in the baseball world, but she could see him building bridges much more happily than he would have been selling houses. But Vietnam?

It would be interesting to see what he ended up doing when he got back from the war and started taking life seriously.

Because he *was* coming back someday.

"You want to move out. And do what?" her father asked her.

"I'm going to make something of myself."

He huffed through his nose, then he set his pen on his green felt blotter. "You're not talking about the music thing again, are you? I love you, Susan, but as I've told you many times, there is no future in that kind of career. No money, either. There are millions of girls just like you who want to be a star. You'll never get to the top of that mountain."

She'd heard it all before, but his words only encouraged her to try harder.

"I'm twenty. I want to live my own life in my own place."

"You can't afford it."

"That's why I'm speaking with you. I need a loan, Dad. I'll pay it all back with interest."

"You'll never be able to afford that, either," he muttered, scowling down at his desk. He paused, thinking it through, then he slowly raised his head. "I'll make you a deal. If you get a full-time job and keep it, I will pay for an apartment for you. It has to be a full-time job that has nothing to do with your guitar or your voice. Something practical, in an office. You can type. I'll find you a job at one of my clients' businesses."

Her stomach rolled at the idea of a nine-to-five job, but her dad was watching intently. She started visualizing what colour she'd paint her apartment walls.

"Are you being for real, Dad?"

"For three years, I will pay your rent for an apartment of my choosing, as long as you are working full-time at a real job."

"Why?"

"Because you might have talent, Susan, but you also have a brain. You forget that you need to turn it on once in a while and use it for constructive work. So you will get a job, and when you are paid, you will keep that income. I will pay your rent, and every week you will write me a summary of how it went. If you quit or lose your job, all the money dries up. I will not pay for you to waste your life. Is that agreeable to you?"

It seemed too good to be true, but he had kept his word. He had chosen 105 Isabella Street for her because an old friend from the war was living there. Mr. Moore had lost part of one leg and badly damaged his spine, so he mostly stayed in his apartment with his wife. Other than her father's requirement of holding down a full-time job, all he asked of Sassy was that she visit the veteran on occasion.

The arrangement worked out for everyone. She was working and making a bit of a living, the Moores were cheered when she visited, and her father seemed content to have the huge, quiet house to himself. She thought he might even be dating a little.

Miss Drummond waddled by and set three pages in Sassy's basket without looking at her. Sassy strained to see what was written on them then gave up.

"Five minutes."

Sassy hated Mr. Brown, one of the firm's partners. She had never felt comfortable around the short, balding man. Two months ago, he had said he wanted her in his office to take dictation every Tuesday at four thirty sharp, and he paid her an extra dollar for doing it. Every penny counts, she kept telling herself. Working was tedious, but spending was simple.

"Of course, sir."

Mr. Brown's office was oak-panelled, his floor carpeted. The lamp and ashtray on his imposing oak desk were polished brass, and the chair behind it was leather. The odorous smoke from his cigars had ingrained itself into the wood and the flooring. It all seemed a little much for such a small man, but truthfully, he was a skilled lawyer. That was obvious from the status of his clients.

As Sassy went to her small chair and typewriter to take dictation, Mr. Brown observed from behind his desk. She pulled out the chair, tucked her skirt behind her knees, sat, then waited. She knew the routine. Once she was prepared, he strolled across the room toward her and clamped one bony hand over her shoulder. At first she'd flinched at his touch. Now she just rolled her eyes.

"Now then, Miss Rankin. Are you ready?"

Sassy had no idea what his letters were about. He composed them in his head, hands clasped behind his back while he dictated, then he flipped his fingers in the air and said, "Now sign," which meant she was to put in the *Sincerely* part, leave a space for his elegant signature, then type his name. Sassy was there to type and get paid, and she didn't care what he was going on about. Probably wouldn't have understood it if she tried. Which she didn't.

After the fourth letter, she pulled the paper from her typewriter then froze, feeling both of his hands on her shoulders. This was new.

"Um, Mr. Brown?"

His fingers squeezed, in and out, in and out, then he leaned over, his breath stirring the hair on the top of her head.

"Have I mentioned how pleased I have been with your work, Miss Rankin? Both professional and conscientious."

She didn't move. "Thank you, sir."

"There is an opportunity for you to do very well here. Financially, I mean. I wouldn't think your income is substantial at the moment, but we can work on that, if you're interested."

"I'm sorry, sir. I don't understand."

Oh, but she did. She squeezed her eyes shut and thought she might be sick when he leaned down and pressed his cold lips to her bare neck, near her right ear. "The president of the company will be looking for a new secretary in a couple of weeks. I'd like to recommend you." His fingers dug in a little deeper. "Let's discuss it over dinner, shall we?"

"No, thank you, sir. I . . . I have plans."

"You should change those plans, if you want to improve your position in this firm. I can explain all about it over dinner."

Tears burned. She had heard girls complain about their bosses and the corners they'd been backed into, but Sassy hadn't had to deal with that in all these months. This man was a toad. He revolted her.

And he was offering her a prime new job.

What if she said no? Would he fire her? If she lost this job, her father would stop paying for her apartment. Then what?

She inhaled and held her breath. "No, thank you, sir."

His breath tickled her neck, and she shuddered. He must have misinterpreted, because in the next moment, she felt his mouth on her neck again.

"Well, I can explain it to you here, I suppose. The president will be pleased to meet you, once you receive my personal recommendation," he said, kissing closer to her clavicle. Goose bumps rose involuntarily all over Sassy's body.

"Sir, please stop."

"Don't be stupid, Susan." His voice felt like a hum in her ear. "I can make you a wealthy woman. Well," he said with a chuckle, "relatively wealthy, anyway. Besides, girls these days—"

Done with this awful thing, she put her hands on the edge of the desk and began to rise, but he shoved her back into her seat. His hands slid down the front of her awful tweed jacket and she shot out of her chair, shoving them off her.

"Stop!" she cried. "You . . . you have no right to do that, Mr. Brown." She blinked away tears. This was no way to represent a strong feminist, crying in the hands of a man taking advantage. Still, she couldn't stop her voice from shaking. She gritted her teeth. "You have no right."

She backed toward the door, watching his greasy, patchy face turn the colour of a spring tomato.

"Now, Miss Rankin—"

"Don't you touch me, you dirty old man," she hissed. "I liked this job, but I don't need it. I'll find another where my boss has some respect."

"Respect! For a girl wearing makeup and short skirts? You wanted special attention, didn't you, Susan?"

She didn't miss the emphasis on her given name. He was trying to make some kind of point, but she was way beyond caring about that. "I came to do my job. That's all. You should be ashamed of yourself. You're disgusting."

She spun at the last minute and grabbed the door handle, wondering what on earth would happen next.

The problem solved itself. Mr. Brown's choked voice caught her on the way out. "You're fired. Don't even think about coming back."

She stumbled to her regular desk, ignoring the bug-eyed stares around her. She grabbed her purse and dashed to the door, out of breath and dizzy. Bursting into the sunlight, she stopped and took a shaky breath. The familiar street felt foreign. Everything felt different. In the past five minutes, so much had changed. First, she now understood the terror and humiliation other women had talked about. Second, she was unemployed. And third, she would have to face her father. According to their deal, he could pull her out of her apartment and force her to come home. He could cut her off financially. He could do whatever he wanted.

She walked slowly down the sidewalk toward Queen's Park, where she'd often taken walks at lunchtime. A knot filled her throat as she realized she wouldn't be walking here as often after today. The park was so pretty, even with the sight of a transient lying on a bench in front of her. Especially in the spring, with purple and yellow crocuses opening up around the still-waking shrubs. Feeling a little wobbly, she sank onto a different bench across from the huge bronze statue of Sir John A. Macdonald and pulled a pink box of Good & Plenty from her purse. Sir John A.'s life would have been much quieter than hers, she imagined vaguely, without the city noises and car horns she barely noticed anymore.

Maybe she should go back and ask to speak with one of the other lawyers about what had happened. See if they were looking for another secretary on their team. Surely they'd understand. They'd reprimand Mr. Brown, and . . .

Oh, for goodness' sake. Who would take her word over Mr. Brown's? Would either of the other two even be surprised if she told them? Were they just as guilty?

And what about the other girls there? How would they regard her, having crashed out of the building like a crazy person, only to come crawling back? The way they'd eye her: curious but too shy to ask, so they'd make up rumours instead . . . All over something that she hadn't done. Something she had prevented from happening.

She shook a handful of licorice candies into her hand and threw them in her mouth. She would never go back to that office. Wouldn't pass through those doors even one more time. They didn't deserve her. She'd show them. She'd find a better place to work—

Except she had no idea how to do that. She wasn't going to get much of a reference from Mr. Brown.

"Where are you, Joey?" she whispered to Sir John.

Her brother hadn't been there to lead her out of the darkness this time. He'd promised he would always be there for her. Peanut butter and jelly. Better together.

It was all a lie. Sassy was on her own.

Still, she let his face come to her, let him ask her the question. "What are you gonna do now? Figure it out. You have to."

She had no other choice. "It's easy. Just two little steps," she whispered.

Step one: Figure out how to tell her father that she was out of a job. By choice.

Step two: Beg for mercy.

W ith her mind on the day ahead, Marion stepped into the Administrative Building and greeted Miss Prentice, who was sporting a bright new shade of pink lipstick.

"Very pretty colour," Marion said, smiling at her.

"You think so? I saw it behind the counter at Eaton's, and the girl said it suited me."

"It certainly does," Marion replied, picking up her charts. "Any messages for me?"

"Not this morning, Dr. Hart."

Down the corridor, Dr. Bernstein was frowning at his work under a flickering lamp. Marion made a mental note to mention to Miss Prentice that the old doctor needed a new bulb.

"Good morning, Barbara," she said, knocking on the first door to her left. "It's Dr. Hart. May I come in?"

The door was already partially ajar, which Marion took as a positive sign. Barbara was normally an extremely private person.

"All right," came a reluctant response.

A nurse was with Barbara when she entered. "Good morning, Doctor.

I'm just finishing here." She rolled her eyes for Marion to see, then muttered, "It's one of those mornings. Full moon or something."

That could mean practically anything in a place like this, Marion thought, pulling a chair to Barbara's bedside.

"How are you feeling today?"

"I'm awfully concerned, Dr. Hart. They say I am to have a roommate soon. I don't want a roommate."

"Most people here have roommates. The hospital is undergoing changes," Marion said, trying not to say too much and send Barbara reeling. "We talked about this before, remember? We are moving from this facility to more open-community health centres, and the administration is now moving patients around to make that possible. I know you don't like change, but you've been fortunate so far."

Reasoning didn't help. Barbara's eyes shone. "What if she and I don't get along?"

Marion would have to monitor the situation. Barbara had been doing well recently, not showing acute signs of anxiety, but her stricken expression was a little concerning.

"Barbara, I have not met your new roommate yet, but they would not put her with you if they do not believe you would be a good match. I understand it can be an anxious time, meeting new people, but you have gotten very good at managing your emotions lately. Should we talk about this some more?"

"No. I'm all right." She exhaled heavily. "I was thinking I might join the art therapy class this afternoon."

"That would be an excellent activity for you. Some others have found it to be extremely helpful. I am looking forward to seeing what you create."

Barbara scowled. "I said I was *thinking* about it. I don't need added pressure from you."

Next on Marion's rounds was Alice Sumner. The young woman sat on her bed, sunlight beaming onto her, and yet Alice had draped an unfolded newspaper over her head. She seemed annoyed.

"Some weather we're having," she said, clearly put out. "I think there's a leak in my ceiling. See it?"

The room was bone-dry. "Someone once said that 'into every life a little rain must fall,'" Marion prompted gently.

"'Some days are dark and dreary.' Longfellow. That's who said it."

Marion knew that, but she also knew Alice liked to show off. She might be unhappy with the current state of the weather, but Marion was pleased with how her thoughts were staying on track.

"Why, you're right," she said. "Thank you, Alice. How are you feeling today?"

"Wet."

"Warm enough?" Wary of Alice's fists, Marion carefully tugged a blanket over the woman's lap. Her fingers clamped onto its edge like claws.

"Nurse Agnes said we are having chocolate pudding later."

"That sounds delicious. Do you like chocolate pudding?"

"Yes."

"Are you going to art therapy today? I understand Barbara might go as well."

As she'd hoped, Marion saw a solemn clarity settle over the girl's expression. Alice liked to talk about what she knew, and she liked to suggest that she knew a lot. That was fine. Anything that kept Alice in the real world was helpful.

"I believe, Dr. Hart, that once Barbara sets her creative mind free through the medium of art, she will feel relief. I have experienced a similar awakening, you see."

Beyond impressed with her patient's sudden lucidity, Marion pretended to flip through Alice's chart and write something down. The shift in her dosage must be helping. Her awareness and empathy suggested the group therapy was doing what it was supposed to do as well.

"Very perceptive, Alice. I'll make sure to keep that in mind."

The newspaper on Alice's head lowered slowly, then she blinked at her window. "Looks like the rain stopped."

"It has."

"I think it will be a good day, Dr. Hart."

Marion smiled. "I think you're right. Can you give me another word to describe how you're feeling?"

That took a moment while Alice searched her memory. "Optimistic."

"Oh, Alice. I love that word."

Marion's head was deep in her notes as she walked down the wide corridor then turned a corner, colliding into a solid chest. She jumped back, mortified.

"Dr. McKenny. I am so sorry. I wasn't paying attention."

"Nothing to apologize for, Dr. Hart," he said, laughter in his eyes. "I wouldn't mind at all if you made a conscious effort to bump into me more often."

Her face burned.

"Actually, this is great timing," he said, leaning against the wall and looking like a model in a magazine. "I was wondering if you might like to have dinner with me one of these nights."

This was not the first time Paul McKenny had asked her out. Marion knew she should be flattered. He was young and smart and terribly attractive. Nurses fluttered around him like little white moths, but Marion couldn't get interested, no matter how she tried. She had graduated one year after Paul had, and she'd been aware of him the whole time. How could she not, the way he watched her? He'd even joined her at a small café one day, making himself comfortable and talking all about his life for a half hour. All she'd wanted was coffee and a quiet place to read. She had smiled and nodded in all the right places, but she kept wishing he'd move to another table. Everyone said Paul was exciting, always doing new things outside of hospital hours, like travelling, and whatever else. Marion thought he was as boring as dry toast.

"That's not a good idea, Paul. You know. Mixing business with—"

"With pleasure?" he finished when she faltered. "Come on, Marion. Those are old-fashioned rules. Times, they are a-changing, didn't you hear?"

"Bob Dylan," Alice volunteered, wandering past them down the hall.

"There's a great Italian restaurant nearby. Giorgio's," he said. "Do you know it? Best carbonara in the city. After, we'll go to Yorkville and have some fun. Give me a good reason why we shouldn't. Come on. You like me. Everyone likes me."

Marion had run out of excuses. In the past, she'd claimed she was feeling sick or had a headache, whatever she could think of to put him off, but he kept on coming. Maybe he would tire of the chase if she went out this once.

"When?" she asked reluctantly.

"No time like the present. Thursday night work for you? Or do you feel a headache coming on?"

Of course he'd known she'd made those excuses up. He was a psychiatrist, for heaven's sake. "No, Paul. I feel fine. Tomorrow sounds . . . fun."

"Don't strain yourself, Marion." He chuckled. "Who knows? You might even enjoy yourself, if you allow it. I'll take you to dinner, then we'll hit the Riverboat. If you can still stand the sight of me by then, that is," he said, flashing a perfect smile. He looked like he couldn't imagine that ever happening.

"Fine," she said, continuing to the old building. "You may pick me up at six thirty."

Marion didn't like to date. Or at least she hadn't liked the few she'd been on. Trying to fake interest in someone else's conversation was exhausting. She did that for a living all day long. If tomorrow went as she expected it would, Paul would talk about himself all night.

"I can do this. It's just dinner," she muttered to herself as she pulled open the door to Ward 6B.

"Good afternoon, Dr. Hart."

"Hello, Burt. What day is it today?"

"Wednesday," he announced gleefully. "Wednesday afternoon, because we had lunch."

"Well done, Burt."

"Are you going to see Big John?"

"Yes, I am."

"He's having a sad day, I think."

"I'm sorry to hear that. Thank you for letting me know in advance."

She wound her way through the room, dodging a couple of men who had planted themselves in the middle and appeared to have forgotten where they were. Along the way, she returned the chorus of "Hello, Dr. Hart. Dr. Hart. Dr. Hart," with her own "Hello, Bruce, Francis, George," and whoever else called out.

John sat at the far end of the room, as usual. Today he was alone, and he had turned his chair to face the glazed window, with its pattern of black metal bars. His chin hung over his chest.

Marion pulled up a chair and set it beside him. "Good afternoon, John," she said. "Burt said you're having a sad day. Can I do anything to help you?"

He lifted his face almost right away, not after his usual delay. His expression seemed brighter, though a string of drool hung from one corner of his mouth. She had been right about lowering his dosage.

"I want to go home."

Her mind briefly went blank, she was so shocked to hear him speak in a complete sentence. If only she didn't have to disappoint him. Whether or not the medicine was working, John did not have the physical or mental capacity to live outside of the institution. She planned to keep him in it as long as she could. She glanced at his chart out of habit, but she knew all the facts by heart. Big John had lived in this building for fifteen years. He had never left the premises, not even on a day pass, and no one had come to visit. He probably wouldn't recognize his old home if he was standing on its front lawn.

There was something about this man that broke Marion's heart. She tried to imagine him twenty years before, young and laughing and full of life. No one could have imagined he would end up here. But the little version of Big John had been struck by a car one day while riding his bicycle, and something had been damaged in his brain. He went from being a regular high school student to a maniac who stabbed the neighbour's cat to death. Days later, he attacked his father, who landed in the hospital with stab wounds that barely missed his kidney. John didn't remember doing either of those things.

If John went home, his family, if they agreed to take him in—which they wouldn't—would have to monitor him constantly. Which they wouldn't.

"What would you do there?" she asked.

"See all the leaves. Leaves are soft. I would touch them." His hand moved sluggishly to his shirt pocket and drew out a pack of cigarettes. He stuck one in his mouth and turned to her, waiting. "I want to drive Grandpa's car."

Marion reluctantly drew her lighter from her own pocket. She had never smoked, but many of the patients did, so she carried it around for them. They weren't allowed to have their own lighters, for obvious reasons.

"John, do you remember what the doctor said about smoking? He said he was concerned about your cough and how it's getting worse. Cigarettes are very bad for your health."

He didn't register the advice. She clicked the little flame to life and held it out.

"I have a rabbit," he offered, a vague sort of smile lifting his mouth. "I forget its name."

"That's all right, John. We all forget things. We have many other things to remember."

"I remember nothing."

"That's not true," she assured him. "You remembered your rabbit, and you remembered the leaves. That's not nothing. Let's try an exercise, John. Close your eyes and take a deep breath. Good. Now, tell me about your rabbit. What colour is he?"

"Brown," he replied softly, sinking easily into the simple memory with the aid of his medications and his familiarity with the exercise.

"Can you imagine him on your front lawn right now? You can? That's very good, John. What colour is that grass? That's right. Can you feel the grass? It's soft and cool, isn't it? Now touch the rabbit. Stroke him gently down his back and tell me what his lovely brown fur feels like."

She continued, keeping her voice in a soft, hypnotic cadence, taking him back to his childhood and the sensations he longed for. Everyone wanted that, didn't they? To return to greener days without demands, days when one could lie back and appreciate the sunlight warming their skin without feeling like they should be somewhere else. To breathe in and out and imagine the whole world open around them, so that they became a part of the whole.

Marion craved that sometimes. Days in the sunshine with nothing on her mind, just the itch of the grass beneath her thighs, the tickle of an ant taking a shortcut over her knee, the bounce of a nearby robin tracking its meal. Smiling when her father came out to see her, walking in the comfortable lope she recognized so fondly. He was happy. He was calm.

"Hello, Bunny," he had called her back then. *Bunny.*

In her memory, a cloud passed over the sun. The shadow stole her father's easy smile, as it so often had. He spun on his heel, striding back to the house without another word.

John was rocking slightly. "Mother is shouting." A frown creased his wide brow. "Mother took the rabbit. She's crying."

Alarms went off in Marion's head. "Can you tell me why she's crying?"

"The rabbit is floppy." He smiled. "Wiggly. Like a worm."

She took a deep breath, sweeping away her childhood memories. She was here for John, not herself.

"All right," she said, trying not to visualize the poor rabbit. "Let's move on. Your mother took the rabbit, but you are still on the grass. Now, the next part of the exercise is not about your memory. It's something different. I want you to keep your eyes closed—"

"They are."

"Good. Now lie down in the yard, and rest the palms of your hands on the grass. Feel the sun on your face. Doesn't that feel good? Take a deep breath and imagine you are breathing in all that happy sunshine."

John's confusion was swiftly replaced with guileless calm.

"Good. When you feel ready, open your eyes. How do you feel?"

"I feel hungry. I'm going to leave now."

"All right, John. You did very well today. I will see you later this week."

"Okay."

They turned from each other, then he called out, "Don't forget, Dr. Hart. I want to go home tomorrow."

To her shame, Marion left the ward and pretended she hadn't heard him. A man with John's problems should never be allowed to leave these walls; however, Dr. Bernstein and the board had gone against Marion's advice and cleared him, based on his model behaviour—behaviour that was, of course, controlled by the barbiturates and the other medications he was on. These walls would soon come down. After John left this place, who would make sure that he took his medications? That he ate? That he slept in a warm place? Without those things, he could become a risk to the public.

When Marion thought about John's future outside of the institute, she prickled with panic.

Done for the day, she walked down the wide corridor, dotted with patients talking among themselves, and let their conversations wash over her. Some were making sense, some made sense only to themselves. Already unnerved, Marion's heart began to race, set off by a familiar fear that everyone here needed a part of her she couldn't afford to share. She felt an almost overwhelming urge to flee.

She ducked around a corner, out of sight of the patients, and stopped walking. As she exhaled, tears filled her eyes. The nurse was right about the full moon, she told herself. She visualized it as she calmed, taking in the lunar lines and shadows, its perfect silver curve. Someday soon, the newspapers said, America would put a man up there. What would that be like? Cold, she imagined, consciously slowing her pulse. And quiet. So quiet.

BANG! The door to her left shook with impact, and a roar came from within. Startled, Marion peered through the window and saw Daniel Neumann, the man recently returned from Vietnam. He paced the small room like a lion in a cage, digging his fingers into his hair with frustration. When he turned, she stepped out of his view then lifted his chart and looked over Paul McKenny's notes.

Acute situational maladjustment. Combat fatigue.

Caution advised. Unpredictable outbursts. History of violence.

When lucid, patient is intelligent. Recommend slow lifting of sedatives based on physical actions to further explore mental state.

"Acute situational maladjustment." No wonder, she thought, studying the man through his window and recalling photographs of the war, both on the cover of *Life* magazine and in the news. She doubted anyone could return from that hell unscathed. His face was broken and bruised. His fury was a living thing barely contained. One day, tens of thousands of men would come home from Vietnam. How many with similar symptoms to Daniel's? How could society possibly take care of them all?

At the back of his room, Daniel faced the wall, his hands braced against it like he was trying to shove it away.

"Let me out of here!" he yelled, lifting his face to the ceiling.

Marion sensed his anguish in the set of his shoulders, the flex of his back. So much pain. So much rage confined. She knew Paul was doing what he believed was the right thing for his patient, but suddenly she wanted to go in and speak with Daniel herself, somehow ease the agony that so obviously squeezed his soul with every breath. She wanted to work with him, not just stand by and observe.

Daniel spun, and his wild gaze locked with hers. She drew back with a gasp, but couldn't look away from the dark bruises colouring his face. He strode toward the door and stopped only when his breath touched the glass, inches from her. She saw the intelligence Paul had noted in his chart, trapped behind a deep sense of urgency.

"Let me out," he said firmly. His voice was muffled by the door, but she heard him clearly. "They need me."

He didn't shout, but his tone was definite. She could tell he believed to his soul what he was saying. She yearned to ask him about that, to find out what he needed and who needed him, but she could not carry out a conversation here in the corridor, through a door. And he wasn't her patient, anyway.

"Please," he implored, lowering his voice. "Please let me out. They need me."

"I'm sorry," she said, her heart aching. "I can't help you."

The rage was back, burning in his eyes. "But they'll die! Call for air support!"

She heard the efficient tread of Nurse Thelma's white shoes approaching from behind. She was accompanied by two burly orderlies, and Marion stepped out of their way. She said nothing, and they did not acknowledge her presence. Nurse Thelma's key slid into the lock, and a wave of sympathy for the man within washed through Marion.

"Get me out of here!" Daniel shouted, desperate now. "They'll die, damnit! They need help! I need to—" His voice dropped. "No! Please. Get off me. No more. I'll be quiet. But if I can't help them, they—"

Marion couldn't make out what Nurse Thelma's muffled voice was saying. The big orderlies crowded around Daniel, blocking her view, and she saw them struggle to gain control over him. Once Daniel was contained, they moved quickly, tying him down so the nurse could jab the needle into his arm. The sedative, Marion knew, would work fast.

In that moment, he looked directly at Marion, still standing uselessly in the doorway.

"Please," he said, his voice dwindling to a whimper as the drug took hold. "They'll die. Please send help."

The pain in his voice was too sharp to ignore. It dug its hooks deep into her, anchoring itself to her heart. She couldn't stop thinking about him as she left the building for the day.

On her way home, she stopped at Jack's Variety Store to pick up a few things. The location was convenient, though the short blocks from Yonge Street to her place felt like a long way in bad weather. The little store had everything she needed, and she liked the owners a great deal. Tonight, she pulled open the door and smiled at Esther Weisbroad, the owner's wife, standing by the counter. She was a sweet, quiet woman with tucked-back brown hair and an apologetic smile. Most of her vocabulary was Polish and Yiddish.

Marion had been shaken up on her first visit to the store. Esther was packing Marion's groceries into a paper bag when her sweater sleeve had slid toward her elbow, revealing a dark smudge on her forearm. When she lifted her arm again, Marion peered closer and felt her stomach roll. It wasn't a smudge at all, but a dark, hateful, twenty-year-old tattoo made up of six inked numbers. The easiest thing for Marion to do would have been to pretend she hadn't seen the indelible mark, but she didn't feel right doing that. As she paid for her groceries that night, Marion smiled gently at the woman. She told her she was very sorry for her past experiences, and that she hoped her life in Canada was a good one.

Today, Marion headed to the back of the store for eggs and milk. She passed Esther's nine-year-old daughter, Roshelle, at the magazine rack, where she often dawdled—much to her mother's chagrin. One of her two long brown braids had come partially undone, and Marion spied chocolate on the corners of her full lips.

"What are you reading?"

The little girl closed the cover of a bright yellow comic book, covered by a cartoon drawing of a puppy. "Scamp. He's one of *Lady and the Tramp*'s puppies. Scamp is very naughty." She leaned intently toward Marion. "Sometimes he even talks to the junkyard dogs."

Marion feigned horror and was about to ask more, when Esther's scolding voice travelled over. "Roshelle! *O kurczę! Oy vey!*"

Roshelle's shoulders jumped up to her ears, and she bit her bottom lip. "Sorry, Mama!" She gave Marion a guilty little smile, put the comic book back where it belonged, and skipped outside.

Marion set her eggs, milk, butter, bread, and jam on the counter then waited patiently for Esther. She was busy with another customer, a woman with a thick mess of chestnut hair falling over a stylish brown tweed suit.

"Just a minute. I have more in here," the woman said, shaking her purse and peering inside.

She was young and quite pretty, but the quick glimpse Marion got of her profile made it obvious that she was not happy. There was a patchy red flush on her cheekbones and a definite redness around her eyes. Her mascara was mostly washed away.

"Oh, I know I have more in here," she was muttering. She pulled her hand from her purse and opened it to reveal a few coins, but not enough.

"May I help?" Marion asked, her heart going out to her. She took out her wallet and paid the difference.

The woman turned, regarding her with wide, surprised eyes the colour of spring grass. Her fingers were shaking. "I don't know how to thank you," she said with a sniff. "I've . . . I've just had, oh, the worst day at work. I got fired."

There was the tug Marion always felt, the psychiatrist in her, wanting to know how she could help. But she was tired. It was time to close up for the day.

"There's no need to thank me." Marion had already calculated her own bill, so she put the correct amount on the counter, smiled at Esther, then slipped past the other woman. "I hope your evening gets better," she called over her shoulder.

Marion hoped the same for herself, but it was not to be. Daniel's plea filled her thoughts: the panic in his voice as the needle approached, and the way his face had melted into submission under the influence of the medication.

Let me out. They need me. They'll die.

What was he seeing?

Daniel had a story he needed to tell. Something that was tearing him apart. He had stared at Marion with such hope in his tortured expression, and she had walked away without lifting a finger to help. She had a terrible sense that she had let him down in the worst way.

That's when she remembered that her date with Paul McKenny was the next night. Paul was Daniel's doctor. Maybe this was her chance to make things right.

six

SASSY

❧

Every minute of every day since she'd left Jamieson, Baines, and Brown, Sassy's gut had churned. She'd tried to tell herself it was the flu or something, but she knew perfectly well what it was. Sassy had never lied to her father before, and she had always insisted with Joey that omission was the same as lying. She should have told her father about her job right away, or rather the lack of one, but having delayed her confession for a whole week, she was now stuck in the middle of an even bigger omission.

Out of guilt, she went the next morning to visit Mr. and Mrs. Moore, her father's war buddy and his wife. She rarely saw them outside of the building unless it was Mrs. Moore carrying groceries. Whenever she saw that, Sassy carried them for her. Today she went to visit, but Mrs. Moore turned her away, saying Mr. Moore was feeling out of sorts. So Sassy returned to her room and tried to keep her mind off the inevitable meeting between herself and her father. Like the Moores, Sassy spent as much time as she could in her apartment, watching television, trying to concentrate on books, eating potato chips, and playing guitar.

Music had always been Sassy's happy place. Her father had no musical talent whatsoever, meaning that when she encouraged him to sing with her, his version sounded nothing like hers. He was tone-deaf, he couldn't maintain a rhythm, and he was content with spending a day without listening to a radio or a record player. But Joey and Sassy were born with music dancing through their veins, just like their mother.

In the large glass-domed parlour of their massive old house stood a Heintzman mahogany baby grand piano. Years after her death, her father told Sassy that her mother had been able to play anything by ear on that piano. Of the very few memories Sassy had of Rita Rankin, she clung most tightly to one. It felt dreamlike, but it filled her with such nostalgia, she knew it had to be real. Every night, her mother had played soft, sweet music after the children had been put to bed. But on one special night, Sassy snuck out of her bedroom to listen, tiptoeing as quietly as she could. Her mother hadn't seen her there, tucked underneath the piano, barely breathing in an attempt to keep quiet. Sassy was held spellbound by the majesty of the instrument vibrating all around her, and the wonder of the chords and melodies her mother created. The sweetness of the memory was tied to one clear image: soft brown slippers beneath cream satin pant legs, slowly lifting then lowering on the pedals.

After her mother's death, and before they were tall enough to reach the pedals, Sassy's father signed both children up for piano lessons. Scales and arpeggios were torture for Sassy, but they were even more agonizing for Joey. After six months, their teacher, Miss Lilly, frostily informed their father that Joey refused to play a note during lessons. The little boy's protest eventually won out over his father's insistence and Miss Lilly's weak objections, and Joey happily shifted his attention to baseball. Sassy stuck with Miss Lilly, forcing herself through the tough stuff so she could get to the fun. She even learned music theory and history, though the whole concept of chord progressions initially baffled her.

What Sassy hadn't expected was that during those long, repetitive scale sessions, she would fall in love with the mindless intricacies of the process. While her fingers worked, her mind sang, creating vague little melodies that wrapped around the arpeggios and wound through the scales. One by one Sassy added to her colourful stack of John W. Schaum piano method books, working all the way through until she finished the Grey Book. That's when

Miss Lilly finally gave in to Sassy's campaign for sheet music of current pop-ular music. "The Great Pretender" and "Smoke Gets in Your Eyes" were the first two, since Miss Lilly enjoyed the Platters, but the notes on the paper were simple and felt dull to Sassy. She asked for more, and Miss Lilly chal-lenged her with a stack of Rodgers & Hammerstein musicals. Sassy melted into the romantic songs, livening them up with chords she'd perfected through learning theory.

One night in October 1964, she turned on the television to watch *The Ed Sullivan Show*, excited to watch a band from England that everyone was talking about. At school the next day, all the girls were swooning over Mick Jagger. For Sassy, it was all about Keith Richard's guitar.

The next day, her father bought Sassy the most gorgeous guitar she'd ever seen. He'd bought it off a client, who guaranteed she'd love the clear sound. Right off the bat, she noticed the trademark gold "Martin" written above the pegs." Jazzed, Sassy carried it to a girlfriend's house, since Nicky had been playing guitar for a year already.

"Sassy!" Nicky cried, astounded. "This is the same guitar as Bob Dylan plays!"

It took a while for Sassy to memorize the placement of the frets and to harden the new calluses on her fingertips, but over time, the guitar re-placed the piano. She returned to the eighty-eight keys and polished the ma-hogany whenever she felt the urge, but those six strings, strung across the sensuous maple shape of her guitar, had won her over. The instrument was freeing, compared to the anchor of the piano. She played for girlfriends on the school's football field, and they all sang along as the breeze lifted their hair. When the women in protests called for liberation, she smiled, because she had already found her own version.

But it had been two years since Sassy graduated from high school, and her friends had moved on. A pregnant Nicky had gotten married after grad-uation to some boy Sassy had never met, and a couple of others had left for college. There was nowhere for Sassy to play guitar anymore, except by her-self, and she craved an audience. If only her father understood. She needed to express herself, and for that she needed freedom from his demands.

Then again, there was rent to pay.

She had a couple of choices about what to do next, she figured. Or maybe three. Try and find a new job, somehow make it big with her voice, or crawl back to her father and beg for forgiveness. She liked the middle option best, and she truly wanted to believe it was possible, but while Sassy might be a dreamer, she was also a realist. She knew the truth.

There was a knock on the door. She swallowed a lump of apprehension as she turned the knob, though she doubted it was her father.

"Davey," she sighed, letting him in. He curled a warm arm around her waist and drew her in for a kiss that temporarily took away her anxiety.

"Got you something." He handed her a bunch of red tulips, which she was pretty sure had been growing in front of the building.

"Thanks. Where you been?"

"Work. You know."

"Did they move you up from dishwashing yet?" she teased.

He'd started working in the kitchen at Chez Monique, one of the coffee-houses in Yorkville, and though he'd had to start at the bottom, he claimed that it was only the first step to his career as a chef. Sometimes he brought her leftovers, which she appreciated.

"Yeah! I chop onions now. Are my eyes red?" He put his face right in hers to make her laugh.

"I can smell them on you."

"And I've been hanging on Baldwin Street, too. There's a hip new pad there with plenty of cats like me. You know. Resisters."

His fingers snugged around the curve of her body, sending a thrill through her. She wasn't deluded that the closeness she shared with Davey was love, but for now, all she wanted was comfort. With her eyes on his, she skimmed her tongue over her upper lip.

Evidently, Davey wanted something else. "Sassy, I got a problem." He took a step back and turned his jeans' pockets inside out. "I'm broke."

"That's why you're here? You came to sponge off me? What would make you think that was a good idea?"

He held out his hands, indicating the apartment. "You gotta have green to live in this choice pad, baby. Everyone else I know is living on top of each other in rooming houses." His sensual smile curled beneath impossibly golden eyes. "But no, that's not the only reason I'm here."

"You can crash here, Davey, but I have no money." She held the words in as long as she could, then she blurted, "I lost my job."

His lips made an O shape. "Bummer. Sorry, man. What happened?"

Her gut rolled, and she turned away. "My scuzzy, chrome-dome boss got all handsy. I nearly puked on his fancy carpet."

"Oh man. That's heavy. Then he fired you?"

She was a little put off by his response. Maybe he was smoking too much weed and his perception was off. "No, Davey. That's when I *quit*. I wasn't gonna hang around there another second."

"That's tough."

"Yeah, well." She sat then picked up her guitar and strummed a chord, picked out the first few notes of "Turn! Turn! Turn!" "It is what it is."

"Don't sweat it. You're talented. You'll get a job." He followed her to the couch. "I don't know about me, though. I'm kind of lazy. I'm really good at lying down. Wanna see?"

He was so cute, reclining on her couch and looking at her like a puppy. She'd thought about him a lot over the past few days. She'd missed him and the ease she felt when she was with him. Giving into temptation, she put down her guitar and lowered herself into the welcoming basket of his arms with a deep sigh, she laid her head on his chest.

"I gotta get a job."

"Bummer," he repeated gently, his voice vibrating under her cheek. His fingertips skimmed up and down her back. "Do you want to go look for one right now, or maybe you and I could chill first?"

She let herself relax, if only for a little while. "Let's chill. We can find a job later."

When later came, it was already dark. Too late for job hunting. While Davey snored, Sassy got up and made grilled cheese, knowing the aroma of frying butter would wake him. She was right, and a few minutes later she heard him on her telephone, though she didn't listen in. As she flipped the sandwiches, he nestled up behind her, encircling her with his arms.

"You smell nice," he said, resting his chin on her shoulder.

She grinned. "I thought you were a chef, mister. What you smell is burnt butter and cheese."

"Yeah? Well, I got you a job."

She stepped out of his embrace and gazed into his careless good looks. His hair was tousled from sleeping, sticking up like a rooster tail in the back. "Oh yeah? What kinda job?"

"It's a gig."

"What?"

His smile was smug. "Yeah. I asked the boss. Eddie says he's got an opening for tomorrow night. Amateur night. Technically, I guess it isn't a real gig, because you only get one song, but it's something. Nine thirty, he said. What do you think of that? Did your boy do good?"

"Seems too good to be true."

If you get a full-time job, she heard her father say again, *I will help you pay for the apartment. Something that is not to do with your guitar and your voice.*

This gig had two strikes against it already. It was not full-time, and it had everything to do with her music. But she couldn't help wondering where amateur night might lead. Her father hadn't said she wasn't allowed to try.

One song. Her mind raced through her inventory, picking her favourite. She popped up onto her toes and kissed him. "My boy did good."

seven
MARION

‿❦‿

Marion left work early on Thursday in order to be ready for Paul when he came to pick her up for their date. He'd mentioned Yorkville, so for a change of scenery and to clear her mind, she took a different bus route home. As they jostled past Bay and Bloor, she studied the Victorian-style homes converted into coffeehouses. Colourful people crowded the sidewalk.

If a person in Toronto was young and free and looking for fun, Yorkville, she had heard, was the place to be. If a man wanted to wear long hair without being called names, if a girl wanted to kiss another girl, if a person was hunting for drugs of any kind, or perhaps some musical, artistic, or literary entertainment, this was where they congregated. On a sunny day like today, they lined up outside the coffeehouses or sat in contented little circles on the sidewalk, clouds of fragrant smoke suspended over their heads.

Their parents' generation, they declared through bullhorns and songs, had ruined the world for generations to come. It was time for a revolution, they claimed, strolling across a busy street in bare feet to meet up with friends. It was time for change, they cheered, shaking tambourines over their heads and dancing in circles. From the bottom of their flared jeans to the petals of the flowered wreaths encircling their heads, hippies lived their lives as they wanted.

Marion supposed she had been born ten years too early to really connect with them. Her sister, Pat, had gleefully joined in. Embrace the movement, she had suggested, but Marion didn't see a movement. She saw a fad.

She also saw both sides. She agreed in theory with what they were saying about the need for progress, but she didn't see the hippy generation doing anything constructive to fix things. Signs and slogans were not productive.

On the other side of the conversation, she disagreed when they claimed everything that came before had been bad for the world. Knowledge gained from past experience was always valuable, just like with medical history. Mistakes had been made, but scientists learned from those then sometimes created miracles, like antibiotics.

As for the protests, which thankfully were less violent than the ones in the United States, Marion mutely encouraged the participants from the sidelines. Women's rights, opposition to racism, ending the war in Vietnam, all of those were causes she fully supported.

The first two matters, women's rights and fighting racism, seemed to be making headway both here and in the States. After all, she was a doctor, and a Black man had graduated among her class as well. She wondered if he was treated differently at his work, too. She suspected so.

But of those causes, the war raged on. Kids the same age as the ones dancing on Yorkville's sidewalks were being slaughtered in a hellish nightmare called Vietnam.

Her thoughts went to Daniel Neumann, a big man in the physical prime of his life. She had no doubt he had been a powerful fighter out there, before he'd lost his eye. Even with his loss, he was strong and determined. There was so much restlessness in him. So much barely controlled energy. She thought again of a lion pacing, trapped in a cage.

Through the bus window, Marion spotted a mother holding the hands of two little girls wearing matching pink sweaters. She thought of Pat wandering the grounds of Expo 67. Her sister had sent a postcard of the U.S.S.R. exhibit, which looked to her like a snow-covered hill swooping over a wall of glass. In her tiny, neat handwriting, Pat had written how much fun they were having, riding a monorail to get around, going inside to learn about

Soviet space technology, even sitting in special armchairs, where they got to experience the sensations of space travel itself.

It's incredible to see the Soviets' technological advancements set out for all to see. Then we entered a large area devoted to their rural way of life, art, international relations, and even a fashion show in their six-hundred-seat theatre. The contradiction was quite jarring. I thought a lot about you in there, wondering what you would think of the display and the communists' message: "In the name of Man, for the good of Man." The Canadian exhibit on the waterfront was no slouch, but I found the Soviet one more impressive. I am taking lots of pictures with my fancy new Nikon. I'll show you everything when we're home.

Marion was quietly envious of her sister, taking in such a spectacle, then she remembered Barbara and Alice and John and all her other patients, each one unique and challenging in their own way, and she was glad she had decided to stay. They needed her, and she needed the routine.

Tonight, however, Marion would challenge herself. She got off the bus and walked the rest of the way down Isabella Street to the apartment, battling nerves. In two hours, Paul McKenny would arrive to pick her up and take her for dinner. She felt slightly nauseous at the thought. Not because of him. He wasn't that bad. It was the idea of making small talk for hours that made Marion uncomfortable.

"I will be fine," she reminded herself, riding the elevator up, then stepping onto the fifth-floor corridor.

The door of 509 clicked shut as she passed, making her smile. "And so will you, sir," she told him. "We will all be fine."

eight
SASSY

❧

Chez Monique. Amateur night. Sassy could hardly believe it was happening. Dear Davey, with his straightforward attitude toward life. She never would have had the nerve to approach the manager like that. This afternoon, she had changed outfits at least four times before finally settling on a white peasant blouse with delicate navy and orange embroidery over a pair of perfectly faded denim flares. She layered a multicoloured macramé poncho on top, though she was slightly nervous about the fringe possibly getting tangled in the guitar strings. It never had before, but it just seemed like Murphy's Law might apply. She tied her hair in two braids so it would be out of the way.

This would be Sassy's first real performance. Oh, how she wished Joey could be there to hear her.

Even a year later, it seemed impossible that he was in Vietnam. She still couldn't understand his reasons. She wanted him home, safe and sound and sitting in the front row. If Joey was still in Toronto, she had no doubt he would be at Chez Monique tonight. She had no idea what he'd be doing for a job, but he wouldn't be working for their father. Joey was more about helping others than making money. Which was why, she supposed, he was in Vietnam. Surely there had been other options available, though. Options that didn't put him in a jungle, dodging bullets and machetes.

If only he was here.

How could he have left her?

Her father had refused, in the end, to see Joey off at the bus station, but Sassy had gone. She couldn't imagine not being there for him. He had climbed onto the Gray Coach bus to Buffalo without fanfare. With tears streaming down her face, she watched him walk down the aisle until he found an available seat, then he waved through the window. The bus crunched into gear, and she feared she might collapse with grief. She knew what happened to boys who went down there. She watched TV and read the news. If she ever saw her brother again—and honestly, she feared she might not—he'd be different.

His first letter arrived about a month later.

> *Training is dog-eat-dog tough. We run a mile before breakfast every day. One guy couldn't manage the parallel bars, and he was bringing down the PT score for the whole team, so they had a "blanket party" for him. Sounds cool, doesn't it? Wrong. They cover the fool with a blanket, then everyone beats the hell out of him to teach him a lesson.*
>
> *We're shipping off in a couple of days. I know you hate that, but I'm ready. I want to see what it's all about, and I can't do that here.*

She didn't hear anything more for another six weeks or so. That time, the paper was mud-smeared and wrinkled, but she knew his printing like she knew her own.

> *Food's bad, but better than nothing. C-rats are meat, bread, and some kind of dessert. They all taste the same. There's only one other Canadian in the unit. Mostly I hang out with a big guy named Tex. You'd like him. Handsome as hell, and boy, can he make us laugh with that drawl. Hal is a farmer from Ohio with six sisters. I told him that was nuts, because it's too much work with just one! Ha ha. Stu is the quietest of us. He wants to be a lawyer. I think he's from Seattle.*

The people here are grateful for our help. They aren't strong enough to fight back. They need us.

Sassy couldn't bear the weight of his words by herself. That night, she had gone to see her father. She said nothing at first, just watched him read a book in the living room, a glass of whisky in one hand. He finally glanced up, brow lifted in question, and she told him she wanted to read him Joey's letter. He put down his book and didn't object. Afterward, she set the tattered page on the table beside her, waiting for his reaction.

"It's true," he said after a quiet moment. "If the people in South Vietnam want freedom, they need the strength and support of the American military machine. But the U.S. needs Vietnam, too."

"Why?"

"American industry relies on Asia's natural resources, and that includes Vietnam. Americans love freedom, but someone else usually ends up footing the bill for them. In this case it's Vietnam." He sipped at his whisky. "War's great for business."

"What an awful thing to say."

"Why? It's the truth. No good ever comes from ignoring the facts. The U.S. manufactures the weapons they're using over there. In fact, I'd warrant a guess that both sides of the conflict are using weapons made in the U.S."

She hesitated, taken aback by the idea. She'd never thought about it like that. "So Americans are extending the war and killing thousands of people on purpose? For money? Shame on them."

"It's not just Americans, Susan. We can't go blaming everything on them. We sit up here in judgement, feeling morally superior because we didn't agree to send our men to fight, although some of the stupid ones like Joey went anyway. War is good for our business, too. Guess who supplies the basic material for those weapons, and who picks up the slack—and makes the money—when American factories are overwhelmed."

Sassy had never forgotten that conversation. It had shifted her perspective, and whenever anyone brought up the topic of how "bad" Americans were, she made a point to correct them. There was enough blame to go around when it came to war.

She slipped her poncho over her head and looked into the mirror, trying to envision the woman onstage she would become in a few hours. Her first real performance. Her first real audience. Maybe if she tried really hard, she could imagine Joey sitting up front, cheering her on. But no good came from ignoring facts, she knew. In reality, Joey was half a world away.

There was a knock, and Sassy broke out of her daze. Mrs. Levin stood at the door with a pot of flowers, smiling. Her neighbour was around sixty years old, with long black hair streaked liberally with silver. The bangles she wore on both wrists jangled every time she moved. With her warm, maternal personality, Mrs. Levin was one of Sassy's favourite neighbours.

"My dear. Look at you," the woman said, instantly concerned. "Are you all right?"

Sassy took the potted plant and placed it on the counter. "I am. Thank you, Mrs. Levin. I was just thinking about my brother."

"Is he all right?"

She puffed out a breath. "As far as I know."

"War is a terrible thing," Mrs. Levin said, her soulful eyes deep on Sassy's. She put her open palms on either side of Sassy's face, holding her tenderly, in a way Sassy thought a mom might do. She couldn't recall if her mother ever had. "One does what one must. Sometimes the worst part is not knowing."

Sassy nodded and bit her lip, holding back emotions. Mrs. Levin must have seen that, because she stepped back, bangles clinking together, and made a show of admiring Sassy.

"Enough about that. Look at you! You're a vision. All this colour. Are you going on a date?" Her eyes teased. "Is it that handsome David boy I met before?"

Sassy's nerves swooped back into place. "I'm playing guitar at a coffee-house tonight! At Chez Monique. It's my first time."

Mrs. Levin clapped her hands together. "My dear! How wonderful. I have to tell Mr. Levin. He will be so proud. I wish we could come, but the family is coming for dinner. Next time, we will be there." She nodded once. "I will let you get ready. I just wanted to give you this. You know Mr. Levin and his dear little plants. He believes every home should have plants in it, so he sent you this calendula. He says to put it on your balcony with your geranium and water it once a week. It should bloom all summer."

Sassy felt a rush of gratitude for the older woman and gently touched a sunshine-orange petal. "Thank you. This is exactly what I needed."

Mrs. Levin leaned closer, and Sassy caught the woman's spicy scent. She'd been cooking. Something with oregano. "You will be wonderful to-night, I'm certain of it."

Sassy held on to her smile as she closed the door. Yes. That's what she needed to remember. She would be wonderful tonight. With or without Joey.

Davey would be working in the kitchen, he'd said, and he would meet her there. He told her to arrive around nine, because Ed, the manager, wanted to meet her by the bar before she performed. At eight thirty, she stepped into the fifth-floor hallway and set out to Yorkville.

It was a lovely, warm evening, and the streets were active with cars and people enjoying the summer weather. Sassy walked between them, catching snatches of conversation and fighting the urge to invite every single person on the sidewalk to come and listen to her sing. When she reached the en-trance to Chez Monique, with its dark brick exterior, she was startled to see a line outside the door. A shiver of nerves passed through her, but she set her head on straight and snaked her way through. She wasn't the only performer, after all. These people had probably come to watch their own friends or family. They didn't know Sassy—yet—but they would love her. She would make sure of it.

Hugging her guitar case to her chest, Sassy went to the counter and asked for the manager.

"So you're our new little star, are you?" Wiping his hands dry, a man emerged from a back room then shut the door against the unwanted light. He was tall and bony. A dark halo of hair was all he had left on his head.

"I'm Sassy Rankin. Are you Ed?"

"That's me." He sniffed with amusement, his thumbs dug into his pock-ets. "Sassy. I'll bet you are. All right. Lemme look at you."

Sassy stood awkwardly, not sure what she was supposed to do while he inspected her.

"Do you want to hear me play?"

"I'll hear you soon enough." He walked behind her, then circled back and gave her a pat on her backside. "Yeah. Yeah, that's good," he said, nodding appreciatively.

Sassy set her jaw. This was *not* going to happen again. Not here, on her special night. "Just tell me where to put my case."

For the first time, Ed met her gaze. "I can show you the back room right now, if you'd like."

She squeezed her guitar tight, revolted. "You are disg—"

"Sass! Hey, Sass!"

She could have cried, seeing Davey's goofy smile coming toward her. "Look at us, working! Hey, you look great." He hugged her, and she clung to him a little longer than usual.

"This guy's a creep," she whispered.

"Yeah, but he has a lot of connections," he replied quietly. "Don't worry about him." Louder, he said, "Tonight'll make you a star."

"Right," she replied, stepping back.

"You don't believe me? Who knows who might be in the audience? I hear scouts come in here sometimes."

Wouldn't that be a thrill? "What about you? Busy cooking?"

His head angled from side to side. "Not quite. I'm peeling potatoes tonight."

Ed closed in on them. "Shouldn't you be scrubbing plates or something?"

"Sure." Davey's arm wrapped protectively around Sassy. "I just came to show my old lady where to leave her stuff. Come on, babe. Let's get you set up."

Grateful, she followed him through the room, sensing Ed's glare on her back. Would she ever get another gig after this? If kissing up to Ed was the price she was expected to pay, her dad was right: she needed to get out of this business. She hoped he was an anomaly among club managers.

Davey stopped before a closed door. "Here you go. They call it the greenroom, which is weird, since everything in here is basically orange and brown, but it's where the performers go before they play." He kissed her on the cheek. "Maybe because you'll make lots of green here. Have a blast, babe."

There was a cozy room behind the door, its two small tables littered with overflowing ashtrays. A stained orange love seat was shoved against the far wall. A tall man with a droopy moustache was already in there, attempting to pace, but he could barely manage two steps without bumping into a wall or table. He glanced up when she entered, then he looked down again abruptly. Baffled, she peered more closely at him and realized his lips were moving, though he wasn't saying anything.

The door behind her swung open. "Poet? The poet's next."

The tall man stared straight ahead, shoulders back, then he strode past both the director and Sassy.

"You Sassy? You're after him."

Sassy's mouth was suddenly as dry as dust. As she unpacked her guitar, she glanced around the room and spotted a couple of empty glasses with a half bottle of vodka standing behind them. Upon inspection, the glasses weren't entirely clean, but she figured alcohol would kill the germs and her jitters. With shaking hands, she poured an ounce or so into one of the glasses and slugged it back.

"Liquid courage," she told herself, closing her eyes as the booze burned down her throat.

Slightly calmer, she sat on the orange love seat and tuned her guitar, rotating the pegs to make sure everything was as exact as it could be. Beyond the door, she heard the drone of the poet speaking on the microphone, punctuated by the occasional cough and scattered applause. The audience had to stay quiet so they could hear him, but the lack of noise made Sassy nervous again. She shook out her wrist so blood rushed to her fingers, then she practiced a little, soothing herself.

The director popped his head in. "Sassy? It's time."

He left her in the wings, and while she waited she took in the sea of faces, obscured by cigarette smoke. A dozen or so pairs of glasses reflected the stage lights as heads bobbed along with the poet's words. She doubted she knew anyone out there, other than Davey. She was on her own tonight.

When the poet finished, he lifted his face toward the light and stretched out his hands. The room rewarded him with a round of applause.

In a blur, the director called her name, then Sassy was under the lights, buzzing with adrenaline. She was aware of wolf whistles, but she was too preoccupied with climbing onto the high stool they'd set out for her to react. Finally settled and with her cheeks burning, she reached for the microphone and flinched when feedback squealed through the speakers. She spotted Ed standing at the side of the room, arms crossed, waiting to judge her, and she felt a little smug. She hadn't fallen in line with his little "audition," but she would win him over with her music.

"Sorry! Sorry about that," she said, pulling the microphone closer and squinting against the bright lights. Her voice sounded unexpectedly loud to her, but she was thrilled with how clear the sound system was. "Um, thank you, everybody, for being here and for letting me sing for you. Like he said, this is my first time here. I'm hoping it won't be my last."

"You got it, babe!"

Davey had escaped the kitchen and was sitting up front. She gave him a grateful wink then turned her attention back to the audience. A deep breath brought back her confidence, and she dropped her gaze to her fingers, already placed where they were supposed to be. She knew how they would move, how they would feel, how the vibrations of the strings would accompany her voice. How her heart would sing. After days and months and years of practice, she was ready.

nine
MARION

M arion spotted something on the floor outside her apartment door and picked up her step, curious. She smiled, realizing it was a potted plant packed with bright orange flowers. She knew immediately who had brought the gift. On the floor beside it was a note. *Calendula. For the balcony. Water every Tuesday, not too much.* Cheered by the thought, she carried the pot into the apartment and set it down before taking care of the hungry cat winding around her ankles. She'd slip a thank-you note under the Levins' door later.

"Yes, yes," she murmured, squatting to pet Chester. "Just a minute."

She placed his bowl of food on the floor, and the cat lowered himself into a comfortable position, digging into his supper as if he hadn't eaten in a year. She carried the flowerpot to the balcony and placed it on her little table so she could see the blooms through her window. This was the third plant her neighbours had given her. Besides this one and the geranium already on the balcony, she had a very healthy spider plant in her living room. She must have done something right with it, because babies had begun to spring from the mother plant. She had to remember to ask Mr. Levin what to do when it got too big.

She liked the different hues that the plants brought to her apartment.

Since she had moved in, she had done nothing to build upon the apartment's original bland, understated shades, but the vivid green helped. Maybe that could be the beginning of a colour scheme, she thought. She didn't have much of an eye when it came to art or design, but she reminded herself that this place was only for her. She could do what she wanted.

She had a little time before Paul arrived, so she poured herself a cup of tea and flipped on the television to distract herself. The Zenith colour console television set against her living room wall had been the first unnecessary item Marion had bought for her apartment. At first she had considered the cost to be exorbitant. Especially since she had been watching black-and-white television for so long and learning the same information. Why spend on something needless like that? But after seeing the first colour television broadcast last April, she couldn't resist. People suddenly appeared more like they should, not like black-and-white cardboard cutouts. She walked past an electronics store almost every day on her way to work, and she'd admired the television screens in the window, flickering with colour. One day, she gave in to the store's siren call.

Now she turned on the news and almost immediately wished she hadn't. It was always the same: a mishmash of explosions, protests, sirens, ambulances, and speeches from scowling public figures.

As awful as the conflict was, the phenomenon of what she was watching was fascinating. The concept of a faraway war raging in this exact moment in time—while she sat here, sipping tea in peace—seemed absurd. The human race had always fought and always would. Countries, continents, religions, races: cavemen fighting over scraps and territories, the Greeks in Troy, the Crusades, the War of the Roses, the French Revolution, both world wars, Korea, and now Vietnam. In school, she had studied the conflicts, and yet it wasn't until recently, with the television screen broadcasting reality at her, that she fully comprehended the scope of what humans could do to each other. What they were still doing. Television had opened the world's eyes to so much.

Chester hopped onto the couch beside her, rubbing insistently against her side, but Marion's eyes were glued to the screen.

Tonight, she watched Vietnam footage taken by a cameraman who had followed soldiers into a river of thigh-deep brown water, sharp-edged grasses trembling a foot above their helmets. Even in the river, Marion could tell the men were sweltering. They had stripped to vests and trousers, offering their bare arms and necks to the swarms of mosquitoes. The camera followed them into the gloomy depths of the jungle, winding through thick, twisted knots of trees, and she couldn't help wondering how anyone could tell where they were going in all that. How could they defend themselves against hidden attackers? The television screen closed in on a soldier squatting by a tree, and it came to her that his hands seemed small, clutched around the stock of his gun. When he unknowingly faced the camera, she saw his soft face and frightened eyes, masked by filth. He looked too young even to shave. Much too young to be in a place like that, killing other boys.

Daniel Neumann had been there. What had he seen? What had he done?

When she couldn't ignore the ticking clock any longer, Marion turned the television off and got dressed for dinner. She had decided to wear her light blue dress with the pleated skirt, because it was simple and comfortable. She'd wear her white cardigan as well, since she didn't want to encourage Paul by going sleeveless. He had told her to watch the street for his shiny blue Chevette, so she unlatched the door to the balcony and stepped out. She placed her palms on the banister's smooth surface and dropped her gaze to the ground, where a hint of warm summer air whispered through the cherry trees.

Seeing them, she recalled John's simple request to go home so he could touch the leaves. Right now, he was safe within the walls of the hospital, waiting for supper, or possibly visiting the physical therapy room for exercise. That was exactly where he should be.

The sad truth was that there was nothing simple about his request. If John—or rather, *when* John was discharged from the hospital, he would not have a home. No one would take him in. There was no way his family would be able to handle him while carrying on with their own lives. John was a sociopath with chronic antisocial behaviour and a complete lack of empathy.

Not all sociopaths were dangerous, but John had a history. He showed no sign that he either understood or cared that he had killed the rabbit that day in his memory, or that he had stabbed his father.

Recently, Marion had received a memo reminding physicians to update their files with regard to the hospital's eventual closure, sections of which had already begun. Marion had not been informed of specific dates, but she knew it might be a matter of a few short weeks before John and the others were discharged. She had put off responding to the memo for as long as she could. Every time she picked up her pen to write down the specifics of her patients, she put it down again, weak with cowardice. She should have spoken up long ago. She should have gone to Dr. Bernstein to register her deep concerns. If she had brought Paul with her as a witness, regardless of how he felt about both her and the issue, Dr. Bernstein would have been forced to listen and write down Marion's arguments.

She would have told him so many important things.

She would have said that once the hospital building was demolished, any anchor John or the others ever had to a community would be swept away. No one would make sure Big John swallowed his pills or ate a meal. No one would make sure he visited a community health centre.

She would have made it very clear that giving John and others like him the "freedom" the media and the general public cried out for endangered him, which would, in turn, endanger society. Off his medications and without the reliable support he had known at the hospital, John and many others would become confused and desperate, inevitably spiralling into a life of addiction, crime, and violence.

She would have pointed out that deinstitutionalization was happening everywhere all at once, and it was simply too much for cities to handle. It had started in the United States in the 1950s and spread. In this immediate area, the Lakeshore Psychiatric Hospital in New Toronto would be closing at the same time as where she worked. Everything she was predicting for her patients would be repeated in countless facilities across the country.

After that, Marion would have made it clear that saving the government's money by shutting down the facilities would undoubtedly be cancelled out by the rise of incarceration costs. Because that's where many of their patients would end up. There was no doubt in her mind.

Everyone would suffer, she would have told him in no uncertain terms, because of deinstitutionalization.

But Marion had never gone to speak with Dr. Bernstein, either on her own or with Paul. She had been too afraid of jeopardizing her hard-won career. Of standing in the spotlight, possibly revealing her inadequacies.

And now that it was happening, she was ashamed of that selfish weakness.

All she could do now was damage control. When she had first learned of deinstitutionalization two years before, Marion had promised herself that she would keep tabs on her patients afterward. She would not abandon them. Alice, Barbara, John, and all the others would need her when they were released. But as that day came closer, she still had no idea how she could do it. She would be working in the health centres by then, and she would have no access to the records of her past patients. She knew their home addresses, but that might mean nothing in a few weeks. It was such an easy thing to open a door and wander blindly into the unknown.

The vastness of what was happening threatened to overwhelm her.

Looking down from her balcony, Marion spotted Paul's car parked against the sidewalk five storeys below. She was only slightly surprised to see it was a convertible. He leaned against it, arms crossed, observing people as they walked by, looking like a magazine model. Any other woman would have been excited about tonight. If only Marion was any other woman.

The wind from the convertible would make a disaster of her long blond hair, so she swung it into a high ponytail, checked the mirror, then grabbed her purse and took the elevator down.

"Look at you!" Paul exclaimed as she walked out the main entrance. "You do not look anything like the doctor in the lab coat I saw in today's meeting."

"I hope that's a compliment."

"You are a fox, and you know it." He stepped back and opened the passenger door, revealing white leather seats. Paul knew how to impress. If only she liked him the way he liked her, things might be a lot easier. Or a lot more complicated. He walked around the front then climbed in, shining that big, bright smile on her.

"Chill, Marion. We're gonna have a gas tonight."

"I'm chilled."

"Whatever you say." His gaze travelled up the wall of the apartment building. "Bet you have a cool pad up there. What floor?"

No, I am not inviting you in. "Fifth," she said. "Are we going to sit here all night?"

Giorgio's was a snug, homey restaurant with red-checked tablecloths and accordion music playing through speakers. Paul introduced Marion to all the waiters, who appeared to know him well.

"It's my favourite place to go," he explained, perfectly at home. "Wine with dinner?"

"Sounds nice."

He signalled a waiter then rattled off the name of the wine he'd chosen. Marion didn't mind his ordering for her. In fact, she found it old-fashioned and a bit charming. She liked wine, but she didn't know one from another.

"I recommend the fettucini Alfredo," Paul said, leaning across the table to point it out in her menu.

"I feel more like lasagna," she replied, closing her menu and leaning back. When the waiter returned and poured their wine, she said, "*Grazie.*"

Paul raised his glass. "I didn't know you spoke Italian."

"A little. Lots of things you don't know about me, I guess."

She couldn't miss the change that came over his features as he tapped their glasses together. "I'd like to learn more."

"Oh dear, Paul. That's too smooth. The one thing you have never been is subtle."

The food was delicious, the atmosphere comfortable, and the wine was both. Surprisingly, their conversation was also pleasant. Maybe she should give him a second chance, she thought. He was trying hard, asking questions about her rather than going on about himself. That was new. Someone must have suggested the idea to him.

"Where do you stand on shutting down the hospital?" he asked at one point, ordering more wine with the flick of a hand. "I know we talked a little about it months ago, but now that it's happening, I can't believe we haven't discussed it more. You've been pretty quiet about the whole thing. Now that we're outside of the office, you can tell me. I promise not to tell Dr. Bernstein."

She flushed, embarrassed that he had read her so well. *I won't tell* was such a juvenile inducement, like something a child might say to another to elicit a confession. He was right about it working, though. Marion had kept her mounting anger about deinstitutionalization bottled up so tight, she reached for the chance to let some of it out.

Still, it was difficult to admit everything right away. "It doesn't matter what I think."

"No?" His eyes narrowed. "I don't buy it. Come on, Marion. Loosen up. Let me in on what's going on in that brilliant mind of yours."

She was right that it didn't matter what she thought. So why not think it out loud?

"I think it's a terrible mistake."

He leaned back and folded his arms, rapt. "Aha. Interesting. Over a hundred years of guesswork and leg irons for people who often didn't need treatment at all, and you think we should keep that?"

"You're suggesting that treatments today are the same as they were in 1850? Considering the progress that has been made since then, I feel safe in disagreeing with your antiquated and simplistic approach."

"Simplistic. Interesting again. All right. I'll bite. Please continue, Doctor. You're hot when you're bothered."

She rolled her eyes. "And you're ridiculous. Do you want to continue this or not?"

"I do. I do. I apologize. Please go on."

After all this time, it felt good to line up all her thoughts on the topic, organize them in a manner that would make the most sense, then finally say them out loud. She waited for the waiter to finish pouring, then she took a deep swallow of wine for strength.

"I will not claim that our hospitals are perfect," she said, "but they are not the institutions from a century ago. We used to sedate or confine anxious or morbidly depressed patients—"

"—or punish them for not conducting themselves in a normal way."

"Exactly. Very different from today. Now we have imipramine, meprobamate, and others. Work out the correct dosage, and that person can often live a pretty steady life."

He frowned. "So? If they close the hospital, they continue on those meds and live a 'pretty steady life' along with the general population."

"Don't be dense, Paul. I'm talking about the most severe cases. How many of your patients would remember when to take their meds or how much? Can they discern chlorpromazine from haloperidol? Many have no idea what day it is, let alone the hour." She shook her head. "To rely on their own competence means we have been treating them unnecessarily all along, which we know isn't the case."

He was paying attention, encouraging her with his expression. She sipped more wine, automatically analyzing his expression as she swallowed.

"Group therapy. Psychoanalysis. The old Watsonian and Skinnerian conditioning has finally led to constructive behavioural treatment. Patients are no longer Pavlov's dogs, but individuals who identify a cue and are able to adjust their actions accordingly. Then there's the miracle of neurochemistry, and electron microscopes capable of exposing the most miniscule details of neurons. All of that will lead to therapies and medications that will only improve over time."

"All right," he said. "We have progressed. So?"

She dabbed the corners of her mouth with her napkin. The wine was delicious. "The answer's obvious. Outpatient therapy in community health centres may work for the people who are suffering from manageable afflictions and who have progressed to the point where they can look after themselves, at least in basic ways. But serious inpatients need a central location where they are cared for and can function properly. In its infinite wisdom, the government is demolishing those places."

He nodded slowly. "I am so glad I asked. This is fascinating, coming from a woman who barely says three words in a staff meeting. They're demolishing them because of cost, and those savings are being redirected to new protocols like community centres. Isn't that good, at least?"

"Government costs will skyrocket. Those with the worst problems and no support will turn to crime and become inmates instead. I can't imagine jails are cheaper to run than our hospitals. Much of our work is done by volunteers. I could be wrong, but I don't think volunteerism is a major contributor to improving life in prison."

"You could be right about that."

"*Could* be? Come on, Paul. There are far too many factors we haven't addressed for this to go well. The proponents of this foolish idea believe the latest antipsychotic medications will offer a cure. Ridiculous! A cure to what? Do all these people have the same problems? Can they all be fixed by the same drugs? Of course not. It's so wrong, Paul. The other day, one patient of mine was paralyzed at the thought of leaving her room, then another—a violent sociopath—wanted to go home immediately, even though he can barely remember his name. When we open the doors and push them both out, what will they do?"

"Maybe she'll find courage. She'll have to. And there will be community centres, so she could drop in there if she needs help."

"Or maybe this new course of action destroys all the courage and confidence she has worked on for months. And what about the other guy? He's in 6B. He doesn't know how to do anything on his own. He barely feeds himself. Everyone's talking about freedom this and freedom that. Freedom to live independently with dignity? Or freedom to die on the street?"

He nodded and sipped his own glass of wine. "So tell me, Marion, why didn't you say any of this before? Why didn't you talk to Bernstein about it?"

That was the question she had sat on for so long. She dropped her gaze. "Because I'm a coward."

"Really? Something that rouses you this much, and you didn't want to fight it?"

"It's not that I didn't want to. I just . . . You've never had to worry about protecting your job or your reputation. I am constantly working just to maintain my status."

"You're one of the best doctors in the hospital. What are you talking about?"

"Doesn't matter if I'm one of the best. I'm the only woman. I go against the grain."

He leaned on one elbow and rested his chin in his hand, frowning. "Here's another thought. Maybe you have your own personal fear of losing the hospital. Maybe you are comfortable with what we do there and how things are run. You know what to expect. Maybe you're afraid that once the building is gone, you might end up as lost as your patients."

She stared at him, shocked, because maybe he was right. "We're not talking about me."

"No?" He shrugged. "Okay."

"Change of topic," she said, draining her glass. "I have a favour to ask."

"Lay it on me. I'm all yours." He held up a finger and glanced around, asking for the bill.

"You are looking after that Vietnam vet in the old building. Daniel something," she said, trying to sound vague. "What's going on with him?"

"Daniel Neumann. Yeah, Daniel's angry as hell, and frankly, he has every right. Smart guy, but he had extreme head trauma, and as a result I don't think he fully understands where he is. We had to lock him up alone and sometimes tie him down so we can medicate. At other times, he's like a lamb. What about him?"

"I wondered if I could trade cases with you. You can pick who you want. I'd like to work with him."

He looked surprised. "Why? What are you hoping to find out?"

"I have been interested in battle fatigue for a while, probably because of my father and his ongoing troubles. Mr. Neumann seems to have some similar symptoms. I've read so many articles about the topic, but nothing compares to the real thing. These men have built up walls to protect themselves from whatever unspeakable trauma they witnessed, and I want to find a door through those walls. I've spoken with Mr. Neumann once, and I've observed him a couple of times through the window. I'm intrigued."

"And what do I get in return, Dr. Hart?"

"Choose someone from the roster. Alice is nice."

"What if I want something else? Like a second date?"

Marion scowled. "I thought we were talking business. I don't know about a second date yet. Give a girl a break."

"All right, all right. Yeah, I'll switch with you. Let me know what you find out about him. I'm curious, too." The bill arrived, he put down some cash, then he dropped his napkin onto the table. "Ready to go? Let's see if we can get into the Riverboat."

All of Yorkville's lights were on, and a pleasant blend of music and laughter spilled from the old Victorian houses onto the sidewalk. Dodging occupied tables and chairs set up outside, Marion took in everything with a quiet little thrill. She'd never been here at night, and there was something about it that felt a bit wicked, in a good way. More than the clubs and the music, it was the people. She'd expected to see hippies, but she also saw people in business suits and conservative dresses. Every Jack and Jill had tumbled down the workplace hill and ended up here, and Marion was swept up in their energy.

Based on the crowd outside the Riverboat, they could see right away the two of them wouldn't get in. Paul apologized as if it was his fault. "I should have known. It's Thursday, after all. Let's find someplace else."

"What's that place over there like? 'Penny Farthing.'"

"It's all right." He shot her a glance. "They've even got a pool in the back, but the waitresses wear bikini tops, so I don't think it'd be your thing. I have an idea, though. I've been wanting to see this place, Chez Monique. Amateur night," he read out loud from the sign in front. "Wanna try?"

They managed to claim a table on the right side of the room, which was packed with tables and chairs, all facing a well-lit stage at the front. On it, a young man with a long moustache and sleepy eyes was passionately reciting poetry. They'd arrived just in time to hear the end of his performance.

As the audience applauded, the director stepped in. "Ernie Molnek, folks. That was 'White Sky, Blue Clouds,' his own composition. Far out, man. Moving on, tonight we have a first-timer playing for us, a real—"

"I'll be right back," Paul said, turning. "We need coffee."

The crowd applauded to welcome the next act, creating the illusion that they were cheering for Paul as he crossed the room. He would enjoy that, she thought, watching him. He seemed at home here, among these people. He leaned down to speak with a couple, and a beautiful woman wrapped her arms around his neck. Marion felt an unexpected flicker of jealousy when she gave him a kiss, but she wasn't resentful of the woman's affections. What she envied was Paul's familiarity with this world and the people in it. He was laughing when the woman released him, and when he glanced back at Marion, she averted her eyes.

Catcalls and whistles trickled through the room as a girl with long braids walked toward the middle of the stage, carrying a guitar. She settled onto a stool then began to pick out an unforgettable, Eastern-style melody in a minor key. "Paint It Black," Marion realized with surprise. She hadn't been able to get that song out of her head after she'd heard it in her hallway last week.

The girl on the stage began to sing, and Marion's jaw dropped. It was the same smooth voice she'd heard before, coming out of her neighbour's apartment. She was watching the audience while she played, her eyes a startling green.

Marion was still smiling when Paul returned with their coffees.

"You look stoked," he said. "What's up?"

"Did you hear that last performer?" She reached for her cup, oddly elated. "I can't believe it. In the middle of all these people I don't know, in a place I've never been, I just met my neighbour from across the hall."

ten

SASSY

☙

Sassy was riding a huge high. She never wanted to come down. One song at Chez Monique had turned into an encore of two more, and when she finally lay down to sleep hours later, she could still hear the applause. She bounced out of bed the next morning then sang the whole time she was making coffee and burning toast.

She'd been a hit. Ed had come to the greenroom after and asked her to play again the following week, which had given her great satisfaction. Davey, who had begun to think of himself as her agent, said he was going to visit other coffeehouses and see if he could stir up more interest.

Right now, he paced in the living room, impatient.

"Let's go!" he hollered.

From her bedroom, Sassy made a noncommittal response, spinning with happiness and checking her reflection in the mirror. She'd taken out the braids from the night before, and now the kinky waves fell like an accordion. She wrapped a bright red kerchief over the top to keep it out of her eyes, then she decided to match that with some lipstick. She felt like a completely different girl from the one who had been so worried the day before. She *was* a different girl. She was—almost—a star.

"Sassy!"

She threw back the last of her coffee then poked her head out of the bedroom. "What?"

"Come on!"

"What's the rush? The protest doesn't start for another hour."

Davey sighed. "The party's already started, and I'm on the committee. I don't want to be late. Come on. Let's go."

She blinked into the hallway mirror one last time, adjusted her kerchief, then headed out with him. Like always, the neighbour's door clicked shut as they passed, but she hardly noticed. Last night had been wonderful, and today was going to be extra groovy. Davey had convinced her of that, though it hadn't taken much. Her first real war protest.

Davey'd become part of an organization called TADP, or Toronto Anti-Draft Programme, providing aid and support to war resisters arriving in Canada with little more than the clothes on their backs. TADP was the largest group of its kind in Canada, he told her, and it was a full-time volunteer job for dozens of people, since the demand increased daily. Seven days a week, trained counsellors were on hand to advise Americans who wanted to immigrate to Canada. They also gave guidance once they arrived, including helping them find employment, and even temporary places to live. For that, the TADP relied on two hostels, as well as a network of almost two hundred people around Toronto who offered rooms in their homes. When it came to deserters—as opposed to resisters—it became more of a sticky political situation, but the TADP had lawyers to help them as well.

Tens of thousands of resisters had crossed the border into Canada since the war had begun, seeking refuge. What Sassy hadn't known, until Davey told her, was that almost half of those were women.

Today's protest had been set up almost single-handedly by Davey, she knew, though he humbly insisted everyone had a hand in it. He was becoming an excellent coordinator, no matter how lazy he claimed to be.

"Are you what they call a conscientious objector?" she asked as they walked.

He shook his head. "No religious reasons, no political reasons. Just moral ones, and those don't count. So I left. People in Canada are pretty accepting of resisters, for the most part. They prefer us to deserters, anyway."

"What was your moral reason?"

"I don't feel like there's any justification for us to be down there, fighting in a faraway war that has nothing to do with our country. So I cut out."

"My brother said it's our duty to make sure communism never reaches our borders, so North Vietnam has to be stopped. What do you think of that?"

He shrugged. "That's what a lot of people say, and, if they believe that, then power to them. Your brother went because he is an idealist. He thinks he can make a difference. He figures the chance of his being killed or having to kill others is worth it to stop a political system from possibly coming to our country. Good for him. I guess I'm doing the same thing, except opposite. Like him, I think I can make a difference. My belief is that if communism gets closer, we worry about it then. Right now, there's no reason for us to be there. The war's been going on for years already, and nothing has been accomplished. More people dying on both sides, that's all."

"I bet that was a hard choice to make, standing up to the entire military machine," she noted.

His expression fell. "Not all that bad for me, but you know what they did to Muhammad Ali this spring? The heavyweight champion of the world? He's Muslim, and he refused to fight or go to jail because of his beliefs, so the World Boxing Association took away his title and banned him from boxing for four years. Bravest man in the world, to stand up to all that pressure. He's an inspiration."

"Yeah, but you're brave, too. It must have been hard to leave your family and come up here on your own."

"I'm not sure my dad will ever get over it. He was in the army in his time. He still has a buzz cut, and he has his medals framed on the wall. He thinks fighting is our patriotic duty. I could never look at a war that way. Sure, a man can do brave things and be a hero or whatever, but in every war, innocents are slaughtered. Nobody should win a medal for doing that."

She couldn't argue. Her dad had a medal, too, she recalled. She pictured it hanging on his office wall and wondered what he'd done to earn it.

"What would have happened to you if you'd stayed home?" she asked.

"I'd have to hide, but the FBI goes after anyone who goes underground. I had a friend who refused to serve in the military even though it would mean he'd end up with a five-year prison sentence. I guess he thought he was making a statement. Jail's not for me, man. There's no shame in moving here. Canada's beautiful, and I got my whole life ahead of me."

She liked thinking of her country that way, as safe and welcoming and offering a future, but she'd never forget what her father had said about Canada making and selling weapons for war. It was difficult to reconcile both sides.

They heard eager, raised voices when they were about a block away from the TADP office, and Davey picked up his pace.

"What's the office like?" she asked, keeping up.

Davey was practically glowing with excitement. His olive-coloured shirt was unbuttoned halfway down his chest, a headband wrapped around his head to keep his long brown hair out of his golden eyes, which shone with anticipation.

"It's swinging, man. Not too big, but it has a groovy vibe." He grinned. "We got a map of the United States on the wall, and we stick a pin in every spot where an American is coming from. On another wall we have a big peace sign made of old draft cards. Some are charred on the edges, like they tried to burn them. So cool."

When they arrived, she realized that he'd held back in his description of the place's decor. The first thing she saw was a plastic chicken hanging from the ceiling with the phrase "Chicken Little was right!" written on it. One wall held a huge poster of Bob Dylan, surrounded by posters, cartoons, sketches, poetry, and more. Brochures lay stacked on the windowsills. On top of an old bookshelf, she spotted a photograph of a soldier in uniform. The poor man looked exhausted. She couldn't help thinking of Joey and the horrific scene he had drawn for her in his latest letter, and a knot tightened in her throat. Joey had done more than his time down there. Extending the original six months to thirteen had been insanity. He should come back now, before it was too late, if it wasn't already.

"Here. Take this outside. I'll be right there," Davey said, handing her a placard. MAKE LOVE NOT WAR, the flowery sign suggested. The *o* in *love* was drawn like a heart, with a downward fork cut straight down through it, forming a peace symbol.

"Did you choose this sign specifically for me?" she teased. "Because I'm happy with another theme, you know."

He kissed her on the cheek. "I hadn't thought of that, but it suits you. Can I bum a smoke?"

She reached into her bag for her cigarettes, and he stuck one in his mouth as he grabbed another placard.

"Davey?"

Sassy stepped out of the way as a small blond girl with a severe look about her mouth entered the office then walked directly to Davey. He lit up at the sight of her. Just as quickly, that happiness melted into an expression of guilt.

"Hey, Christine." He bent down to give her a kiss on the cheek. "So cool that you came. Thanks." He glanced at Sassy, and it dawned on her where the guilt was coming from. "Christine, this is my, uh, very good friend, Sassy. Sass, this is Christine. I've told you about her, right . . . ?"

He hadn't, but she let him off easy. She'd had a hunch. She had smelled cheap perfume on him before, and it was the same as the scent wafting off Christine right now.

"Of course. Far out."

Davey might once have been laid-back about things, but these days he seemed more like the Tasmanian Devil in the Looney Tunes cartoons, and not just because he was always hungry. Outside of being with Sassy, he was working evenings in the Chez Monique kitchen, organizing protests and functions at the TADP, and now she knew about Christine.

With her hunch confirmed, she reluctantly accepted that she and Davey were better as friends and said nothing more about it.

A half dozen kids came into the little office then, squeezing her against the wall, and Davey nodded a welcome. "Pick a sign and wait in the back. There's a crowd there already."

They followed his orders without hesitation, and she felt a rush of pride for him.

Christine stood unmoving, watching the goings-on. "What should I do?"

"It's almost time," he told her, scanning the office with a frown. "I just need to . . ."

Sassy recognized his expression. It was kind of like when she was in a rush and had to go somewhere but couldn't remember what she was forgetting.

"Your bullhorn," she suggested.

"Far out, Sass. You're the best." He grabbed it off a shelf. "All right. Let's go."

Sassy didn't miss the way he took Christine's hand in his—or the victorious expression on her face when she glanced at Sassy. The two of them headed out, and Sassy followed, wondering how on earth Davey had connected with such an arrogant girl.

For a while, Davey walked between them, striding up Spadina Avenue with a bullhorn in one hand and Christine's hand in the other. At the back of the group, some of the girls carried bundles of daisies, which they handed out to people they passed along the way. Eventually, Davey and Christine moved up to lead the two dozen or so protestors. Sassy lagged behind. Backing off was the right thing to do, but still, it was hard to see him so happy with someone else.

From the front, Davey started calling out slogans on his bullhorn, and the group eagerly parroted his words.

One, Two, Three, Four! Tell me what we're fighting for! Sassy yelled over and over, more sure of herself with every step. She only stopped when her voice started to crack. She had to make sure she didn't strain it, since she was singing again in a few nights. Someone lit up a joint and passed it to her, restoring her enthusiasm, and Davey switched to *Make Love, Not War!*, so she waved her sign and chanted along.

Like the love-in at Queen's Park, their peaceful protest felt dreamlike, with all the colours and smiles and brotherly love that held the group to-gether, all the singing and chanting and daisies, all the fingers held up in Vs. It was as if society's rules didn't matter for a day, and the protestors owned the city, preaching the message to everyone they met. Pedestrians paused midstep, taking in their procession, and when they turned east onto Bloor Street, Sassy saw photographers aiming at them. Still buzzing from the mar-ijuana, she made sure to wave and smile.

Near St. George Street, a beautiful blond woman across the intersec-tion caught Sassy's eye. She was wearing a suit and walking the opposite way, though she'd stopped to observe the protest. Still following the group, Sassy admired the woman's elegant, organized appearance. Something about her reminded Sassy of the yellowing photographs of her mother, once upon a time, framed liked museum pieces on her father's mantel. She wondered where the woman was headed, with her shining hair drawn into a disciplined roll and her hand curled around the handle of a serious-looking black brief-case. She looked important. Sensible. Poised. Such a contrast to the messy joy that emanated from the protestors. For just a beat, Sassy wondered what it might be like to switch places.

The group stopped walking, and because she hadn't been paying attention, Sassy bumped into the boy in front of her. From her tiptoes, she saw Davey in the lead, with Christine standing beside him, but he was blocked by a half dozen policemen. When one of them moved his hand to the baton at his belt, Sassy started shoving her way through the protestors to stand at Davey's side.

"Don't you dare hit him!" she shouted at the policeman.

The young officer blinked, looking confused. "I wasn't gonna. Not un-less he asks for it."

"He's not asking for it! Why is violence your first resort?" She felt em-powered and righteous, standing up for Davey and representing them all. They had every right to be here.

"Sass," Davey murmured. "Let it go. Nothing happened."

The weed was taking over her thoughts, playing protest music in her brain and suggesting to her that Davey was only saying that to keep her quiet, so she refused to be silenced. Had he missed the importance of this showdown, preoccupied as he was by Christine? They were standing up against The Man! This was a big deal!

"Of course something happened!" She stood toe-to-toe with the bewildered policeman. "I saw you. You were going to hit him with that stick. If you think the fuzz can just beat up innocent citizens, you're wrong!"

"Miss, please step back."

Davey sighed behind her as Sassy moved even closer. "I'm allowed to be wherever I want to be. I live here. This is my city, and I—"

"Miss, if you don't move back, I'll have to take you in."

"Sass. Come here," Davey muttered, tugging on her sleeve.

She felt a twinge of concern, then she disregarded it . . . and did the wrong thing.

"Oh yeah?" She put both hands on the policeman's chest and shoved. "Go ahead!"

The next thing she knew, her wrists were cuffed, and her elbow was gripped by a policeman. She looked to Davey for guidance, but he appeared completely lost. As did everyone around him.

She was led to a police car, and the officer opened the back door then waited for her to climb in and sit. The cuffs pinched and bruised. The moment the car door was closed, Sassy's world became very quiet. Sick with shame, she watched out the window as Davey gestured toward her, negotiating with the police. He shot her apologetic glances while he did so, but she was painfully aware that none of this was his fault. She'd let herself get out of hand. She had to stop smoking pot. It always made her do stupid things. This time, she had really done it. She was petrified about going to jail. How was she supposed to tell her father about this? She was already keeping mum about the loss of her job.

Some of the others in the group were speaking with the police now, and her mortification grew.

Davey, it ended up, was powerless to save her. He pressed his face to the window and stared uselessly at her. The policeman returned to his car, and she burrowed into the back seat, wishing she could disappear from sight as he drove away from the crowd. He looked young, she thought. His straight black hair, neatly trimmed above his collar, carried no grey, and the eyes reflected in the mirror were not yet lined by age. Her father would have approved: a young man with a responsible job.

"What's your name?" he asked.

"Susan."

"That was a dumb move, Susan," he said flatly. "We weren't even going to stop the protest. Just letting the leader know the parameters."

Her shackled wrists ached. "I'm sorry I pushed you. You're right. I was dumb. What happens now? I've never been arrested before."

"You get one phone call. Call your lawyer, and he'll tell you what to do. Maybe next time, think first, okay? You could still be out there handing out flowers if you'd kept your mouth shut."

Inside the station, she was led to a telephone at the back of the police station, and the officer gave her a dime to make her call. Feeling painfully small and slightly nauseous with nerves, Sassy clutched the phone to her ear and dialed her father's number.

"Hello?"

"Hi, Dad," she said, feeling her resolve give way. So much for being strong and independent. She gasped in a breath. "They told me I am entitled to one phone call."

"Who told you . . . " There was a pause. "Where are you, Susan?"

"I'm, um—"

"Please don't say you were arrested."

"I'm sorry, Daddy," she whispered.

"What happened?"

"There was, uh, we were . . . I was at a protest."

A long, exasperated sigh travelled through the receiver.

"I never thought that—"

"I can't believe this."

"I'm sorry! Please, Dad. Don't leave me in here. I messed up. Please give me another chance."

"Susan, it's Friday. It's a workday. How are you at a midday protest on a weekday? What's going on?"

"Oh, Dad. I . . ."

She could picture him at his desk, drumming his fingers on the wood surface, torn between his love for her and the sheer frustration he felt. The two of them had been so close when she was small. He'd had such big dreams for her, and he'd always been there when she needed him. But Sassy had let him down many times.

"I lost my job," she said quietly. How could she ever tell him what had happened with Mr. Brown? It would break his heart.

"What?! When did this happen? Why didn't you tell me?"

"Dad, please. Not now. I just want to get out of here. It's awful here."

"I want to know what happened with your job."

"Later, Dad, okay? Please?" She caught her breath, tears burning. "I can't talk about it here."

"But why—" Her heart twisted, hearing his exasperation. "You will explain it to me later."

She was full-out crying now. She faced the wall so no one in the police station could see.

"I'm sorry, Dad. I really am."

He sighed. "Last chance, Susan. I will get you out of there, then you will live up to your end."

She leaned her back against the wall, bracing herself. She felt sure her knees were about to give way. "I promise."

He hung up, and she was led back to a cell. On that long walk down the cement hallway, she silently prayed. *Please, please, life. Don't make me break that promise.*

eleven

MARION

❧

On the morning after her date with Paul, Marion left the apartment at nine o'clock, slung her purse over her shoulder, then quick-walked the twenty minutes to the medical library. Having accomplished the first step in her mission to help Daniel Neumann by securing him as her patient, now she had to see if she could dig up anything that might work for him.

The date with Paul had been all right, she could admit. He was beguiling and amusing, and she claimed victory over their discussion about deinstitutionalization, but the evening's ending had turned her a little sour. She'd gotten such a kick out of watching her neighbour perform a few songs. She'd commented a few times to Paul about how talented she thought the girl was. Paul had nodded, but after the fourth mention, he'd looked a little bewildered.

"I get that you think she's good," he said. "Why are you so excited about it?"

"She's my neighbour. I practically know her! Isn't that exciting? It's like she's a celebrity."

"You're all worked up over an amateur singer in a club who lives in your building. Unreal, Marion. You really need to get out more often."

He couldn't dampen her spirits, though. After the first song, her neighbour played two encores. The last was "Where Have All the Flowers Gone," and everyone in the coffeehouse had sung along. It was beautiful, and Marion decided that one of these days she would work up the nerve to go and introduce herself at the apartment. After the set was done and the girl had left the stage, Marion lost interest in the show. Especially since the next performer was a long-haired, bearded man who looked like he hadn't showered in a week. He hunched over his guitar and sang in kind of a growly, incoherent voice she didn't recognize as English. Paul had laughed at her twisted expression then driven her home.

"Let me walk you up," he offered, his blue eyes sparkling in the streetlight.

"I wasn't born yesterday, Dr. McKenny," she reminded him. "I'll see you at work."

"You don't want to offer me a cup of tea or something?"

"I just had drinks with you for the past two hours. I'm not thirsty anymore. Thank you, Paul. I enjoyed tonight. Now, say good night."

They climbed out of the car and regarded each other over its roof.

He let out a huff, looking resigned. "I'm sorry to say it, Marion, but you're missing out."

"Missing out? Are we talking about you still?" she joked, but he wore a serious expression.

"I'm talking about life. Doesn't matter if you like me or not. You need to expand your horizons. You live at your apartment and at work, and that's it, from what I can tell. As a doctor, I'm suggesting you challenge yourself to do something you wouldn't normally do. Do something that scares you."

"Where's this coming from?"

"Don't take this the wrong way, but you are predictable, Marion. That's not a bad thing. You seem satisfied with your life. But tonight I saw you truly happy, and it was because of something you'd never experienced before. You saw that singer, and you lit up. You must have felt the difference in you."

She had, and his words brought on an unexpected wave of emotion. She took a beat, letting his words sink in. Was he right? Was she completely happy in her life? She'd asked herself the same thing so many times.

"I get your point," she relented, then she gave him a quiet smile. "Who knows. Maybe someday I'll surprise us both. Thanks, Paul. I do appreciate what you're saying."

"You still want that Neumann file?"

She'd almost forgotten. "I do, thank you."

"I'll put it out for you. Good luck with that guy. He has a temper when you let him loose, so watch it."

"I will. Thank you again. You know, Paul, you should go back to the coffeehouse and see if that blond is still there. The one you were watching all night." She laughed at his expression. "I might be square, but I'm not blind. Good luck with her. I'll see you Monday. Thank you again for this evening."

She wasn't thinking about that conversation as she stepped into the library. Today wasn't about her own life, it was about his. Her attention was on finding up-to-date papers and treatment options with regard to "war neurosis" and "combat stress reaction." She wanted to learn the root cause, and how she could help.

From the shelves, she pulled out what sources she could think of, then she flipped through pages and came upon the first known mention of battle fatigue. Three thousand years ago, it was written, the Mesopotamians believed that soldiers' nightmares, depression, amnesia, and other symptoms were brought on by avenging ghosts of those slain in battle. Twenty-five hundred years after that, Herodotus described an Athenian soldier who went blind after witnessing the Battle of Marathon, but who had no physical injuries to either his eyes or his brain. In 1600, Shakespeare's General Macbeth murdered his king. For years, Macbeth had hardened his mind to slaughtering countless men on battlefields, then he suddenly lost all reason by following a dream of witches professing he would be king. *O, full of scorpions is my mind, dear wife!*

From a nearby shelf, Marion pulled out a more recent book, set during and after World War I. That conflict had ended the lives of more than twenty million people, and so many men had come home changed forever by the utter horror of what they had seen and done. The term *shell shock* had come from the Great War, she discovered, because the initial assumption was that close contact with exploding shells was responsible for the damage done to a man's brain. They had no other answers.

The men's symptoms were a puzzle, and the sheer flood of cases arriving after the wars forced the medical field to pay closer attention. Veterans came home with inexplicable symptoms like extreme anxiety, involuntary tics, stutters or mutism, a refusal to eat or drink, and debilitating headaches. There were cases of soldiers experiencing functional paralysis with no physical causes, vomiting for no apparent reason, and suffering unpredictable bouts of hysteria. Dozens of private mental institutions, lunatic asylums, and empty sanatoriums filled to overcapacity with these men. The doctors did what they could, but for the most part, they still had no real explanations.

There were valid reasons why the place where Marion worked, and every other similar institution, was known as a "snake pit" or "house of horror." For about a century, doctors had basically worked in the dark, trying different approaches. But the truth was, the treatments were often worse than the symptoms.

Like Marion, some doctors believed in the moral solution. They encouraged patients to talk about their experiences, and they provided soothing therapy to try to ease the suffering.

Other doctors worked more with the concept that an affected man's behaviour was a weakness, and one that should have a simple fix. Their conclusion was that if a man's brain had gone off track during combat, it needed to be snapped back into place. Unfortunately, that "snapping" was often carried out through brutal methods, like forced and extended ice baths, locking patients in closets, purging, bloodletting, using straitjackets for restraint, injections, electric shock therapy, and even lobotomies.

Riveted, Marion kept reading, and even though she had read plenty of horror stories, some still caught her off guard. Like the account of Henry Cotton, director of the Trenton Psychiatric Hospital in New Jersey in 1907. He believed his patients' troubles were brought on by internal infections, and he "cured" them by surgically removing teeth, appendixes, and colons. Hundreds of patients died, and thousands were maimed for life.

For nine months in 1918, a British psychiatrist named Dr. Lewis

Yealland treated a patient who had not spoken since his return from the front. Regarding the man's silence as a failing, Dr. Yealland decided to treat the problem with force. He demanded that the patient speak as he had before, insisting he "must behave as the hero" he expected, and he was not squeamish about reaching his goal. To elicit any sort of sound from the man, Dr. Yealland applied electric shock to the patient's neck, he extinguished cigarettes on his tongue, and he placed hot plates at the back of the poor man's throat. Frustrated by months of unproductive attempts, Dr. Yealland finally strapped the patient down and applied a powerful and prolonged electric shock to his throat. When at last he removed the charges, the patient whispered, "Ah." Dr. Yealland was so encouraged by the sound that he continued with the shock therapy for another hour, until the patient finally began to cry. In the end, the patient whispered that he wanted a drink of water. Dr. Yealland recorded his treatment as a success.

Then there were lobotomies. Despite having no surgical training, Dr. Walter Freeman II created a "transorbital lobotomy" as recently as 1949. Marion knew all about Freeman, including the horrible fact that he had performed his final transorbital lobotomy just last February. He boasted that the procedure could be performed with neither anesthesia nor operating rooms—in fact, his transorbital lobotomy was a simple office procedure with no need for a surgeon at all. First, he applied electroconvulsive therapy to induce a seizure so the patient felt nothing. Then he inserted an instrument resembling an ice pick under the patient's eyelid, against the top of the eye socket. Using a mallet, he drove the tool through the thin layer of bone and into the brain, where he swept the tip around the area to clear out what he called frontal lobe tissue. Many of his patients died of cerebral hemorrhages. Others needed to relearn how to eat and use the bathroom.

Yes, there were sound reasons why mental institutions had a bad name, but those were mistakes that many doctors—if not all—learned from. Medicine had moved forward, constantly improving. Physical therapy, group sessions, and new medications were among the "new" and progressive treatments that had risen from the snake pit's ashes.

Sometimes, unexpectedly positive results came from unusual methodology. In 1934, Dr. Ladislas Meduna discovered that the brains of patients with epilepsy had greater concentrations of microglia—the brain cells whose job was to search for harmful scavenger cells in the central nervous system— than those of patients with schizophrenia. From this, he surmised that seizures could possibly be beneficial. He injected camphor into a catatonic patient to cause seizures, and after four sessions, the patient was walking and talking on his own.

Seizures, it was discovered, could be brought on more quickly and with fewer side effects through electroconvulsive therapy, and those sessions began to show progress.

So many years of work, producing so little understanding.

Marion closed the last textbook, deep in thought. The general understanding over the years was that people diagnosed with this illness were broken. Marion had a different theory, and she wanted to explore it with Daniel. What if he, and men like him, weren't broken at all? Obviously, he had experienced at least one shocking, life-altering traumatic injury in Vietnam. What if, to maintain his sanity in an insane situation, he had constructed a wall around the trauma in his brain? Was it possible that he was living within that protective wall while undergoing an unconscious process of sorting through what happened? Maybe, rather than being broken, Daniel was searching for the right doorway to get back to where he belonged.

Marion would never punish him for something over which he had no control and for which he was not to blame. The first step she wanted to take in his treatment was to reduce his sedation, if it was physically safe. If they were going to work together, she needed him to be able to think clearly.

Paul was in the front administration office when she arrived at the hospital later. "There she is. Prettiest psychiatrist in the place."

She couldn't help smiling. "And the only female one."

He held out a file, which she assumed was Daniel's. "I believe we talked about an exchange of sorts."

"Certainly. I will grab those other patient files for you."

He wiggled a finger side to side. "We had a different kind of deal, if I recall correctly."

Marion shot a horrified glance at him then at Miss Prentice. The secretary was pretending not to listen, but her fingers were poised suspiciously over the typewriter keyboard. Furious at his lack of discretion, Marion breezed past Paul and headed toward the corridor.

"Dr. McKenny, please come with me."

"Gladly."

She could hear the smile in his voice, the teasing that she no longer found funny. She wheeled on him after they were in the privacy of the staff room.

"How dare you? In front of Miss Prentice, too. Do you plan on telling the entire building that we went on a date?"

"Hey, a deal's a deal."

Her eyes narrowed. "We did not seal any deal on that front. You know that." She reached for Daniel's file, but he whisked it behind his back, out of reach. "You are behaving like a child."

"I enjoyed Thursday night very much," he said, a glint in his eye.

His charm was not working on her today. "I already said thank you, and you agreed to trade patient files. I told you I would get back to you about the second date, but this morning's shenanigans have not helped your cause."

"Sure, they have. They've helped you remember Thursday night and how much you enjoyed it."

"Give me the file. Now."

He did, so she swallowed her pride and felt her resolve weakening. It wasn't worth making an enemy out of Paul. Most of the time he was a pretty good guy.

"What were you thinking of for a date?"

"Dinner Friday. Maybe French this time." He winked. "*Cela pourrait être très romantique.*"

She opened the staff room door and exited into the corridor. "I will let you know, monsieur. Thank you for the file."

twelve
SASSY

ꝏ

Sassy didn't recognize the man sitting near the front desk at the police station, but there was no one else, so she assumed he had come for her. She wasn't sure if she was disappointed that her father had sent someone else to get her or if she was relieved he hadn't come himself.

"Miss Rankin?"

He stood with a smile and rolled up his newspaper, tucking it smoothly into his jacket's inside pocket. Sassy focused on playing it cool, but she couldn't help noticing that the guy was a definite hunk. Way too conservative, and maybe about ten years older than she was, but a girl could still look. His dark hair was cut neat and short, and his eyes were a pale grey-blue.

"I recognize you from your photographs," he said.

"Beg your pardon? My photographs?"

The corners of his eyes creased self-consciously. "That sounded presumptuous. I apologize. I'm Tom Duncan. Please call me Tom. I work with your dad. I'm his new partner, actually. He has photos of you all over his office. Your mother and brother, too, of course, but mostly you."

She eyed him with suspicion. His partner? Joey was supposed to have that job.

"I didn't know he had a partner."

"He asked me last week, and I was honoured to accept." He extended a hand toward the front door of the building, and she saw traffic moving steadily beyond. "I took care of the paperwork. Shall we go?"

She'd been in a cell for only a couple of hours, but as she stepped into the fresh air, she took a deep, restoring breath. "What time is it?"

Tom was in the middle of sliding his sunglasses on, and she couldn't help but think that he looked an awful lot like Sean Connery when he wore those. It didn't hurt that he was wearing a light brown sport coat over an ivory sweater. She was positive she'd seen a photograph of Sean Connery wearing exactly that. Tom lifted his wrist to check his watch, and the sleeve pulled taut against his upper arms. The man was hiding an outstanding set of shoulders in that jacket.

"Five o'clock. Rush hour. Sorry I took so long, but I had another appointment. Your dad did, too, which is why he sent me. My car's parked just up here. I'm supposed to take you to his office."

As they walked, she regarded him covertly. Tom Duncan was taller than average, with straight posture and a confident stride. It was like she was walking beside James Bond. Imagine that. This guy must be smart, too, for her father to bring him in as a partner.

He seemed likable enough, but Sassy had taken a stance months before, vowing never to fall for a businessman. She'd recently discovered how cruel and capitalistic her father's real estate business was, and how ruthless he had to be as the best realtor in the city. The night she found out, she and Davey had been sitting with friends, talking about this and that, when one complained that his parents had lost their house to the bank, and some real estate guy had bought it.

Squinting against cigarette smoke, the young man had said, "I was born in that bedroom. Nothing wrong with it. It was the only pad I ever knew, but The Man trashed it, you know?"

"Bummer. They knocked it down?" Davey asked.

"No, man. They renovated the whole thing. Totally changed it. Then he bought our neighbour's house and did the same. Then, like, three more houses went up for sale, and now the neighbourhood is so expensive no one's got the bread to live there. A whole street, wiped out for profit."

Sassy kept her mouth shut about her father and what he did for a living. "Why'd the other neighbours sell their houses? They must have gotten a lot of money for them."

"Gentrification, man," another girl groaned. "Fat cats killing the whole world with their green. I say we should all just hang on the streets. Screw 'em."

Sassy had to laugh. "Yeah, but only in the summer."

From that conversation, Sassy learned that renovated houses cost too much for most people to afford. Her father did that: buying up old houses, fixing them, then selling them for big cash. After he worked on them, only the rich could afford to own them. Where was everyone else supposed to go? That conversation had changed how she regarded her father. She loved him, but to do what he did, he'd have to be cold. And greedy.

At the same time, she was uncomfortably aware that his income paid her rent. She kept her mouth shut on that, too.

"I have to ask," Tom said. "What's jail like?"

Any good feelings she had started to develop toward him evaporated. "What a question."

"I've never been. Until today, I'd never even been in a police station. I'm curious."

"I don't recommend it." She walked on, annoyed and keen to change the subject. "So lemme get this straight. If you are my father's partner, that makes you a conniving, thieving capitalist like him, right?"

His jaw dropped. "Wow. What a thing to say."

She smiled, pleased with herself, and kept walking. Tie game.

"Maybe he shouldn't have bailed you out," he muttered behind her. "I wouldn't have. I don't usually get along with Marxists."

"You're probably too old to understand what we're all about."

She wasn't sure why she'd snapped like that. She admitted to the occasional tantrum, but she wasn't usually rude. She blamed the hours spent waiting in the police station, all by herself.

His footsteps stopped. "Unless you want to walk all the way, you should come back here. This is my car."

Slightly embarrassed, she went around to the passenger door of his navy-blue Buick and got in. The car smelled new, so she told him that, hoping to smooth things over a bit.

He patted the dash. "Nineteen sixty-six Buick Skylark. Beautiful, isn't she?"

"Uh-huh."

She didn't know or care about cars, but she decided to keep that to herself. She faced the window as he pulled out of the parking spot and made his way into traffic. The new-car smell was a bit strong, so she rolled the window down and let the wind toss her hair. After a few minutes of riding and thinking, Sassy couldn't hold back any longer.

"Is he furious?"

"Who? Your dad? I'd say so."

Tom was resting his elbow out the window, and the sun was beaming onto his sunglasses. From this side she could see a little curled line at the side of his mouth. Not a smile, a smile *line*. She wondered if it disappeared when he got mad. Right now, though, he looked amused.

"What's so funny?"

"You. Your dad lets you live your happy hippy life and pays all your bills, and all he asks is one thing: keep a job. Instead, you skip off work, get arrested, then beg for mercy. Incredible. No kids of mine will ever be spoiled that way."

Sassy's cheeks burned. "It's none of your business."

"That's a good thing," he replied frankly.

She was glad to see Tom reach for the silver dial of the radio, filling the cab with Simon and Garfunkel. "The Sounds of Silence" was one of Sassy's favourites, and the melody almost swept her anger away. Almost. She'd been meaning to learn it on the guitar—it wasn't difficult, just a few simple chords—but she hadn't yet. She didn't realize she was humming along with the radio until the song ended and gave way to the Mamas and the Papas.

"Your dad told me you were a singer. You know this one, too?"

"'California Dreamin','" she murmured, cheered by the music and intrigued. "Sure, I do. My dad called me a singer?"

"Well?"

She scoffed. "I'm not singing for you. I don't perform on demand."

"Fine. Just making conversation."

She wasn't sure why she didn't like this man. He hadn't done anything wrong. In fact, he was obviously making an effort to be nice. Whatever it was, something about Tom Duncan grated on her, so she kept quiet the rest of the drive. She knew the route to her father's real estate office as well as she knew the walk to her apartment building, and the closer she got, the more she withdrew. She glanced sideways at Tom, but he didn't speak again until they reached the building then parked.

"Nervous?" he drawled. That little curl at the side of his mouth was definitely teasing now.

Sassy climbed the three storeys to her father's office then walked in, remembering at the last second to stop at the receptionist's desk. As a little girl, she'd gotten away with dashing into his private office and acting cute whenever she arrived, but that kind of allowance had gone the way of her pigtails.

Miss Sloane had her hair up in a beehive today, and her green-rimmed cat's-eye glasses matched her olive-coloured turtleneck almost exactly.

"You're looking hip," Sassy said.

Miss Sloane glowed with the compliment, but her smile subsided as she remembered the reason for Sassy's visit. "Thank you, Susan. It's nice to see you again. Go right in. Your father's waiting for you."

He was turning pages in a binder, checking them against another piece of paper at the side, and Sassy saw photographs of buildings flip by. She stood still, waiting for his cue.

She knew she was spoiled, like Tom had said. She knew she had it easy, like Davey suggested when he'd come to her for money and a place to stay. She'd never admitted to any of her friends how wealthy her family was, but she'd come close when she told Davey about the deal her father had made about her rent. It wasn't that she was embarrassed about how much money they had, she just didn't see any point in flaunting it.

From the very beginning, she and her father had been close. He loved Joey, but Sassy was the apple of her father's eye. While she couldn't remember a lot from when she was little, she'd seen pictures of him carrying her on his shoulders, pushing her on swings, laughing as they shared an ice cream cone. Those photos, he told her later, had been taken by her mother. Then she died, and Sassy got older. He devoted more time to his business, and she'd seen him less. After Joey left, her father had barely been home at all. She understood that. The big red house was so big and empty it practically echoed with every step, every sound. Now that Sassy was on her own, she imagined he basically lived at the office.

He didn't notice her in the doorway, so she sniffed to get his attention. He glanced up, and her heart broke a little, seeing his initial joy quickly melt away.

"We have some things to talk about, Susan."

"I'm sorry, Dad," she said, stepping up until she was across the desk from him. She bit her lip to keep from crying. She hated disappointing him. "Thank you for bailing me out."

"You assaulted a policeman," he said flatly.

"He was being mean to my friend," she replied lamely.

"You pushed him. A policeman." He shook his head. "Never in my life did I imagine either of my children would be a criminal. I am so ashamed of you."

The floor dropped beneath her. "I'm sorry, Dad," she whispered.

"What kind of peaceful antiwar protestor shoves a cop? You know what that makes you?"

She blinked and her vision blurred. "No, sir."

"A hypocrite, Susan. You are a criminal and a hypocrite. And if the policeman hadn't been so kind, you'd have a criminal record for the rest of your life."

She'd assumed she did have one now, so in the midst of this terrible storm, this was a sunbeam of good news. Not enough to change much with her father, though.

"What do you have to say for yourself?"

"I . . . I got carried away. It was exciting out there, and then the police stopped us and—"

"Were you high, young lady?"

Her cheeks burned. "A little."

"My daughter. Smoking drugs, hitting cops." He turned his face from hers. "I feel sick. What would your brother say? Would Joey think this was such a great idea?"

Joey probably would have thought it was funny, but there was no way she was going to say that. She didn't move. She had no idea what to do.

When he faced her again, he was no less angry. "What were you doing in a protest? You have to be crazy to get into that. Have you seen the news lately? All the race riots in the U.S.? The national guard getting called in to stop riots where people were throwing bottles and rocks, setting fires, looting—"

"That's not happening here, Dad."

"Don't interrupt me." He tapped his pen on the desk then slid all his paperwork to the side. "I have another question, and I sure hope you have a better answer this time. It's the middle of the day on a weekday. You should have been at work, not shouting on the streets, disturbing people. Why weren't you at work?"

A sob caught in her throat. She felt weak and scared and afraid. "I quit on Tuesday, Dad. I'm sorry."

"You *what*? And I'm just now hearing this? Do you *want* to lose your apartment? Why on earth—"

"I had to leave, Dad. Trust me."

"Why should I trust you?" he asked through tight lips. "You, we have established, are a criminal and a hypocrite."

She flinched.

"Tell me why you quit that job. Explain."

"I don't want to," she said weakly.

"Doesn't matter. Against my better judgement, I just bailed you out. You owe me."

He was right. She owed him for so many things. "Technically, I was fired."

"Even worse. What did you do?"

"I . . . I was uncomfortable. My boss—"

"You can't blame your failures on someone else, Susan. You know that. Take responsibility for your own actions for once in your life."

She took a deep breath and felt her cheeks burn with regret. It would hurt him to think of his little girl in a situation like this, but he had her cornered.

"All right, Dad. I'll tell you the truth." She squeezed her eyes shut and kept them that way as she blurted out everything. "Mr. Brown came after me. I was typing for him, and he copped a feel, and I tried to get up but he pushed me back into my chair. I was scared, so I shoved him off and ran out. I'm sorry. That's what happened. Even if you make me live at home again, I will never go back to that office."

When her father said nothing, she opened her eyes. He was staring at her, his face a shade of grey she'd never seen before.

"I'm sorry, Dad. I—"

"Why didn't you tell me? Did you know that he was—"

"There were rumours. Another girl quit before me, and people said he'd been spoken to about it, but I don't know what that means. Evidently, it wasn't enough. I never thought he'd come after me, and if he did, well, I swore I would be tougher than that other girl. But I guess I wasn't."

The lines of his face had softened. She knew him so well, and right now she could tell that what he wanted most was to stop being angry and give her a hug instead. But she knew herself, too. She didn't deserve that hug, and he knew she knew it.

He cleared his throat, struggling for words. "I am sorry you went through that."

"I want to work again, Dad. I will find something. And I promise I'll work hard."

She heard a sound behind her and glanced back. Tom had come into the office and was looking down at his shoes. That was embarrassing. She hadn't wanted him to hear their conversation, but he'd probably taken in every humiliating word.

"I've already found you a job, Susan," her father said, looking pleased at last. He grinned and held out his arm. "Meet my new partner and your new boss, Tom Duncan."

thirteen
MARION

‿✦‿

M arion went first to visit her female patients—minus Alice Sumner, who was now in Paul's charge—and gave them the attention they needed, but her mind raced ahead. When it was time to visit Daniel, she couldn't get there fast enough.

At his door, she stole a look through the window. He huddled on a single cot in his blue hospital-issued pyjama bottoms and a faded white T-shirt. The bed looked far too small for him. His knees were drawn up to his chest, and he'd wrapped his arms around them. Someone had shaved his face, probably yesterday, and his eye was closed. Was he sleeping while sitting upright? She'd read men in combat could do seemingly impossible things like that when there were no other options. She knocked, saw his head lift, then let herself in.

"Mr. Neumann," she said quietly. "I'm not sure if you remember me, but I—"

He turned his head slightly, regarding her. "Guess I'm the one with the good memory. You're Dr. Hart. I am *Major* Neumann. Does that help?"

The deep purple bruising around his face had dulled to a sickly green-yellow, and the swelling was down. The cut on his lip was still there, but it was healing. He made no attempt to smile.

"I'm sorry, Major. May I come in and speak with you for a few minutes? Are you feeling up to a visitor?"

"How am I supposed to know? I say one thing and the people here say another, and they claim they know better. Whatever. Come on in."

"How are you feeling?"

He lifted a shoulder then dropped it. "Sluggish from the drugs, but at least they haven't chained me up again."

"You were never chained."

"Semantics, Doctor. I was cuffed. Just softer chains." He moved lethargically, gestured to a chair by the door. "Come on in. Let's get the party started."

She took the seat, aware of his gaze on her the entire time.

"Major Neumann, I recently spoke with Dr. McKenny about your case. Do you remember him?"

"Vaguely. He thinks he's smart, but he don't know much."

That startled her. "Dr. McKenny is a brilliant psychiatrist. To what are you referring?"

"Calling it as I see it. He kept asking what I was thinking, but I don't think he understood the answers." His voice was cool, composed. He didn't seem to care. "So where is he today?"

"I requested to take over your case, and he has agreed."

She let that sink in.

His back straightened against the wall, and he adjusted so he could look straight at her, not around his patch. "Why would you do that? I thought you were afraid of me."

"Should I be?" She observed him closely, scouting for any sign of threat, but she saw only surprise, then concern.

"I don't think so." His tone had lightened, which was good. She'd caught his attention. "But I'll be honest, I don't know a lot. I got no real idea why I'm here." His fingers crept over the black patch where his eye had once been. "This probably has something to do with it."

"You don't remember how that happened?"

"Not much."

That was interesting. Dissociation often, but not always, included amnesia as a symptom.

"But you do remember some of it?"

It was like she'd flicked a light switch off, the way his expression dropped. There was a flash of . . . something feral, then it was gone. She briefly wondered if she should have come with protection, like Paul had suggested in his notes.

"No."

She could be smart and stop there with this line of questioning. She could get help from an orderly, just in case. Or she could continue, and offer trust by doing so. *Do something that scares you*, Paul had said. So she kept going.

"The other day, you yelled at me to help you. You said you needed to get out and help someone. Do you remember that?"

He shook his head, nothing more. There it was, she thought. The nugget she needed to dig for. A mine in a dark field. If she dug at the wrong angle, it could explode.

She set her file on the floor, reaching for a more personal connection. "I want to get to know you better, Major. That's the only way I can help you."

"You think I need help?"

"You don't?"

She was getting used to his one-sided shrug. It wasn't a motion of not knowing or having no idea, it was a vague, defensive movement. He didn't want to start this conversation, but he wasn't stopping her.

"Why did you go to Vietnam? You're Canadian. You didn't have to go."

"I did, though. I'm a man."

"What does that mean? Just because you're a man, that doesn't mean you have to fight someone else's war."

His expression was one of annoyance. Exasperation, even. She supposed he had fought this particular battle before.

"Of course it does. It's my duty to defend our country and fight for the underdog. My granddad lost a leg in World War One doing that, and my dad fought in the next one. I couldn't just stay home and run the fish plant."

"Is that your job? Running a fish plant?" She bent slightly, checking the notes on the floor. "You're from Nova Scotia? I've never been there, but I have heard it's lovely."

He was all right with this line of questioning. The tension eased slightly from his brow. "My great-granddad started the plant, and the family has carried on the tradition." His tone was calm, his voice gentle. The well-considered words were deliberate. "It's done a lot for the community. Not a glamorous job. A city girl like you couldn't take the stink for very long, I don't think."

"The city has its own smells," she replied wryly, "but I imagine working with fish would be worse. I guess your family has had to do more since you've been gone."

A spark of resentment. "They're strong, my family. They don't need me."

"I didn't mean to infer that they couldn't survive without you. Nothing like that. I'm merely trying to get to know you. What did they think of you going to war?"

He dropped his chin to his chest and said nothing. Clearly, they had not been happy.

"How did you feel about their reaction?"

A weak shrug.

"Do they know you're here?"

"Not unless someone contacted them. I sure didn't."

"Why not?"

"'Hey, Dad. It's me. I'm in the nuthouse. How are you?'" His brow lifted. "You think that would go over well?"

"They might want to be here for you. Do you plan to go home after all this is over?"

"I don't think that far ahead, Doc. I wonder if I'll wake up tomorrow. That's as far as I go."

Depression was no surprise, nor was fatalism. It could be a symptom, or it could simply be that he was unhappy in this place. She couldn't blame him for either. She thought of her father, how he sometimes slumped in his old armchair in the corner of the room, staring silently at the floor, looking like he would rather be dead than exist another moment. The next morning, he'd be himself again, asking if she'd like to go out for ice cream. Maybe take in a ball game. What must it be like to swing to such extremes with no control?

"You said your father and grandfather both served. Did you ever speak with them about their experiences?"

"Grandpa's from that older, tougher generation. He could be run over by a tank and not complain about it. Dad doesn't talk about his war, either."

How many men lived with that ache within, the furious buildup of emotions and no way to release them? Who had decided that men should not cry? One of the more asinine societal values, in her opinion. Then again, she supposed a man possessing enough courage to face a charging predator without sobbing with fear had merit. Who else would protect the families?

"Do you feel like talking about Vietnam?"

He met her gaze, wary. "What do you want to know?"

"Always simplest to start with the weather. I hear it's hot."

He adjusted his position on the bed, letting his shoulders sag a little. "When I first got there, I stepped out of the plane and it felt like I walked into a wall of steam. I couldn't breathe. You want to swim to cool off, but even the river water is hot." One eyebrow twitched with humour. "Beer's hot, too. More like soup than beer. But we drank it like water anyway. I was just starting to get used to the heat when the monsoons hit. The rain didn't make it any cooler, just harder to get around."

There were so many things she wanted to ask, but she had to tread carefully. Not unlike him, out in the jungle. She decided to hold off on asking him about combat. He would tell her what he needed to tell her when he was ready, and not before.

"The cool air must be nice now that you're back. At night, especially. I always sleep better when it's cool."

Any trace of softness left his face. "Don't know if you noticed, but sleeping isn't my problem. I just stick out my arm and they knock me out."

"I'm sorry. That was inconsiderate of me." She hugged her arms around her, suddenly chilled by the small room. "Are you warm enough in here?"

"I don't feel much anymore."

"You've probably felt more than your share," she said gently.

His reaction was slight, but she saw it. "You're talking about my eye."

"Well, that, and other things. I imagine you've seen awful things. That's got to hurt inside and out."

That little shrug. He wasn't taking the bait, but he was testing her a little. "I'm kinda numb all over."

She felt a pull, an invitation in his tone. He wasn't speaking purely of physical sensations. And he hadn't chased her off as her father had; instead, Daniel had shown her a crack of light under a door, if only she could find the right key.

She moved on. "I know you aren't fond of the sedatives you've been given, but do they help at all? Do they take away any of the pain?"

"They knock me out. I feel nothing," he said flatly.

"I have heard that on rare occasions, sedation can encourage other dreams. Of better times."

"I haven't seen anything good for a long time."

"Can we talk about the episodes you experience when you're asleep naturally? The nurses report you shouting in your sleep. Do you remember what you see or feel when that is happening?"

She could practically see him thinking through the question, then seeking the right response. Instinct told Marion that any answer he gave to that would be reluctant. He wanted to deny that he had any trauma at all. That what had happened was a part of war, and he accepted it. And yet, his hesitation suggested that a part of him wavered. Deep inside, he cradled a fragile glimmer of hope. If he shared his memories with her, would the pain extinguish itself? Or would talking about what happened supply the oxygen it needed to burn even hotter?

He wouldn't meet her eyes when he spoke at last. "I don't know."

"That's all right. Do you know if you had vivid dreams when you were a child? Did your parents ever tell you that you yelled in your sleep?"

He shook his head, but he did not slam the door on her questions.

She had to be cautious, take her time. She could be neither overly compassionate nor clinically objective. Neither insincere nor weak. She had to help him believe in her so she could give him the strength he needed to heal.

"You might not remember clearly," she said, "but I get a feeling that you sense something, even under medication meant to dull it. Even if it seems strange, I would like you to describe whatever it is to me, if you can."

He hesitated, thinking it through. "I sense something, yeah," he said slowly. "But it's not real. It's like . . . It's like someone took a brush to one of my grandma's paintings before the paint was dry. I can't tell what's real and what's a nightmare."

"Let's talk about when you're awake. The reason you were initially restrained and heavily sedated was because you were violent and ranting when you were awake. And yet right now, you're not sedated and you're quiet. How do you feel at this moment?"

"Everything's normal—at least, I think it is. I feel like me. Like I always did, I think, except I'm always pissed off these days. And confused, I guess."

"Reasonable. What about during those other times, when the nurses felt you needed restraints? I am aware that it's difficult to talk about, but I want to understand your experience."

"It's hard to describe." He cleared his throat. "Right now, I can describe everything in this place. The cheap cot, the stains on it, the two-inch tear in the blanket. But if you ask me another time, I might be in 'Nam. Wherever I am, it's real. I know that, because it's not just something I see and remember. I *feel* where I am. I'm in 'Nam, and I hear the guns and the bugs and my brothers talking, and I see every leaf and branch in the jungle, like I'm standing right there. I guess that sort of makes sense, because Vietnam's in my bloodstream now.

"But what's not clear to me is how I actually *feel the heat* of the air. When I see fire, I feel it scorching my skin. I smell the hair on my arms burning. When it comes, I feel the urgency to do something, and I have no choice. It's real." His fists clenched on his lap. "But then someone comes in here and ties me down, and that's when I realize none of it was real after all. The needle goes in, and it's like I'm being sucked out of what I know is real, even though I also know it isn't."

She was surprised by how open he was about his confusion and his hallucinations. Maybe her theory had been wrong, imagining that a man in Daniel's position might construct a defensive wall in his mind. He wasn't trying to hide anything from her. Not that she could tell, at least.

He dropped his chin. "I gotta be crazy, talking like that."

"No, Major. Not at all. It's actually very healthy to be able to explain something that complex. Have you heard of 'phantom limb' syndrome? When a person still feels a limb even after it has been amputated? It's similar to that, in a way."

"My grandpa still feels his leg, fifty years later. So strange."

"Exactly. It's no longer there. Nevertheless, it's real, like the heat on your skin. I'm curious. After the sedation is given, does everything go black right away, or does it feel like it's fading, or moving farther away?"

Again, that thoughtful pause. "When I was a kid I fell down a well. I remember lying at the bottom, my leg broke and blood everywhere. I was afraid no one would find me. All I could see above me was blue sky and clouds, but my mind still saw everything else. You know what I mean? I could visualize my house, the dock, the boats, and I could see my old dog, but I wasn't really there. That's what the drugs here do to me. They remove me from what I know. They take me away from myself." His chuckle was self-conscious. "None of that made any sense, even to me."

"It made sense to me, Major."

"Don't patronize me."

"I'm not," she assured him. "What you're saying makes sense to me."

He held her gaze, and she stilled, waiting. "Are you allowed to call me Daniel?"

"If you'd prefer it, yes."

She would have to keep that quiet from Dr. Bernstein, but she was glad that he had asked. He was reaching out. He wanted to find out if he had lost his mind, but he could proceed only if he trusted her. Marion would give him every reason to trust her, and she would never betray that trust. She would be his partner through this struggle. It was up to her to drop a rope to help him climb out of the well where he'd fallen, so he could emerge back into familiar territory.

At the same time, she had not given him permission to use her first name. There had to exist a doctor-patient relationship. She would not tell him that she knew very little about why he was experiencing all this, that she'd not found existing research on the topic nor a definitive therapy. But her title would give him the illusion they both needed.

"How do you feel about the medicine we give you here, Daniel? Does it help?"

"I'd call it a Band-Aid."

"What does that mean?"

His focus softened. "Maybe the meds are covering up what's broken in me, so whatever it is can heal underneath and form a scab. Or maybe the Band-Aid is trapping moisture where it needs air, and the wound is getting infected."

It was an apt metaphor.

"Do you feel like you're broken?"

Shrug. "Do you?"

"I guess we won't know for sure until the Band-Aid's removed," she said. "I'm going to reduce the dosage bit by bit and observe how you do. I obviously can't completely remove the sedatives. Not yet, anyway. You tend to get physical during your less-than-lucid moments. I hope that we can get to a point where you are able to determine what is real and what is a hallucination—"

"It never feels like a hallucination."

"I understand. I do. But what you are experiencing is not what we would call a memory, not really. Memories are not typically that vivid. At the same time, what you see is not currently happening to you. When it happens, I want you to label it as a hallucination. Can you agree with me on that? When we recognize what they are, and give them a name, we get a little distance from them. From there, we can work toward helping to ease them. You may not be able to adjust your thinking while it's happening, but when the episode is done, I would like you to remind yourself that it was a hallucination. Every time. Until you believe it."

"I see what you're doing. Okay, yeah."

She reached for his chart and wrote some of her initial thoughts as well as a new directive for the barbiturates. Then she set the clipboard back on the floor and sat back.

"How does it feel to be back over here?"

"You mean stuck in this closet of a room by myself with needle holes in my arm? Can't say it's the best place for me."

"My question was poorly worded. I was wondering how you felt being here in Canada versus in Vietnam."

"I haven't seen much of Canada since I've been here, have I? It sure is quiet in this place, until some looney goes off in the hallway or something." He exhaled. "But I know what you're asking. It's strange. When you're over there, you miss your family. When you're here, you want to be there again."

"Even though you could easily be killed in that environment? You were there for a year. You know the fragility of human life. You've seen the worst of it, I imagine."

"I have, and I do know it. But I miss my unit. I want to be with them."

It was generally understood that if someone insisted on repeating an action that had already proven to be detrimental, even harmful to them, there might exist a type of psychological disorder. Daniel wanted to go back to a world that had taken his eye and nearly killed him, but Marion wasn't certain why. Was that actually a disorder, or was it something else?

"I'm sorry. I don't understand. Why would you choose to go back to a place that has a high probability of killing you?"

"It's not the place, Doctor. And no, I don't have a death wish. It's my unit. We may not all like each other, but we're brothers. When I was in country, I knew everything about those guys, and they knew me. We were family. I knew who I was, and where I fit in." He hesitated. "Where am I now?"

She felt a lurch in her chest, seeing his eye suddenly shine, but she let him finish.

"My brothers need me. And I need them. That's why I have to go back."

fourteen
SASSY

After about six minutes of boiling, Sassy dumped the noodles into the colander then grabbed milk from the fridge. She lined the bottom of the empty pot with milk and threw in some butter—did anyone actually measure that?—then she tore open the little envelope and poured in the orange dust.

Tom Duncan, she thought for the hundredth time since she'd gotten home. Great.

She slid the noodles into the pot, stirred everything to her preferred consistency of cheesy, then she reached for a bowl and . . . stopped herself. Why bother? She'd just have to wash it after. She slid a spoon from the drawer, carried the pot to the table, and dug in.

Tom Duncan and his stupid question. *What's jail like?* She wished she'd had a good answer for him. She doubted *he'd* ever see the inside of a cell, with his expensive suit, new-smelling car, and flashing blue eyes. He looked like the perfect capitalist. Just like her father. Honestly. Couldn't they see how old-fashioned they were? How the world was changing, and they needed to change with it? How old was he, anyway? Thirty?

She huffed and ate a spoonful of her dinner, barely tasting it. What a lousy day.

Her gaze went to the television, which wasn't turned on, then to the cheery pot of calendula on top of the console. The late-afternoon sun was spilling over the orange flowers like a golden spotlight, and from her seat across the room, she thought she saw one of the buds starting to open. It should cheer her, but not even that was working.

So now she'd be working for Tom Duncan. He was not a fan of hers, obviously. He couldn't be, not after everything she had thrown at him at the police station, then in the car. Talk about starting off on the wrong foot. She would have to go in to work on Monday, sit at her desk, and keep quiet. Maybe, over time, he'd get past her behaviour, and things between them would get better.

She pictured that curl at the side of his mouth. Even with sunglasses covering his eyes, she could tell he'd been laughing at her. That charming smile must work wonders on the poor suckers buying homes from him.

She took another bite of Kraft Dinner then pushed the pot to the side. She'd lost her appetite. With a sigh, she folded her arms on the table and dropped her head onto them, trying not to cry. She needed another love-in, like at Queen's Park. An afternoon of sunshine and laughter with friends, maybe in Yorkville. She could bring her guitar and play for the people there like she had at Chez Monique.

She groaned, feeling a pang of loss. That dreamy part of summer was over. So much time had passed since that perfect afternoon, but it felt like months, not weeks. Then she'd blown her job, and pushed a cop . . . She wasn't looking forward to whatever was around the next bend, but it had to be better than how she was feeling right now.

Someone knocked on the door, and she debated answering. If Mrs. Levin or Mrs. Romano showed up, all cheery and sweet, she wasn't sure she could handle it. But Sassy wasn't the kind of person to hide away from friends, so she went to answer.

"Davey!" she said warmly, then she remembered how he'd let her down and turned back to her living room. "Nice of you to stop by."

He followed her inside, eyed the pot of noodles, but couldn't seem to sit down. Figuring he'd join her, she sat on the couch and pulled her feet up, sitting cross-legged.

He stopped walking, but didn't look at her. "You're okay?"

"Yeah," she said, hurting. He wasn't usually so callous, and she needed his support. "I thought you'd come see me in jail."

He didn't meet her eyes. "Yeah. I got caught up in stuff."

She resented his cavalier attitude. Sure, he'd been busy, but she needed the focus to be on her. She'd been in *jail*, after all. Davey hadn't come to rescue her, and he should have. Why was he skimming over that?

"My dad bailed me out," she said coolly, making no mention of Tom. "So don't worry about me. It's all cool."

He started to pace again, his eyes on the parquet floor.

"What's wrong?" she asked at last.

His head dipped side to side like a boxer's. "I'm ticked off at you."

"What? Why?"

He dropped onto the couch, staring at the television's grey screen, his expression pinched. Sassy grabbed his scruffy chin, turning him to face her.

"Why?"

"The protest, man. What you did totally made us look bad. I mean, we're supposed to be about peace, and you, well, people say hippies are a problem, and because of what you did, they think they're right. Why'd you have to go and do that?"

She hadn't seen him angry before. At least, not at her. Her annoyance at being left to rot in jail was swiftly replaced by guilt. She hadn't even thought of how her little performance might affect the entire movement she was trying to support.

"I . . . I was trying to help you, Davey. You know that."

"Yeah, well, I can handle myself, Sass. I'm a big boy." Then his frown melted into a puddle of apology. "Also, I can't come see you anymore."

Her breath caught. "Why? I didn't mean to mess things up! I said I'm sorry!"

"Nah. It's not that. It's Christine."

Her thoughts flew to that mousy little thing with crooked teeth, bad skin, and no brain. Sassy tried not to be biased, but she couldn't help it. She couldn't see one redeeming feature, except maybe her large breasts.

"Sure, yeah. What about her?"

"I guess we're getting serious."

"You guess?"

"She said she wants to. After the fuzz took you away, well, the whole protest kind of fell apart, then she and I talked for a long time. She said, like, she wants to be monogamous."

She'd caught Christine glaring at her a few times, but this was unexpected. She should have read Davey better, too.

"Is she worth it?" she asked weakly.

He lifted one shoulder, looking like a little kid. "I mean, I like her a lot. But I like you, too."

"I guess you can't have everything."

He dropped his chin. "I'm sorry, Sass."

"I am, too."

He got up and held out his arms, and she gave him a tight hug. "Come see me when she drives you crazy."

"I'll miss you," he whispered. "This is a real bummer."

"Just be happy," she replied, tears burning behind her lids. She refused to cry, though. Not until he was gone. She did want him to be happy. She just wanted him to be happy with her.

She'd never felt so lonely as she did after he left. Normally, if she was sad, Davey was the one she'd talk to. Sometimes she'd go home to her father for a pick-me-up talk, but now was not the time. With Joey in Vietnam, she had no one. She wished she had a friend she could call.

Outside, she heard the leaves swishing in the trees, and she realized that's exactly what she needed. Air. A change of pace. She headed for the door then grabbed her guitar case at the last minute. She'd find a quiet place under a tree, in the wind, by herself, then she'd play, and she'd cleanse herself of this awful day. She headed down to the lobby, then remembered on her way out that she should check her mail. There was rarely anything in her mailbox, but it was worth looking.

And there was something. Of course it had arrived today of all days. A letter from Joey, stained, wrinkled, and bearing a loose, hurried printing she'd never seen before. She hesitated, unsure whether to take it back up-stairs and read it there, then she tucked it into her pocket and went outside, into the wind.

At the park around the corner, she walked past a bench and over to a cool patch of grass beneath the canopy of a maple. She set her case down, sat beside it, then leaned against the tree trunk while she opened Joey's en-velope.

Sassy didn't get many letters from Joey, but she forgave him for that. She knew from the television that he was probably deep in a jungle somewhere, lost in the dark with his military brethren. She tried not to let her imag-ination go any further than that, but Joey was a good, descriptive writer. Over the past year his words had become a journal of sorts, bringing her into the war whether she wanted it or not. His stories about the First Battalion, Third Marines patrolling at Da Nang were so vivid she could almost feel the stickiness of the air and the tension in every heavy branch. The way he talked about his buddies, she felt as if she almost knew them. Then there were the letters he wrote when he got homesick. That's when his tough veneer gave way to the boy she had always known. Last year around Christmas, she had opened a letter from him while she sat by the window, watching fat snow-flakes dance around her yard. Then she read that the thing he missed most at that moment was snow. His simple wish had torn her apart.

She unfolded the letter and stared at printing that hardly looked like Joey's. His hand had obviously been shaking when he wrote it, and she tried not to picture his fingers gripping his pencil.

I got a bad story, Sass.

That's how it started. Her stomach dropped, and she knew the wind would not be enough.

We got ambushed last night. Got into a hot zone and Tex got greased right off. I ran to him, even though that was stupid. We're trained that you gotta look out for yourself first. I didn't, and I was lucky, because one of the others shot a gook who was aiming at me. My brother saved my life. But then he went down and

There was a space between the words. A smudge of what had to have been Joey's tears swept across the dirty paper.

God, Sass. This is so hard to write. Everybody tells you not to make friends out here. They say we should just call each other "Jack," to make it easier. I never could. But I get it now.

Another smear blended the letters, maybe from his thumb, but she saw clearly what he'd written.

I lost my mind. I can't remember much. I shot everything I saw. I was screaming. I wanted to kill everyone. I still want that, Sass. I want to kill them all, because—

He'd scribbled something out.

My buddy's head was messed up bad. I wrapped my shirt around it and dragged him out of the way. I don't remember getting him to the main camp, but I did, and they took him to the MASH unit. I don't know anything else. I gotta believe he's alive.

Sassy's heart was in shreds. Clutching the paper to her chest, she sobbed for her brother, for the others in his battalion, for all the men out there who were trying to survive in a horrible world. She kept visualizing Joey out there, wrapping his shirt around a man's bloody head, the panic he must have felt, the terror . . .

She forced her memory to show her the Joey she wanted to see. He'd been one of the smaller kids in the neighbourhood, his thick curls tumbling to his chin, his face and hands always grubby. His eyes were green like hers, and their corners were creased by so much smiling. His laughter was like a baby's, rolling straight from his gut, and he never seemed to run out of energy.

It made no sense, remembering him like that then reading this. His laughter would have sharpened into screams, his face and hands would have been slick with another man's blood. But she needed that memory. She needed to see him again as he was.

"Please come home," she whimpered into the wind.

Her sobs slowed, and she winced at the steel band of a headache now wrapped around her skull. Her nose was plugged from crying. There was nothing she could do, she acknowledged. Nothing but breathe and hope and wait. But how could she not feel his terror ripping through her? How could she not weep at the very idea of him, alone and in danger? How could she ever get past this?

Breathe, whispered a voice in her head. *Just breathe.*

She closed her burning eyes and inhaled a deep, shuddering breath, which she held as long as she could, focusing on the nightmare visions and the pulse of Joey's panic. When she could bear it no longer, she let everything out in a long exhale that said, *Come home.*

There was a push to the air, a heaviness she recognized with a sense of anticipation despite her own pain. A gust of damp air rushed past, blowing her hair in all directions. A thunderstorm was coming, its bank of dark grey clouds rolling off the lake behind the city's skyscrapers, and she didn't think she had long before it broke. Long enough, though, to gather her thoughts.

What a day.

Davey, watching her public arrest then waiting until someone else bailed her out to tell her he was done with her.

Tom, the stranger she had attacked for no good reason, who would now be her boss.

Her father, who had quite rightly called her a hypocrite.

And Joey. Broken, afraid, and unreachable.

She sighed, picturing each man, one at a time.

"Davey," she said out loud, picturing those lion-gold eyes. "I'm sorry I embarrassed you, and I hope we will still be friends."

She pictured the curl at the side of Tom's mouth, since his eyes were hidden by his sunglasses. "Tom, I hope you'll give me a second shot. I made a fool of myself, and I was mean. I want to prove to you that I'm not like that."

She remembered the look of frustration in her father's expression. "Dad, I'm sorry. The last thing I want is to disappoint you. I messed up. Thanks for giving me another chance. I won't mess up again."

Then she tried to pull Joey's face to mind, but it hurt too much to picture him as anything but that little boy she'd played with so long before. "Come home, Joey. Let me take care of you."

In the distance, thunder rolled.

Still shaky, Sassy got to her feet and grabbed her guitar case. The park was empty, and the trees leaned under the force of the wind. She picked up her pace, feeling slightly better. A tiny bit cleansed. Enough that she could begin to imagine something better on the horizon.

If she could get to her apartment before the clouds burst, she would enjoy the tempest from her balcony, as long as the wind wasn't too strong. Thunderstorms brought the best sort of electricity, and she needed that energy to fill her up. What was it about storms that stirred her? Why did she find herself torn between laughing into the rain and dissolving into tears?

Another gust shoved past, carrying the first spatterings and swirling leaves into cyclones around her. Fat raindrops dotted the sidewalk, filling the air with the warm aroma of petrichor, and Sassy considered the remaining two blocks until she got to Isabella Street. Maybe she could outrun the worst of what was coming. Clasping the handle of her guitar case tight, she ducked her head and sprinted as the rain began to fall in earnest.

fifteen
MARION

❧

Marion burst through the front door of 105 Isabella, careful not to skid on the slippery tiles with her wet shoes. Catching her breath, she untied the little plastic strap of her rain hood and slipped it off, letting rainwater cascade onto the lobby floor. The elevator came right away, but just as the door was closing behind her, someone called out.

"Hold the door, please!"

An arm shot between the elevator door and the wall, and Marion put her hand out to hold it open. A girl dashed inside, carrying a glistening guitar case dotted with pink and orange flower stickers. Marion tried not to stare, but she couldn't help wondering if it was her neighbour. How convenient that would be. She had been hoping to introduce herself sometime. It was hard to tell for sure, though, because the girl's hair was soaked, falling in long tendrils over her face and down her wet sweater. It made her look very young.

"Thanks a lot." She set the guitar case down and gathered her hair in one hand, then she used both to wring it out. "That storm is unreal!"

She glanced at Marion, and recognition dawned for them both. "Hey, aren't you the woman who helped me out at the grocery store the other day? That was outta sight, what you did." She scrambled for her purse. "Here, let me—"

She was young, she saw, probably about ten years younger than Marion.

The corners of her eyes creased into half-moons, but not before Marion noted her wide black pupils. Speed? Marijuana? She sniffed. Marijuana.

Marion held out a hand. "No need. You're going up to five, right?" she asked, pleased that she knew.

"Far out! How'd you know?"

The elevator bumped then began its slow, humming ascent.

"Actually, I live right beside you. I've heard you practicing. I even heard you play at Chez Monique one night. You were great."

"Far out! I'm Sassy. I'm in—"

"Five thirteen," Marion finished with a smile. "I'm Marion. Five twelve."

"Groovy. I can't believe you heard me that night. That's wicked. Did you have a good time?"

"I did. I hadn't ever been—"

All at once there was a thump, and the lights went out. The elevator jerked to a stop, and the tiny space was suddenly pitch-black.

"Oh no," Sassy wailed.

"It's the storm," Marion said, disappointed. She enjoyed storms, but not from inside a box. "I wonder for how long."

"They'll come for us, right? I mean, they know we're here?"

"Of course. But it's a pretty big storm," she murmured. "Might be a while."

Sassy's voice was small. "Bummer. I don't like dark places. Especially small ones hanging in elevator shafts. I'm kind of claustrophobic."

"The electricity could come back on at any moment. Let's not worry."

"I can't even see you," Sassy said.

"Our eyes will adjust," Marion assured her.

There was a pause, then Sassy asked, "Hey, did you see the movie *Psycho*?"

"No!" Marion cried, aghast. "I don't think we should discuss scary movies right now, do you?"

"Cool."

After a while, Marion heard Sassy slide down the wall of the elevator and sit. It seemed like a good idea, since they didn't appear to be going anywhere for a while. She unbuttoned her raincoat then sat on the floor as well, feeling the hard edge of the guitar case beside her and Sassy's foot jiggling with nerves.

"We're safe in here," she told the girl, closing her eyes.

"Are we, though? I mean, yeah. Okay. If we don't run out of air or the cable doesn't bust and drop us."

"Neither one of those is going to happen." But now Marion was going to think about it.

"Okay. It's a downer, though. I've had the worst twenty-four hours. It would have been cool to have something go right. I'd die for a smoke right now. Oh wait." She fumbled in the dark, and Marion heard the latch on the guitar case click. One of the instrument's strings hummed when it was touched accidentally. "There you are, my little darlings. I think a Mother's Little Helper might be just right for this situation. Want one?"

"I'm sorry?" Marion asked.

"Mother's Little Helper. From that song. Mick Jagger, you know? Mother needs something to calm her down?" She stopped when Marion didn't say anything. "No? It's V. Valium. Want one?"

"Oh, diazepam," Marion answered quickly. "Uh, no thanks."

"You sure? You might like it."

For a split second, Marion considered the idea. "No thanks. Not my thing."

"I dig it. Whatever floats your boat." A quiet minute passed, then Sassy sighed. "So lame that I'm freaking out. I'm just real uncomfortable in small places."

"Maybe you could sing," Marion suggested. "Distract us."

"Far out." The guitar thumped as it was taken from its case. "It's a little tight in here, but I'll try. How about 'Sunny Afternoon'? You know the Kinks?" She plucked the opening descending notes then began to sing.

She had a pretty voice. Light and expressive. There was nothing wrong with the Kinks, but Marion preferred the way the song sounded when Sassy sang it.

"Do you know 'Bus Stop'? Seems boss for today," Sassy said, then she plucked the opening notes, putting Marion in the mood. "Bus stop, wet day, she's there, I say."

She seemed more confident now. Maybe it was the Valium, or maybe it was the music.

Marion breathed slowly through her nose, smelling damp polyester and musty carpet, and she let Sassy's music bring colour to the darkness. She'd heard all the songs before, but she'd never really listened. And didn't the kids say that it was "all about the lyrics, man, all about the lyrics"? Marion thought she was starting to understand.

"What a romantic song," she said at the end.

"Yeah. True love. My mom and dad had that."

Past tense? "That's wonderful that you were raised that way."

"I wasn't really. My mom died when I was six. But I know they had it, because my dad never even looked at another woman after. Cool fact: the Beatles just put out a song about her."

"Your mom?"

"'Lovely Rita.'" Her voice was wistful. "That was her name."

"I don't know that one."

"It's from the new record, *Sgt. Pepper's Lonely Hearts Club Band*. It goes like this."

Eventually, Sassy laid the guitar back into its case, and Marion opened her eyes. Her vision had adjusted just enough that she could see Sassy's shape across from her.

"Thanks for the music. It was a nice way to pass the time."

"But we're still here," Sassy groaned. "Oh! I just remembered. I have Cheezies. Want some?"

Marion couldn't stand the things. "No thanks. I have Tic Tacs, if you'd like."

"Mm. That sounds perfect," Sassy replied.

Marion reached across the darkness for Sassy's open hand, then she tapped some mints into it. "We should do something to distract ourselves."

"I'm in. Got any ideas?"

"How about Twenty Questions? I'll ask you something, then I have to answer the same question. Then you ask me a different question, and you have to answer it as well. You have to be honest in your answers. Get it?"

"Right on," Sassy replied. "Lay it on me."

"I'll go first," Marion said, thinking. "What was your favourite subject in school?"

"That's easy," Sassy said. "Music. Oh, and English. Poetry. I love poetry. 'Two roads diverged in a yellow wood, and sorry I could not travel both . . .'"

"Robert Frost," Marion said. "Beautiful."

"I wish I could think up lyrics like they thought up poems."

"You'll figure it out when the time is right," Marion said. "Mine was science. I loved science. And math."

"We would have been at opposite wings of the school. Never would have met."

"You're probably right. Okay. You ask me something."

"Like your favourite colour or something?"

"If that's what you want to know. It's more interesting if you ask a question that needs more than one word to answer."

"I get it." She hesitated. "What is the scariest thing that happened to you when you were little?"

That was an interesting first question, Marion thought, automatically shifting to her psychiatrist role. But the rules of the game were that she had to answer first. It took a second to come up with her answer, then it came rushing back.

"I was six. My family and I were visiting a friend's cottage in Muskoka, and my sister and I borrowed the canoe without asking. We shouldn't have. We were far too little to be out there on our own. A motorboat went by really fast, and our canoe got caught up in the wake. I must have panicked, because I stood up, and suddenly I was in the water."

She paused, feeling a familiar tightness in her chest. "Pat tried to pull me out, but neither of us knew how to swim, and she couldn't reach me from the canoe without falling in herself. It drifted farther and farther away from shore, and all I remember is that when I screamed I kept swallowing lake water."

"Whoa!"

"Thinking back now, there were lots of adults around, so they pulled me out right away, but it felt like forever at the time—"

"No, man! You can't think about it from the perspective of now. We're talking about when we were kids. That's some heavy stuff, Marion."

"I've never swum since."

"Unreal. Good thing there were folks around."

"I was very lucky." She exhaled, surprised by how that memory still made her heart race. "Your turn."

At first, Sassy didn't answer. When she did, there was a colder tone to her voice. "I think I was, like, seven. My dad had taken Joey to a baseball game. Joey's my brother, by the way. I was home with my nanny, and she was super pregnant. We were playing hide-and-seek, and she was 'it'. I hid in my dad's closet under all his coats and sweaters." She paused. "I can still smell that wool. Anyway, she couldn't find me for what felt like a real long time, and then she shouted that she had to leave. Thinking back now, I know it was because she went into labour with her son, but back then I didn't know where she'd gone. At first I was ticked off, because she wasn't trying to find me. But then I couldn't get out of the closet. I can't remember if it was locked or just stuck, but I was little, and I couldn't open the door. I banged on it and yelled until I lost my voice, but no one came. You know how kids have no understanding of time passing? It felt like my dad was gone forever." Her breath sounded shaky. "Yeah. That's my scariest moment."

"But he came home eventually," Marion reminded her gently.

"My little brother, Joey. He found me."

"Sassy, do you understand that your childhood memory led to your claustrophobia?"

"Uh . . . huh. I guess you're right. Never thought about that before."

"I have a little trick for you to try. It won't work all at once, but I think it might help over time. When you feel scared like that, like you might be right now, I want you to force yourself to remember the moment that your brother opened the door. It must have felt so good, seeing him and breathing in that fresh air."

"Uh-huh."

"Can you try that?"

"Right now?"

"Yes. Think of the elevator door as the closet door in your memory. Now imagine that moment when he found you, and the relief you felt."

When Sassy spoke again, her voice was a little calmer. "Far out. How did you know that?"

"I'm a psychiatrist. It's my job to know things like that."

"A lady shrink! That's outta sight." Sassy chuckled. "When I'm feeling looney, I'll come see you."

"Actually, we don't say 'looney' or 'lunatic' anymore," Marion said. "Technically, patients can be diagnosed as insane, but we specify the particular illness to avoid a negative connotation."

When Sassy didn't respond, Marion continued. "What I mean is that we try not to use stereotypes like 'looney' or 'crazy.'"

"Cool."

"Do you want to know where the term *lunatic* comes from? Hundreds of years ago, it was thought that people behaving abnormally were reacting to the natural changes of the moon, which is *luna* in Latin. Hence 'lunacy.' They said those people fluctuated like the moon, waxing and waning."

"Far out. You're wicked smart," Sassy said. "Know what I think? You should try to swim sometime. I mean, you know how to get rid of the fear. You should use it on yourself."

That stopped her. Marion wasn't used to intelligent suggestions that used her own words against her. Sassy was right, of course, but the idea scared her too much to consider.

"Maybe. I don't really like water anymore, though, and I never took any lessons. I'm all right without."

"That's a lousy excuse."

Marion felt her cheeks warm, but it didn't matter. Sassy couldn't see it in the dark. "Want more Tic Tacs?"

"Sure. Thanks."

"It's my turn to ask a question," Marion said. "After that last question, I want to know what you're afraid of now."

The moment the words were out, she regretted them. Why would she ask a question when she didn't want to admit the answer?

Sassy exhaled. "Honestly, sitting in the dark in this elevator is top of the list right now. Even with your advice. Other than that, losing Joey's my biggest fear. He's uh, well, he's fighting in Vietnam, and no, I don't want to talk about that. I just hate not knowing where he is or if he's safe, and I'm constantly afraid that I'm going to hear bad news someday. Also, I'm afraid of disappointing my dad. He wants me to be this successful businesswoman, but that's not me. I'm a child of the sun, you know? I belong outside, celebrating Mother Nature and freedom and flowers and sky . . . Right? Not rotting at a desk."

"But in life—"

"Being a flower child doesn't pay the rent. I get it. But that's where I'm at. Maybe in time. But those two things are kind of like, tied, I guess. I am afraid of losing Joey and disappointing my dad. What about you?"

Marion hesitated, embarrassed. She'd never admitted her greatest fear out loud. But here they sat in the dark, two strangers with completely different stories. And it was her turn to answer. The rule said she had to be honest. She knew the power of conversation, and she hoped she had helped Sassy a little. Maybe speaking her own concern out loud would help her as well.

Lately, Marion's thoughts kept returning to Paul's suggestion last night, that she was missing out on life. And that somehow led to thinking about Daniel, a man who had barely survived the worst, but craved more.

She took a moment to get her thoughts in order. She knew it was paradoxical, since her work was all about getting her patients to talk about themselves and their feelings, but Marion never discussed herself that way. The silent elevator, the inability to escape, and the anonymous darkness crowded in on her, reminded her that it was her turn.

What harm could it do?

"I always wanted to be a doctor, and I put everything I had into making that happen," she said, starting slowly. "But I'm thirty-one. Sometimes I wonder, What else have I done with my life?"

"Probably saved a lot of lives," Sassy put in helpfully.

"I hope so. But what about my life outside of work? I never used to envy my sister and what I considered to be a predictable life, but recently I've wondered. Pat has a husband, kids, and a beautiful house. I have a one-bedroom apartment and a cat."

"What's his name?"

"Who, the cat? Chester."

"Chester. I want to meet him. Sorry. Go on."

Marion sighed. "I've never travelled, I've never gotten drunk, I've never done a lot of things."

"You got an old man?" Sassy asked.

Marion scoffed. "We're not talking about that."

"But do you?"

"No. I, well . . ." She stopped. "See, maybe that's what I'm talking about. I could, but I haven't made time. I think more about work than the future. Now that I think about it, my biggest fear is missing out."

"Sounds like we need to set you up."

An unexpected blush rose, and she recalled the gentleness in Daniel's scarred face, the trust he openly sought and cautiously gave.

"I don't think having a boyfriend's the answer."

"No, but it's a cool start."

They sat in silence, then Sassy spoke up again. "It's okay, man. We feel what we feel because we are sentient beings, and we shouldn't apologize. If you feel that way, then it's real. I guess the next question is, what are you gonna do about it?"

Marion opened her mouth to speak, then she snapped it shut when the elevator lights suddenly went on. She covered her eyes against the unexpected brightness, and Sassy squeaked with relief. They got to their feet as the elevator rumbled back to life, and Marion stared at the floor, wishing the power would shut off again. She had said too much to this stranger. She wasn't sure how to even look at her now.

Sassy noticed. "That was pretty heavy. You okay?"

"I'm fine, thank you." The door rattled open at the fifth floor, and the two faced each other in the hall. "Home sweet home at last."

The mysterious door across from the elevators clicked open and closed. The women exchanged a glance.

"What's he looking for, do you suppose?"

Marion felt an unexpected pang of sympathy. "Maybe he's just lonely."

"Maybe. You know, Marion, it's okay if you're square. Lots of people are. It's fine. We're all different."

Square. Exact edges and straight lines. Yes, that described her perfectly, which only added to her frustration. "Thank you, Sassy. It was nice getting to know you. I'm kind of glad we got stuck in there together."

"Hey, do you wanna come hang in my place and have some wine? It's just me. You might have seen Davey before, but now it's just me."

"Davey? Is that your 'old man'?"

"Nah." She dropped her gaze. "He's a gas, but he has somebody else now."

"I'm sorry. Is that a bad thing?"

"It's whatever. We believe in free love, you know? Nobody can tell us what's right or wrong or good or bad."

"I see." But there was pain behind Sassy's words. Marion heard it.

Sassy laughed. "I can see that you don't. Come on. Have some wine with me. I could really use the company."

A flurry of butterflies beat in Marion's chest at the thought. She was tired, she was melancholy, and she had her defences down. Sassy was so young. Marion wasn't sure she was up for that kind of energy.

"I don't think so. Not tonight."

Both of them turned, hearing raised voices come from behind the next door.

"The Romanos," Marion commented, walking past. "Too much basil in the sauce, probably."

"They make great food," Sassy said, stopping at the end. "Here's me. You sure you don't want to come in?"

Marion thought about Chester, waiting by his bowl for her. Of her quiet apartment and the thunderstorm she could watch through her window, if it was still happening.

"Oh, I don't think so. It's been a long day."

Sassy flung her door open, giving Marion a peek at her living room. "Come on. Live a little. Stay and have a glass of wine with me. We can just hang out."

A flash of bright-coloured furniture and intriguing art on Sassy's walls caught Marion's attention. She spotted a yellow beanbag chair in the familiar, yet very different living room. Vivid blue and green stripes made up the rug in the centre, and yet somehow, the cherry-red couch fit in. She was amazed by how the two identical apartments could be so distinct from each other. The only thing she recognized was a pot of bright orange, soaking-wet calendula flowers on the balcony.

Sassy and Paul were right. Marion needed to live a little. Her resistance crumbled.

"I'd love some wine," she decided.

She stayed an hour, unexpectedly comfortable on Sassy's couch. She wasn't ready for the beanbag yet. Might never be, but that was okay. She was enjoying a simple unwinding evening with a new friend. When was the last time she'd done that, if ever? It felt good. As they sat and talked, with the storm streaming noisily beyond the window, she became aware of the sharp corners in her mind beginning to round. That's how she liked to think of what happened when she had a little too much wine. Soothed by Sassy's chatter, she relaxed into it.

On the table, next to a bowl of pretzels, Sassy had a small pile of books. Marion reach for them, then she examined the titles.

"Are you reading all these?"

"I've read them, but I leave them out as reminders," she said. "You have to take them with you when you go."

"*The Yellow Wallpaper*," Marion read. "What's that about?"

"That's one of my favourites. It's basically a horror story, only it's really about a woman's life and what it feels like to . . . wait. You actually might love this one. Right up your alley." She handed the thin book to Marion. "The woman goes crazy because she doesn't fit into the role of wife and mother, so she's sent away, but they won't let her do what she really wants, which is to write, and . . . Oh, I don't want to tell you any more in case I spoil it. It's really short. You can finish it quickly, I'm sure. And I think you'd like this one, too. *The Bell Jar.* Again, the woman in the book is going insane, and she eventually commits suicide, so it's pretty scary. What's really interesting is that Sylvia Plath, the author, committed suicide a month after she finished writing this."

Marion blinked. "Why are you reading about women who are losing their minds?"

"I don't know. I guess it's kind of a possible story for all of us, if we leave our lives to others. As women, we need to be courageous and forge our way ahead, not follow someone else's rules."

"Huh. And this one?"

"*The Golden Notebook*," Sassy said, adding the third book to Marion's stack. "It's hard to describe. It's about a girl named Anna, and . . . it's . . . You have to read it."

"Thank you," Marion replied. "I haven't read fiction in so long. I can't even remember the last book I read for pleasure, not work." She flipped through a few pages of *The Golden Notebook*, curious. "I think I'll read some tonight."

Sassy's walls were crowded with art. It was nothing like the dry line art hung around Marion's apartment, with the sole purpose of camouflaging the bare walls. Her eye was caught by a large painting done in a smooth amalgam of yellows, reds, and pinks, then overlaid by random floating mushrooms, happy faces, and peace signs. It was warm and fresh. She felt like the artist had been happy when he painted it. She stared at it, trying to decide how she felt when she looked at it.

"I really like that one," she said eventually. "I've never seen anything like it. So bright and different."

"That one? Oh, thank you! I painted that."

"Really! You paint, too?"

"Used to. I have others in the closet if you want to see."

Marion checked her watch then put her empty wineglass down, startled by how quickly time had passed. "I'd love to see them sometime, but I have to get home now. Chester will be hungry."

"I'd love to meet him someday."

"I'm sure you will." At the door, Marion lifted her raincoat off the hook. "Thank you, Sassy. I really enjoyed this evening."

"Oh, me too! Made the whole elevator thing almost fun."

"Almost," Marion said with a chuckle, then she pushed back a rush of apprehension and said exactly what was on her mind. "What do you think about doing this again next week, but at my place?"

PART TWO

There is no such thing as closure for soldiers who have survived a war. They have an obligation, a sacred duty, to remember those who fell in battle beside them all their days and to bear witness to the insanity of war.

—Lt. Gen. Harold G. Moore, *We Are Soldiers Still:*
A Journey Back to the Battlefields of Vietnam

sixteen
SASSY

❧

The following Monday, Sassy bused to her father's office building then climbed the stairs to the third floor, more apprehensive with every step. She dreaded the start of her new job and burned with shame every time she thought of how rude she had been to Tom on their first meeting. It was easy to blame her unpleasant stay in jail, but that didn't excuse the hostility.

At the top of the stairs, she paused at Miss Sloane's desk, waiting for her to hang up the telephone.

"Ah, Susan. Welcome to the office. I think you'll like it here."

"We'll see," Sassy muttered, then she snapped herself out of the mood. She had to start off on the right foot if she was going to get anywhere. "I'm sure I will. I guess I'm a little nervous."

"That's only natural, dear. Why don't you go set up your desk how you like it. It's that one over there, outside of Tom's door. He'll be in soon to see you, I'm sure. He usually arrives at—" She checked her watch. "He gets here just before nine, so about ten minutes from now."

"Thanks, Miss Sloane."

"Oh, please. Now that you're here, you must call me Betty. Otherwise, I'll feel old."

"All right, Betty," Sassy said with a smile. "Thank you. Then please call me Sassy."

A slight scowl. "How will your father feel about that?"

"He won't say anything. He's the only one in the world who calls me Susan anymore."

She walked to her desk and braced herself with a positive attitude. When Tom arrived exactly ten minutes later, she had pasted on a tranquil smile. He took off his jacket then stopped at her desk, and just from the casual expression, she could tell that Tom Duncan was a better person than she was. Without even a hint of a mention of her jail time and their ensuing conversation, he greeted her with a surprise cup of coffee, then he introduced her to her responsibilities and placed a file on her desk. His niceness almost made everything worse.

"This might be a little unprofessional, but I'm hoping you'll call me Tom. I mean, if there are clients around and it seems better to go with Mr. Duncan, that would be all right, but I'm more of a first-name person. How do you feel about that . . . Susan?"

"Sassy," she allowed. "Of course you may call me Sassy, Tom."

She was painfully aware that no matter how polite and professional he was, her actions of last week were imprinted in his mind. Even if he'd planned to get along with her from the start, he now couldn't help but see her as a spoiled little girl who could do whatever she wanted under Daddy's watch. To make matters worse, he was right. She had to change that perception. She set her mind to demonstrating that yes, she had been that way, but she had changed. This sassy cat was changing her stripes.

She got to work, following his instructions, determined not to mess up. And yet every time she looked at him, her mind seemed set on misbehaving. Sarcasm bubbled to the surface when he spoke to her, as if he turned a tap in her head, so she zipped her lips and fought the urge to banter with him. He was her boss, after all. She had to be professional. It was a strange feeling. She wanted to like him, and yet she constantly felt like challenging him.

Working in this office for Tom was a much better fit for her. For one thing, she wasn't in a pool of secretaries. She was the only one, and her desk was just outside of Tom's windowed office. Just like at Jamieson, Baines, and Brown, she typed and filed, but it was more than that. She hadn't expected to enjoy working for him, but the more he talked and the more they worked together, the more intrigued she became. Her desk was physically close enough to his office that she could hear him talking on the phone, and he was constantly dropping things off on her desk, so she started to get a feel for some of what he was doing. She still disliked the overall idea of their business: buying houses, upgrading them then selling for a profit, thereby making neighbourhoods unaffordable for real people, but she kept quiet about that. Tom seemed keen to teach her, so she listened and learned, resolved not to disappoint either him or her father.

Her father worked down the hall in his own office, though she hadn't seen him today. She knew some girls might feel smothered, having to work near their father like that, but Sassy was quietly elated. She had always loved being close to him, and it was even more special now that she didn't live with him.

At lunchtime, Tom showed Sassy the boardroom, where they occasionally entertained clients. On Fridays, he said, either he or her father brought in lunch, and they ate it in there. Sassy was to clean up after, but she had expected that. Thinking of being fed even one day a week was a welcome bonus. There were only so many peanut butter and jelly sandwiches a girl could eat.

At the end of her first day, to her great surprise, Sassy was smiling. Things were looking up. She liked her job, the sun was shining through her very own office window, and last Friday she'd made a new friend in Marion, just when she'd really needed one. Marion was a little older, she guessed around Tom's age, but she was pretty cool. She'd run into her in the hallway on her way out this morning, and Marion had invited her over tonight. Sassy said yes right away, then volunteered to bring wine. Now she wanted to tell her about the new job, see what she thought.

Sassy said goodbye to Tom at five o'clock, and he gave her a cheery nod.

"Good work today, Sassy. Thank you. I think this is going to go well, you and me working together."

"I do, too," she managed, though she couldn't hold his gaze. "Listen, Tom, I . . . I need to apologize after last week." She inhaled a little confidence then lifted her eyes to his. They were a sharp, intelligent blue, and she was reminded of Sean Connery again. "I was incredibly rude. I'm sorry."

That curl at the side of his mouth lifted, and she wished she could read what thoughts it was hiding. She didn't know him well enough yet to ask. She would have to fix that.

"Apology accepted. You'd had a bad day. I get it."

"You didn't deserve that from me."

"Sure didn't."

Was that laughter? Or was that little half smile an expression of acceptance? Either way, his answer struck her the wrong way.

"I said I was sorry."

The other side of his mouth rose as well, curving into a full smile. "Are we starting up again, Sassy? I mean, I can keep up, but it's going to be harder to work together if you're going to freak out at me every time you think I said the wrong thing."

What was it about Tom Duncan that made her want to get in his face and, well, be right? To win every time? It was ridiculous. *Grow up, Sassy.*

"No. We're not starting up again. It's me. I'm tired. Thanks for putting up with me," she said.

"It's not a problem." He lifted a charming black eyebrow. "How about we start over again, you and me?"

"Yeah," she said. "I'd like that." She stuck out her hand. "Nice to meet you, Tom."

"I'm glad to meet you, too, Sassy."

She did like that smile of his.

It really had been a good day, and she was feeling more upbeat than she had been whenever she'd left the law office. Maybe it was like Davey said once, that everything happens for a reason.

After leaving the office, she walked a couple of blocks to the LCBO. As usual, the big room was quiet, and four or five people stood at counters, filling in their order form. The LCBO wasn't much different from a bank, except with booze. With all the paperwork involved, it felt suspiciously like the Liquor Control Board of Ontario was keeping track of what people drank.

She stopped at one of the counters then ran her finger down the list of wines to choose from. Using a pencil chained to the counter, she filled in her name and address, the brands of wine, how many bottles she wanted, and the prices on a specially printed pad of white paper. She brought the paper to the short queue at the till, having signed the bottom line to certify she was over twenty-one, and when it was her turn, she slid her order through a hole at the bottom of the window. She paid the man after he rang it up, and her change jangled down a metal tray as he passed the form back to her. She brought that to the next desk then waited in a second line to hand it to another man, who went back to his shelves and wrapped her two bottles in brown paper bags. What a rigamarole.

On the bus, she held the paper bags on her lap and watched out the window. Her gaze was caught by the sight of a man in a long black coat, walking the other direction. His beard was long and matted, and long hair stuck out stiffly from beneath his cap. He kept stopping in front of passersby with his hand out, but it remained empty. Most people walked around him without a backward glance, but some did give him a second look. Those were rarely kind, and Sassy felt a deep and helpless sympathy for him.

The transient was still on her mind when she knocked on Marion's door after her supper. Marion praised her wine choices, and they settled in with a couple of glasses. Sassy brought the poor man up to Marion right away.

"He looked so tired, you know? Like he maybe hadn't slept or eaten in forever. Nobody was paying any attention to him, but I wanted to, like, jump out of the bus and give him all the cash in my purse."

"Wouldn't have been a good idea," Marion murmured. "You didn't know him."

"Don't talk to strangers, you mean?"

"Well, yes, but these days it might be a little more dangerous. And I expect you'll start to see more and more people like him out there."

Sassy frowned. "Why do you think that?"

Marion finished her wine then held out her glass for more. "The Ontario

Hospital, where I work, is shutting down. It's a huge mistake. They're calling it 'deinstitutionalization.'"

Sassy frowned. "Are you losing your job?"

"No, no. I'll be working at a new community centre."

"But I've heard that's what's best for the patients, isn't it? They deserve freedom, just like everyone else."

"I know that's what people say," Marion replied, her expression tightening with frustration, "but tell me how that can be true, Sassy. Some of my patients are extremely unstable. They are unpredictable, and they don't know how to live outside of the institution. If a patient doesn't know enough to take their medications, if they forget to eat, if they bang their heads against a brick wall until they crack their skulls, how can that be good for them? What's to stop them going out in the middle of a snowstorm and freezing to death? I know what people say, but the truth is that these patients need to be in a hospital."

Sassy's mouth opened slightly with concern. Nothing she'd heard or read in the papers had suggested any of these things. Everyone seemed fully in support of letting the patients out of the hospitals. The picture Marion painted was alarming.

"It's horrible how this whole transition happened with so little thought to consequences," Marion continued, "because there will be plenty of those."

Sassy swallowed some wine. "Like what?"

"Do you really want to hear me complain about this all night?"

"Absolutely. If it matters to you, it matters to me."

"All right. Well, as they are discharged, the patients will mostly be released to their families, but in many cases, their families won't be able to care for them. They won't know how. Then what? If their families kick them out, where will they go? The community health centres are like regular offices, only open during the day. There is nothing set up to provide full-time care for those who need it, and so many will be in need." Her fingers curled around the stem of her glass. "It's not just our hospital that's shutting down, remember. Lakeshore will be emptying out at the same time, with the same problems. And what about the veterans returning from Vietnam, and the generations of suffering veterans before them? I'm not exaggerating when I predict that in the near future, hundreds of transients with psychiatric troubles will be wandering around the streets, sleeping on sidewalks or in parks with no protection, no food, no medicine, or anything. Some of those could be dangerous to the public if they aren't monitored. Others will be tossed in jail, where they will get lost in the system."

"So the government is more keen on saving money than people?"

Marion gave Sassy a flat look. "Sure feels that way, but I can't imagine that overloading the jail system will save any money."

"But there are some places for them to stay, aren't there? What about social housing? The government is supposedly building twenty thousand houses across Canada every year."

"Of course," Marion replied. "Affordable housing. Like when they built Regent Park back in the forties. But those don't provide what so many of our patients need, which is specially trained doctors and nurses to help them survive. Otherwise, it's not freedom for them, Sassy. It's a life sentence."

"What about rooming houses?"

"There is no care at all for the patients in those houses, just slumlords, basically."

Sassy shook her head, thinking of the man in the black coat. "What will he do in the winter? Where's he going to sleep?"

Marion raised one cynical eyebrow. "On park benches or in alleys, probably."

As they did so often, Sassy's thoughts went to Joey. "You said that some of those patients who are being let out of the hospital are veterans."

"Yes. Of different conflicts. We even have men from the Great War with us."

"Do you think Joey will be all right when he gets home?"

Marion observed her over the rim of her wineglass. "In what way?"

"I don't mean physically. Nobody can predict that. But what about . . . the other thing? Will he be crazy? Will he be like one of those rubbies in the street?"

"Those 'rubbies' are people, Sassy. People who need help."

"Sorry. You know what I mean."

"I can't say if Joey will come back all right. It varies with every man. Some of them live at home with their families." She hesitated, deliberating what to say. "My father has had trouble for twenty years, and yet he has lived what many would consider a normal life."

"I'm so sorry, Marion. Thank goodness he has you."

Marion's cheeks reddened. "I wasn't always the most supportive daughter. When I was young, I felt embarrassed by him. I saw him as weak, which I suppose is natural. We're used to men being, for lack of a better word, bulletproof."

"But now you help him."

"When I can."

"If Joey comes back . . . that way . . . what can I do to help him?"

Marion let out a long breath. "I wish I had better answers for you, but that varies, too. You will have to wait and see what he needs."

Would she still know him when he returned? Would he know her? Would there be room for her in his life? Would he even want her help? Would she know what to do?

Every time she wondered about how he would be, the inevitable question cut through the noise in her head. A question she would never ask out loud.

Would he come home?

She dropped her gaze to her glass, not wanting Marion to see the doubt in her expression, but her friend seemed aware of most things that were going on around her. She probably knew exactly what Sassy was thinking.

"You have to think positively," Marion said.

Sassy had been doing that for so long. Without any answers, it sometimes felt like she was lying to herself. But Marion was right. There was nothing else she could do about it, and living in fear would ruin her life.

So she ordered herself to be positive. Sassy *would* see Joey again. He would be all right, and even if he wasn't, she would stick with him. She couldn't let herself think any other way. She needed her brother, whoever he turned out to be.

seventeen

MARION

❦

Marion had never really had a best friend before. Pat had been the so-cialite in the family, the one invited to parties and wooed by football players. Marion hadn't been interested in meeting people. Her mind craved facts, and she wanted little more than to learn. Everything. In high school, instead of sitting with friends, she spent her time in the school library, reading.

Marion had completed grades nine to thirteen, sheltered in that quiet haven. She had been happy, but she couldn't deny having had moments of envy in those tender teenage years. Of sadness even, that she'd never bothered—or dared—to try anything else. At the end of school every day, she'd passed by the field, where students congregated in little clusters, but their conversations never interested her.

Sassy would have been one of those girls on the high school field, surrounded by friends. Had she carried her guitar to school and performed for them? With those dancing green eyes and her way of making people feel good, Marion had no doubt she would have been popular. Sassy had been right in the elevator: they probably never would have met if they'd been in school together.

Now that Marion was getting to know her, she could see what a waste that would have been. She'd never had a close friend, then all of a sudden

Sassy turned up, eager to get to know her. She left Sassy's apartment on that first night with her arms full of books and her mind buzzing with input. The next Monday, Sassy came to her place after supper and exclaimed at all the differences in their decor, declaring that Marion's plain white walls were calming.

A week after that, Marion was sipping wine and listening as Sassy stood by her record player, moving from one album to the next, carefully dropping the needle onto the songs she wanted to explain.

"This is 'Early Morning Rain' by Gordon Lightfoot," Sassy told her, looking serious. "I actually heard him play a few years ago at the Purple Onion in Yorkville. He was in a duo then, called the Two Tones. His voice is kind of nasal, can you hear it? But his poetry's great. Now this one," she said, moving to the next record, then the next, leaving Marion in a contented stupor. The girl was a whirlwind, and even if Marion didn't ingest all she was saying about the music, her energy was contagious. She made Marion long for a record player of her own.

Between the songs and the books and the wine, Sassy told Marion about Joey. Left without a mother, in the care of a father who had never stopped grieving, the children had formed a deep bond, finding security in childhood games, and trust when they needed it most. Joey's decision to go to war had shattered Sassy. Some nights, she sobbed on Marion's shoulder, thinking of him there, wondering if he was all right.

Marion never said it out loud, but she didn't think he was. He might have found purpose, fighting communism with his band of "brothers," but he would have lost so much more. Marion knew what that kind of violence could do to the body and mind of a man. Especially a good one. Sassy asked her once about the topic, wanting to know what she'd seen in her practice, but Marion had little to add to what Sassy already surmised. Men like Joey were not built to withstand the brutalities, the cruelties, the inhumanities of war.

But now Marion had a new source for answers: Daniel Neumann.

"How did you do it?" she asked him one day. "How did you keep going in the face of enemy fire? It goes against human nature not to flee a threat like that."

His expression hardened at the question, but she saw something deeper within him falter. "I did my job," he said. "I wasn't there to run."

"Do you remember your first encounter with the enemy?"

They were sitting on uncomfortable plastic chairs in her office, and her door was closed. They'd come a long way from those days when he'd been shackled to his bed. He was bent over, his forearms resting on his thighs, his heels flat on the ground. He wrinkled his nose at the question.

"I do. I've never been so scared in my life."

"What do you remember?"

"I was fresh out there, you know? I was the FNG. Seems like forever since that day."

"FNG?"

He started to speak, then he stopped himself. "The *NG* stands for 'new guy.' I'll let you guess what the *F* stood for. Sometimes we called them Cherries."

She made a sound of acknowledgement and encouraged him to keep going, but in her mind, she couldn't help but appreciate the different sides to this man. A warrior, a killer, and a gentleman.

"I was by a stream, filling my canteen. The heat out there, it drains every drop from you. The other guys were somewhere behind me. I heard them laughing at something, then someone yelled. All of a sudden, bullets were whipping into the grass around me. Sounded like sharp whispers, you know?"

She thought she could hear them, his description was so clear.

"I got into the water, but that was no good. The stream was dappled by all the bullets, and it wasn't deep enough for me to dive."

"What did you do?" she asked, forgetting briefly where she was. He'd brought her with him into the jungle, and his terror rushed through her veins.

"I don't know how long I stood there, frozen, basically waiting to get shot. Then one of the guys shouted, and that cut through the bullets. It was like a window opened, and I heard everything: the men, the guns, and the enemy screaming something I didn't understand. I stopped panicking and ran head-long into the fight. I mean, I was trained for that, right? I didn't go all the way to Vietnam to hide. I started shooting, my hands so sweaty I was afraid I'd drop my gun. I barely even knew what I was doing. It was sheer desperation."

Her own palms were damp just hearing the story. "What happened?"

"I was standing out there like a target, shooting like an idiot, then Tex ran over and shoved against me, making sure I was paying attention. The authority in his voice saved my life. I followed him, I dropped into underbrush when he did, and I got back to work."

As he grew quiet, Marion leaned in. "Did it ever get easier? Being out there?"

His shoulder lifted. "Sure. I mean, it's always a surprise, but we tried to be ready. That's what it's all about, right? Getting there first, taking the enemy off guard, getting out alive. I was a pretty good shot. I used to hunt as a kid, and that came back to me almost right away. I wonder if I can still shoot now. I've never tried with only one eye."

Marion paused, considering the question she wanted to ask. Was it the right time? "This is a tough question, and you don't have to answer. I'm wondering how it felt to kill someone."

There was no change in his expression. "I know what you're asking. Am I a man or a monster? It's not that simple, Doc. Nothing is out there. Fact is, someone's gonna get killed, and you don't want it to be you. They die or you do. That's all. Every man in every war understands that."

She waited, because he'd lost focus. He was remembering something.

"I used to think I'd have a problem killing someone. That didn't last. Over there, you're always hunting, always trying to stay alive long enough to do it. I've thought about that a lot. I can picture talking to my dad and my grandfather about it now that I've lived it. That'd be interesting."

Her own father's face came to her, strained and unsure. Would *he* ever tell her how it was?

"What about the fear? Did it get better?"

He chuckled lightly. "Oh, that never goes away. If you're not scared, you're gonna die. I've seen men die because they were too confident. They forgot to listen for the things that didn't fit. The breathing. A twig snapping under a boot that's not yours."

She shuddered. "So basically, you are constantly in fight-or-flight mode."

"Flight's not an option."

"And yet you wish you were still there."

"I told you. It's not the place or the fight. I dream about the jungle and the fighting, but what matters is my brothers. I'm a part of them, and they're a part of me. It's like, oh, I don't know. I had an aunt who used to weave baskets. Every straw held the next one in place. That's how it is."

"So the brotherhood is the thing?"

He nodded.

"Some men can move past these war experiences, but some never do." She swallowed, preparing to share. "My dad still fights his war. I see how scared he is when it comes back to him. But I'm learning from you that maybe that's a good thing. He's still scared, and maybe that's why he's still alive."

Daniel said nothing.

"You're calm now," she noted. "You're aware. What does it feel like to find the sense of calm after all that chaos? To return to what you were before?"

"But I'm not who I was. I remember that guy, and I miss those simpler days, but I'm different. I'm stronger. People might not see that when I freak out. They might see me as sick in the head, but I know what I'm capable of. I have moments, sure, but most of the time, I'm a stronger, more reliable me."

Knowing he felt that way made it a little easier for Marion to accept his impending release into society. Daniel should have been discharged already, but he had developed an infection around his eye socket, and she had used that as an excuse to keep him in the hospital's care for as long as she could. She was concerned, as she was for all her patients, about how he would deal with living on his own, but she had a selfish reason, too. Every time they spoke, she felt strongly connected to him, and she wanted more. More of his stories, more of his perspective. More of his company. More of *him*.

When Sassy came over to Marion's apartment later that week, Marion shared some of Daniel's thoughts on life after war, hoping Sassy could think of Joey in that light. When he came back, he would be different, she told her, but he would still be himself inside. And he would crave a brotherhood of veterans. Sassy listened in silence, her eyes locked onto Marion as she drank in her hope. When she finished, they didn't speak for a little while.

At the other side of her living room, Marion's brand-new record player clicked off, so she stood to flip the record over. She'd gotten used to the routine of sliding a record out of its sleeve, placing it over the post in the middle of the spinning turntable, then carefully lowering the needle onto the vinyl.

She'd never planned to buy a record player. A few weeks before, on a sunny Saturday, Sassy had knocked on her door and said she was dying to buy *Help!*, an LP put out two years before by the Beatles. She asked Marion to grab her purse and go with her. Initially, Sassy's impromptu ideas had knocked her back a step. Marion's usual reticence was at odds with Sassy's impulsive nature. But over time, her reluctance gave way to a new, invigorating curiosity. Now she rarely questioned Sassy's plans. On that Saturday, they bundled up against the December chill and walked from the apartment to Yonge and Elm, where Marion noticed the huge yellow A&A sign for the first time.

When they entered the record store, Marion thought immediately of a library. Thousands of records stood inside trays, lined up in rows that stretched the length of the store. About twenty people milled around them, flipping through albums. Some of the shoppers were talking to friends, others were silent in their searches, but around all of them wafted music that Marion had never heard before. When a man's smooth, warm voice soared from the speakers, violins stretching melodies around it, Marion stopped short.

"What's that?"

Sassy tilted her head, listening. "Nat King Cole."

"I could listen to him forever," Marion breathed.

Sassy strode down the row, sorted through a stack of records, then plucked one out and handed it to Marion. The cover was light brown and featured a portrait of a smiling young Black man wearing a yellow tie.

"*Love Is the Thing,*" Marion read. She turned it over and read through the list of songs, landing on "When I Fall in Love," the song that had just played. "Are you going to buy it?"

"Yes. For you."

Marion chuckled. "All right. Every time I come over, you have to play it."

"No, no," Sassy said, walking on. "You'll play it on your new record player. That's our next stop."

Marion had balked then surrendered. Why shouldn't she have music in her home? The most difficult thing about a record player, Sassy claimed, was choosing which record to play. Once they brought it home, Sassy loaned her other LPs, and Marion began to rely on music to bring her calm at the end of the day. She had not expected the impact the little box would have on her life.

Now she lifted *Mr. Tambourine Man* off the turntable, flipped it over, and started side two.

"Would you like more wine?" she asked, heading toward the kitchen to refill her own.

"Tell me about Daniel," Sassy requested from the other room. "Not Daniel the patient. Daniel the man."

Marion brought the bottle out and filled both glasses, frowning. She wasn't really supposed to talk about her patients, but with all the conversations she was passing between Sassy and Daniel about Joey, it seemed all right. Besides, she never gave out any medical or private information.

Sassy was insistent. "He sounds cool. I hope to meet him someday. You're, like, so stoked when you talk about him."

"I've learned a lot from him."

"Maybe so," Sassy replied, her gaze soft, "but there's more there. Your aura is so warm when you think about him. Talk to me, Marion."

Marion had to adjust her thinking, taking Daniel out of the hospital examination room and bringing him closer to home. As soon as his image appeared in her mind, she felt lighter.

"He's like you, in a way," she realized. "He's opened up windows in my mind and shown me life from different perspectives. With you, I am braver about trying new things. With him, I feel like . . . like I want more excitement out of life."

"There it is," Sassy grinned. "Can you feel that glow in your cheeks? I can see it. Marion, he's your Sonny!"

Marion stared at her.

"Sonny! You know. Sonny and Cher! He's got you, babe!" she sang.

Sassy kept grinning, and Marion laughed, her heart full. She didn't know about the whole Sonny thing, but Sassy's reaction was enough. Growing up, she had wondered if she'd missed out, never having had a best friend. That question no longer mattered.

Now she had Sassy.

eighteen
MARION

‹ ◦ ›

Marion made sure she was at work early on Wednesday. She had prepared for this day, and yet she felt completely at a loss. When she walked into the staff room, Paul was leaning back in a chair, reading what looked like a letter.

"Good morning," she said with a smile, pouring herself a cup of coffee.

"Good for you, being upbeat. How many of yours are leaving today?"

"I wasn't being upbeat, just polite. Two more. I submitted the last of their paperwork this morning. Six left last week. Two of those were taken in by family, but the others were not welcomed. Hardly a surprise." She sipped her coffee and with a studied nonchalance said, "Your former patient, Daniel Neumann, is leaving soon."

"They assure us," Paul said, studying the tattered arm of his chair, "that we don't need to worry."

"In all our years at med school and beyond, I don't remember learning who 'they' is."

They heard the sound of Dr. Bernstein's footfalls approaching, and Paul chuckled softly. "Speak of the devil. Here comes 'they' now."

"Doctors," Dr. Bernstein acknowledged, reaching for the coffeepot. "How are we feeling today?"

"Actually, we—"

Paul's hand clamped onto her forearm. "Can't complain. It's a fine morning."

Dr. Bernstein's eyes narrowed at Marion. "Seems a bold place for the two of you to meet, right here in the open, doesn't it?"

Marion's jaw dropped, and she whipped her arm out of Paul's reach. "Pardon me?"

"I do not encourage fraternizing among the staff, but seeing as you are both professionals, I—"

"Dr. Bernstein! I object to your assumption. Dr. McKenny! Tell him."

Paul smiled. "Unfortunately, I'm afraid your conjecture is incorrect, Dr. Bernstein. As charming and beautiful as Dr. Hart unquestionably is, she and I are only friends and colleagues. We have well-established boundaries."

Those boundaries had been set months before, when she'd finally agreed to go for dinner with him a second time. After a delicious meal, he had chased after a different kind of dessert, and she'd surprised both of them by slapping his face. He had sheepishly admitted she'd warned him, then he backed off and apologized. Since then, there had been no suggestion of a third date, but she was glad they were still friends. Plus, he was someone with whom she felt comfortable discussing cases, and sometimes that could be hard to do.

Still, her face burned. "Dr. McKenny, I find it disrespectful when you refer to my charm and beauty. I am your colleague and your equal. I would appreciate it if you would keep that in mind."

The men exchanged a glance then turned back to her. Apology softened Paul's expression.

"Understood," Dr. Bernstein said, his lips slightly pursed. "I do hope you will not reprimand me for pointing out that your job is not to sit around, talking. Your patients are waiting."

"A lot fewer of them," Paul muttered as their boss walked away.

At first, Paul had been like so many of their generation, caught up in fashionable new ideas about treating people with psychiatric problems: a clean sweep of these old institutions, and a fresh start with community health centres. The plan had been popular until recently, when the consequences Marion had feared had started to occur: increased vagrancy, addiction, crime. Now Paul was completely on Marion's side, but it was too late.

"None of it makes sense to me," she said.

Paul rolled up his letter and was tapping it thoughtfully against the arm of his chair. "I'll tell you what else doesn't make sense. My friend wrote to me about hospitals in Vietnam. Did you know they're being targeted out there?"

"What do you mean? The hospitals specifically? Aren't there rules in war? Like no bombing medics or field hospitals?"

He unrolled the paper. "He wrote about this woman, Claire Culhane. She was a medical administrator at Grace Dart Tuberculosis Hospital in Montreal. Last spring she felt moved by a front-page photograph in *Weekend Magazine* that showed a young Canadian nurse caring for orphaned infants in Vietnam. She decided to go there herself and see what it was all about."

"Gosh. That's brave."

"It's either courage or delusion." He twisted his mouth to the side. "Or a little of both. Miss Culhane told my friend that Saigon is disgusting, crowded with beggars, overwhelmed by poverty, and the whole city stinks. She started working as a nurse in a tuberculosis hospital, but then she learned of a rehabilitation centre being built entirely by Canadian funds in a coastal town"—he checked the paper—"called Quy Nhon. Apparently, that hospital is entirely unprotected in the midst of rockets, gunfire, and mortars. All essential medical equipment—like bandages, morphine, X-ray machines—were on back order when she arrived. Even the generator was on back order."

"How can they function?"

Paul read out loud. "They have twenty-three beds and sixty patients, on average, with twenty more arriving daily. Many suffer from tuberculosis, but about eighty per cent suffer horrific wounds from bullets, fire, poison gas, and napalm."

Marion hadn't allowed herself to think about what the medical situation might be out there. She'd seen enough just watching the news.

"Yvon—"

"Who?"

"Sorry," Paul said. "My friend who wrote this letter. Yvon says there's another big hospital in Quảng Ngãi with two hundred beds and seven hundred patients. Many of those are women and children. Miss Culhane started tracking everything, and since it's Canadian-funded, she wrote to Canada's External Affairs minister and demanded an increase in the budget as well as an end to the red tape that was holding all the medical equipment hostage." He frowned. "Looks like they got some of the money, but spent most of it on bribes, to keep the deliveries safe."

"What a disaster. Why isn't our government getting involved?"

"Listen to this. It gets worse."

A few weeks ago, the hospital was visited by the ICC, and a new head doctor was put in place. Upon his arrival, this Dr. Jutras designated the hospital for tuberculosis patients only, and he expelled all other patients, whether they were sick, wounded, or dying. Claire strongly objected, citing the Geneva Convention, but he paid no attention.

Soon afterward, she discovered that Dr. Jutras was sharing Claire's detailed patient files with the CIA. Why? So they could weed out any possible Vietcong among them, then descend upon those patients' villages for the purpose of interrogation and torture. As a result of Dr. Jutras's actions, they have burned down entire villages, including everyone in them. It's mass murder, Paul. Claire confronted her superior, but she was ignored.

"Oh my God, Paul. That's horrible!"

He nodded. "Canada has given millions of dollars to the government of South Vietnam. That sounds good in theory, but we have also taken American defence contracts, supplying raw materials and manufacturing weapons. Think about that. The napalm, grenades, aircraft engines, and whatever else we're sending is putting those patients in hospitals." He pushed his chair back and got to his feet. "Miss Culhane's right. We are basically an American weapon."

Marion dropped her hands to her lap. "This is shocking. Everything we're being told about Canada's contributions to the war is a lie."

She sat a bit after Paul left, stewing in her thoughts. The lies of the governments, the needless destruction of lives—there was a terrible parallel to the war in Vietnam and deinstitutionalization at home. There was no napalm here, but there was ignorance, and that would kill people one day.

"All in the name of freedom," she said softly, then she got to her feet and headed down the hallway. The empty rooms around her felt strange. Where were those patients now? Were they all right?

When she arrived at Daniel's room, he was sitting on his bed, reading a book with his back against the wall. When she entered, he jerked forward, then he spun from view and his hands went to his nightstand. She watched him struggle to set the eye patch in place, then he got up, still facing away from her.

"I'm sorry, Daniel," she said. "I didn't mean to startle you."

He turned back, his smile sheepish. "I wasn't dressed for visitors."

"I should have knocked."

"Doesn't matter." He lifted one shoulder. "I just don't like to flash this around."

"I understand. Is it more comfortable when you take the patch off?"

"Yeah. A little air feels good, no matter if it's fresh or not. But it sure ain't pretty to look at."

She had done her best not to study his scars, but sometimes when he got lost in his stories, she couldn't help but see. That smooth, invincible skin of a strong young man, the lines at the corners of his eye that should have creased when he smiled, the dark shading of his beard on only one side, the eyebrow that should have drawn down to mirror the other.

He was right. It wasn't pretty. But somehow, to her, he was beautiful.

"How's the book?" she asked.

He held a copy of *Catch-22*, and he frowned at the cover. "It's all right. Pretty depressing, though."

"Do you want to come out to the community area so we can talk? There's hardly anyone there."

He was up and at her side in no time, keen to get out of the tiny room. They walked together, and she felt a sense of contentedness just being with him. She supposed they could be called friends, in that he had shared his innermost thoughts and feelings with her during treatment, but he didn't know much about her. Once in a while, he asked questions about her life, but she kept her answers brief and always returned to the original point. After all, no matter how much she was learning about herself from him, this was his therapy, not hers.

They had been working together for a few months now, and Marion felt better about his well-being after every appointment. Through meditation techniques, he had gained better control over his physical aggression. He was coming to terms with things in his past and learning to control his episodes. He had begun to attend art therapy classes, and she was stunned by his talent, though the scenes he painted were dark with menace.

"My grandma's an artist," he told her. "She paints portraits, mostly."

"Does she know you can do this?"

"Sure. She taught me."

"I'm still trying to get you moved to a bigger room," she said as they walked to the end of the hallway. The area was set out like a T, with the top of the letter against a bank of windows.

"It's not a problem. I've been in less comfortable places in my life. Can you get me more books?"

"Let me know what you like to read, and I'll see what I can do."

"You mentioned a spy book by a French guy—"

"John le Carré, yes. *The Spy Who Came In from the Cold*. I'll look for it. Anything else?"

"Surprise me."

"Have you read any of the James Bond novels? You'd love them, I think."

"I've heard of the movies. Sure. I'd read those. Thanks."

"Interesting trivia: the author of those books, Ian Fleming, trained at Canada's spy school not too far from here during World War Two."

He frowned, clearly doubting her. "Spy school?"

"It's true. It was called Camp X. Amazing story."

In the common area, she chose a table with two chairs. Nurses frequently passed by, and an occasional patient shuffled along the corridor, but she and Daniel would be left undisturbed.

He sat facing the window so he could watch a winter storm as it blew in. Early flurries danced in the dwindling light.

"Pretty, isn't it?" she asked softly, admiring his profile. "So calm."

He nodded, looking thoughtful.

When a nurse walked past, he asked her, "Can we have something to drink?"

The nurse bobbed her head at both of them. "Tea or hot chocolate? They're making up a big pot of hot chocolate in the kitchen. With marshmallows."

"Tea!" shouted one of the men at the neighbouring table. "Tea, please! Tea for Stanley, too! He wants milk in it."

"All right, Henry. I will bring those right out. How about you two?"

Marion and Daniel glanced at each other. "Hot chocolate," they said together.

After the nurse left, Daniel smiled. "I haven't had hot chocolate in years. Makes me think of home. My mom always made it."

"I've never been to Nova Scotia."

"So you said. You need to do some travelling, Doc. I've got you two for two."

"I have a question about Vietnam."

He kept his gaze still, observing the snowflakes. "Are you asking me about the place or what I did there?"

"I was asking about the place, but I'm open to whatever you'd like to talk about."

"Why?"

"Because your stories are interesting."

He winced, remembering. "I know what I haven't told you about yet. I've been putting it off. There's a whole other world underground. Tunnels the Vietcong dug years ago, filled with booby traps and gooks we called tunnel rats. I was in one once. That was the most terrifying experience in my entire life. I would prefer to get shot over taking my chances in one of those again. I don't want to talk about that."

"I don't need to hear about it."

"Sometimes we humped through the worst of the jungle in silence, only to hear the scream of an explosive just before it hit and blew everything up. We saw so much. In the beginning, I puked a lot. I saw parts of men that should never be seen. But I was with my brothers, and we kept each other relatively sane. At some point I guess I toughened up. I had to. You gotta keep moving, or those body parts could be yours."

"A friend of mine just got a letter about a Canadian nurse in Vietnam. She discovered some horrific things over there, and I wondered if you'd heard of them."

"Like what?"

She decided to skip over the part about the Canadian government funding targeted killings. She wanted to learn more about that before she started spreading talk.

"She talked about villages getting burned, of civilian men and women and children being slaughtered. Did you see that ever?"

He nodded and looked away. A young man in a greying bathrobe strolled past their table, humming to himself.

"She hinted that sometimes it wasn't the North Vietnamese that killed them, but the CIA."

"Wouldn't surprise me. Vietnam is crazier than the craziest sucker in this building. And every man over there is a product of the insanity."

She had avoided directly asking about combat for a while, but he was so calm now that it felt like the right time, so she did.

"Can you tell me more about what your unit did over there?"

"We walked, we hid, we killed, we blew things up . . . we laughed sometimes. And other stuff."

"Like what?"

He narrowed his eye, thinking back. "I'll tell you about recon. Five or six of us would go humping in the boonies for four or five days at a time, locating enemy base camps and reporting their movements. We had to move like snakes through those trees, because Charlie was always listening. It was his neighbourhood."

"Charlie. That's slang for the North Vietnamese?"

"Yeah, among other, less friendly names. And there are also the Vietcong, the communists in South Vietnam." He puffed out a breath. "On recon, we were supposedly hunting, but really, we were the ones being hunted. Everybody knew that if you walked into an ambush, you probably wouldn't come out. Flak vests and metal helmets were too bulky to wear on those missions, so we wore regular camo without protection, and we smeared grease on our faces. We couldn't let our rifles jingle against our backs as we walked, so we cut the slings off and carried them by hand. Everything we needed to survive was in our packs, plus one of the men always carried a radio so we could report what we found. That thing weighed twenty-five pounds. It's nearly impossible to carry it without making a sound."

"How do you know where you're going in that jungle? I've seen it on television. Everything looks the same. How can you communicate with each other? How do you know if you're being seen?"

"Well, if they see you, it's too late," he said flatly. "We communicate through hand signals mostly." He stuck his fingers together and extended them, then he bent his elbow so his hand fell in a chopping movement. "That's 'fall in line,' meaning get back in formation before you step on a claymore. A land mine." He dropped his flat hand, palm side down, toward the ground. "That one's obvious. It means to get down, whereas if you raise it in a fist, you're telling everyone to freeze. And if you are indicating the position of incoming enemy fighters, you use the numbers on a clock. Like straight ahead is my twelve. Directly beside me on my left would be my nine, and behind me is my six. Get it?"

"So you are sitting at my ten?"

"Exactly."

She was spellbound, listening to him. What did his facade of calm suggest? Was he the smooth surface of a lake with a sea monster lurking beneath, or was he the ocean after a storm, the churning sand within slowing and settling?

The more time Marion spent with Daniel, the more she thought of her father. What had he seen during his combat days? What had he done? What kind of strain was he still suffering with? And yet, he lived a relatively normal life. He did his job, went out with friends, came home for dinner. He'd raised two daughters.

Why was Daniel here in this place, while her father was in his home? Daniel had calmed immensely since he'd first arrived at the institute. He hadn't had an episode in two weeks. Together, they had worked on differentiating between nightmares and hallucinations, then helping him find his way through both. He needed to be prepared. They were going to push him out of the hospital soon.

She tried to ignore the ache she felt, knowing he would be gone. It was unprofessional. She'd gotten far too attached to Daniel. As he spoke, she watched his lips and listened to every syllable. She held her breath when he described a perilous occurrence, stared openly into his remaining eye. She even felt a girlish rush in her chest when he flexed his fingers, imagining the strength in them.

In fourth year at university, her favourite lecturer, Dr. Perkins, had talked about the ethics of physician-patient relationships, including the clear rule that there be no sexual bond at all. At the time, Marion hadn't considered that to be anything with which she must deal. Now it weighed heavily on her conscience.

"I don't expect I could bum a cigarette."

"Sorry," she said, shaking her head to break her reverie. "I don't have any."

"That's okay." He hung his head. "You know, I think of my unit every day. Who's been killed since I left? I wonder if I'll ever see any of them again."

She waited for him to continue.

He hesitated. "I know what you're thinking—that seeing them would bring back bad memories—but nobody knows those like me and my brothers."

"When you think of your buddies over there, how does it feel? Physically, I mean."

He gnawed on his lower lip while he thought that over. Automatically, Marion noted that it was not a compulsive action. Nothing irrational or concerning. Just an ordinary man, making an ordinary movement, thinking about the least ordinary thing.

"My body hurts," he replied gruffly. "Like I got ripped out of a place where I should be. They need me."

"You've said that before. You'd still go back."

"In a heartbeat."

"You are a braver person than I, my friend. The Canadian Red Cross just put out a call looking for more surgeons to go to Vietnam, but I can't imagine doing that."

"You're not a surgeon, though."

"Actually, I am. I loved doing surgery. Especially in an emergency room."

"How'd you end up a shrink?"

"I got sick in school and was unable to physically continue the specialty. I still wanted to be in the medical field, so I changed direction and studied psychiatry instead."

"Well, if you change your mind about going, I'd be the best security guard you could ever imagine."

She smiled. "I'll keep that in mind. Daniel, I need to ask you one more question."

"Shoot."

She pushed past the pang in her heart. "Do you think you will be all right, living outside of the care you're being given here?"

His brow lifted. "I was ready weeks ago, Doc. I'm just saving money with free rent and meals."

Just then, the nurse walked through the doorway carrying a steaming tray of tea and hot chocolate. "Here we are!"

Henry, the card player at the next table, shot out of his chair and raced toward the nurse, overcome by thirst. The nurse stepped out of his way, Henry kept going, and the tray of hot drinks crashed to the floor, shattering the cups.

When Marion glanced back from the disaster, Daniel was crouched under their table, his expression blank. He'd been facing away, she remembered, so he'd been unprepared. With shock, she realized she saw her father in Daniel's face in that moment.

"Daniel?" Marion whispered. She crouched beside him. "You're all right."

He didn't move. It was a moment before he even blinked.

"Daniel? It's me, Dr. Hart. I'm with you. You're all right. You're safe."

Focus slowly returned to his gaze, like ice melting, and his hands began to shake. He closed his eye, ashamed, and Marion's throat swelled with sympathy. So much strength and courage and dedication, now so small, huddled beneath a table.

"Why are you behind the furnace, Daddy?"

Her mother entering, taking her hand. "Come along, Marion. Let's leave your father in peace."

Marion set her fingertips on the back of Daniel's right hand, and it stilled. Without looking at her, he gently turned his hand over and interlaced his fingers with hers. Marion's pulse raced at the contact. They both sat motionless, waiting for their hearts to slow.

At last, he let out a breath. "I'm sorry," he said softly, and she felt his hold ease.

She tightened hers, unwilling to relinquish the unexpected touch and the feelings it had released in her. There was something connecting their palms, and it felt vital. A kind of electricity built on trust. He needed her, but it was more than that. She needed him. She couldn't bear the thought of letting go.

"You have nothing to apologize for."

"That hasn't happened in months," he told her. A veil of sweat shone on his brow. "I thought I was doing well."

"You are. And if you ever wonder again, find me. Sometimes wondering causes more fear than knowing. I am here for you, Daniel. I want you to know that. Even after they release you from this place, I want to be there for you."

Bit by bit, his face turned to hers, the light scruff of his beard shadowed by the table over his head. He didn't speak, but she felt as if she could hear his tortured thoughts.

"Am I crazy?" he asked at last.

"No, Daniel. You're in pain. But you're going to be just fine."

Too soon, she went to meet Daniel in his new, larger room. Beside him on the cot was a small rucksack, in which he had packed his few belongings. When he rose to greet her, he stood a little taller.

"How do you feel?" she asked, wishing he would ask her the same thing. She had been miserable all week, pacing the hospital corridors and the rooms of her apartment, picking things up and putting them down, all because he would soon be gone. She wanted to reach for his hand again, but she kept her own at her sides.

"I got a question," he said.

What on earth were these feelings? What was it rushing through her heart, burning through her face? She felt like a teenager in high school again, suddenly shy.

"You never told me your first name. Since I'm not a patient here anymore, is that allowed now?"

"Marion," she replied.

She was accustomed to reading his glances and body language: the tilt of his head, the tightening of his brow, the sarcastic smile that made him look devilishly handsome. But the way he was watching her now, with vulnerability softening his expression, that was new. His mouth opened slightly.

"Marion, do you think I'll do all right out there?"

Her name on his lips sent a thrill through her. "Do you?"

"Give me a straight answer."

"I think you'll be fine. You have the information about the legion, right? They will help you find a place to stay and get you going again. And you have the letter about the community health centres in your area. It's important you go to those appointments and call them if you need anything else. Here, I brought you a heavy coat and a cap . . ." She trailed off, swallowing the knot in her throat. "Daniel, it's been wonderful getting to know you. I truly mean that."

He hesitated. "I almost wish I still needed help. So I could be with you."

She was the one who needed help now. She held the coat toward him and took a step back.

"I'll walk you out," she offered.

It was cold and grey outside, with random snowflakes twisting slowly downward. Daniel stood in the entrance to the Administration Building, folding his cap in both hands and staring out at the bleak winter day. He was good at standing very still. He'd perfected that skill in Vietnam.

Marion couldn't speak, seeing him there.

"All right," he said at last, taking a deep breath and pulling the wool cap low over his ears. He gave her one last smile then held out his hand for her to shake. "Thank you. I feel like my life has changed, being stuck in this place with you. For the better."

Me too, she thought. "I'll miss you, Daniel. Be careful out there." She sniffed, wondering where on earth she'd left her professional detachment. "Do me a favour?"

His gaze travelled over her hair, her eyes, her lips, as if he was trying to commit it all to memory. She felt the strongest sense that he wanted to kiss her. "Whatever you need, Marion."

"Never be afraid to ask for help. Find me if you need me."

He nodded.

She didn't move. She stood on the edge of a cliff, waiting to fall into him if he made the slightest move, but then a car horn sounded out on Queen Street, and they both stepped back.

"Goodbye, Daniel."

"I'll see you, Marion," he replied, then he walked off into the greyness and joined the anonymous crowd.

nineteen

SASSY

❧

During Sassy's first couple of months working at Raskin Real Estate, she heard a lot. Friday lunches in the boardroom—usually a plate of sandwiches and pickles Betty ordered from the deli downstairs—often turned into discussions about the industry. Sassy rarely said anything while they went on, but she was learning, day by day. Her father had a lot to teach. He knew all the ins and outs of sales and the technical aspects of real estate. Tom's approach was more about how to work with clients on a personal level. He was a smoother, more outgoing man overall. Both styles worked, apparently. She enjoyed being included in the conversations. It made her feel smart, and she wanted to learn more.

The trouble was, she'd never forgotten that her father had called her a hypocrite months before. She'd deserved it then, and she deserved it now. How was she, an advocate for socialism, supposed to admit that she was interested in business?

Sassy finished typing Tom's latest listing onto a stencil then pulled it carefully off the roller. At her last job, she had gotten used to using carbon paper to make copies of letters. Now she used a mimeograph machine with a hand crank to churn out copies of flyers.

She loaded the paper then set up the machine, turning on the fluid to keep the wick moist inside, engaging all the pressure knobs, then fitting the master copy onto the cylinder. Once she'd checked the first copy to make sure everything was centred, she set the dial for twenty copies and started up the hand crank. As the damp papers shot out onto the tray, she inhaled the weird, chemical freshness emanating from the purple ink. What was it about that smell? She'd noticed Tom surreptitiously sniffing a page after she set it on his desk, so it wasn't just her.

He hadn't come into the office yet today, so she imagined he was out at meetings. He'd taken her with him before, and she was sorry she wasn't with him this time. To her surprise, she had discovered she enjoyed talking with clients, finding out what they needed and wanted. Tom seemed genuinely impressed by how good she had become at the business in such a short time.

Tom was a levelheaded boss, and he read Sassy well. To keep her happy, he kept her busy, trusting her with increasingly challenging tasks. She often found herself drawn into his words, and his gentle, rational thoughts. She liked the way the ends of his phrases seemed to curl a little, like the edges of his smile. Like he couldn't help being a positive person. He got a kick out of making things happen. She liked that energy.

What she didn't like was how she had begun to feel around him on a non-work level. His attitude was not the only thing she liked about him. Instead of starting arguments, as she had initially been tempted to do, she often found herself trying to make him laugh. More recently, their conversations at his desk had wandered off topic, and she easily lost herself in those icy-blue eyes. They talked about movies and music, and she chided him for having old-fashioned favourites. He seemed to get a kick out of her little barbs.

"You're calling Elvis Presley old-fashioned?" he asked one time. "I have trouble with that. You gonna tell me you aren't one of those girls who sits there with her chin on her fist, sighing when he's singing on those Hawaiian beaches, moving the way he does?"

"No, I'm not 'one of those girls.' You haven't noticed that about me yet?" She chuckled. "To be honest, I've never even been to one of his movies. I like some of his songs, though. He's got a great blues feel."

"You've never seen any of his movies? That's unbelievable." He hesitated just enough that Sassy predicted what he was about to say. "Maybe I should take you to one. See what you say when he's singing and dancing and wearing some kind of uniform."

Her face roared with heat that she tried to hide by lifting her chin with a dare. "Maybe you should."

It had been two weeks since that conversation, and neither of them had broached it since. She was relieved and disappointed all at once. Of course she shouldn't date her boss. But what if he hadn't been her boss? What if he was just a regular businessman? What then? Would they drive each other crazy, or might they find common ground? The moral dilemma of dating a capitalist was new to her.

She patted her hair into place with her free hand and secured it with a bobby pin. The bun she'd tied that morning wasn't as tight as it should be, and it was starting to fall apart. Marion had shown her the technique. They'd agreed that it was up to her to practice, which she hadn't done. She preferred leaving her hair down, but Marion was right; having it up and out of the way was a smarter way to wear it at work. Marion had also insisted on taking her shopping for work clothes last week, since Sassy was always complaining about that tight tweed suit. At first she had been reluctant to go, since Marion was so different from her and so much older. She didn't want to say anything about that, but the last thing she wanted to do was change her style and suddenly become all fuddy-duddy. Marion had only smiled and promised she wouldn't do that to her. Once she was in the changing room, it took Sassy by surprise how much she liked the look of a couple of pastel-coloured skirt suits that fit just right. She'd assumed they would make her look too conservative, but she loved the style.

And what an unexpected bonus to hear Tom's sweet compliments on how she was looking these days.

Over the past couple of months, her opinion of him had turned around completely. The more she got to know him, the easier it was to admit that she had jumped to conclusions based on the expensive cut of his suit. Behind all those perfect stitches and rich wool, beyond what she still regarded as slick sales techniques, he was a decent man. A good one, even. He worked well with her father, and, considering her father's demanding character, that was saying something.

In an attempt to push Tom from her mind, Sassy concentrated instead on her work. She had mastered all the forms and filing and whatever else he asked for, but she was a little restless. A couple of days ago, she overheard Tom and her father having a brief discussion about commercial spaces in strip malls. She had never thought about who might own those unremarkable, sometimes dingy clusters of stores. They were everywhere, and yet they were almost invisible most of the time. Of course someone had to own them, she reasoned, feeling stupid. She'd just never thought that through. But now that the buying and selling of properties was right in front of her every day, she wanted to get the facts straight in her head. She decided to do some research on her own.

When they met for lunch that Friday, she had a lot of questions, but Tom asked the first one.

"Where's that mall you bought?" he asked her father.

"You bought a *mall*?" Sassy exclaimed. No wonder they'd been talking about the strip malls. She knew her father was wealthy, but that was beyond what she'd believed.

"Southwest corner of Bayview and York Mills," her father said, looking pleased as he reached for a tuna sandwich. "Made sense to me."

"Seems like a good opportunity," Tom replied. "Fairly affluent family homes around that area. They need access to a mall like that."

"It's been around a few years, and it's been popular, but the owner's on his way out. I was speaking with him about some of his tenants, and he told me he'd had enough of the business. So I just flat-out asked him."

"Perfect timing," Tom said, biting into a roast beef sandwich. Those were his favourite, Sassy had noticed. "You're going to hang on to it this time? Or sell?"

"I think I'll keep it. Something different on the side."

All of a sudden, Sassy felt very smart. She waited until they were both enjoying their lunches and had forgotten all about her, then she spoke up.

"What do the stores there pay for rent?" Sassy asked her father, nonchalant.

Both men glanced up, taken off guard, but it was her father's gaze she held.

He folded his arms and leaned back in his chair, observing her. She knew the stance. He was preparing to defend his position. Sometimes, when she was behaving belligerently, he could get a little nasty, and she knew she was like him in that way. This time was different. She had a surprise for him, and she knew he was going to like it.

"Based on the square footage, two hundred and thirty dollars."

"Are you planning to raise it?"

"That's how business works, Susan." He gave her a guileless smile. "Their rents help pay for your apartment."

"Of course. I was just wondering, because Sunnybrook Plaza at Bayview and Eglinton has a much higher volume based on similar square footage. Makes me think you might be getting close to outpricing yourself. That one's a little dated, about fifteen years old, but it was the first strip mall in Toronto, and it has plenty of parking."

Tom and her father stared at her in shock, then Tom did a poor job of hiding his delight.

"I see," her father said, expressionless. "Do you happen to know what their rent is right now?"

"Two hundred forty-five dollars. Principal Investments, the landlord, raised it six months ago by two per cent." She reached for a ham sandwich and sat back with a shrug, relishing the moment of stunned silence. "But what do I know?"

Her father graced her with a wonderful smile, and she felt his pride like a hug. "What do you know, indeed? There's my girl."

He had always tried to get her interested in business, but she'd never given him anything to hope for. Why should she worry about a steady career when he gave her everything she needed? Except strangely, she'd found that the more satisfied she became with her job, the more she looked forward to getting up in the morning and doing more. Maybe she'd been too young when he'd tried to persuade her. Maybe she'd had to grow into it. Whatever it was, this new appetite for practical information felt invigorating.

At the same time, it was a little confusing. Considering everything she'd ever believed and protested about, it bothered her that capitalism made so much sense. Done right, it could help everyone, it appeared.

The concept of gentrification stuck in her mind, though. As pleasing as renovations and upgrades appeared, those who could not afford the bettered homes would always need places to live, too. When she'd spoken with her father about it, he'd assured her that improving buildings, and not just aesthetically, helped a lot of people. Purchasing, renovating, then reselling homes brought up the increased value of the houses for families trying to improve their situations. It also paid salaries to tradespeople hired for the construction. And for those still in need of a home, the government was building thousands of homes every year.

Between her father and Tom, and their different approaches to the job, Sassy had figured out a lot of things.

She loved seeing the pride on Tom's face when he closed a sale. The way his laugh lines suddenly appeared. Yes, he was handsome, but it was more than that. He genuinely enjoyed what he did, eager from the first step, then plainly satisfied at the end. She could tell it was about more than money with him. What was it about real estate that appealed to him so much? And why did Sassy find it so interesting? A vague, unsettling question started up in the back of her mind. What if maybe, someday, she tried this job herself? Could she do that? Would she be any good at selling? Was it hypocritical even to consider the idea? Because when she saw that satisfied expression on Tom's face, she realized she wanted to feel the same thing.

On the final Friday before Christmas, Sassy finished her last bit of filing, then she grabbed her coat, hat, and boots and stopped at Tom's desk. He was working with his head down, marking up a chart.

"All done," she said. "I need to cut out."

He glanced up, and she could tell he'd been concentrating awhile. His hair was mussed where he'd dragged his fingers through it, and she was tempted to smooth it down. Except when it was messy, he looked younger, which she liked.

"Already? What time is it?"

"Early. Four o'clock."

He blinked and faced the window, seeming to recall where he was. "That's a lot of snow. You okay to get home in this?"

"Sure, but I have to leave now." She smiled sweetly. "I'm entertaining this evening."

"Tell me you're not going on a date in this weather."

An unexpected blush rose to her cheeks. No matter how hard she tried not to see her boss as attractive, it was a lost cause. More and more, every time she looked at Tom Duncan, Sassy felt butterflies.

"No date tonight," she said. "Remember I told you about my neighbour friend, Marion? And how we alternate dinners in each other's apartment every week? The two of us decided to have a dinner party tonight at my place for Christmas, and we invited more neighbours. I need to get home and get ready." She frowned at her watch. "So if it's all right with you, I'm leaving early."

"It's all right with me. Oh, before you go, I meant to ask. Did you finish that file on the house on Berkshire? Were you able to get all the neighbourhood information? I know some of it was out of the way."

"I got it all. It's in that big box on the shelf. I couldn't lift it, so I left it there for you."

He got up and headed to the shelf, and Sassy glanced at her watch again, a little annoyed.

"What do you think of the property?" he asked.

"Me?"

"Well, sure."

As he stretched to reach the top shelf, she couldn't help but notice the lines of his starched white shirt tightening against his shoulder blades. Usually he wore a jacket, so she didn't get the same kind of view. She didn't mind this one at all, and though it was probably wrong, as far as workplaces went, she let herself admire the sight. She figured there was about ten years between them, but gosh, thirty-ish sure didn't look old on him. Without so much as a grunt, he lifted the heavy box and placed it on the table while she watched.

"You did all the research," he said. "You know it better than I do."

She forced her brain back to the file, which she'd completed that morning. She dug through the box and handed it to him, but he didn't look inside. Instead, he waited for her answer.

"It's a middle-income area that has seen better days," she told him, "but the community has been active recently in restoring the adjacent park. It's about seventy per cent young families, maybe twenty per cent people over sixty."

"And the other ten per cent?"

"Young married couples. Oh, and there's a new school going in. Should be ready by the end of next summer, they think."

"Perfect. Thanks a lot for this. You're making my life much easier." He squinted briefly, thinking something through. "Do you want to get out of here sometime and see some of these places? Obviously not when the weather's like this, but some time when it's clear? We could drive around together, and I could show you how I figure out where to look."

She started to say no, then she stopped herself. The truth was, she did want to go.

"I'd like that," she told him.

"Good. After the holidays, we'll pick a date." He froze. "Uh, I didn't mean date, date. I just meant—"

She laughed, trying not to let on that she wished he did. "I know what you meant."

"Have a good time tonight," he said. "And have a good Christmas. I'll see you next year."

He was right about the weather. The snow was so deep it was higher than her boots, which she discovered when a cool trickle of snow tumbled inside, soaking her stockings. The bus took an achingly long time to shove through the drifts and the traffic. It took so long that she wondered if she'd have been faster just walking, but that would have been exhausting, and she needed energy for tonight's party. As soon as the bus reached her stop, she rushed home then dripped melting snow all over the elevator floor. At her apartment, she shrugged out of her coat and stuck her key in the lock, but the door swung open before she could turn it.

"Davey!" she exclaimed. "What are you doing here? And how did you get in? Do you still have a key?"

She hadn't seen him in months. Not since Christine had given him the ultimatum.

His mouth twisted slightly with embarrassment. "Do you want your key back? You never said."

She hung her coat in the closet, stuffed her mitts in the sleeves, trying to figure out how she felt about seeing him there. "It's fine."

"I like your Christmas tree," he said.

She grinned at the little tabletop shrub, around which she'd strung a length of red beads. "I wanted something a little festive for the season. So what brings you over here? It's been a long time."

He held out his arms in invitation, and she happily stepped in for a hug.

"Way too long, man. It bums me out, not seeing you, Sass," he said, his familiar voice sweet in her ear. They were both smiling when he stepped back. "I had to grab something for the TADP, and it brought me out this way. Then all this snow . . . and you were right here . . ." He grimaced. "I know it's been a while. I hope it's okay."

"It's fine, Davey. I've missed you, too. But tonight's a little crazy for me. I have things to do."

"I get that. Let me help."

"Nah, that's cool. I got it."

He cleared his throat. "Hey, Sass, can I crash on your couch tonight? The snow is too much, man. If I leave now, I won't hit Christine's for hours."

"Won't she freak?"

"It's cool. I'll just—"

"You'll tell her you slept somewhere else, right? Anywhere but here." She shook her head, scolding. "Cool. Whatever. But I can't hang out with you like usual. I have friends coming over for dinner in about an hour."

"Outta sight. A party."

"They're not your kind of friends. They're my neighbours."

"I smelled turkey down the hall when I came in. Don't worry about the cheese straws. I saw you had everything ready for them in the fridge. I'll get those. I'm practically a master chef," he joked.

"Of course you are," she called from her bedroom.

Sassy loved the end of a day. She loved getting out of serious, uncomfortable fabric and pouring herself into something that felt more like her. The apartment was chilly tonight, so she pulled her favourite white angora sweater over her head and unrolled it over a comfortable pair of flared denims.

She called out to Davey as she ran her brush over her long chestnut hair. "How are you doing out there?"

"Spilled the flour," he muttered. "Don't worry. I've got it."

Smiling, she twisted her hair around hot rollers and left them in while she did her makeup. When that was done, she brushed out the big curls, wrapped a Christmassy-red bow around the top of her head and let her hair cascade over it.

"How are you doing?" she asked again, joining Davey in the kitchen. She pulled an apron from the drawer, tied it on, then grabbed a rolling pin. "That looks good. Now roll it out to a half inch, like this, then cut them into two-inch sticks. Bake them fifteen minutes, and they're done."

"If I ever have my own kitchen, I'm going to make those, like, every day."

She kissed him on the cheek then rubbed off the lipstick she'd left behind. "You left your blue shirt in my closet, if you want to change."

He headed off, humming to himself, while Sassy set out her recent purchases of six glasses and three bottles: rye whiskey, sweet vermouth, and Angostura bitters, in case anyone wanted a Manhattan. She was developing a taste for those. She poured a few maraschino cherries into a bowl in case her friends wanted them for a garnish, but she held her breath as she did it. As cheerful as they looked, Sassy would rather drink poison than eat one of those cherries. She'd gorged on an entire jar as a child then brought it all up on her grandmother's white rug. Even now, she could barely stand the smell of them.

"Want me to turn on a record?" Davey asked just as there was a knock on the door.

"Yes, please. Oh, and can you please pour those M&M's into a bowl and set it out?"

"Got it."

She walked past him toward the door, hearing the click of the record player being turned on, then a crackling sound as the needle dropped onto the Byrds.

Marion was at the door, holding out two bottles of wine. Her friend was dressed beautifully as always, with a classy elegance that made Sassy feel a bit like a slob. She wore a light blue knitted dress with a short navy jacket over the top, and she'd let her long blond hair down for a change.

"Your hair! You're a knockout."

Marion handed Sassy the bottles then touched her brow, self-conscious. "You think so? I wasn't sure."

"Oh, it's fab. You gotta wear it down more often. Come on in. You've met Davey, haven't you?"

"I don't think so," Davey said, walking across the room with his hand out. "This is far out. Sassy's told me all about you."

Sassy laughed. "You're, like, my only classy friend," she explained, then she paused, thinking of Tom. "You and my boss."

"I've heard lots about you, too. Are you joining us for dinner?" Marion asked Davey.

He grinned. "Sassy said I could. The snow's pretty bad, you know?"

All three gazed out the balcony door at the thickening blizzard. "I hope everyone has a place to stay tonight," Sassy said, then she saw Marion's stricken expression and immediately felt bad. Right away she realized her friend was thinking of her patients, out there in the cold when they should have been safe at the hospital. She curled her arm around Marion's waist and drew her close for a gentle hug.

"I'm sure Daniel's warm somewhere," she said softly. "He knows how to take care of himself."

Marion's smile battled back onto her face. "I'm sure you're right."

"I'm glad I'm here," Davey put in, having no clue about what was going on around him, as usual. "Thanks for letting me stay, Sass."

"No flying your freak flag," she warned. "We're eating at the grown-up table tonight."

"I'll even do dishes after. Thanks, ladies. This'll be cool."

Having Davey around would add a different dimension to the gathering, Sassy thought, pouring Marion a Manhattan. She poured one for herself at the same time.

"Cherry?" she asked.

"Please."

She had never thrown a dinner party before, and she hadn't been sure how her guests would get along, but she needn't have worried. Once the other two couples arrived, each with food and a bouquet of flowers, everyone started up their own conversations. She had invited Mr. and Mrs. Moore as well, but they had graciously declined, saying they weren't up to it.

"I brought music," Marion said, producing Ella Fitzgerald's Christmas album, and suddenly, everything felt festive.

Halfway through the Romanos' big, stuffed turkey and Mr. Levin's debate with Mr. Romano about hockey, Marion excused herself. Both bottles of wine were empty, so she headed off to grab more from her cupboard.

"I'll be right back," she promised.

"I'm telling you, that Punch Imlach is bad for the team," Mr. Levin was saying. "Nobsody likes him. Mahovlich can't stand him. Mark my word sixty-seven will be the Leafs' last Stanley Cup."

Mr. Romano nodded sagely. "The players are too old. What is it, eight of them over thirty-six already?"

"Giovanni," his wife scolded. "That's not old. Thirty-six is nothing."

"Yeah, they're old. What do you know about hockey?"

Mrs. Romano threw her hands up. "You think I don't hear you talking all the time about Leafs this, Leafs that, Stanley Cup, penalties, whatever? I know way more than I wanna know."

Mrs. Levin chuckled. "We should have our own ladies' nights when they're playing. I hear hockey talk all the time. What about you, Davey? You a Leafs fan?"

"No way, man. Hockey's, like, an aggressive expression of masculinity, you know? Women are just as strong, and—"

"What are you talking about?" both older men exclaimed, making Sassy laugh. Marion returned just in time with more wine, and a subdued Davey refilled all the glasses as everything devolved into loud talk about how ridiculous the world was today.

Somewhere in there, Mrs. Levin retrieved her dessert from Sassy's refrigerator then set it down on the table. The plate held a number of delicate pancakes rolled over something sweet, Sassy guessed, then fried to a golden brown.

"This smells wonderful, Mrs. Levin," Marion said, inhaling. "What are we having?"

"Cheese blintzes," Mrs. Levin replied, serving them one by one.

Her husband lifted an eyebrow. "My wife thinks these are good for dessert, but me, I prefer them at breakfast."

"Pah," she replied, waving a hand at him. "I like them anytime, so there. I didn't see you stepping in to cook. You got complaints? You make dessert next time."

Her husband looked contrite. "You're right, dear. I love your blintzes. They're good anytime."

"Wise man," Mrs. Romano teased, making everyone laugh.

"These are outta sight, Mrs. Levin," Davey said, licking his lip. "Can I have the recipe?"

"You like to cook?" she asked.

"I do. I'm hoping someday—"

"When do you got time to cook if you're out on the streets, protesting?"

Everyone stopped midchew and blinked at Mr. Levin.

"Harold," his wife cautioned under her breath.

"Well? You go to protests, yes? You carry signs and march around, so maybe you got no job so you got time for cooking, yeah?" Mr. Levin shrank a little under his wife's scowl. "What? I can ask, no? I just wonder about kids these days."

Davey gave him a wry grin. "I wouldn't argue with you, Mr. Levin, except I do have a job. I'm a cook at Chez Monique."

"And he runs the Toronto Anti-Draft Programme," Sassy put in.

Mr. Levin sat back as his wife served him a second plate of dessert. "Anti-Draft. What is this? In my day, we all went to war. Our fathers went to war. Men went to war without question. There was no anti anything."

Davey opened his mouth to respond, but to Sassy's relief, Mrs. Romano jumped in.

"Did you serve, Harold?"

"Sure, sure." There was a slight flare of Mr. Levin's nostrils. "How could I not? The Nazis were killing our people. Does a man stay home when his family's getting slaughtered?" He glanced at Davey. "Thousands of us left Palestine to volunteer with the British Army. We never asked no questions."

Sassy stayed quiet, interested in the conversation and a little sorry for Davey, but she didn't interrupt. He was a big boy, as he'd told her before.

"Cool, but that's not Vietnam," Davey said quietly. "The Vietnamese don't need us down there. It's their war. It's not our families they're killing."

Mr. Levin nodded reluctantly, accepting Davey's point, but Sassy shuddered, recalling Joey's latest letter.

Mrs. Levin laid a warm hand on Sassy's, noticing her reaction. "Let's not talk about all this killing," she suggested, but the others weren't paying attention.

Mr. Romano took over where his friend had left off. "You don't know communists," he told Davey, his face darkening. "They're insid . . . insti . . ."

"Insidious," his wife murmured when he couldn't find the word.

"Yes. This." He pinched his thumb against two fingers and jabbed the air, emphasizing his point. "They take control of everything. They kill people you love. Communists don't care who you are." His voice was cold. "From communism there is only one small step to fascism. Nothing is worse than fascists."

"At least Mussolini didn't kill Jews," Mr. Levin muttered.

"No. Mussolini wasn't specific in who he killed. Just anyone who wasn't him," agreed Mr. Romano. "Sassy's brother is doing the right thing over there. We gotta defend ourselves against communists and fascists, Davey, wherever they are. You kids think you will change the world with your free love, but so did those people. And now they're dead and buried. I saw the bodies myself."

Davey lowered his gaze to the table, and Sassy could see he was debating whether or not to speak up, or at least how best to do it. She knew he couldn't resist, but she appreciated the fact that he was respecting her guests. If he said his piece the right way, she would support him.

"I understand what you're saying. I do. But I believe the war in Vietnam is a war in Vietnam. It is not in America. I believe America should not be sending men down there to fight."

There it was. Plain and simple. Sassy approved. "They shouldn't be sending weapons, either." She quoted her father from so long before. "But war is good for business."

"We're making things worse by being involved," Davey agreed, nodding. "And we're losing, no matter what the television says. It's been over ten years and the war's still on. We should have either won it right away or gotten the hell out years ago."

Silence stretched across the table.

"I tell you what," Mr. Romano said, his dark eyes boring into Davey's, "if those communists in Vietnam win the war because there weren't enough brave American men to defeat them, you will remember this conversation."

"Enough," his wife said tightly. "Stop all this talk right now. You and your talking. All the time about the war. That was years ago. We're safe here. No Vietnamese communists are coming—"

Mr. Romano's shoulders lifted, and he held his hands out. "How do we know this? How is anyone safe?"

She slapped her palm on the table. "I said stop. This is Christmas, for crying out loud. Enough. This is a delicious dinner, and Davey's a good boy."

Davey gave a weak smile, and Sassy recalled her responsibilities as a hostess.

"Mrs. Levin, Davey's right. These blintzes are absolutely delicious. You have to give him the recipe."

Mrs. Levin beamed, and Sassy saw relief in all the women's expressions. And in Davey's.

"I'd like your recipe for the turkey dressing," Marion said to Mrs. Romano, picking up her cue. "It was the best I've ever tasted."

"My mama, may she rest in peace, she taught me this."

"You all spoil us," Sassy said. She turned in her seat, toward the living room. "Speaking of, I've been meaning to ask you, Mr. Levin. Have you seen your spider plant? It's doing so well in the window, just like you said."

"Oh yes," Marion added, getting up to clear plates. "I wanted to ask about that, too. What should I do with all the tiny little plants growing out of it?"

"Sassy, you got paper and pen?" Mrs. Levin asked. "Come here, Davey. I'll write that recipe down."

Everyone moved to the living room and settled comfortably in Sassy's limited furniture. The older men lit cigarettes, and Sassy was gratified to see Mr. Levin offer one to Davey. She plugged in the kettle for coffee, then she joined Marion in the kitchen entryway, her arms folded as she regarded the scene.

"I love that we're able to do this," she said. "We're so fortunate to live here."

"We have great neighbours," Sassy agreed.

Marion held up her glass, and they clinked them together.

"Merry Christmas, Sassy. May 1968 be a year to remember."

twenty

MARION

ɔ⊕c

January was the coldest month. In contrast to December's windy sweeps of snow, January's sharp, cruel teeth forced Marion to bundle from the top of her head to the soles of her boots, leaving only a small slit in her scarf for her eyes to peek through. Even then, she tried to cover them with her mittens when she didn't need to see, because on particularly stormy days like today, her eyelashes froze together.

She climbed out of the bus outside of the new community health centre, with its cheery redbrick face and large windows, safely shuffling like a penguin to the front door, careful not to catch her heels on invisible patches of ice. The windows were frosted to opaque, telling her the furnace was turned way up high. She could hardly wait to thaw out with a cup of coffee.

The cozy staff room was empty, but she was getting more used to that every visit. She didn't share any shifts here, since the few doctors alternated days. Aside from a couple of nurses and the support staff, she expected solitude. Paul hadn't been assigned to this centre, and she discovered she missed him.

All of Marion's patients had been released from the hospital. The only bright side was that her own practice had expanded to include two of the community health centres. Many patients that she had never seen before now came to her there. Having read their backgrounds, she was relieved that many appeared to be doing better than expected, though she did adjust prescriptions for a couple. As for her former patients, she saw a few. Barbara Voss was supposed to meet with Marion at the health centre every Friday, but she hadn't shown up for her first two appointments. From her records, Marion knew Barbara should be staying with her sister, but Marion had never met the woman. She wondered how it was going between the two. Not knowing was the hardest part.

Like with Big John.

And Daniel.

She had heard nothing from or about either of them since they'd left the hospital, and she was scared to death with all this cold weather. Did they have somewhere to go?

At the end of the day, Marion pulled on her winter coat again then tied the scarf so it spread wide over her face. Sliding on her mitts, she stepped into a raging blizzard and squinted through the snow, waiting for her very late bus. When it arrived, she joined the similarly cocooned people crowded inside, and since there were no seats left, she stood and hung on to the back of one, letting the bus's motion rock her into a semi-stupor. Her thoughts travelled to Daniel, and she felt a now-familiar sadness. She no longer had access to his records, and he was not assigned to her health centres. After they'd said goodbye, she'd hoped that she would forget her silly—what was it: a *crush*?—but she missed him more than she'd expected to. If only she could find out where he was, and how he was doing. But Toronto was a city of more than two and a quarter million people. The chances of finding him now were next to nil.

She wasn't sure if it was the heat from the bodies in the bus or if the weather had actually warmed a little, but when they arrived at her building, she was able to lower her scarf as she stumbled across snowy Isabella. She rode the elevator to the fifth floor, peeled off her winter clothing as Chester purred around her wet boots, then she turned on the TV and clicked to NBC, only to be horrified by what she saw and heard.

"Earlier today," stated the white-haired anchor, "South Vietnam's President Thiệu declared martial law. It all amounts to the most ambitious series of communist attacks yet mounted, spreading violence into at least ten provincial capitals, plus American air bases and civilian installations stretching the entire length of the country. None had greater psychological impact than the assault on the American embassy in Saigon."

"What?" she gasped.

The newscast switched to a reporter in Tokyo. "Two hundred thirty-two GIs killed and nine hundred wounded makes this one of the heaviest weeks of the Vietnam War."

She couldn't help but recall Daniel's quiet, heartbreaking question. "Who's been killed since I left?"

The coverage swapped abruptly from the cool blue studio to alarming footage of U.S. soldiers rushing from post to post outside the American embassy, evading the Vietcong. The enemy had managed to get into the eight-storey building as well as set up around it. Mortar and rocket attacks had blasted huge holes into the walls.

"Snipers and suicide commandos," the reporter called them. The coverage went to bodies on stretchers being carried to ambulances. "Two U.S. Marines tried to fire on the Vietcong through the embassy gate and were killed by automatic weapons fire."

Two U.S. Marines, she thought, feeling sick. Sassy would no doubt be watching this footage as well, her heart in her throat as she sought out a fleeting image of her little brother.

The reporter ducked reflexively, and Marion leaned in, absorbed in the action. The cameraman's lens followed an FBI man rushing to the building and glancing through a window. He dropped down then blindly fired his semiautomatic weapon through the window in a wide, sweeping motion without looking.

Marion had watched plenty of footage of the men "humping" through the bush, as Daniel called it. It had started to feel almost routine. This footage was different. The attack was happening in cities from Da Nang to Saigon and many in between, with pavement and sidewalks and buildings not too different from Toronto's infrastructure. There were civilians trapped in that building, regular administrative staff doing their jobs, wondering if they would ever get home again.

The coverage shifted to another reporter, hunched behind a wall at the Saigon airport, his voice temporarily overpowered by a barrage of machine-gun fire. Soldiers sprinted down the street, and Marion noticed Red Cross trucks in the background. Of course they would have had to be in the thick of things, she reasoned, but it was nearly impossible to imagine working in those conditions.

The news anchor in the studio returned, backed by the safe blue screen. In ominous tones, he announced that forty to fifty thousand enemy troops were poised to attack near the U.S. Marine garrison base at Khe Sanh. A map appeared, illustrating that location, about halfway up the eastern coast, near the dividing point between North and South Vietnam. Fighting had resumed in the north, at Laos, he said. Forty thousand additional enemy troops waited there for orders.

Dread pooled in Marion's gut. Were the good guys actually winning the war? She recalled Davey's words at Sassy's dinner party before Christmas, convinced that the Americans were losing, despite what the media said. Today, that seemed chillingly true.

She jumped when the telephone rang, then she picked up the receiver.

"Marion?" It was Sassy. Her voice was shrill, panicked. "It's Joey. My brother's missing."

twenty-one
SASSY

❧

Sassy sat stone-still at her desk, her mind completely blank. She'd tossed and turned for hours last night, imagining Joey somewhere in the jungle, hurt and alone. In the morning, she managed to make it into the office only because her father would be there. She needed to be near him. He would never say so, but she knew he needed her, too.

She pried her gaze from her typewriter and faced his office door. It had been shut all morning. Seeing that made her feel cold. And alone.

She rapped one knuckle on it. "Dad? Can I come in?"

He was holding a picture frame when she entered. She assumed it was a photograph of Joey, but when he placed it on a shelf behind him, she saw she was wrong. It was a picture from the last war, one she'd seen many times. Her father was sitting on a jeep's hood with a couple of other men, and all were smiling, smoking cigarettes. His young face looked so much like Joey's.

She sat across from him without waiting for an invitation. "Who's that in the picture?"

"A couple of friends from the war." He pointed at one. "Recognize him?"

She squinted at the man's face and added forty years. "That's Mr. Moore. I visit him like you asked, Dad. About once a month. He's doing all right."

The hint of a smile touched his lips. "I'm glad."

He took his glasses off and looked at her. Really looked. It was the first time he'd done that in a long time, and it warmed her straight through.

"How are you, Susan?"

Her eyes filled. "Where is he? What's happening?"

"The Vietcong carried out an unprecedented attack yesterday. They're calling it the Tet Offensive, and it took the U.S. by surprise. They're still fighting their way out of it. There's no way to find out anything about Joey yet."

He swallowed hard, and she felt a jolt of panic. He was afraid. She had never seen that expression on his face before, and it frightened her as well. Determined to help somehow, she walked around his desk and planted a kiss on his bristled cheek, feeling a terrible ache in her chest. He hadn't shaved that morning.

"He'll come home," she assured them both.

He offered her a sad smile then got back to work. She left him alone and shut the office door behind her.

A few days after the news came about Joey, Tom came to her desk.

"What's with the long face?"

She let out a huff of air, feeling defeated. She hadn't meant to speak with Tom about it, since this was a workplace, after all, but he'd asked.

"It's my dad. He doesn't want to talk, and I miss him so much. I feel like I don't even know him anymore."

Tom lowered himself onto the corner of her desk. "He's still the same, just keeps to himself more."

"I know he's worried about Joey, but what about me? I'm still here, and I need him. He doesn't even remember that I exist."

He studied her. "He knows you're there. Of course he does. Maybe he doesn't want to talk about it yet. You have to be patient." The corner of his mouth curled. "I know that's not your strong suit."

"I shouldn't have to be patient. He's my father. We need to be together around something like this."

"Sassy, your dad is who he is. He's done pretty well in most things, you know? He survived the war, he came back and picked up his dad's business, he raised you after your mom's passing, and now this. With Joey missing, he's moved to a new level of pain, and he's doing his best to survive that as well."

"But what about me? Maybe *I* want help," she said softly.

"You're both stubborn. And you're both tough. One of you will have to bend, and it doesn't look like it will be him. Maybe try to think of what *he* might want, not you. Maybe that will help both of you."

It was annoying advice, but Tom was right. The trouble was, she didn't know her father very well these days. She had no idea what he might want. Then it struck her that someone else might. That night after work, she stopped in at Jack's Variety Store and bought some flowers, then she went to visit her father's friend in 517.

"Hello, Mrs. Moore. These flowers are for you."

"Why, thank you, dear. It's lovely to see you."

"I've been thinking of you and your husband. Are you busy? May I come in?"

The older woman smiled. "Of course, Susan. I just made fresh buns. Would you like one?"

The apartment was a bachelor, barely enough room for the two of them. Basically, it consisted of a sitting area big enough for three chairs with a small table between them, a television on a stand, a tiny kitchen, and a curtain closing off the bedroom section. Every time Sassy visited, she felt guilty for all the space she had in her own apartment.

"Hello, Mr. Moore," she said as he hobbled into the sitting area on his crutches. He was a slender man, and his eyes were always sad, like a basset hound's. Pain had etched lines around his mouth.

"Hello, Susan. Very nice to see you," he said.

His wife helped him into a chair piled with thick pillows, trying to ease the pain in his spine, if only a little. What a life they led.

Tom was right. Sassy was spoiled.

Mrs. Moore brought them both a cup of tea and a roll, and sat with them for a little while, then she excused herself, saying she had to write some correspondence. She wasn't fooling anyone. Anything Sassy and Mr. Moore talked about would be overheard in the tiny space. They had no secrets.

"I didn't know if I'd told you that I started working for my dad a while back. In real estate," Sassy began.

Mr. Moore's pinched expression eased a little as he shifted a pillow. "You hadn't. How is the old boy?"

"He's . . . Business is good," she said, letting her eyes crinkle at the sides. She wasn't here to complain, but to help someone feel cared about.

"Ah. And he's doing all right?"

How could she answer? With honesty, she decided. "We haven't spoken much lately."

"Why?"

She shrugged. "I wish I knew."

A shadow crossed the veteran's expression. "Your brother's still over there?"

Straight to the point. Her dad used to be like that, too. Maybe they learned not to mess around when they were there. Just get it done.

"Yes, sir. Joey's been there eleven months now. He signed up for six, but the marines offered some kind of incentive, and now he's there for thirteen months." She took a deep breath. "Actually, it's worse than that. Joey's missing. It happened after the Tet Offensive. Nobody's heard anything about him since."

He observed her for a beat, and his sympathetic gaze loosened her fragile hold on her tears. When it let go, she put her head in her hands and let them come. He said nothing, only waited, then he handed her a Kleenex.

"I'm sorry to hear that, Sassy. I really am."

"What can I do, Mr. Moore?" she sniffed, dabbing at tears. "All I want is to talk with my dad about it. I *need* to talk with him. But he barely even looks at me." She caught a sob. "I miss him so much."

He exhaled, and she calmed slightly. "All you can do is try to understand. It's not easy, I know."

"I hope you don't mind my asking, but do you get like he does sometimes? Remembering the war like that? Do you, I don't know what you'd call it. Do you shut down?"

"I'm different from him, I guess." He gestured at his missing leg. "My memories of the war are always right here, in front of me. I can never phys-ically forget. I'm lucky that I don't have the nightmares that so many have." He hesitated, then he focused fully on her. "I do have memories, though. I have a lot of memories of your dad."

Until tonight, Sassy and Mr. Moore had stuck to superficial topics. She asked how he was getting along, and she offered to pick up groceries or whatever. Sometimes they talked about Sassy's childhood, because he seemed interested, and she loved to talk about those times. For some reason, they'd never talked about his past, and how he knew her father.

"I've seen the photo of three of you," she said, encouraging him. "Dad keeps it on his desk. You and dad and another guy. You sure were young."

He chuckled. "Young and stupid. Yeah." A smile flickered. "I've known him a long time. You know, he and I went to high school together."

"I didn't know that."

"It's too bad you didn't know him before. Your dad was a funny guy. And reliable. If anyone needed anything, they could talk to Jim Rankin. He could talk his way into a crowd and leave everyone smiling. He was Mr. Con-fidence."

Sassy smiled. She liked hearing that.

"I don't suppose he's told you anything."

"About what? The war? No, not really."

He let out a long breath. "So he didn't say anything about Italy."

"I don't think so. Why? What happened in Italy?"

Mrs. Moore breezed into the room, reminding Sassy that they weren't alone.

"Would either of you like another bun, and a little more tea?"

"I think we'd both enjoy that," Mr. Moore said, lifting an eyebrow when Sassy's stomach spoke up. "Maybe a little meat and cheese on Susan's? She must be hungry after her day at work."

"Ham, dear?"

Sassy nodded gratefully, and Mrs. Moore headed to the kitchen area. Every movement she made was fluid and easy, almost as if she wasn't looking at what she was doing.

"May I help?" Sassy asked.

"No, no, dear," Mrs. Moore said, reaching for the whistling kettle. "I have it all under control."

She tucked an errant grey curl behind one ear and slid her gaze to her husband as if asking a question. Sassy saw him smile slightly and give a gentle nod. *It's all right*, she read in his eyes.

"You were asking about Italy," Mr. Moore said.

Now that he'd brought it up, Sassy was dying to know. There must be a reason it hadn't been spoken about before. She bit her lip, unsure. "Is it all right to ask?"

Mrs. Moore cast a glance over her shoulder, reading her husband. "Maybe Jim doesn't want her to know."

"Maybe not," he replied, "but I was there, too. He can't keep my story to himself."

Mrs. Moore brought over their tea and sandwiches, and Sassy did her best to eat slowly. Mr. Moore left his food on his plate and waited for his tea to cool a little, his gaze wandering slightly past her.

"It was after the Battle of Sicily. Do you know your history?"

His wife settled in the third armchair in the room, keeping to herself but always there if he needed her. From the little table beside her, she pulled out a crochet needle and a skein of thin white yarn.

"I wasn't a great history student," Sassy admitted, "but I know about some of the major battles. I know about that one. You were there?"

"We all were. Me, Jim, and Marcus. That's the third guy in the photo."

It was interesting, being able to put her father in an actual physical location in the war. The concept of his fighting had always felt so unclear.

"Our platoon was in the initial landing, then we were sent to liberate some of the small villages beyond. The Germans and other fascists fled the scene. Most of them, anyway." She watched his face soften, going back in time. It was as if his eyes got younger, but the rest of him aged. "That's where all this happened," he said, gesturing to his partial leg. "It happened so fast. Jim and I were clearing out an alley. It all looked good, so we, well, we forgot to be cautious, I guess. I recall very little except it was a hot, gorgeous day, and your dad and I were laughing about something. It was a good time in our lives. We were young and free, and we were living, at least for the moment, in Italy. The war was almost over. We had the enemy on the run at last."

From the corner of her eye, Sassy saw Mrs. Moore's needle slow. She knew what was coming, it seemed.

"I'm sorry to interrupt," she said. "Did you want to tell her about Mr. and Mrs. Romano?"

Mr. Moore glanced up, and they held each other's gazes, then he nodded.

"You go ahead," he said.

"Our neighbours, Mr. and Mrs. Romano, you know them?" she asked Sassy.

"Of course! They're wonderful. What about them?"

"Your father and Mr. Moore helped liberate their village. They never forgot that. When they came to Canada, your father helped them find this apartment. He—" She glanced at her husband again, but he did not stop her. "He helped us as well. Really, your father has taken care of all of us."

Me too, Sassy thought, smiling as she thought of the Romanos like that. She'd had no clue they were somehow connected. Wait until she told Marion. What an amazing thing, to know her father had taken care of all of them.

"I had no idea. That's such a beautiful story."

"Your father is a hero in many ways," Mrs. Moore said.

Sassy nodded, a little overwhelmed. "He's a great dad."

"I'm sure he is, but there's a lot more that you don't know," Mr. Moore said calmly, resuming the conversation. "On that beautiful, sunny day, as he and I were walking down the street, completely oblivious, there was an explosion. That moment ruined my life, but your father saved it."

Sassy stared. "I beg your pardon?"

"I don't remember much after the explosion, but I do remember looking up and seeing your dad's face. He was pulling me back, out of the street. He saved my life."

Her jaw dropped, and her mind went to the framed medal on her father's office wall, as well as the commendation notices from the mayor and the army that hung on either side of it. Her father had shrugged off all her questions about them. Why? Why wouldn't he have told her that he saved his friend's life?

"I never knew that," she said at last, her chest tight. "He never told me."

"He didn't like to talk about it. He was always very humble about that day. He never did any newspaper interviews when they asked, and I never saw him wear that medal." He exhaled. "So I imagine that having his son fighting in a different war is hitting him hard. The news out of Vietnam is awful. Worse all the time, and it doesn't seem to be ending anytime soon. Knowing your brother is MIA must be eating your father up inside, and I bet it's bringing up a lot of memories he'd rather forget."

"What can I do?" she asked, tears blurring her vision. "How can I help him?"

Mrs. Moore smiled kindly. "He knows you're there, dear. Even if he doesn't say anything, he knows. The war took them far away from us, and some of them lose parts of themselves over there. Sometimes whatever they lost pulls them back. All you can do is be there for him when he returns. Never let him forget that you love him."

twenty-two
MARION

There was little Marion could do but sit with Sassy and offer comfort. No one could guarantee that Joey would ever come home, and she refused to make empty promises. Late one night, Sassy padded down to Marion's apartment, bleary-eyed, saying she couldn't sleep, so Marion prescribed Librium for her to take at night. During the day, she said nothing when Sassy pulled out her bottle of Mother's Little Helper. Those magical white pills lulled Sassy into a comfortable state of nostalgia.

Marion didn't say anything to Sassy about it, but she was having trouble sleeping as well. Certainly she was concerned about Joey, but she didn't know him, so that was secondhand worry. What kept her awake was thinking of Daniel, somewhere in the freezing city and no doubt hurting deeply. And getting so little help from her. If only she could be sure he'd found shelter, she might be able to sleep.

As a doctor, all Marion had ever wanted to do was help and heal. To be useful in a damaged person's life. When she operated, she used her mind and nimble fingers to repair what was broken. As a psychiatrist, she offered therapy and prescriptions when needed.

Right now, watching her best friend suffer, and having no idea where Daniel might be, she felt useless.

Trying to distract herself with television didn't work. When she saw the news and its predictable coverage of Vietnam, she no longer saw strangers. Sassy had shown her many pictures of Joey growing up, and these days Marion had trouble not seeing his shadowed face under a metal helmet. There were other faces in her mind now, too, thanks to Daniel. After all his stories, she felt as if she practically knew his "brothers."

Sometimes when she thought of Daniel, she also reflected on her father. She hadn't been to visit her parents for over a month, though she had joined them for their annual Christmas dinner, bearing dolls and toys for the children, a couple of Sassy-recommended books for Pat and her husband, and new sweaters for her parents: a soft pink one for her mother, and a camel-coloured cardigan for her dad. When they were washing dishes after supper, Marion had her mother to herself, and she used that time to ask about her father. Her mother assured her that he was doing well. The "episodes," as she called them, didn't happen as often anymore. But when Marion dug deeper, her mother admitted that she'd gone out shopping in November and come home to find him weeping and unaware.

"But he swiftly returned to himself," she said brightly. "I sat with him and held his hand, like you suggested, and he remembered me right away. I was very quiet and calm when I told him where we were."

Almost all their married life, her mother had tended to her father. When Marion thought of that, then saw the way she strove to see everything in a positive light, she couldn't help but feel sorry for her mother.

As much as Marion adored her family, she was relieved to get back on the bus after a few hours and return to her quiet apartment. Seeing her father quietly engaging with his grandchildren reminded her of when she was small, and she didn't like to think about that. She wasn't proud of who she had been back then. A few times, he'd collapsed in public, and she still burned with the shame she'd felt as a child, aware that strangers and some of the family's friends were witnessing a grown man crying. They were judging him, she knew, and the rest of the family as well. As Marion matured, she adjusted to his behaviours and was sometimes able to help him recover, but it wasn't until she began to study medicine that she understood his reaction was an involuntary condition he could not help.

Her shame now came from recognizing how cruelly she had thought of him for so long.

The other night, Sassy had come to see her, looking brighter than she had for a while, and she'd proudly told Marion what she'd learned about her father's role in the war. He had a framed medal on his office wall alongside letters from the mayor and other officials, Sassy said, all congratulating him on his exemplary service.

"He saved Mr. Moore's life!" she kept exclaiming. "I had no idea!"

When Marion asked, Sassy said no, her father had never displayed any suffering postwar. Not like Marion's father had.

Once again, Marion burned with shame. It was awful to be envious of her best friend, but she couldn't help it. Beautiful, talented Sassy had a wealthy, heroic father who paid all her bills. In contrast, Marion had worked for years to get where she was. Sassy's father had come home with a medal; Marion's had brought only nightmares and panic and hopelessness.

This morning, tired from another nearly sleepless night, Marion dressed and prepared to head to the community health centre. Before she called the elevator up to the fifth floor, she pressed her ear against Sassy's door, listening for any sounds. She didn't hear anything, and she hoped that meant her friend was fast asleep, oblivious to the world. The day after Sassy's news about Joey, Marion had gone to visit each of the neighbours to let them know what had happened, and why Sassy would be different. Both Mrs. Romano and Mrs. Levin quickly declared they would cook for her, so Marion suggested they arrange a schedule between them that wouldn't overlap. They said they hoped she wouldn't need them to cook for long. Everyone wanted Joey found. Everyone wanted Sassy to breathe again.

twenty-three
SASSY

⁓

Sassy squinted at the clock by her bedside: two thirty a.m. Who on earth would call her in the middle of the night? With a groan, she dragged herself out of bed and slumped into the living room.

"Hello?" she said into the phone.

"Miss Rankin?" It was a woman's voice. Calm, detached, efficient.

Sassy was in no mood. "Listen, lady. I don't know what you're selling, but this is a terrible time to phone people."

"Forgive me." The woman's tone softened a bit. "Am I speaking with Susan Rankin? Daughter of Mr. Jim Rankin?"

Instantly, Sassy felt cold all over. She dropped onto the couch. "Yes?"

"I am calling from the Toronto Western Hospital, Emergency Department. Your father was admitted here an hour ago following a car accident. We need you to come in right away."

Numbness enveloped Sassy, from her lips to the tips of her fingers. *Come in right away.* She wrapped herself in her winter coat and boots and ran to the elevator. On the ground floor, she tore out the door and sprinted toward Yonge Street, where she hailed a taxi. At the hospital entrance, she thrust cash at the driver then rushed to the front desk. There, they directed her to a room just off the Emergency Department waiting area, where she was told to wait.

"Someone will come to speak with you," a nurse said.

"Can you tell me something? Anything?" she begged.

But the nurse knew nothing more.

Sassy paced between worn, plastic-upholstered chairs, trying not to hyperventilate. There was a buzzing in her head, louder and softer with her breaths, but it was not coming from the fluorescent lights. She dropped her gaze to the floor and covered her ears, barely registering the faded sparkles in the tile floor. She didn't hear the doctor enter the room. Instead, she saw his shoes stop in front of her, and she sat straight up.

"Miss Rankin? Your father just got out of surgery." His quiet monotone barely broke through the humming in her head. She opened her mouth to ask, *Is he all right? What happened? Can I see him? Can we go home now?*, but the doctor spoke first.

"His injuries were severe, Miss Rankin. We will do what we can to keep him comfortable, but the truth is, he has very little time left."

The buzzing stopped. Surely she'd heard him wrong. "What?" she whispered. "What do you mean?"

He was older, his hair almost entirely grey. Slim, with deep lines cutting across his brow and around the corners of his mouth. His surgery scrubs were a dull sky blue with a small trail of dots near the neckline. Blood, she realized.

Her father's blood.

"I'm sorry," he said gently. "Your father was in a very traumatic accident. We did everything we could, but his internal injuries were too severe. He will not recover."

It made no sense. She'd seen him yesterday, walking and talking with Tom. He'd been fine. There was no way this was happening.

"No. That's not . . . You don't know him, Doctor. He's strong. He can recover from this. There has to be something more you can do."

"We did all we could, but there was too much damage. His organs are failing, and we cannot help that. They will not heal. He is sedated now, to spare him pain. It's the best we can do."

The buzz started again, low and persistent. She shook her head, but it was still there. A hive of bees in the distance, coming closer. She couldn't get enough air. "I don't understand. Please, Doctor! You need to do something!"

"I'm very sorry, Miss Rankin. Your father will likely pass within the next few hours." He stepped back. "Nurse Holly will take you to him."

Sassy hadn't noticed the nurse arrive. Could still barely register her presence. "But wait! Please!" she cried as the woman took his place. How could he just walk away?

The nurse put a gentle hand on Sassy's shoulder. "Come with me, dear, and you can say your goodbyes."

Sassy recoiled from the woman's touch. "Don't say that! My father is going to be fine. He just needs . . . Please, please, can you ask the doctor, can he . . . can he . . ." Her breath was coming in gasps now. She clutched at the nurse's arm with violently shaking hands. "He's all I have left."

The nurse's gaze was a deep well of sympathy, and her voice soft and soothing. "Miss Rankin, please come with me."

The corridor was a blur, the fluorescent lights a dusky yellow. A million thoughts, a million *empty, useless* thoughts whirred through Sassy's head, but she couldn't grasp any of them. She had no answers. She had nothing. This wasn't happening. Couldn't be.

Nurse Holly pushed open a door, entered first, then looked away.

A sound between a cry and a sob broke from Sassy's throat as she stood paralyzed in the doorway. Tubes and wires connected her father to machines that beeped and blinked, and somewhere in the confusion, his bruised, broken, swollen features lay still on a pillow. Beneath it all was his handsome face and loving soul, the man who had quietly taken care of everyone.

Through a blur of tears, she rushed in and grabbed his hand. It was cold, so she started rubbing it for warmth.

"Daddy?" she whispered, then a little louder. "Daddy? Wake up."

A slight motion of his eyelids, then she saw the dark slits of his eyes. He closed his fingers slowly around hers, and she saw dried blood hardened on his fingers.

"Susan," he breathed. "I'm sorry."

She drew his hand to her lips and kissed it. He smelled like blood and dirt and sweat, but something much sharper tied it all together: the reek of alcohol.

After Joey had gone missing, Sassy had popped into her father's office every day to visit, but she'd been quickly dismissed. She'd invited herself over for dinner more than once, but he had been distant, even cold. The house was uncharacteristically messy, and nothing appeared to have been cleaned or even tidied in a long time. She was bothered enough that she decided to spend almost a whole day there doing laundry, changing his sheets and towels, then washing up the entire kitchen.

That's when she discovered the reason behind his change in behaviour.

When she was cleaning the kitchen, she'd found a cache of empty Scotch bottles. Alarmed, she found more in his bedroom and bathroom, some half full, a couple unopened. Alarmed, she gathered every one of them, debated facing him about the sheer number, then decided to throw the evidence away.

But the drinking hadn't stopped.

"It's okay, Daddy. You're gonna be okay." Her smile kept quivering, like it didn't belong, but she forced it to stay. "You just need to rest."

In his tight expression, she saw pain and regret. The corners of his bruised eyes were wet with tears. He knew he was dying.

"Oh, Daddy, please. Please don't. I can't—" A shuddering sob tore through her, and she thought, *I will never be the same.*

"I'm sorry, Susan," he whispered.

She laid her head on his chest and wept. When his hand came to rest on the back of her head—a comfort she would never feel again—she couldn't breathe.

Eventually, the door to the room opened again. "I'm sorry, Miss Rankin." She recognized the kind voice of Nurse Holly. "I need to change his dressings. I'll send someone to the waiting room for you when it's time."

Sassy didn't want to leave him, but he had fallen asleep again. She wiped her eyes, kissed his hand again, and fled the room. Outside, in the corridor, she leaned against the wall, puffing for air and aware of a sharp, tightening pain around her head. The wall itself seemed unsteady, and stars drifted across her closed eyes.

This wasn't happening. This wasn't real. She needed to wake up from this nightmare.

But when another nurse walked past, she had to accept the truth, because now she wasn't the only one in the cool, echoing corridor. Suddenly, she couldn't bear to be alone. She staggered toward a pay phone and fumbled in her pocket for change, then she hesitated, the receiver held inches from her face. Whose number did she know? She inhaled deeply, needing to think clearly. Marion, she knew, would come without hesitation, but she had looked exhausted the last time she saw her. No, not Marion. Who else could she call at four in the morning?

"Operator? I need the number for Tom Duncan." In a flash she remembered a mention he'd made in passing of his apartment building. She gave the street name to the operator.

His voice was hoarse. She pictured him then, his beautiful eyes barely open, his hair sticking out in every direction.

She sucked in a sob. "Tom. My dad."

"Sassy?" Then again, more alert. "Sassy? What's happened?"

All she could do was breathe at first, a desperate panting in an attempt to answer him without collapsing. How could there be words for this?

"He . . . he . . ." She wanted to tell him everything so she'd no longer be the only one facing the emptiness. She needed him here, to help her manage, to stop the floor from moving under her feet. In the end, all she could say was "Please come to the Western Hospital. He's dying, Tom."

Her legs felt like jelly as she returned to the waiting room. She sat, then dropped her head into her hands, her mind blank with panic.

"Miss Rankin?"

A policeman stood before her. "I'm very sorry, ma'am," he said kindly. He held a small notebook in one hand and drew a pen from his pocket. "I know this is a terrible time for you, but I need to go over the details of the accident with you for my report. Do you feel you're up for this?"

She stared dully at him, thinking, *No, I'm not. Go away. Leave me alone.* But she said, "I want to know."

In a daze, she heard him recount everything about the scene of the crash, the condition of her father, and the ambulance ride. The way the policeman spoke was so matter-of-fact, it almost felt like it had happened to someone else. Then he was gone, and she stared at his receding back, wondering how she got to this place.

The nurse had not come for her yet, so she drew her knees to her chest, needing to hold herself together somehow. Her brow rested on them, and she closed her eyes, welcoming the darkness that helped ease her throbbing headache.

What felt like minutes later, a pair of warm, strong arms gathered her up against a solid, wool-clad chest. The light scrape of a beard brushed her brow.

"I'm here, Sassy. Tell me what I need to know."

Tom's voice rumbled through her, and she clung to him for a moment. Then she pulled herself together as best as she could and held his gaze. "I should have said something. I should have stopped him."

"What happened? Were you with him?"

"No. He was alone, but I found out last week that he'd been drinking a lot ever since Joey went missing. Last night he had way too much, then he drove his car into a building. I don't know if he was drinking at a bar or at home, and I have no idea where he was going in the middle of the night. He was going so fast the police think he might have passed out with his foot on the accelerator. They told me there's nothing left of the car."

"Miss Rankin? You can come in now." The nurse eyed Tom. "Family only."

"He's my old man," Sassy blurted.

Whether it was for show or for need, she didn't care which, Tom took her hand and helped her to her feet, then they walked in silence to the room where her father lay. Her breath caught when Tom pulled the curtain back, though nothing had changed other than clean white bandages. She could never get used to seeing that, and she already knew she would never forget it. Together they sat on either side of her father's bed.

"Can he . . . can he hear us?"

"He spoke to me," she said, though his whispered apology had been almost too faint to count.

Tom bent forward, his face pale. "Jim?"

Slowly, her father opened his eyes. His mouth opened slightly, but nothing came out.

"It's all right, Jim. I'll take care of everything."

Sassy pressed her hand hard against her mouth, needing to hear it all, see it all, feel it all, *remember* it all, and if she let herself weep, she knew she would never stop. Her father's eyes rolled toward her, held her, then returned to Tom.

Tom nodded. "I'll take care of her, Jim. I promise."

He died just before seven o'clock, when the rest of the city was coming to life. Sassy sat beside him the entire time, fighting sleep, needing to be with him every second. Tom left and returned a couple of times, bringing her coffee and something to eat, but he never said a word. When the time came and the doctor entered the room, they stood together. Tom wrapped his arms around her as the nurse drew the sheet over her father's face.

And he held her tight as she convulsed with grief.

—————————

The funeral was three days later. As he'd promised, Tom took care of everything. Sassy was vaguely aware of things happening around her, but no more than that.

The night before, Marion had come over to help her pick an outfit. She freaked out that she had nothing black to wear, so Marion went back to her place then quietly returned with all Sassy needed, including a pair of practical black shoes.

After she dressed, Sassy stared into the mirror. She didn't recognize herself.

Except for the puffy redness around her eyes, the girl in the mirror was very pale. Sassy had a fair, freckly complexion, but this girl was almost grey. She supposed she should put on some makeup, but she couldn't even bring herself to wear lipstick. She brushed out her hair and pulled it back into a bun, then she looked at herself again. Leaned in closer and stared right into those swollen eyes.

"I can do this," she whispered to her reflection. She was a performer, after all. She could sing a sad song with a smile on her face, couldn't she?

Her green eyes looked back, searching. "Can I?"

There was a knock on the bedroom door, then Marion led her downstairs. Tom waited at the curb in his blue Chevette, and he drove them to the church in silence. They sat in the front pew with her, Marion on one side, Tom on the other.

Joey wasn't there. Maybe he was dead, too. She tried to picture him sitting beside her, but she couldn't imagine him in a black suit.

A stranger stood at the front of the church to read the eulogy. *Jim Rankin was a pillar of society. An inspiration to many. An innovative businessman with a deep love for family. A good friend.*

Mr. Moore, leaning heavily on his diminutive wife, said a few words, too. *Jim Rankin saved my life. He was a hero. The world has lost a great man.*

When Sassy rose at the end of the service, she felt Marion drape her winter coat over her shoulders. They followed the casket out, and she was startled by the number of people sitting or standing in pews behind her. She spotted Betty, her father's secretary, right away, then she recognized others from business meetings. A few of her former neighbours were there as well. When she spotted her childhood nanny, Minnie, she had cried out without meaning to. So many memories came with that familiar face. Her father and Joey laughing with her. *You two kids are peanut butter and jelly.* Minnie dissolved at the sound of Sassy's pain. In the back row, Davey gave her a careful smile, and it was hard not to go to him for the hug she knew would be there.

At the church exit, Sassy stood like a cardboard cutout, observing all the life around her and feeling none of it.

twenty-four
MARION

❧

Sassy didn't say a word in the limousine as it drove from the cemetery to Isabella Street. She sat pressed against the window, watching freezing rain stream down the glass, watching people and places Marion knew she would not remember. She was very pale. Very still. Grief stole the energy out of the living, and that seemed even more profound when it struck someone like Sassy.

Marion and Tom kept quiet as well, though Marion longed to hear her friend's voice. Her heart broke every time she looked at Sassy. If only she could talk with her about what she was feeling and how she would survive this. But that time would come, she knew. Marion would be ready when she was needed.

Tom sat on the Cadillac's jump seat, facing them. He had not moved throughout the service, but he had kept Sassy's hand in his, whether she noticed it or not. When it was time, he shouldered the coffin and led the pallbearers from the church to the hearse that waited for them in the sleet. As soon as it was loaded, he was back at Sassy's side with an umbrella. He held her hand securely where it curled through his elbow. The chauffeur held open the back door, and Tom eased her in like she was fine china.

The cemetery was miserable. The freezing rain was relentless, and everyone shook from the cold beneath their umbrellas. About two dozen people stood at the graveside, which was an impressive crowd for this weather. Marion estimated just as many had chosen to forgo the wet part of the ceremony. Among the mourners, she recognized a couple of politicians from newspaper photos, wearing expensive trench coats over expensive suits. Marion's gaze drifted over the shivering crowd, and she wondered how many of them really knew Jim Rankin. How many had been friends? Did they know how lonely he was without his son? How he'd avoided his daughter for so long and chosen liquor instead of talking about the truth? Did they realize they could have helped him if they'd tried?

Afterward, Sassy held on to Marion's hand, so Marion became the receiver of the well-wishes.

"Thank you for coming," she said over and over, but she did not shake any hands. "Thank you. We appreciate your kind words. Yes, it was very sudden. Thank you. Thank you."

On Sassy's other side, Tom appeared solid as he acknowledged the businessmen he knew then thanked them for their condolences. He was being as strong as he could, for Sassy. They all were. But Marion saw the pain in Tom's eyes.

Sassy stood in a daze, mute.

Now, in the elevator, on the way up to her apartment, Sassy let out a long sigh.

"I wish Joey was here."

Marion bit her lower lip, trying not to cry. It wasn't fair. None of it was fair.

twenty-five
SASSY

Sassy rolled over and eyed the clock on her bedside table: ten thirty-five. The last time she'd looked it was nine twenty. She assumed it was morning, but she didn't really care. She wanted to stay here forever, wrapped in her rumpled sheets and blankets, the floor littered with scrunched-up tissues. There was no window in her bedroom, so she didn't know if the sun had come out after all the rain. Her head felt like cement, and her feet were heavier than that. She wasn't going anywhere, and she didn't care.

Then it all rushed back; the reason she was here, curled into her sheets like a snail. "*Daddy!*" she gasped, and the volcano of emotions erupted through her again, leaving her sobbing, then whimpering when she could catch her breath once more.

It still didn't seem real. It couldn't be, her inner voice insisted. He couldn't be . . . gone. She would wake up from this nightmare, and her father would be at his desk. He would check his watch and scowl when she came in late. He had to be there. That's where he belonged.

Not in a grave.

Her mother's body was probably no more than dust now, she thought absently.

And Joey? Buried among the thick foliage of Vietnam?

She'd thought about that last night, about how alone she was now, about how her whole family was gone. In one desperate moment, she decided she wanted to be with them, so she'd taken all of Marion's pills at once. When she'd swallowed the last one, she heard a small voice inside of her, breaking through her desolation, reminding her that *Joey might be all right! What will he come home to if you're gone?* So she ran to the washroom and stuck her finger down her throat. She'd fallen asleep beside the toilet, then she'd crept back to bed while the rest of the world slept.

She recognized a knock at the door as Marion's quiet but firm hand. She wanted Marion to come in, but she couldn't get out of bed.

The apartment door opened, and she remembered that she hadn't locked it the night before.

"Sassy?" Marion poked her head through the bedroom door and squinted through the darkness. "I brought breakfast."

"I'm not—" she started to say, then she stopped, unsure. The earthy aroma of coffee seeped through her door and twisted into the air. Had she eaten last night? She couldn't recall. Didn't care. Didn't have the energy to say anything more.

"I made muffins. And coffee. I can make eggs, too, if you want."

With effort, Sassy peeled back her eyelids and sat up. "Thanks."

Marion stood at the side of her bed. "Did you sleep?"

"Yeah. Thanks for the pills."

"You only took one, right?"

"Yeah," Sassy lied.

She flipped back her sheets and dragged her pyjama-clad legs over the side of the bed. The strangest vibration travelled through her arms and legs, and her hands felt almost like they'd been asleep. She wondered if that came from the pills she hadn't thrown back up. Before she stood, she looked at Marion and met an awful, sympathetic gaze that tore her apart again. She dissolved into tears, but Marion was there, and that was neither a nightmare nor a dream. Marion was real, and she was not going to leave her. Sassy gripped her tight, needing the stability, and was a little surprised to feel Marion's body bumping with quiet sobs as well.

"I need a bath," Sassy muttered, uncomfortably aware of that fact. "How long has it been since the funeral? I probably stink."

"It's been a couple of days, but you're fine," Marion said, dabbing away a few of her own tears. "Come and eat, then we'll see about that bath."

"Oops," Sassy said as they entered the kitchen. She'd left the pot of chicken soup on the counter last night, untouched. Mrs. Levin had brought it, and Sassy hadn't had the heart to tell her she wasn't interested in eating.

Marion covered the pot with a dishcloth. "I'll look after that. She won't even know. Go sit. I'll bring in the muffins."

The two of them had sat at this table so many times. They'd discussed everything under the sun, from music to politics to food to wine, from television to weather to books to school. They shared stories about their families, both good and bad. Sassy told her about her dreams to become a famous singer, but she'd also admitted that she was interested in learning more about her father's business. Marion told her she had once thrived in an emergency room, up to her elbows in blood, but Sassy hadn't been able to picture that. She told Marion about her unexpected attraction to Tom, and Marion had eventually confided in her about Daniel. She said she had never intended to fall for anyone, let alone an emotionally damaged patient recently back from a war zone. But there it was.

At one point at this table, weeks ago, Sassy had broached the topic of sex. Marion had spotted Sassy's copy of *Tropic of Cancer* by Henry Miller on the table, and she asked what it was about. She passed the book to Marion, saying little, only "Oh, it's sort of a fictional memoir." Marion had opened the book at random, and her eyes had popped open with shock. Sassy had dissolved into gales of laughter that eventually had them both gasping for breath.

"All right," Sassy had said when she could speak again. "He was a tiny bit obsessed with sex."

Now Marion placed two cups of coffee on the table then slid a plate of oatmeal raisin muffins toward Sassy. "Just baked this morning. They're still warm."

"Thank you for being here," Sassy said, watching her. "I mean it. I wouldn't be getting up if you weren't here."

Marion smiled gently. "You'll feel stronger once you eat something. Go ahead. I'm a pretty good baker, if I do say so myself."

She took a bite of the muffin, and the next thing she knew she was dabbing at crumbs and licking them off her finger. Marion went to get more coffee, and Sassy bit into another muffin.

"These are really good," she said.

"I'll bake blueberry another day. Those are even better."

Sassy swallowed, but it was difficult with the lump in her throat always there. "What am I supposed to do now, Marion?"

"You live, Sassy," her friend said calmly. "One day at a time. You are going through a terrible, traumatic time, and now you have to survive it. You're not alone. Tom and I are here with you. So are all the neighbours. We all love you, Sassy."

She felt herself weakening again. "I can't believe he's gone."

"It's a horrific thing. I am so sorry you're suffering."

A thought Sassy had planned to keep to herself for the rest of her life popped to the surface. It came out with more force than she'd thought she had. "I am so angry at him. And I'm ashamed of what he did, because I think it was on purpose. And I know I shouldn't be angry because he's *dead*, but I can't help it. It hurts so much, what he did."

"All your feelings are valid, Sassy. It's all right to be angry. When he died, he took part of you with him, and there's no way you could have prepared for that. His death changes everything you knew." She held Sassy's gaze. "And it's all right if you feel ashamed of him, but keep in mind that you don't truly know what he was thinking. You don't know the real reason for why this happened. It's not as if he left you a note detailing his plans."

"If he'd written me a note, or if he'd told me, I could have stopped him."

"Could you? I don't think that's fair to either you or him."

"I could have. If I'd told him I needed him . . ."

"He knew that. He loved you so much, Sassy, but this was about him, not you. If you're right, and he did it on purpose, it was a last resort. Your father was a complicated man. He was your father, but he was also a decorated war hero. Before he was a dad, before he had any idea what his life might become, he put his life on the line for others, and he saved lives. It doesn't matter how many medals a man might earn, he isn't impervious to the pain his experience caused." She sighed. "He must have been torn apart by everything happening, but he never would have left you alone. Not if he'd been able to think clearly enough to stop himself."

"I know what you're talking about," Sassy said. "You've told me about Daniel and your dad, and the things they have to live through. But my dad never had problems like that. He was fine all his life."

"Some of the men I've read about keep their problems buried their whole lives. They hide them away because they're ashamed, or they don't want anyone else to know. Or they just want to forget what happened." Marion lowered her eyes to the empty plate before them. "My dad suffered his whole life after the war, and he's still suffering. Your dad just kept it contained, I guess. With Joey missing, it might have all come back."

"Joey." Thinking of him brought back a whole other level of misery. "I hate feeling this way. I feel like I'm not even here."

"Grief is the most painful of all human emotions. It's the price you pay for loving and being loved."

Sassy took a deep breath and let it out very slowly, fighting exhaustion. How could she still be tired? She'd slept for three days already.

"I don't remember if I ever grieved my mother's death," she admitted. "I didn't know her."

"You were so young. You probably went through a lot of confusion rather than typical grief. In a way, you have always grieved her, but her loss helped shape you into the strong person you are now."

"I have a snapshot in my head of her funeral," Sassy said, surprising herself. She'd forgotten all about it until this moment. "I remember being with my father and Joey in that big, cold church. So many people were there, all of them wearing black. I had a friend back then—no idea who she was, I just vaguely remember her face—and she was in the row behind us with her family. I remember seeing her little hand in her mother's. I could almost feel the softness of the woman's skin as she comforted her daughter, and I remember feeling really, really pissed that she had a mother and I didn't." She inhaled, and the air shuddered through her. "Now I'm an orphan."

Marion's eyes shone. She took Sassy's hand in hers and held it between them, pulling Sassy out of the darkness. "But you're not alone."

twenty-six
MARION

❦

One week after the funeral, everyone mentioned in Jim Rankin's will was called to a lawyer's office. Tom drove, and though Marion wasn't officially invited, she went just to be with Sassy. From the back seat, she watched her friend stare out the front passenger window as they drove. She could practically feel the longing in Sassy's chest, her desperate need for life to go back to what it had been.

Marion and Tom stayed close to her, but there was only so much they could do. The person Sassy needed the most was the person they had buried only days ago.

The lawyer's meeting room was dark and formal, with old wood floors that creaked underfoot. Deep oak wainscotting lined the walls beneath perfectly stacked bookshelves, and many of the book spines glimmered with gold lettering and lines. Everything looked as if it came from the last century. Smelled that way, too. Sweet. Like the wood had been cured by old pipe smoke.

The lawyer, Mr. Godfrey, sat on a tufted leather chair behind an ornate walnut desk. A number of forward-facing, wood-framed chairs had been arranged for the guests. The whole room radiated wealth and history.

Sassy was led to the front row of chairs, along with Tom and Marion. At the side of the room, Marion spotted another couple she remembered from the funeral. The man was propped on a stack of pillows, his wife at his side.

After they sat, Sassy leaned toward Marion. "That's the Moores," she said, in case Marion didn't know. "They live down the hall." She frowned. "See the man just coming in? Sitting beside Mr. Moore? I'm pretty sure he's one of the three men in my dad's photo. From the war."

Marion glanced over, and her heart stopped. "No . . . that's *my* dad."

Sassy stared at him, then at Marion. "Your dad knew my dad?"

Marion couldn't take her eyes off her father. As if sensing her stare, he lifted his head and gazed directly back at her. She didn't recognize the taut expression on his face, and unease coiled in her belly.

"Ladies and gentlemen," Mr. Godfrey began, jerking Marion's attention forward again. "May we begin, please?"

He welcomed them, offered condolences, then he said something legal-sounding that Marion didn't catch. After that, he opened a file folder and pulled out a few sheets of paper. Marion glanced back at her father in confusion, but he was watching Mr. Godfrey.

"Before we begin the reading of the will, I have a letter that the deceased has requested I read in advance to everyone here."

Beside Marion, Sassy seemed to burrow deeper into her chair. Someone cleared their throat. Mr. Godfrey observed them all, then nodded to himself before he began.

Dear friends and family,

There are some things you need to know.

If he is here today, and I really hope he is, there is only one person in this room who knows the secret I have kept for the past twenty or so years. I apologize from the bottom of my heart to him and to any others present who have been affected in any way by what you are about to hear.

Over the years, I have received honours and privileges based on my actions in Italy during the war. I am grateful for all the attention. My business has prospered in large part due to the opportunities those accolades have provided me. After so many years, to my great shame, I had almost come to accept the story as truth. Do not think I am being humble when I confess to you now that I deserved none of those tributes.

On July 17, 1943, one week after Operation Husky brought me and over twenty-five thousand other young men to Sicily, my brothers-in-arms and I found ourselves in a bitter engagement with the Germans while fighting to liberate the small village of Valguarnera.

Marion heard a long sigh from across the room. When she looked, her father had closed his eyes, and his head hung over his chest. Beside him, Mr. Moore observed Mr. Godfrey with interest. Sassy had gone even paler than before. Marion clutched her friend's hand, needing her to know everything was all right. Sassy didn't respond.

The lawyer continued.

It was a long, difficult battle, but in the end, we were victorious. Victory in those days did not always taste sweet. We had lost many friends, and though there was relative peace where we were, there was a lot of work still to be done. The heat was sweltering, and we were all beyond exhausted. If he is here today, my friend Hank Moore will remember how the two of us stood alone on that hot, dry street corner, complaining about our thirst and dreaming about a nice cool beer.

Everyone turned to look at Mr. Moore, who wore a quiet smile. Sassy slipped her hand from Marion's so she could wipe tears off her cheeks.

Hank joked about heading to a local restaurant, then he stepped into the street and onto a mine. I saw it happen. I stood in a daze and saw the pool of blood spreading from where his leg had been. I saw the odd angle of his body. And I did nothing.

"What?" Sassy sat up tall, heat suddenly radiating off her. Her grey cheeks blazed red.

Mr. Moore was shaking his head. "That's not true," he said to his wife.

Everyone else held their breath.

Hank was unconscious, and he was rapidly losing blood. My friend was dying right in front of me. The explosion drew enemy fire, and despite all my training, I did not move to help my friend. I was paralyzed with panic. Only one thing could make me move, and that was the voice of a man I have betrayed for years. He ran toward us, screaming at me to move Hank to safety and tie up his leg, all the while returning fire, protecting all three of us. I heard a bullet hit the wall by my head. I still remember the sound it made. It would have hit me if that selfless man had not shoved me away. That was the moment I finally came back to life and dragged Hank out of the way.

I apologize to you, Hank. You have always believed that I was responsible for saving your life. Afterward, when we joined the others, Hank sang my praises, and a legend was born. The other man, the true hero, did not ask for credit. In fact, he did not want it.

In the years that followed the war, the third man withdrew from society, and he seemed content. He was a good man, but reserved. When I repeatedly offered to tell the truth, he said he saw no point in doing that. He said he would not benefit from the story being retold, and my business and I would suffer. My conscience did not allow me to rest completely, so we struck a deal. I kept the medals, but I also paid for his daughter to go to medical school.

Marion felt a tingling down her spine, a numbness in her lips. She turned to look at her father.

He gazed back, his eyes shining. "I'm sorry," he mouthed.

She didn't understand. She waited until she could feel her body again, then she rose and went to his side. She knelt beside his chair, holding his gaze and shaking her head with disbelief.

Mr. Godfrey cleared his throat. "If I might continue. There's not much more, then I will get to the will itself."

Marion's father gripped her hand, and together they listened.

I owe Marcus Hart my life, and I have tried to live in a way that he would approve of, though he never asked for anything. When last we spoke, he asked if I could find his daughter a good place to live. I suggested the same apartment building where Hank was living with his lovely wife, and where I later sent my daughter, Susan. It fills my heart to know our two daughters are now close friends.

To everyone in this room, again, I apologize. I lived a lie, and I pulled you all into it. I hope you will someday find it in your hearts to forgive me.

As far as my will, Mr. Godfrey will tell you that I am bequeathing generous sums to the Canadian Legion and the Canadian Red Cross. Mr. Godfrey is in possession of a cheque for Hank Moore. It is a hollow apology for letting him live in the dark for so long.

The rest is as follows:

I apologize to my partner in business, Tom Duncan, for allowing you to believe you worked with a war hero. You have more business acumen than I ever had, and I am proud to leave the business to you. I wish you great success.

For my son, Joey. I'm tortured by the thought that you went to war because of me. That you saw me as some kind of hero and decided you should aim for that as well. If that is why you went, I pray to God you someday understand that you were so much more courageous than I. When you come home, you will have half of my wealth to do with as you please. I know you will do something good with it, because you have a heart of gold.

Lastly, I ask forgiveness of my remarkable daughter, Susan. In the past year or so, and increasingly so after her brother's decision to go to Vietnam, I have become selfish. I chose my own misery over her happiness, and I regret that deeply. To you, my wonderful, spirited, talented Sassy, I bestow all the rest, including the house, knowing that all you ever really wanted was my time. I hope you will use this money to make yourself happy, and I hope that means you will play your guitar and sing like a nightingale for the rest of your days.

twenty-seven
SASSY

❧

Everything Sassy had believed about her life was a lie.

Oh, there was so much she needed to talk with Joey about, but even if she could manage to get her thoughts onto paper, where would she send a letter? There had been no news of him. Deep down, Sassy knew the silence didn't mean much. The entire country was in flames, and with the Vietcong descending on U.S. bases and South Vietnamese villages, word about one specific soldier wasn't going to arrive quickly.

She refused to accept the possibility that Joey had been killed. That was unthinkable. Joey was just missing. He would be found. She *needed* him to be found.

She couldn't tell Joey anything. Not yet.

And now she couldn't talk with Marion, either.

After the reading of the will, Marion stayed with her father. Tom drove Sassy back to the apartment building, and neither of them had spoken throughout the drive. She imagined Tom was as confused as she was. When they got to 105 Isabella, she asked him to come inside; she couldn't bear to be alone. He followed her into the elevator and stood silently at her side as they rode to the fifth floor. In her apartment, she went, out of habit, to make tea, and he walked around the living room, studying her paintings.

When she brought out the tea, he was gazing through the balcony door.

She placed the tray on the coffee table then sat. She'd brought a few cookies as well, but she didn't imagine either of them had much of an appetite. Still saying nothing, Tom joined her on the red couch.

"I miss him so much," she said quietly, starting the conversation. "I want to go see him or have lunch with him at the office like we used to. I want to hug him, and I want to help him stop drinking, but I'll never get a chance to do any of that."

Tom kept his eyes on the table in front of them and said nothing. That was all right. She didn't really want to hear anything.

"I don't have my mom, I don't have Joey, and now I don't have my dad. It's just me, and I'm not ready for that." She faced him, studying his profile. "It's not fair."

Now she wanted him to talk.

"You're right. It's not." He sipped his tea. "Sassy, this might not be what you want to hear, but I'm kind of pragmatic when it comes to things like this. I lost my parents years ago, and I remember how scary that felt. Like I was floundering without a life preserver. But Sassy, you are your own person. You always have been. You're strong and independent, and that's not going to stop. So the way I look at it, technically you don't need them. You can stand on your own. You *want* them, but you're in control of yourself, so it's not a need."

"Feels like it," she sniffed.

"Of course it does." He placed a comforting hand on her back, giving her exactly the amount of connection she needed in that moment. "I'm sorry you're hurting, Sass. If I could do anything in the world to help you, I would."

He was such a good man. She didn't deserve him.

"He called me Sassy," she said.

"What?"

"In the will. That was the only time he ever called me Sassy." She exhaled. "Today messed everything up in my head. I'm so confused."

She leaned back in the couch and stared up at the ceiling. She needed to get her thoughts in order. Right now, none of them were lining up.

She rolled her head toward him. "Are you angry? You know what I mean. About today."

He thought about it. "Not angry. Surprised, yes. Not angry."

"I am." At least she thought that's what she felt. No, she felt *betrayed*, she realized, but anger was an easier emotion to manage. "All my life, I got used to people looking up to him, calling him a hero. They all wanted to be on his good side."

Tom shrugged. "Honestly, a lot of that had to do with him being an outstanding businessman. And he gave back to them, remember. He was always donating to causes and making company speeches when they invited him to come. He did a lot. Maybe too much, now that I think of it. Maybe he was overcompensating."

"He didn't overcompensate with me," she grumbled. "Pretty much left me in the wind."

He nodded sympathetically.

"Will it hurt the business, do you think? I mean, if the press hears about what he did? Or his clients?"

"I don't see why they'd hear about it. It was your dad's choice." His eyes held hers, willing her to understand. "As far as I'm concerned, the only people who will ever know the truth were in that room today."

That helped ease the cramp in her gut, but something still bothered her. "Is it cool that I'm angry? Marion says all my feelings are valid, but, I mean, he just died. Seems like I shouldn't have feelings like that."

He raised his brow. "I don't know, Sassy. Do you feel justified in that anger?"

"I feel like I've been lied to all my life. So yeah. But I'm also ashamed. I've seen that medal on the wall since I was tiny. I believed my dad was better than all the other dads, and I am afraid that maybe I behaved that way sometimes."

He picked up a cookie. She watched him eat, then she had a sip of tea.

"That's kind of ironic, isn't it?" she thought out loud. "Me thinking he was so great for being a war hero, and me being against anything to do with wars. I guess he was right all along about me being a hypocrite." She paused. "I'm mostly embarrassed, I think. To be honest, after learning all that, I don't have any idea how to talk to Marion. She's my best friend, and it's like we switched places."

"How do you mean?"

"I don't know. Last week, my dad was a hero. Now he's dead, and it's her dad who's a hero. Mine's just a liar."

"Hold up," he said, lifting his hand. "I'm not sure you can say your dad was a liar. He never claimed to be a hero. It sounded to me like Hank Moore volunteered the information he had, and your dad merely let it happen. So technically it's not a lie."

She side-eyed him. "You think so? I'm not buying it. Omission is still lying."

"That's up to interpretation, I guess. But Sass, it's not right for you to paint him as nothing but a liar. I bet a lot of men lied about different things over there for a lot of different reasons. Think about who he was the rest of the time. Your dad was a good man, and he loved you like crazy. Even before I knew you, he was always talking about you."

She wished she had known that.

"Tell me honestly, Sassy. If you'd known he wasn't a famous war hero, would you have loved him any less?"

"Of course not."

"Then why worry about it? Everyone has secrets. He did what he could."

"He let you believe it, too. How does that make you feel?"

Tom's gaze dropped to the floor, and his jaw flexed. "I'm okay. Like I said, I'm surprised. But it doesn't matter to me if he was a hero or not."

"Do you wish he'd told you?"

"He had his reasons."

Her heart twisted. He was trying to be strong for her, but it must be killing him as well.

"He thought you were terrific," she said gently. "I never heard him talk about having a business partner, so you must have really impressed him. And the way he spoke with you, it felt like he saw you as an equal."

The curl in his smile twitched. "I'm glad. I enjoyed working with him, and I liked having him as a friend. That's how I'm going to remember him. He was a good man, Sass."

It felt good to let someone else win for a change. Especially when it was Tom. If she could do as he suggested and remember her father as the man she'd loved all her life, without worrying about the rest, she'd be stronger for it.

"I wonder what Joey's going to say." She left off the question about if he would ever come home to hear about it.

Tom did, too. "I guess we'll find out when he's back."

twenty-eight
MARION

❧

Marion didn't hesitate, and she didn't ask permission. She followed her father to the parking lot and got in the passenger's seat. He waited until she was in, then he turned the key. He made no sign that he'd seen her there, simply put the car in gear and headed home. They drove a while in silence, and she waited for him to say something. When he didn't, she realized he was waiting for her.

"Does Mom know?"

He kept his eyes on the road. "She does."

"She never told me."

"Why should she? It was my secret to keep, and she respected that. Besides, she knew it wouldn't change anything."

"But it does, Dad. It changes everything."

He glanced in the rearview mirror then pulled over to the side of the road and parked. Without changing his expression, he turned off the ignition and faced her.

"Explain to me how it changes everything."

Marion knitted her brow, trying to pin her thoughts down. There was so much. How had her father gone from being someone that few people even noticed to being a hero? She didn't think she'd ever been so incredulous or felt so proud as she did in the moment she'd learned the truth. But she'd also felt . . . betrayed.

"Why wouldn't you want Pat and me to know that you saved a man's life?"

"What would that have done? Would I have been a better dad? Would you have loved me more if you'd known?"

She shook her head right away, frowning. "Don't be ridiculous. It wouldn't have affected any of that."

"Then what does it change? My life was your mother, your sister, and you. That's all I needed. If I ever wanted to boast about anything, it would be about you, not me." He shook his head. "That day wasn't something I planned, and what I did didn't deserve a medal. I was in the right place at the right time, but it could just as easily have been me in Jim's place. Or Hank's. We were all brothers over there."

She thought of Daniel, of the loyalty she'd seen and heard when he talked about the men he'd fought with in Vietnam. Daniel wasn't shy like her father, but he didn't boast, either.

They were my brothers. I did whatever I could.

"But people deserve to know you were a hero."

"Why? For whose sake, Bunny? Not mine. I never denied anything, did I? I never lied. I just didn't feel the need to dwell on what happened. To be honest, I didn't want people coming around with expectations. I just wanted to be left alone with my family. Jim was comfortable making speeches. He was always good at that. And most of the time he was as good a soldier as any other. He just froze up that one time, and I was there. The truth is, they'd have done the same if it had happened to me." He nodded, smiling. "And then he went and paid for your schooling. Really, if I'd ever needed anything, that would have been it. Why would I need a medal when I could watch you flourish instead?"

Marion tried to find a weak spot in his argument but couldn't. Thinking as a psychiatrist, she briefly considered asking him if he thought today's revelation might help his episodes. Would the public acknowledgement of the truth ease his troubled soul when he couldn't remember where he was?

When he curled up in terror, believing he was still on the battlefield, would it help him get past that fear? In the end, she decided against it.

"So tell me, Bunny. Now that you've heard my thoughts, does Jim's letter change anything?"

Marion exhaled, suddenly understanding. Sassy. It changed things for Sassy. After she'd gotten over the shock, Marion's sympathy all flowed to her best friend. What had it done to Sassy to learn the truth at a time when she was already so weak? Her brother was missing, her father had killed himself in an alcoholic haze, and she'd just learned the truth about his war heroism. Sassy would feel very alone right now. And broken. She would need Marion more than ever. She felt an urgent need to get back to the apartment and to her friend.

"Actually, Dad, it does." She smiled. "You may not think jumping in front of enemy fire and saving Hank's life was heroic, but I do. Even more inspiring, I suppose, is the fact that you never wanted any thanks for what you did. You were satisfied with who you were, so you took it all in stride. You lived life the way you wanted, not waiting for anyone's approval. That makes you an inspiration to me."

His eyes sparkled with tears. "That means more to me than any medal ever could. My darling Marion, you have been my greatest joy. I'd love to say you were my greatest accomplishment, but you did it all by yourself."

There was more that should have been said, and all the way home, Marion thought about the shame burning in her chest. As a child, how many times had she walked away from her father when he needed her, mortified that other people had witnessed him behaving strangely? How many times had she scorned the sight of him, paralyzed by his thoughts or huddled behind the furnace, wishing he could just be like her friends' strong, reliable, *normal* dads?

Marion hadn't admitted any of that tonight. Instead, she had convinced herself that confessing her ignorance to him after all this time could make matters more painful. Maybe he hadn't noticed her embarrassment years before. He had never mentioned it, after all. If he wasn't aware of how she felt back then, and she apologized for it now, wouldn't that hurt him more?

So she kept her embarrassment to herself, and she told herself that it was better that way. He didn't deserve to be hurt by her childhood prejudices.

Her father was a hero; he was a good, honest man who had sacrificed himself for his friends.

Like Daniel, he called them his "brothers."

What had Marion done for her own friend? She'd talked with her, fed her, cheered her as much as she could, but what had she really done? Sassy was more than her friend. She was her sister.

It was time to do more.

Back in her apartment, Marion grabbed the phone book. She flipped past a handful of pages, and when she got close to what she wanted, she stopped and let her finger slide down the list of names. Impatient for his supper, Chester strolled over and skimmed his tail across her face, demanding attention. Without taking her eyes from her work, she lifted him off the desk and placed him on the floor. He kept doing figure eights around her legs, but Marion had no time for cuddles.

"Ah. There you are," she said to the book. "McKenny, Charles. McKenny, David J. McKenny, David P. McKenny, Fred. Where is . . . Ah! McKenny, Paul, M.D."

She picked up the telephone and dialed his number, uncertain. She didn't want him to think that she—

"Hello?"

"Paul? It's Marion."

His surprise lasted only a blink, then she heard a crunching on the other end of the line. Was he eating *potato chips*?

"Well, well, well! Good to hear from you, Marion. How are you?"

She decided she couldn't just leap in with the point of her call. A little small talk first. "I hate to admit it, but I've missed you."

"It's just not the same anymore, is it?" More crunching.

She scowled. "Are you eating chips?"

"I am."

She thought that was a little rude. And now she was hungry. With everything that had happened today, had she eaten anything? Trapping the phone between her ear and her shoulder, she opened the kitchen drawer where Sassy had left an emergency supply of candy.

"Don't put that in there. I don't eat candy."

"It's Smarties, Marion. They make you smart."

"Are you enjoying the community health centre work?" she asked, popping a couple of Smarties into her mouth.

"It's fine," he said noncommittally. "Kind of a solitary activity though, right? Waiting for appointments has never been my thing, and most don't even show up. I mean, why would they? Do any of them know what a calendar means? Do they wear watches? You were right all along, Marion." He crunched on a few more chips then paused. "Listen, it's always nice to talk with you, but what are you really calling for?"

"I need help, and I'm wondering if you're the right person to speak with."

"Want to talk about it over lunch tomorrow?"

"Stop it, Paul. I need help right now. Besides, I thought you were dating someone."

He chuckled. "You're right. Old habits die hard, I guess."

"My good friend is going through a lot. Part of it is that her brother's in Vietnam, and he went missing at the end of January."

"That's tough."

"It is. She's a terrific girl, and she's really suffering." She deliberated over how much to share then went ahead. "Her name's Sassy. She's a hippy."

"You have a hippy friend named Sassy? Well, good for you."

"I do," she said, unexpectedly proud of that. "Oh! You saw her! She performed the night you took me out."

"I remember that. You freaked. So Sassy's encouraging you to do new things? I like her already."

"She does. In a way, she's changed my life. And, uh, she's actually the reason I called you." She took a deep breath. "Here's the thing, Paul. I read that the International Red Cross in Geneva put out a distress call to doctors from neutral nations because of the Tet Offensive."

"I read that, too."

"How does one get in touch with the Red Cross?"

"Why would you ask me that? I'm not a surgeon," he said, sounding confused.

"No, but you know a guy who knows that woman, Claire Culhane, and you know some surgeons, so I thought you might point me in the right direction." She swallowed. "I . . . I want to go."

This time she felt his shock through the phone. "To Vietnam?"

"As a VPVN. A volunteer physician in Viet Nam."

"Listen, Marion, when I suggested you live a little, this wasn't what I meant. That's nuts."

She couldn't stop now, or she might lose her nerve. "Do you know anyone in the Red Cross, or don't you?"

"Listen, even if I did, I wouldn't tell you. That's insane, Marion, and you and I both know insanity pretty well. Even if I was a surgeon, I'd think long and hard on this, and I'd probably decide against it. But if I was a *woman* surgeon, I would accept that the idea is beyond far-fetched. Probably suicidal. You're not even a surgeon."

"But I was, almost. I'm going, Paul. With or without your help."

There was silence on the other end of the line, then he sighed. "I have a friend who's going. Lee Willard, neurosurgeon. I'm not too surprised about him, to be honest, because he enjoys doing things that should kill him. He goes parachuting for kicks on weekends."

"I want to talk with him," she said quickly, her pulse hammering in her temples. "Please, Paul?"

She held her breath, practically hearing him consider the idea.

"I'll tell you what. You might be nuts, but I do admire your courage. I'm sure the answer will be no, but I'll call Willard and plead your case. He can talk with the CRC. Hang tight, Marion. I'll let you know as soon as I hear anything."

twenty-nine
SASSY

Sassy felt sick with shame. Here she was, curled like a pathetic snail, too chicken to answer the door when her best friend knocked. All along, Sassy had been so happy when Marion promised she would always be there, but now Sassy was hiding from her. What kind of friend was she?

But there was so much in her head. How could she explain it all to Marion?

Tom could call her father a good man a hundred times, but Sassy wasn't convinced. She kept trying to bring happy thoughts to mind about him, how he looked when he laughed, how proud he'd been of her in that meeting about the strip malls. But the pretty pictures didn't last.

Jim Rankin was a fraud. And his deception had made Sassy a liar.

Marion's father, the quiet, humble plumber no one talked about, was the real hero. Marion had told Sassy about her father's "episodes," those dark times when the war found him again and dragged him under. Sassy had sympathized, saying how awful that must be, and how sorry she was for it, but inside, she couldn't deny feeling just the tiniest bit smug. Until today, Sassy's dad had been the hero, and he'd never suffered "episodes" to embarrass her. She hated the competitive edge she felt when they discussed their fathers, but she couldn't deny the satisfaction her father's status gave her.

Until the reading of the will.

Marion's father was the true hero, and he was still suffering for it. Jim was just a man who had taken the credit then killed himself.

Just a few days ago, Marion had come to Sassy in her time of need, bearing muffins and encouragement, and had called Sassy's father "complicated." A loving father and a war hero, she'd said, giving Sassy a sense of family pride. That had given her what she needed to emerge from her deep well of grief.

Now she couldn't face Marion. At least with Tom, he'd been lied to in the same way Sassy had. He'd thought Jim Rankin was his friend, but Sassy didn't buy that. Friends didn't lie to one another.

"I don't know what to say to Marion," she'd said to Tom.

He encouraged her to tell her everything she was thinking, but Sassy couldn't see that happening. She was too scared, too humiliated to broach the subject, even though she knew Marion would help her with it.

By ignoring Marion's knock, Sassy had put their meeting off for tonight, but there was no way she could avoid her best friend forever. What should she do, then? Apologize? Beg for forgiveness? But what for? Her own ignorance of the truth or her cowardice to face her friend?

She hugged her knees closer to her chest, feeling very small. And ashamed. And alone.

In the morning, she stayed in her apartment until she heard Marion's door lock behind her, then the mechanical swoosh of the elevator door. When Marion came home later that afternoon and knocked again, Sassy hid. Another day down, another night of feeling guilty. She did the same the next day and night, though her heart broke a little more every time she heard Marion at her door.

On the third morning, once she was sure her friend was safely out of the building, Sassy extricated herself from her couch. She couldn't stay home today. The day promised to be as dull as watching paint dry, but she couldn't ignore it. She'd been delaying the meeting, put off by the long bus ride to the lawyer's office to sign papers regarding her father's estate. Once she arrived, there was all the paperwork, then the torture of Mr. Godfrey droning on and on, advising her about money and legal stuff and whatever else. Honestly, she missed most of what he was saying and almost fell asleep halfway through.

Finally done there, she climbed back on the bus then got off early, reminding herself to stop and pick up some much-needed groceries. On her walk home after that, she reminded herself that she had better get some laundry done. She was running out of clean things to wear. Oh, a bath would be nice, too. It was a relief to finally get home. Just inside the building's front door, she checked her mailbox, which was empty, then stepped inside the elevator.

"Hey!" Marion rushed in just behind her, flushed and smiling. "My goodness! Where have you been? I've been looking for you for days now. How are you doing?"

Sassy gave a weak shrug and tried to look happy, but she was uncomfortably aware of the beads of sweat popping up on her brow.

"Oh, nothing much. I've been out, you know, working and"—she lifted the envelope in her hand—"and dealing with lawyer things. You know. Stuff like that."

Marion looked unsure, and Sassy felt even more embarrassed. Not only was Marion smart, she was a psychiatrist. She would easily see right through her flimsy excuses. She poked the button for the fifth floor a few times, trying to convince herself that if she could get up there fast, she could disappear again and avoid the conversation she knew was coming.

"How are you doing?" Marion asked again. It was not just a passing question. She *really* wanted to know.

Sassy *really* didn't want to tell her. She kept her gaze on the elevator buttons. "I'm fine. How are you?"

The elevator chugged past the second floor. Only three more to go.

Marion frowned at her. "What's going on, Sassy?"

She forced a laugh as they left the third floor behind. "Nothing! Everything's cool. I'm just, you know, getting by. Getting used to being an orphan and all that."

At last, the fifth floor. Sassy practically tumbled out the door.

"Sassy, I—"

She couldn't stand it. She thought she might explode from all the tension inside, so she wheeled on her friend. "Let it go, Marion. I'm fine, okay? Don't flip your wig. I've been busy, that's all."

She bugged out down the hall, aware that Mr. Snoop's door had clicked open. Sassy wanted to die. He was listening. Probably the whole floor was listening. All she needed now was for the other neighbours to come out and ask what was going on.

"Sassy," Marion said behind her.

Sassy kept her gaze straight ahead and aimed for her door. No way would she let Marion see the tears streaming down her face. She pulled out her key as she approached, opened the door, and stepped inside . . . But she couldn't close it over Marion's planted boot. Reluctantly, she met her friend's furious gaze.

"What is happening?"

Sassy closed her eyes. "I . . . I can't talk to you, Marion."

"What? Why? What did I do? And why are you crying?"

"You didn't do anything." Her face burned. "I just don't know what to say to you."

Marion's jaw dropped. "You aren't talking about the other day, are you? What the lawyer read? No. You can't have been thinking about that all this time." Her lips tightened. "Step aside. I'm coming in."

Before she could object, Marion strode past her into Sassy's living room and spun around to face her.

"Do you want wine?" Sassy asked, walking directly to the kitchen. She kept her gaze anywhere but at Marion, who looked pissed. She'd never seen Marion pissed before. She was pretty intimidating that way.

"I don't know. Will we need wine?"

"I'm getting two glasses."

She poured, and when she returned to the living room, Marion was inspecting one of her paintings, hands behind her back. She didn't turn around. She was forcing Sassy to start the conversation, and Sassy had to admit, that was only fair.

"I'm sorry," she whispered.

Marion faced her, but she wasn't smiling.

Sassy held out her full glass, her face warm with shame. Marion glared into Sassy's eyes and made no move to take it.

"I really am sorry," Sassy said. "I've been acting like an idiot. I've been afraid to talk with you about what happened."

Marion's eyes narrowed. "So I was right. You've been hiding from me."

"Yes."

Marion accepted the glass and took a long drink, never looking away. "Why?"

"I'm so embarrassed, Marion. Everyone was going on about what a great man my father was, when all the while it was really *your* father. I bragged in front of you, and I probably said mean things without meaning to, and it all came back to hit me in the face. I just . . . I'm so sorry. I didn't know how to talk with you about it."

Marion sipped again. "First, why on earth would you be embarrassed? This has nothing to do with you and me. I mean, yes, we heard some surprising things—you could have knocked me right over when I learned about my father. All my life, I'd never known. Just like you."

"Weren't you furious at him for lying to you?"

Marion inhaled. "Let's sit. We should have been talking about this from the start."

The weight that had been pulling Sassy under for days was gone the moment they sat together on the cherry-red couch. What had she been thinking, questioning how Marion would regard her after all those revelations? She should have trusted their friendship.

"I spoke with my father about it that day," Marion said, setting her glass down. "Yes, I was angry. I felt like I didn't know him at all, and I'm thirty-one. But everyone has a right to their own secrets. There are reasons they're called secrets, and we don't always get to know them. Finding out the truth about my dad was upsetting, but it didn't change who he is at all. And yet, when he told me his reasons for what he did, I saw him differently. I'm proud of my dad, but I was proud of him before. So the only reason I had to be angry was that he hadn't told me his secret. And there was no reason he should. It was his."

Marion always had such a beautiful way of thinking of things. Sassy envied her that. Every time they finished a serious conversation, she felt like she understood herself and everything around her a little better. Marion was a better person than she was. A better friend.

"The thing is, Sassy, it's never been a competition."

Marion also read her mind sometimes. That was a little alarming.

"Our fathers reached an agreement, and they were both satisfied with what they got out of it. They were friends, not competitors. Just like you and me." Marion exhaled. "On that note, I wish I could have met your father, just so I could thank him for paying for my education. He changed my life! He made it possible for me to follow my passion and find my purpose. My parents never could have afforded med school."

Tears welled in Sassy's eyes. "I'm glad he did that. He owed your dad. And it was the right thing to do."

Marion shook her head. "Your dad didn't have to do what he did, writing that letter for the will. I think he suffered much more than my father ever did over the arrangement. He would have felt guilty for carrying on with the illusion, but he respected my father too much to challenge their agreement. He set the record straight without embarrassing my father. Don't you see that was a final kindness in a long line of kindnesses?

"And he did so much more," Marion continued. "He paid for Hank Moore's apartment, he helped the Romanos when they came to Canada, and I'm fairly sure he did something for the Levins as well. He's the reason I'm living in this building, so he's the reason I met you." She drained her wineglass. "Your dad was a good man. He just didn't want anyone to know it."

Sassy let all of it sink in. As usual, Marion was right.

"As soon as I found out, I wanted to apologize for my father," she said, "but I didn't know how. I felt sick about his lie, and I was so embarrassed. But I get it now. I've only embarrassed myself. So now, what I am really apologizing for is not trusting our friendship enough to talk with you about it. That was a pretty stupid thing to do."

Marion nodded, smiling through a sheen of tears. "Yes, it was. Apology accepted."

"Oh, good. Because I have missed you so, so much."

thirty
MARION

❧

Marion hadn't heard from Paul in over a week. He had promised to contact her as soon as he heard anything about the Red Cross, but the anticipation was killing her. She called him four times, but he never picked up the phone. At one point, she considered going to his house.

The next day, the phone rang.

"Marion, it's Paul. I can't believe I'm saying this, but I found a way for you to get to Vietnam, if your heart's still set on it."

She felt the earth move beneath her. "Of course it is."

"Willard was set to go, but he broke his leg skiing. He agrees with me that you're crazy, but I told him that if you had your mind set on being a VPVN, he wasn't going to be able to talk you out of it. So he spoke with the CRC about you. Since you haven't gotten blood on your hands in a while, he told them you are basically a very advanced surgical student. Apparently, they're so desperate for doctors, they agreed." He waited. "Marion? You still there?"

"I . . . I am."

"I have all the information here for you, but there's one issue that could mess things up. Obviously, it's not safe for a woman to travel alone to Vietnam then work in a combat zone. Especially a civilian like you, who basically has no idea how to take care of herself."

"Hey!"

"So the Red Cross is trying to find someone to go with you. Basically, a bodyguard. They are speaking with some of their volunteers this week about it. Trouble is, that person will have to pay their own way."

Daniel's words flashed in her mind. *If you change your mind about going, I'd be the best security guard you could imagine.* She almost laughed. If only she knew where he was.

"They will find someone," she said, positive. Everything about this trip felt so right. There was no way any of it could go wrong.

"I gotta say, Marion, I really am impressed. These are not the actions of the woman I took to dinner months ago."

That made her smile. "I certainly hope not. All right, Paul. Tell me what I need to know. I have paper and a pen."

Marion's hand was damp as she wrote down all the information. She hoped she could read her writing later.

"Paul, I can't thank you enough."

"Thank me when you come back alive, all right? I'll even let you buy dinner this time."

She hung up then looked in the mirror. "Guess what, Dr. Hart?" she said, unsure whether to laugh or cry. "I hope you remember how to stitch up a body, because you're going to Vietnam."

thirty-one
SASSY

❧

The phone rang, and Sassy reached for it, distracted by a form she'd been reading. "Good afternoon. Rankin Real Estate. How may I help you?"

"Sassy? Is that you? You sound so serious!"

"Marion! Far out. You never call me at work. What's up?"

"I got some news today, and I can't wait until tonight to talk with you about it. Do you have some time?"

"Of course. It's just me here right now."

"Okay. Um, it's pretty big news."

"Let me have it."

"After the funeral, I did a lot of thinking, and I've made a pretty radical decision. Um, you know how I'm always saying I wish I had more courage? Well, I think I just claimed the lion's share."

"What are you talking about?"

"Are you sitting down?"

"Don't freak me out, Marion."

"I don't think I'm going to be able to prevent that this time."

"What are you talking about?" Sassy repeated.

Marion took a deep breath. "Because of this Tet Offensive, the Canadian

Red Cross announced that they need more doctors in Vietnam. So I made a phone call to find out more."

Silence. "You're not thinking of going."

"I am. I know it probably won't help Joey, but—"

"No one in their right mind would let a woman go to Vietnam."

"Did you know there are thousands of American nurses down there?"

Sassy couldn't actually register that news right now. "I did not."

"Nobody talks about them, but it's true. Anyhow, I just got a phone call, and I . . . I've been approved. I'm going to Vietnam in a couple of weeks. I will be there for two months."

Sassy stared at nothing, trying to make sense of what she'd just heard.

"Sassy?"

"This . . . this is for real?" She got up and strode to the window, needing to move. "Like, you're actually going down there?"

"I really am."

Sassy's gaze dropped to the street beyond, mushy with melting snow. "But you're not a surgeon."

"No, but I have surgical experience, and they're pretty desperate. The Red Cross has approved it, as long as they can find a volunteer bodyguard to come with me." She hesitated. "Sassy?"

"Sorry!" Sassy returned to her desk and sat with a thump. She picked up a pen and started drawing circles on a pad of paper to keep her hands busy. "I'm not thinking straight right now. I was imagining that my best friend just told me she's going to Vietnam in a couple of weeks."

Marion's nervous laughter tinkled through the phone. "Far out, huh?"

"That's heavy, Marion. Are you sure about this? How do you feel?"

The line was quiet for a beat. "Excited, pleased that they actually agreed to it, but kind of in shock, I guess. I'm a little scared, too."

"You'd be nuts if you weren't."

"It feels surreal. I keep saying it out loud to myself. 'I'm going to the Vietnam War.' I'm not sure it's really sunk in yet."

"It's so massive, Marion. Help me understand. Why are you doing this?"

Marion took a breath, then she said, "First, because I'm a doctor and I believe

I can help. Second, and maybe more important, I'm going because you're my friend. I haven't thanked you for everything you've done for me, and now I can."

"I haven't done anything."

"You just don't know what you've done, because it comes so naturally to you. When you took me to places and shows and introduced me to people, you were giving me a whole new outlook on life. The way you enjoy life has changed who I am. I think that because of what you have given me, I am now the kind of person who would like to test herself and do something good at the same time."

"Marion! Stop that!" she cried, sobbing. "You've given me so much, too. I've never thanked you, either."

"You just did."

Adrenaline shot back into Sassy's bloodstream. "But I don't want you to go! What if something happens? I can't lose you, too!"

"I will be fine."

"Gosh," Sassy said, leaning back in her chair. Marion was calm. Sassy needed to get to that state, too, and Marion had taught her how. She exhaled slowly, counting to four. "All right, Marion. I will try to believe that. What can I do to help? I know. We'll get you some new threads for the jungle. Shopping this Saturday."

"Good idea."

The door to the office opened, catching her attention. "Tom's here. I'd better hang up. Can I tell him?"

"Sure."

She swept the tears off her face with her sleeve, sniffing loudly. "See you tonight? My place?"

"I'll be there."

Tom was checking his mail as he approached, picking through envelopes without watching where he was going. It gave her the opportunity to admire his navy-blue herringbone jacket, unbuttoned over nicely fitted dark trousers. He'd loosened his blue-striped tie so he could undo the top button of his crisp white shirt. He didn't like wearing ties, he had confided once. Coats were fine, but ties made him feel like he was on a leash.

She cleared her throat, stopping him from walking into her desk.

"Oh, hey," he said, popping out of his stupor. "How was your morning?"

"I can't even think straight. Marion just called me. She had the craziest news."

While she told him the story, she watched his expression soften from polite interest to bewilderment then harden to concern.

"To a war zone?" he asked in disbelief. "What is she thinking?"

"I'm so proud of her," Sassy said softly. "She's braver than I'll ever be."

"Braver than me," Tom agreed. "You said she's a psychiatrist, right? Doesn't it seem ironic to either of you that a shrink is doing something so insane?"

She laughed. "We're both aware."

He stood back and folded his arms, thinking through those dazzling blue eyes. "I'm going to make a donation to the Red Cross to help her out."

Gratitude rose in her chest. "That's righteous, Tom."

"I'm sure it costs a lot to send volunteer doctors. And all the medicine and machines."

"I hadn't thought of that. The financial aspect. But I am learning to think more like that every day, thanks to you and Marion. And Dad. I'll donate, too." Then a thought struck her, and she paused. "Actually, I have an idea."

"What?"

She faced her desk, seeing nothing but the ideas her mind was suddenly bringing to light.

"Sassy? What's the idea?"

She smiled vaguely at him. "I'll let you know when I figure out the details."

The idea stayed with her all day, feeling more promising by the hour. As soon as she was done at work, she got on the bus and went straight to Chez Monique to see Davey. If anyone could do what she was thinking, it would be him.

Thinking about Davey led to more thoughts of Tom. What was she going to do about Tom? She was way over her head with that guy, she'd realized. Normally, she wouldn't have hesitated to approach an attractive man with questionable suggestions about what they could do together, but not this time. There was something different about Tom. His regard for her meant so much. He respected her. Through Tom, she had begun to see a different, more mature image of herself. And that had helped her understand how important it was to offer respect in return.

Then again, if he wanted more from her, all he had to do was ask.

The coffeehouse was filling up when she arrived. She asked for Davey, and he came out with a big grin, wiping his hands on a tomato-stained apron.

"Sass! God, it's groovy to see you, man!" He wrapped her in a bear hug. "Out of sight!"

"Can we sit for a sec?"

He asked one of the servers to bring over some coffee, and she heard him quietly promise that he was taking only a short break with an old friend. Then he led Sassy to an empty table and leaned on his elbows, giving her that undivided attention she remembered so fondly.

"You first," she said, pretty sure her news would take longer than whatever he had to say. "What's going on with you? How's TADP?"

"Busy, man. So good."

"How's Christine?"

His mouth twisted to the side. "She flaked off, man. Yeah. She was, like, totally into Ned. Remember him? Guy looks like a beaver, man."

Her heart squeezed with sympathy. "She never deserved you, Davey."

"I should've stayed with you. I was always happy when I was with you." His brow lifted. "Speaking of which . . ."

"That train has left the station, bud."

He slumped a little. "My fault. Huge mistake."

"It's okay," she assured him. "You're gonna find a little fox soon. I know it."

"Enough about me. Sock it to me, Sass. What's up?"

She took in a deep breath, and it shuddered. "There's a lot, honestly."

Concern flooded his eyes. "I'm here for you, man."

She thought she had herself under control. She didn't. Her throat closed up like a necktie that kept tightening. In a heartbeat, Davey was around the table and crouched beside her, and she clung to his hug, crying like a baby.

"I got you, babe," he said. "I'm here. What happened?"

"So much," she said, sitting up and swiping tears off her face. "I have to thank you, Davey. I didn't get a chance before. Thanks for coming to my dad's funeral. It meant a lot to me, seeing you there."

"Of course I was gonna be there."

"We didn't really get to talk about what happened. Weren't you curious?"

He gave her a light shrug. "Only if you want to tell me. Honestly, it's none of my business. I was just there for you."

She knew he'd say that, but she decided she wanted him to know the rest. "He was drinking a ton before it happened. You know, after Joey went missing and all. The night he died, he was wasted, and he drove his car into a building." She squeezed her eyes shut for a beat. "I hate thinking this, but I feel like he crashed his car on purpose."

"No! Why would he do that?"

"He had too much on his mind. I don't think he knew what to do," she said with a sniff. "After Joey went missing, I think my dad lost control. I went to see him at the house, and I found, like, so many empty booze bottles."

She considered telling him about the lie she'd lived with her whole life, thinking her father was such a hero, then finding out it hadn't been him after all. Did she really want to get into that? Another time, she decided.

"Oh, man. Sass, I am so sorry. How's your brother? Any news on him?"

"Nothing."

She grabbed a napkin and blew her nose, then she stared at the tabletop until her emotions calmed. Once she felt able to speak again, she offered Davey a cautious smile.

"So there's some crazy good news, too."

"Go on."

"Marion has gone and done the wildest thing."

Davey's expression was almost comical when she told him about Marion going to Vietnam. She couldn't help laughing at him, which was something she sorely needed. She thanked the server when the coffee arrived, then she poured in a teaspoon of sugar.

He shook his head the whole time she stirred it in. "That is far out."

"I know. She's amazing." She deliberated about how much to say about Tom and her feelings for him, then she decided to stick to the point. "When I told my boss, he said he was going to make a donation to the Canadian Red Cross to help her get over there. So then I started thinking how great you are at organizing things with the TADP, you know? Putting things together? And I wondered—"

"Right on! Yeah!" he exclaimed, grinning. "I totally get what you're gonna say. Let's have a party and make some money for Marion and the Red Cross. Leave it to me, babe." He slammed his palm on the table, excited. "Oh, man! I know exactly who to call. I got some singers, that weird poet—remember him? And you—tell me you'll perform, please. I miss your singing so bad."

"You are amazing, Davey," she said, her throat in a knot. "Of course I'll sing. You figure out when you want to do this, and I'll use my dad's mimeograph to print off posters."

"It's gonna be righteous, Sass."

Davey made piles of apologies, saying he had to get back to work, so Sassy wrapped her bright orange scarf around her face and headed out, leaning into the cold wind as she walked home from Chez Monique. Her mind was going a hundred miles an hour, thinking about Marion, then about the plans she and Davey were pulling together, but she was totally stoked. No, a fundraising concert for the Red Cross wasn't going to bring either Joey or her father back, but the love she was feeling from her friends felt almost overwhelming.

How could she have gotten through the past couple weeks without Marion?

The wind sheared across the street, whipping her scarf loose, but she grabbed it before it took off. Deciding to take a shortcut where the wind might not find her as easily, she turned a corner into an alley, and a patch of ice caught her boot heel. She wheeled her arms, trying to stay upright, but just as she managed to regain control, one of the transients sitting on the sidewalk lunged for her. She drew back with a cry, more afraid of him than of the ice. Then she saw the side of his horribly scarred face, and she walked away so fast it was almost a jog. After half a block, she slowed and glanced back, but he wasn't following. She saw the vague outline of his body, sunken back onto the sidewalk, curled in on himself to protect his face from the wind. Relieved that she'd escaped unscathed, she faced forward again and cut around another big patch of ice, keen to get home and safe.

There were a lot of people living on sidewalks and in parks now, and she found herself feeling divided every time she saw one. Winter in Toronto was brutal, and more than once she'd wished she could invite some of those men out of the cold so they could warm up in the apartment's front lobby, but she didn't. Right now, she was very glad of that, having narrowly avoided the scarred man's grasp.

She looked back again, wondering about him. Thank goodness she'd paid attention to Marion's explanation about the institutions shutting down. A few of the patients who were being released, she'd said, could be very dangerous. Better that she avoid any of the transients she saw, she figured.

She crossed the street, concentrating on maintaining her balance as she navigated the ice in her high-heeled boots, so she was unprepared when two arms clamped around her chest from behind. She screamed, squirming in her attacker's grip, but she couldn't anchor her boots on the ice. He dragged her backward, and she kept wrestling, but he was so strong she couldn't move.

"Let me go!" she shrieked. She curled her mittens into claws around his arms, trying to pry them off her, but he barely seemed to notice. "Somebody! Help me!"

Still trudging backward, her attacker clamped one hand over her mouth. "Quiet," he said, his voice a light singsong. "Let's go play, pretty kitty."

"Help!" she screamed against his cold hand, petrified now. "Let me go! Do you want money? I can give you money!"

"Quiet!" he roared, and she burst helplessly into tears.

Her cry was cut off when the man jerked backward and suddenly released her. Sassy dropped to all fours in the snow, wheezing and gasping for air.

"*Dung lai!*" a man yelled. "*Dung lai!*"

A woman nearby shouted, "I'm calling the police!"

With her world still spinning, Sassy stared in disbelief as two big men faced off beside her. Both were menacing, wearing almost matching, dingy winter coats, black wool caps, and tattered boots. Which one had grabbed her? Could the other really be defending her? Or was he just there to fight? As soon as she could breathe, she told herself she'd get up and run.

The larger of the two had a long, thick beard, and he hunched like a grizzly, with his legs bowed. His arms dangled at his sides, and he barely flinched when the other man drove his fist into his stomach. The only sign that he'd felt anything was the emergence of a loose-jawed smile within his beard and a faint sound she thought might be a laugh. He lurched forward, and the smaller man—who still had to be over six feet tall—punched the grizzly's face so hard Sassy heard a snap. The man stumbled back, rubbing his jawline with a big paw and frowning with bewilderment.

"Done?" the other man barked, but the grizzly shoved him to the ground then dropped on top of him. Sassy caught a flash of metal, then she glimpsed the tip of a blade aimed at the smaller man's throat. Both men's hands gripped its handle, and the blade shook from the tension between them. Suddenly, the man on the bottom snarled, his teeth a slit of white in his grimy face, and he thrust all four of their hands straight up so their arms were extended over his head. That threw the grizzly off balance, and the man on the bottom took advantage. He rolled on top and took control, resting the tip of the blade against the man's wide, hairy neck.

"*Dung lai!*" he repeated. When the grizzly didn't stop struggling, he tried again. "Stop moving, or I'll drive this through your miserable throat."

The man on the ground went limp, and the other one turned his face toward Sassy. There it was, that awful scarring that had made her want to run. Up close, she realized he was wearing an eye patch as well. His fingers were dark, almost burgundy, sticking out of fingerless gloves.

"You okay?" he asked.

"Thank you," she squeezed out. "I think you just saved my life."

He scowled down at her attacker. "Who are you?"

The man's mouth hung open slackly while he considered the eye-patch man. "John. I'm John."

"What were you doing?"

"Walking. Taking kitty for a walk."

Lifting his lip with disgust, the eye-patch man got to his feet. When the big man began to move, he placed his boot firmly on his throat.

"Don't," he said calmly.

The big man did not budge until the sound of a siren split the air. Even then, no one moved until a policeman jumped out of the car and pointed his gun directly at the smaller man.

"The other one," Sassy told him, pointing. "This guy saved me from that one."

The muzzle of the gun shifted to the man on the ground.

"I don't know how to thank you," Sassy said as the eye-patch man helped her up.

"No need. You okay?"

"Just scared, I guess. He came out of nowhere."

He eyed the captive as handcuffs clasped around the thick wrists. "I think he's *dien cai dao*."

"Um, what?"

"Sorry." He dropped his hands into his coat pockets. "Vietnamese for 'crazy in the head.'"

"You speak—" She stared at him, unexpectedly aware. The only reason someone like him would know Vietnamese was if he had been there. That would explain—would Joey come back with a scar like that?

"Heart!" John shouted. "Heart! Heart!"

"What's the matter with you?" the policeman demanded. He shot a bemused look at the other two, but John kept yelling.

"Heart! Heart! Doctor! Heart! Doctor!"

"You in pain, mister? You ain't having a heart attack or nothing, are you?"

"Heart! Doctor! Heart!"

The man with the eye patch perked up then strode over to John. "Dr. Hart?"

"Dr. Hart! Dr. Hart!"

Sassy's jaw dropped. Why would he—she stopped, stunned. Could this be one of Marion's patients released from the institution?

Some will be all right. Others can be extremely dangerous.

The policeman studied both men. "You know what this is all about?"

"He's from the institute on Queen Street," the one-eyed man replied. "I need to find his doctor. She'll know what to do with him. I don't think he understands what's going on, honestly. But hang on tight to him. He's dangerous."

The police car drove off with John in the back. Sassy watched them turn down the next street, still dazed.

"I gotta make a telephone call," the eye-patch man said to Sassy. "Can you lend me a dime?"

"Uh, yeah. Of course." She dug in her purse. "I'm Sassy, by the way. And you are . . . ?"

"Daniel." He glanced around. "I need to find a phone booth."

Daniel! Of all the men in this city, she'd just been rescued by Marion's Daniel? "Let me buy you a coffee instead," she said, unable to contain her grin. "It's the least I can do. We'll call from there."

"You don't have to—"

"No, no. I insist." She shook her head with wonder. "I'm dying to hear how you know my best friend, Marion Hart."

thirty-two
MARION

Marion had just finished tidying her apartment and was sitting down to make a dent in *The Bell Jar* when the telephone rang, and Sassy's incredulous voice burst through. Stunned, Marion listened to her account of the attack, then asked after Sassy's well-being.

"Never mind that," Sassy said quickly. "I'll tell you about it when you get here. You gotta come right away. There's a guy here with an eye patch, says his name is Daniel . . ."

Marion clutched the receiver to her ear. "Where are you, Sassy? I'll be right there."

Daniel.

She hung up then rushed to her room, heart pounding. How should she look when she saw him? Not like a doctor, she decided. She was no longer his, so why carry on like that? She peered into the mirror, feeling like a nervous teenager. Sassy said she liked Marion's hair down, so with her heart pounding in her temples, she brushed out the long blond tresses then pulled on a light blue sweater that Sassy had insisted she borrow. Feeling bold, she followed her friend's instructions with the new makeup she'd purchased, though she wasn't ready for false eyelashes.

"Not bad," she said, blinking at her reflection.

Long ago, in that cramped elevator, Sassy had asked Marion what scared her the most. She was afraid, she reluctantly admitted, that she was missing out. Well, she wasn't going to miss out this time. She grabbed her winter coat and scarf, wriggled into her boots, then stepped out and locked her door. The adrenaline streaming through her made her feel like a whole different woman.

She headed for the bank of elevators and heard the mystery neighbour's door click open then close, just in time to block her view of the inhabitant. Marion didn't care. She was going to see Daniel. What a world, where Sassy and Daniel were having coffee together, waiting for her!

She decided not to wait for a bus and hailed a taxi instead. The driver pulled in front of the Riverboat Coffee House, and Marion descended the set of stairs. Paul would be impressed that she'd finally gotten in, she thought.

She spotted Sassy waving to her from a table at the corner of the room. Across from her sat Daniel, and he rose when he saw her. Marion couldn't get to them fast enough. Sassy had already assured her that she was fine, so she evaluated Daniel as she wove between tables and chairs. He looked all right, she thought, but he could definitely use a shower and a haircut. His coat was draped over the back of his chair, and despite the dimness of the room, she saw his shirt was dirty. Was she imagining it, or was he thinner than he'd been a month ago?

"I thought I would never see you again," she said, holding out her hands.

He took them. "This city's so big," he agreed.

"I disagree! It's a small world after all!" Sassy put in, wiggling her eyebrows at Marion. "This is far out. Come and sit. You two can talk, and I'll get us some coffee."

Marion's brain went straight to doctor mode. She couldn't start with questions about his living conditions. Not yet. Those might be answered defensively, and she didn't want to begin on the wrong foot.

"Sassy said you saved her life. I can't believe it. I mean, I believe you are capable of it, but how incredible that the two of you even met up. What happened?"

Daniel turned to the side to cough, and Marion noticed his eye patch looked dirty. That couldn't be healthy. She would get him a new one.

"I was going to find a phone and a phone book to call you, but Sassy reached you first," he said.

"Why were you going to phone me?"

"What happened actually involves you. You're going to need to intervene with the cops somehow. You remember a patient called Big John? Because he sure remembers you."

John! "Of course I do. How is he?"

"He's currently behind bars for attacking your friend."

Marion felt the blood rush from her face to her toes. She glanced toward the coffee bar, where Sassy stood. "John did that? Is she all right?"

"Seems to be fine. Just, well, a bit shocked. She's tough."

"I warned the board that John was dangerous," she said, her voice sharp with anger. "I can't tell you how many reports I filed, but they still released him. I'm not surprised he attacked someone. I just wish it hadn't been Sassy."

"What'll happen to him now?"

"There might be space for him back at the institute in one of the smaller buildings. They are putting the most severe cases in there for now. I'll make sure he gets the care he needs. But poor Sassy. She must have been terrified. And you—she was right. You're a hero."

He rolled his eye. "Not exactly. Just good timing."

Sassy was still at the bar, chatting with a waitress, purposefully taking her time. Bless the girl. Marion took a calming breath and tried to think more clearly.

"Tell me about you," she said, holding his gaze. "How have you been?"

The one-shoulder lift. "Same old. You?"

"No. You don't get off that easy. I've thought of you constantly since you left the hospital. Tell me what it's like for you out here."

"I'd rather not." When she didn't look away, he sighed. "I'm still the enemy, it's just a different battlefield. When people find out I've been in Vietnam, they call me a baby killer. Me! One guy spat at me." He dropped his chin. "I spent a night in jail after I pounded him senseless."

To be alone, targeted and traumatized, was too much for anyone to take sober. She wondered if he was drinking, but when she leaned in, she didn't smell it on him.

"The news hasn't done the returning soldiers a service, that's for sure," she said. "I'm sorry you had to go through that. Where have you been living?"

"Here and there."

Nowhere, she thought with alarm. "Do you have a job?"

"Nope." He scowled. "Don't tell me to get one, either. I'll find one when I'm good and ready."

"Have you been taking your—"

"Not all the time, no." He dropped his gaze to the wooden table between them and followed a crack with one finger. "I . . . I had a bad night a couple of days ago, and I took a couple extra pills. Poor choice. So I stopped taking them altogether."

Marion was holding her breath, trying not to visualize what he'd done. She watched his finger slide across the tabletop. "And how has that been?"

He kept his gaze averted. "Let it go, Marion. I'm all right. I can do it. 'Nam was worse. Just not so cold."

His hands were dry and cracked from living outside. She longed to reach over and warm them in hers.

"I'll get you some warm gloves. Those ones look useless."

"You don't have to."

She gave him a gentle smile, though he still wasn't looking at her. "I may not officially be your doctor anymore, but that doesn't mean I can't try to take care of you."

At last, he lifted his gaze to hers, and she saw something sad in its depths. Or was it fear? Resignation? It reminded her of when he told her how useless he felt, stuck in the hospital instead of being with his friends in the jungle, facing death.

"I wouldn't say no to that," he said quietly.

Her heart squeezed, hearing his pain. "You'll be okay. I'm with you now."

Sassy returned to the table with coffee and a plate, which she set between them on the table. "They had some groovy-looking butter cakes up at the counter, so I got us each a slice. Go ahead, Daniel. I want to hear how it is. You first."

His mouth turned in a way that suggested he felt awkward taking the first one, but he was clearly hungry. Marion turned to Sassy, giving him privacy, and from the corner of her eye she saw him practically inhale the cake. She held her friend's gaze, and a silent solution was agreed upon.

"That looks so good," Marion said, reaching for a slice. "Thanks, Sassy. Are you okay? I hate that you had to go through what you did. How awful." She took a bite, and her lips twisted. "Do you like this, Daniel? I'm sorry, Sassy. It was nice of you to buy it, but this is too sweet . . . I don't like it."

She held it out to Daniel.

"You sure?" he asked, then the slice disappeared.

Sassy happily passed hers to him as well.

"When's the last time you ate?" Marion asked gently.

"Yesterday? The day before? I don't remember. Doesn't matter."

"Of course it does," Marion said, hurting for him. "You matter."

"More coffee, please!" Sassy said, holding up a finger for the waitress. "And maybe some apple pie? Oh, yes. Three big slices. With ice cream, if you have it. Thank you."

Daniel dropped his gaze, clearly embarrassed.

"I just came from Chez Monique," Sassy said, keeping the conversation off Daniel. "I went to see Davey at work."

"You haven't mentioned him in a while," Marion noted.

"No, I . . . I had an idea I wanted to ask him about."

"Sassy's been having a tough time lately." She glanced at her friend. "Do you want to tell him?"

Sassy bit her lower lip. "My brother's missing in Vietnam."

Daniel straightened. "Missing? Recently? Where was he last?"

"Somewhere around Nha Trang. I'm not good at geography," she admitted, "but I don't think that's a great place to be."

He leaned back in his chair. "No, it isn't. Who is he with?"

"He's a marine. First Battalion, Third Marines."

The change that came over Daniel's expression was immediate. His whole face opened up, seeking information. "What's his name?"

"Joey. Joey Rankin."

Daniel froze in place, his mouth slightly open.

Marion couldn't look away. "Daniel? What is it?"

"First Battalion, Third Marines. That's my unit." He swallowed and looked directly at Marion. His eye shone with a new light. "Joey's one of my boys."

Nobody moved, then Sassy looked directly at Marion, willing her to ask the obvious. Marion couldn't believe what she was about to say.

"Daniel, I have something to tell you."

He waited, staying perfectly still. In contrast, Marion was suddenly vibrating inside.

"I am going with the Red Cross to Vietnam."

He blinked. "You're going to 'Nam?"

"I am. But the next part's even harder to believe. The only way they'll let me go is if I have a bodyguard."

Daniel was entirely focused on Marion. From the corner of her eye, Marion saw Sassy beaming.

"I'm sorry," he said calmly, though she sensed the elation behind his neutral expression. "What, exactly, are you telling me?"

"I'm not telling you anything." She took a deep breath, still holding his gaze. "I'm asking you."

He lifted his chin, the quietest sort of smile coming to his lips. "Then ask."

It was harder than she thought it would be. The absolute best thing would be for Marion to have Daniel by her side, and they both knew it. But what she was asking of him, especially after all his troubles, went way beyond—despite the fact that he wanted to go back to his unit more than anything.

"I am asking an impossible question. I know you're ready to jump in headfirst, but I need to know something vital. Only you can answer it. Daniel, are you well enough to go with me? I would need to know I could count on you every step of the way."

He did not leap in with an exuberant yes, as she'd half feared he would. Nor did he show uncertainty, as he had every right to do. Instead, tranquility descended upon him like a veil.

"Vietnam will do all it can to kill you, Marion. I will be your shield."

PART THREE

You don't have to save me, you just have to hold my hand
while I save myself.

—Unknown

thirty-three
MARION

— March 1968 —

Marion stood paralyzed at the Toronto Airport departure gate for Canadian Pacific Air Lines, sweat rolling down the sides of her face. The passengers behind her had chosen not to wait any longer, so she had become an island, jostled between two rivers of impatient travelers. She apologized to every one of them, but she couldn't make her feet move either forward to board or back to the safety of the waiting area.

Daniel was late. Had something happened?

Marion was living a nightmare of her own creation. Ever since the idea had dropped into her head that she should go to Vietnam, she had been flitting around like a chickadee, uncertain where to land. The whole idea of boarding a plane and flying thousands of miles to get to a jungle where hospitals were blown up all the time had seemed exciting and heroic. Now it just seemed stupid. And if Daniel didn't show up, she'd be doing it all on her own.

"Hey." Daniel's face appeared in her peripheral vision. "Sorry I'm late."

She turned to face him. "It's okay," she managed breathlessly. "I've decided not to go."

He glanced toward the desk, where the line of passengers was dwindling.

Everyone else was already on board. "Too bad, Doc. We're up. Can't hold up the entire plane."

Still, her feet felt rooted to the weathered carpet. The first stop in their journey would be Japan. It struck her that her life would be complete without seeing Japan.

"We're gonna be fine, Marion. What's scaring you?"

"To start, I've never been on an airplane before."

"This is the easy part of the trip."

"That does not fill me with confidence."

"Well, we're not walking to Vietnam." She jumped when his hand curled over her shoulder. "What did you tell me, months ago? Something about taking deep breaths and picturing yourself on solid ground, I believe. Picture yourself sitting in a relatively comfortable seat beside me, possibly getting a glass of wine from a stewardess, if they're serving. You don't even have to sit by the window if you don't want."

"My ticket says I'm sitting by the window," she said, reaching for any excuse she could find.

"Let me see. Aha." He kept ahold of it and handed her his ticket instead. "Now it says you aren't. So you can choose. Come on, Marion. Time to practice what you preach. They're waiting."

She kept her eyes squeezed shut and her hands like claws over the armrests as the Boeing 707 rocked and bumped, picking up speed on the runway. Then she felt a sense of lift in her stomach. Almost like the elevator on Isabella, but way stronger.

"Open your eyes," Daniel said gently.

In the end, he had talked her into taking the seat by the window, and now she gawked beyond it. Buildings and cars rushed beneath them, becoming tinier with every second.

"How fast are we going?" she asked in a whisper.

"For takeoff, I think it's around two fifty or three hundred miles per hour. Up here, cruising speed is double that."

For a full minute, she stared out the window. The minuscule city and the surrounding farms shrank away gradually then were gone all at once when the plane entered the clouds. She felt a jump, as if the plane had gone over a hurdle, then a drop that left her breathless, and she wondered if she might get sick. Or if she was about to die.

"Air currents," Daniel explained. "They come and go. If the weather gets bad, the pilot will probably reroute. This is just a light cloud cover, I think."

She took some long, deep breaths, letting her body sink into the seat cushion, then she became aware that Daniel was humming softly to himself. When she turned toward him, he was leaning back, facing the ceiling, his eye closed.

"Who sings that?" she asked, admiring his profile.

"The Box Tops. I think it's called 'The Letter.' Heard of them?"

She hadn't, but she'd heard the song. "You have a smile on your face, Daniel."

"Do I?" He kept his eye shut. "I'm on a high like you wouldn't believe, Doc."

This was the first time she'd seen him truly relaxed. Ever since she'd asked him to go with her, he'd been a different man. Cool, efficient, and resolute, reminding her that he was, in every sense but nationality, a marine. He was driven, focused on details, and paying close attention to whatever she said. Everything to do with the journey was now his priority, and he took that very seriously.

It had all happened so quickly. Due to the nature of their travel, her passport and their two visas had been expedited by External Affairs, and she carried a letter of introduction from the External Aid Office of the government of Canada, certifying that they were going to Vietnam as Canadian Red Cross medical specialists. The letter was formally embossed by the national commissioner. To make today worse, Marion still suffered aftereffects of the vaccines and immunizations she'd taken against yellow fever and cholera, two deep muscle injections of immune gamma globulin, and pills for antimalarials, including quinine. Daniel was sympathetic. He was spared the shots, since he'd already gone through them a couple of years before.

He didn't have much in the way of clothes, so they went to the military surplus store to outfit them both. She had been issued a light blue gown and a white apron with a red cross on the front, but Daniel shook his head at that.

"Makes you a target," he said. "You can wear it for these folks here, but we're going to get you something more practical for real life."

When she first saw him in olive camouflage, his black lace boots shining, wearing a flat-brimmed hat he called a "boonie," he seemed larger. He was definitely more confident, as if he'd slipped back into his skin. He'd insisted she dress similarly. She felt silly pulling on trousers made for a small man then tucking in the tail of an olive shirt, but he approved, and that was good enough for her. He found her a boonie as well, then he opened her eyes to yet another threat of their destination when he attached a suffocating mosquito netting to the hat.

The next day he brought her to a shooting range outside of the city and produced a pistol. She snorted, uncomfortable with even looking at the cold, black metal weapon.

"What am I supposed to do with that?"

"That's what I'm gonna show you. Vietnam's not Disneyland, Marion. You need to know how to take care of yourself if anything unexpected happens."

"Like what? You're going to be with me." She wrinkled her nose. "I really don't want to touch that."

"I'm sure there's a psychiatrist word for what you're doing now. Delusion?" He offered that slow, one-shouldered shrug. "This isn't up for discussion. You have, for whatever reason, decided to go to a highly charged war zone. Time to face reality. This is a Colt M1911. It's what I used over there. Pretty standard, but there are some things you need to understand about it."

"Really? Can't you just—"

His lip pulled up like a snarl. "Enough, Marion. Now watch. The grip goes right here, between my thumb and first finger. When I do that, this hammer pulls back, but even if I pull the trigger, it's not gonna fire. See that? I haven't loaded it, and I haven't unlocked the safety. Here. Hold that. It's perfectly safe."

He slid it into her hand, and she wrapped her fingers around the grip like he said.

"Think of the barrel of that gun as your pointer finger, okay? It's gotta be straight, lining up with your arm, or it won't hit anything. Got it? Good, now keep a tight grip and lock your elbow, then raise your arm straight up to your eye level. Use your left hand to steady it, flat under the butt so it's supporting your right hand. That's it. That's the basic setup. Look straight down the barrel and line up that dot between the two sights. Can you see those? Yeah. And your target is lined up with the dot. Now you're ready to shoot. Your finger is on the trigger, but the safety is still on. Try it."

Something about holding the weapon gave Marion an unexpected rush of adrenaline. She was almost disappointed that nothing happened when she pulled the trigger.

"Next is the complicated but necessary part. You gotta load the weapon if it's going to do anything."

She rolled her eyes. "I'm not stupid."

"I would never say that about you. I'm just talking you through this so you will see it step by step if you ever need to use it. So to get started, put your hand over the top of the slide. It's called that because you push this button on the side so you can slide it back until it clicks. See how that leaves a hole here? That's the 'magazine well.' Look through it and you'll see it's empty, right?"

She was glad he told her what to expect, because she had no idea what she was supposed to look for.

Next, he pulled a thin rectangular metal block from his pocket. "This is the magazine, and it holds the bullets. Usually seven or eight. Push the flat end here into the butt of the gun then shove it in hard, all the way. Now put your hand back on the slide, pull it back toward your chest, and let it go. That locks the magazine in place. You are now loaded, but you still can't fire, because of the . . . what?"

"The safety?" she asked tentatively.

He smiled. "See where your thumb is, near the top? See that little lever? That's the safety. When you lift the gun to your eye level, your thumb needs to push that down." He stepped back. "Point it at the ground, would you? Not at me. I mean, unless you wanna kill me. Can't miss at this range."

After she'd practiced moving the safety a few times, he came around behind her. "Now hold that grip tight and raise your arm like I told you, and brace your legs."

She felt his body press against her back, and his arms went around hers. "I'm gonna do a couple with you so you don't get hurt. After you shoot, the gun recoils." He put his hands on hers and adjusted her wrists so her thumbs lay toward the barrel. "You don't want your wrists to bend up with that recoil, and that means you have to hang on tight. Someone taught me years ago to focus on your baby finger. If it's tight, your wrist won't bend up, so make sure that baby finger is as tight as you can get it. The recoil is a pretty solid kick, so I'll stay here while you get used to it. Okay. See that tree straight ahead? Match that with the dot, then line them both up between the little sights. Got it? All right, then. When you're ready, pull the trigger. Remember to keep your baby finger tight around the grip."

Marion ran through the whole procedure in her head, aimed, then fired. The recoil shoved her back against him, and she felt the shock of it through her wrists and shoulders.

"Feel that? Try it again, but this time, concentrate on the strength in your forearms and your baby fingers."

That time, the recoil was much less violent. She grunted and was still shoved back, but it didn't hurt.

"Yeah?" he asked.

She nodded, keen to go again. "Yeah. I get it."

He stepped back, encouraging her to do it on her own. She missed a few times, but Daniel said nothing. He was waiting, encouraging from the side. She didn't want to disappoint him, and even more, she wanted to accomplish this for herself. So Marion closed her eyes briefly and imagined herself standing in the emergency room. The enmity coming from the weapon was the chaos. She was the calm. She breathed in, remembered everything he'd told her in exactly the right order, then she fired. And she hit the target dead centre.

Elated, she lowered the weapon and faced Daniel, savouring the approval on his face.

"But I'll never need to use it."

"I hope not," he said, but he had her practice over and over, making sure.

Another day, he took her to a park for more basic training. "I'm not going to show you much, because you don't have time for drills or anything, but I want you to know a few things in case you're ever in close contact with the enemy." He frowned slightly, looking apologetic. "Though in all likelihood, if you are faced by a Vietcong intent on fighting, you're in big trouble."

Marion had never been in a position where she'd had to defend herself, other than with Paul, who had given up the chase after one angry slap across his face. But it was always better to be safe.

"Yes, please," she told him. "What you teach me would work anywhere, not just in Vietnam. Where do we start?"

"Let's pretend I'm trying to strangle you. I'm way heavier, way stronger." He put his hands around her neck. When she felt his hold tighten, she put her hands on his arms and tried to pry them apart.

He released the pressure. "Do you think you're as strong as I am? Are your arms going to beat mine? Never. Now, watch this. Put your hands around my throat, Marion, and squeeze."

His skin was warm, his pulse hammering loyally beneath her fingers.

"Your thumbs are the weakest connection. Remember that, because it's true in every case. All I have to do is duck straight down between your thumbs. Once I'm bent over, I spin out of your reach."

He very slowly showed her the move, then he turned the tables on her, his strong hands circling her throat. Her first reaction was panic, but the steadying sense of controlling an emergency room returned, and she ducked between his thumbs then spun free. It was an exhilarating feeling, learning that she could save herself if needed.

"Now that you're out of my grasp, kick your heel to the back of my knee, and I won't be able to stand up. Or, well, you tell me, Marion. You're the doctor. If you were able to shove your palm as hard as you could straight into my nose, what would happen?"

"I could kill you."

"Lesson learned. Let's do this exercise again then try another." He hesitated. "Speaking of which, what happened to Big John? You know, after the cops came to get him."

Despite everything John had done, it still made Marion smile, knowing he was being taken care of. "I called Paul McKenny. Remember him? He was your first doctor at the hospital. Anyway, I asked him to help me have John readmitted to the institution. So now John's hospitalized again, and back on his meds. He most likely will never leave."

"Better for him," Daniel murmured.

"For everyone," she agreed.

He exhaled, moving on. "Okay. Back to what we were doing." His hands went to her throat. "Get me off you, Marion."

Every day leading up to their departure, Marion learned more about herself. She was stronger, smarter, and braver than she'd ever thought. She'd never known what she was missing before, and with Daniel's lessons her confidence soared. The night before she and Daniel were set to leave, she pulled on the boonie hat and marched down to Sassy's apartment. Her friend gasped with surprise then laughed, which was exactly what Marion had hoped for.

"I brought us a bottle," she said, producing a bottle of red from behind her back. "Your favourite."

"You'd better not drink too much of that," Sassy said, carrying it to her kitchen. "You have an early flight."

Marion shuddered at the thought. Flying was at the top of her list of things she wasn't looking forward to.

Sassy was already pouring into two wineglasses. "I'm gonna miss you."

"I wish I could be there for you tomorrow," Marion replied.

Sassy just shook her head. "You are flying to Vietnam because of me, Marion. The fact that you are going to miss the fundraising concert we're throwing to help pay for you and Daniel to go is nothing to apologize for."

"What are friends for, if not to fly across the world for them?" Marion teased. "Cheers."

They regarded each other over the rims of their glasses, and Marion watched Sassy's eyes fill with tears.

"I really am going to miss you," Sassy whispered. "You better be careful out there."

Marion swallowed past a knot in her throat. "I promise. It's only two months, but I'm going to miss you, too. Gosh, this seems much more like an adventure fit for you, not me."

"If only I was a doctor," Sassy replied sadly.

"You've been through so much in such a short period of time. I hate leaving you right now, but this is the only window of time I could go."

"I know."

"You'll be okay," Marion said again. "You have Davey—"

Sassy's smile turned mischievous. "Yes, but even better, I think I might have Tom."

Marion elbowed her playfully. "Now I know you're going to be all right. I see that look in your eye. Poor Tom. He has no idea what he's in for."

"I think he does," she said, wiggling her eyebrows. "I just hope he's prepared." She took a sip. "Did you tell your parents you were going?"

Marion nodded. She'd called ahead, then taken the long ride up to their house to join them for Sunday dinner. Pat and her family had come as well, which was good. It meant she could tell everyone at the same time.

"What did they say?"

Marion chuckled. "Well, I thought my mother was going to faint, honestly. Pat got mad at the mention of Vietnam, so she didn't listen to much after that. Her husband did, though. He was nodding, and I think he understood that I'm not going there to support the war. I'm going to support the men involved. He'll try to explain it to her later, but Pat's not great at listening sometimes."

"What about your dad?"

They both knew that was the real question. Joey's departure to Vietnam had been the beginning of the end for Sassy's father. Marion had been well aware of that the whole time she had made her decision to go, but she knew her father better now. She thought he knew her better, too.

She smiled faintly, recalling his expression. "He didn't say much at first, but he watched me as I talked it through. I explained that I would be in a safe compound, I was with the Red Cross, and I would have Daniel. I needed to know what he was thinking, so I just asked him straight out. He told me he didn't want me to go for obvious reasons, but mostly he wanted to understand my motivation. That was hard, because I wanted to tell him he had inspired me to be courageous, but I didn't want him to feel responsible in case anything went wrong."

Sassy nodded. She understood that all too well, Marion knew.

"So I told him that I wanted to do more with my life, and an opportunity had presented itself."

You hadn't planned that day in Italy, she'd reminded him gently. *Would you change what happened if you could?*

He had held her gaze, a gentle understanding in his expression. *Not a thing.*

Sassy waited, knowing there was more to the story, but Marion was relieved she didn't ask. Something about the look in his eye, the pride she saw, had felt deeply personal. She wanted to keep it for herself.

She had tried not to watch the news leading up to their departure, but at the same time, the rational part of her needed to know what she was getting herself into. The Tet Offensive, the organized and vicious attack on southern points, including U.S. military bases, was tentatively controlled for now. Other than the news media reading their talking points to the camera, no one seemed confident the invasion would continue uncontested. Hundreds of military and civilian casualties had resulted from the battles, including nurses, physicians, and surgeons. Mass graves had been discovered, holding corpses of teachers, doctors, civil leaders, and other enemies of the North Vietnamese. Some of the murdered had been shot in the head, some had been buried alive. Others had died of asphyxiation due to the plastic bags tied over their faces.

She'd brought all those points up with Daniel, and he'd nodded coolly. "There are atrocities everywhere. On all sides. But that's why we're going, right? To do what we can to ease the suffering."

There were no more terrifying bumps on the flight, and Marion eventually nodded off to sleep. She had no idea how long she was out before she woke up with her face in Daniel's sleeve.

"Sorry," she said.

"What for? Look." He pointed out the window. "That's Mount Fujiyama."

She stared in awe as they approached over Tokyo Bay. The angle seemed impossibly low, but they landed with barely a bump. After refuelling, they were off again, this time for Hong Kong.

"Sleep some more," Daniel advised, balling up his jacket to use as a pillow. He placed it on his arm and patted it, indicating she should lean in. When she did, he dropped his head back on his chair so he faced the ceiling. "Next stop is Saigon. Trust me. You want to be awake for that."

Almost immediately, his face relaxed into slumber. She stared at him, as confused as she always was about this man. So young and gentle, breathing calmly beside her, and yet behind that soft exterior was the hunger of a lion. It was obvious he couldn't wait to get his boots on the ground and head into the violence.

As a psychiatrist, she found the dichotomy fascinating.

As a woman, she was experiencing something new. Daniel was the very picture of a warrior. To both her dismay and her selfish delight, he had already said he would die without hesitation to protect her. Her job was surgery, he said. His job was her.

But, like most women, Marion held feminist views, like demanding equality and fighting back against exactly the kind of male strength that he represented. Marion had experienced chauvinism firsthand, so she understood the need for progress. And yet here she sat, propped comfortably against a tall, rugged, handsome soldier determined to be her champion. She was surprised by how content she felt, letting him take care of her. How it filled her up inside, knowing he kept her safe.

He made a little sound in his sleep, and a scowl flickered across his expression. He had come so far from the tortured man she had first met, screaming in panic whether awake or asleep. He still suffered, though. Recently, she had seen him flinch on occasion, but it was nothing like the soul-stealing episodes he'd had before.

His jaw loosened slightly as he dropped deeper in his slumber. How on earth was Marion supposed to sleep when her whole nervous system vibrated? But the combined flights added up to almost twenty-four hours, and she knew he was right about being prepared for the next landing. Neither her body nor her mind argued when she closed her eyes.

She was jarred awake by the thud of the plane's wheels touching down at Saigon's Tan Son Nhut Air Base. Daniel was already wide-awake, his gaze on the view beyond her window.

"I read this is the busiest airfield in the world right now," she said, scanning the scene. "Look at all those helicopters!"

They stood in lines like huge, lethal dragonflies. Warplanes were parked beside them, awaiting pilots and commands. Men in dark green jumpsuits milled around the machines.

"Look," Daniel said, pointing across the runway. "A Phantom. The fastest fighter jet there is. I knew one of those pilots once. He said their slogan was 'Speed is life.' I wonder where that guy is now."

If the helicopters were dragonflies, the camouflage-painted Phantom was a wasp.

"Are those . . . on the wings . . . ?"

"Missiles," Daniel confirmed. "Air to surface. These birds can carry thermonuclear weapons, if required. Don't worry. They're not right now. But they could."

"And over there?"

A giant plane stood in the sunlight. If the Phantom was a wasp, this was a bumblebee. It struck her that she must not have gotten enough sleep if she was classifying warplanes into types of insects.

"That's a bomber. The Boeing B-52 Stratofortress. Those things saved my ass more than once."

Their own plane jerked to a stop. Marion caught a glimpse of scattered, charred metal off to the side, the burnt remains of aircraft. She squinted beyond them at a pillar of smoke.

"What's that?"

"Artillery fire," Daniel murmured, then he straightened and stretched his neck, tilting it one way then the other. "Ready, Marion? We're almost there."

His calm statement shot adrenaline through her, and she felt the compulsion to cry. What in the world was she doing out here? She held her breath all the way to their plane's eventual parking spot, then she watched the other passengers rise calmly and grab their bags.

Daniel stayed in place. He faced her, and it struck her for the first time that he looked uncertain.

"I know you're frightened," he said. "If you weren't, you'd be nuts. This is alien to you. But you're doing the right thing, Marion. You're going to save lives. I'm not gonna lie: it's going to get scary, but I know you pretty well. You can do this. Just keep pressing forward, no matter what. If it gets dicey, do everything I tell you to do. That's the only way I can protect you. Do you understand what I'm saying?"

"You're trying to tell me not to panic," she replied softly. "It's not working."

"I'm trying to tell you that we will get through this. I won't let anybody hurt you."

She nodded, wide-eyed.

"Do you know what our slogan is? The U.S. Marine's slogan?"

She shook her head.

"*Semper fidelis.*"

"Always faithful," she translated.

"That's me," he told her. "You are my sole responsibility here, Marion. You can count on me. Always."

thirty-four
SASSY

Three weeks had passed since her father's funeral, and the world still felt strange. Everywhere Sassy looked, she saw her father. She called out to him a few times, heart racing, only to receive confused glances in return. But still, she saw him walking into a store, his stride so recognizable. She spotted the back of his coat, then his shoes as they passed inside. There he was again, talking with a stranger on the sidewalk, but when he turned, the face belonged to someone else.

The worst was in the office. When Tom told her to take time off, she didn't listen. "If I don't work now, I might never do it again. After all, he left me all this money," she hinted, but it was only partially a joke. To her surprise, work had become a satisfying part of her life. She understood now why her wealthy father had kept working his entire life. Besides that, she loved being near Tom. His energy fed hers.

But sometimes, sitting at her desk, her mind played tricks. The crack of her father's office door easing open. The sound of his voice at the reception desk, greeting a client. His sly little smile, the one he gave Tom when a deal was almost closed. She saw it all. She missed it all. She clung to it all. She hated the impromptu bouts of misery that overtook her. She might be walking along a sidewalk, thinking of nothing in particular, when the truth would hit her, and she'd wander into a hidden doorway for privacy, torn apart by grief.

Grief was the opposite of joy, Marion had said. What Sassy needed most was joy, and to her, music was joy. The fundraising concert wasn't about the money. Financially, she didn't need anyone's help anymore. It was about coming together. Trying to find happiness in the saddest of times.

The concert was the next night, so she decided to stop at Chez Monique to see Davey, make sure he didn't need anything. On her way, she passed a man huddled on a bench, wrapped in a worn overcoat, and she couldn't help thinking about the first time she had met Daniel. She'd learned something shameful about herself that day. She had judged him unfairly right off the bat. Now that she knew him, she understood he had only been trying to help her step safely off the sidewalk ice. But out of reflex, Sassy had been repelled by the scarred, patched man sitting on the frozen sidewalk. She had assumed the worst. Sure, Big John had turned out to be exactly what she had feared—she was so glad Marion was getting him the care he needed—but Sassy couldn't forget that she had been entirely wrong about Daniel. He was a warm, intelligent man down on his luck. He was even handsome, despite the disfiguring marks on his face. Not like Tom's Sean Connery look, but he had the face of a natural, hardworking, outdoors kind of man. Marion had told her he was a fisherman in Nova Scotia before he'd gone to Vietnam. Sassy could picture that easily.

"Everything's going so well!" Davey exclaimed when she walked into the coffeehouse. "Tickets for tomorrow night are almost sold out. We've made nearly four hundred dollars already, and there's lots more coming at the door. Oh, and the coffeehouse is going to donate half its take as well."

"Far out!" She gave him a hug. "Know what I remember? That day we met, at the love-in? You said you were going to someday organize a big event, and here you are."

"So cool that you remember that. I barely remember anything from that day, man. I don't know what we smoked, but it was awesome." He grinned, and she inhaled his joy. It was exactly what she needed. "But this concert, man, it's gonna be twitchin'. The performers are psyched. They think it's unreal about Joey being MIA, and now that Marion's gone, they're super keen to help out."

"I can't thank you enough for all this, Davey. Marion's going to be blown away when she finds out we've paid for Daniel's trip. She was counting pennies at the end."

"Doing this has been a gas," he told her. "So many people are supporting you. They love you, and so do I." He gave her a kiss on the cheek. "You doing okay?"

She stiffened, keeping all the misery at bay. "Please don't ask me that."

"Right on." Quick as a wink, he changed direction. "Have you picked out what you're playing?"

"It's a surprise." She had decided she was going to perform all of Marion's favourite songs. Sweet songs to make people smile for a change. She handed Davey a box of Smarties, knowing they were his favourite. "What can I do to help?"

"No way, Sass! Thanks." He opened the box and popped a couple into his mouth. "Nah, there's nothing for you to worry about, man. It's all done."

"Want to come to my place for dinner? I bet you haven't eaten all day."

A beat of indecision, then he asked, "What are we having?"

"I don't know yet. Something with noodles."

"You have cheese, right?"

It felt good, hanging with Davey after so long. Sorrow was a confusing, exhausting emotion, and she hadn't yet figured out how to handle it. There were moments when all she wanted was to be alone, but most of the time she found herself craving company. Especially in the evenings, after work was done. Easy company, like Marion, or Tom, or Davey.

Marion had already flown across the world. Marion, the hero neither of them had ever suspected. Gosh, Sassy missed her. She kept wanting to go to her place and tell her about her day, and her absence felt like a wall.

Tom, well, she spent the whole day at the office and sometimes at lunch with him, and even though they had a great time, she didn't think he'd appreciate being hounded by her every night. Besides, he needed time alone, too.

Davey was just right, with that warm smile and his lion-coloured eyes. She was occasionally tempted to grab him and revert to old times, but the urge wasn't too strong anymore. More like an echo of what they'd had. Sassy had Tom firmly in her sights now. Her tragedies hadn't affected her attraction to him. She didn't want to scare him off, though, in case he wasn't looking at her the same way. So Davey spent the night, but he slept on her couch, each of them content just to be around the other.

He was gone early the next morning, needing to make sure everything was ready for the concert. She grabbed her guitar then got into a bus and sat by the window, feeling strange. Sassy arrived at the coffeehouse at five thirty, dressed in her best, but wrapped like a gift in a cozy winter coat. Tent dresses were all the rage, so she'd picked up a bright pink one along with a matching pair of pantyhose. Her hair was swept back from the front, and she'd let the rest hang free with a big, happy curl around the bottom. Her makeup was perfect. She was ready.

She was riding a huge wave of adrenaline and was almost euphoric about the night to come. But deep down, all she could think about was Joey. Joey was why Marion was gone. Joey was the reason for tonight. God, she wished he was here.

Then she arrived at Chez Monique and shoved her blues away. There was a sign on the door that read: CLOSED FOR PRIVATE EVENT AT 6:00. TICKET HOLDERS ONLY. With a grin, she headed to the greenroom to see if any of the performers had arrived and was surprised to see the little room was packed tight and lit with energy. When she wriggled inside, a dozen musicians and poets all cheered.

"Thank you all for being here!" she said over them. "This means so much to me."

"We'll get your bro back, Sass," one called, and they all cheered again.

Stepping out of the room, she spotted Davey standing by the bar and went to see how she could help. She slipped off her winter coat as she walked.

"Look at you! You look like a piece of Dubble Bubble! Outta sight, Sass!" He glanced at his watch. "It's almost showtime."

"Can I do anything?"

"Why don't you go stand by the entrance? Tonight's all for you, so everyone's gonna want to see you."

She was happy to oblige, though the cold night seeped through her little dress every time the door opened. Then Tom walked in, and she felt warm all over. She watched him slip off his brown leather coat, revealing a cream-coloured Irish knit sweater over a pair of jeans. He scrubbed his fingers through his hair, brushing off snow, then he spotted her and gave her a gorgeous smile.

"I'm so glad you came," she said. She pointed. "That's Davey. He's the one who put this all together."

"We'll thank him later," Tom said, holding her with those Sean Connery eyes. "He looks pretty busy right now, and these tables are filling up fast. I should grab a seat before they're all gone." He leaned down so she could hear him better. "I'm looking forward to hearing you sing, Sass."

Her heart did a little jump. "I'll sing one just for you, boss."

"Maybe you and I could go out for a drink after," he suggested carefully. "We could pretend I'm not your boss."

Tom was about ten years older than she was, and he was a dyed-in-the-wool capitalist—but she didn't mind that so much anymore. He was smart, funny, and thoughtful, never mind that he was movie-star handsome. She'd learned about business from him, and while she was still bothered by the fact that the poor did not benefit from gentrification, she judged the concept less harshly now that she understood the reasons for it. Most importantly, Tom had been there for her when her father died. She would never forget that.

Any other time, she would have beamed and agreed effusively to his invitation, but something had changed. No matter how happy she was at that moment, she was not the carefree girl she'd been before. She'd grown up. His invitation, combined with the cautious sparkle in his eyes, didn't feel like just a drink. It felt like it could be the next step into her future. She let that feeling rush through her then shine onto him.

"I would like that very much," she said. She stayed with him as long as she could, enjoying the performances and his subtle reactions to them.

Ernie Molnek was just finishing his recitation when Sassy realized she was on next. Her heartbeat quickened.

"I gotta go," she said breathlessly.

"Knock 'em dead, Sass," he replied with a smile.

She stood by the stage, waiting for Ernie to finish and getting her nerves in order. The lights overhead prevented her from making out individual faces in the audience, but even so, she thought she saw Tom's profile. Was he looking at her or simply enjoying the poetry? Then he turned his head and held her gaze for a good ten seconds, only breaking it off as Ernie finished speaking and the audience applauded. She closed her eyes and took a deep breath, calming the urgent desire burning in her chest.

Davey went to the microphone next, holding his fingers up in Vs. "Hey," he said, a proud smile on his face. "I'm Davey, and I'm amped that you're all here. We have one more performer for you, and you know she's the grand finale! She's gonna blow your mind. Ladies and gentlemen, please put your hands together for my best friend in the world, Sassy Rankin!"

Beaming, she walked toward the stool he'd put out for her and pressed a kiss on his cheek. "You're too much, Davey," she murmured into his ear. "Thank you."

"I'm guessing," he whispered back, "that we're closing in on a thousand bucks. That ought to cover some expenses."

"Amazing!"

"Yeah," he said, pushing her away. "Now it's your turn. Go wow 'em, Sass."

Settled on the stool with the guitar on her knee, Sassy leaned toward the mic. Her gaze went to Tom, and for just an instant, she saw her father sitting with him. Emotion rushed in, so she took a beat to calm herself.

"My brother Joey made a mistake," she said to the crowd when she was ready. "When he went to Vietnam to fight, he believed he was doing the right thing, but I never agreed."

Beyond the lights, she saw slow nods. These people understood.

"None of that matters now. He's my brother, and he is all that remains of my family. I love Joey like I always did. Part of me died when we heard he was missing."

She paused, recalling Marion's voice when she'd told Sassy over the phone about her plan to go to Vietnam. Sassy hadn't known whether to cry with disbelief, fear, or gratitude. In the end, it had been all three.

"The toughest thing for me has been coming to terms with the fact that there's nothing I can do for him. He might never make it back. But my friend Marion saw I needed help, and she showed me what it means to be a true friend. She's a doctor, and she has gone to Vietnam for my sake and to help those in need of medical care. I don't expect her to find Joey. That would be impossible. But no matter what, she's my hero just for going. Every penny you paid to get in here tonight, any extra donations you feel like dropping into that box on the bar, and half of the proceeds from your coffee and food are all going to the Canadian Red Cross to help cover expenses. Marion has gone to help men over there who might die without her. So on behalf of all of them, thank you."

She dipped her head to her guitar, tears blurring her vision, then she sucked in the emotions and spoke again.

"Safe travels, Marion."

She started with "Leaving on a Jet Plane," imagining her best friend in the sky with Daniel at her side. Did Marion see the way Daniel looked at her? Did she realize she held her breath when he spoke? The romance of it all made Sassy smile as she switched keys to "Never My Love." She and Marion loved that song.

"I have a very good friend with a really nice car," she said after that, glancing at Tom. He nodded appreciatively. "He thinks I don't know who Elvis Presley is." The audience laughed, and she played a quick, complicated riff on her guitar, smiling coyly the whole time. "So this is for him. 'All That I Am,' from Elvis's movie *Spinout*, is about a race car. Does that work for you, Tom?"

After that, she played Louis Armstrong's new one, a poem to goodness and to all the best parts of life. "What a Wonderful World," she was certain, was going to become a hit.

When that was finished, she took a deep breath then smiled broadly at the audience. "My last song for tonight is something a little more upbeat,

and I hope you take the message home with you. Thank you again for helping the Canadian Red Cross with your donations. I hope you all had a gas
tonight."

She started to play, then she caught a glimpse of Davey's happy face in
the wings. He was beaming and swaying and singing along.

"All we need is love! Whap-bap-buh-duh-duh!"

After it was all done, and her whole body was still pulsing with adrenaline, Sassy set her guitar aside and smiled at people approaching the stage.
She couldn't get off before well-wishers came to congratulate her, shaking
her hand or hugging her. She knew a lot of the hippies, but there were others
as well. Women and men dressed in business suits, and some in between, like
Tom.

"I dropped another hundred dollars into the box," a stranger in a white
collared shirt said. "Great cause, great show."

"Out of sight," exclaimed a girl she recognized from the TADP protest.
"I was totally bawling. You're like Joan Baez, only sweeter."

"Your brother's an idiot for fighting," a long-haired man in a headband
told her gently, "but he's got a dynamite sister."

"He's not an idiot," Sassy bridled. "He's trying to do the right thing, just
like we are."

"Right on," the man replied, looking sheepish. "No offence meant."

"None taken," she said. She was aware that a lot of people in the room
felt the same as he did. "Thanks for coming. I really appreciate it."

Tom waited behind the cluster of fans, distracting her. She was overwhelmed by all the attention, but really, she was dying to hear his thoughts.

"Well?"

"Incredible, Sassy. I knew you were good, but that was unreal. Your dad
would've been so proud." He glanced around at the noisy crowd. "You probably have other things to do besides that celebratory drink. We could do it
another—"

"Don't you dare back out now, mister," she purred, lifting one eyebrow.

That brought out the Sean Connery flash. "Tonight it is." His eyes
darted to just beyond Sassy's shoulder, and he lifted his chin so she'd look.

"Oh! Tom, this is Davey, the mastermind behind tonight. Davey, this is Tom."

Davey stuck out his hand. "Hey, man. Sassy talks about you a lot. Thanks for coming." Then he faced her, and something in his expression drained all her joy. "Uh, Sass, can I speak with you a moment?"

"Lay it on me. You look like somebody died."

His mouth opened, and for a panicked moment she feared he might cry. "Somebody bagged the cash."

Sassy stared at him, disbelieving. "No. How could that happen?"

"It's gone, babe. I had it safely hidden behind the counter, I thought. It was tucked behind a bunch of boxes. I was only away from it for a second, when I came out to watch you. When I got back, it was gone." His face squeezed tight with regret. "Somebody must have seen me. I'm so sorry."

She was having trouble getting her brain to work. Who, in this generous audience, would be so desperate as to steal from them?

"You're sure?" she asked feebly.

"I've looked everywhere. Like a hundred times."

"All the work you did," she said, feeling slightly ill. "What a waste."

"No, man. It was an amazing experience anyway. I just can't believe all the money is gone."

"How much was it, do you know? Did you get a chance to count it?

He groaned. "Yeah. Just under $850."

Tom whistled quietly. "Somebody's going home a lot richer."

With a knot in her throat, Sassy's gaze travelled over all the happy people. Some had returned to their seats to enjoy a cup of coffee. Others had left already. Was the thief still here, staring back at her? She couldn't imagine the gall that would take. The longer she watched them, the angrier she got.

"I guess we should call the cops," she said uncertainly.

Davey's expression didn't change. "I guess so. I don't know what they could do, though. We don't know who was here, and a lot of people have already left."

She slumped, and he opened his arms for her. "Oh, Davey."

"It's all right. We'll figure this out." He squeezed her. "Such a bummer."

A hand touched her back. "Sassy."

She pulled away from Davey and wiped her palms across her eyes, smearing tears and mascara everywhere. It didn't matter.

"I can go with you to the police station tomorrow," Tom offered.

"Okay. Thanks, Tom. Oh, I feel sick. And I'm so angry. What kind of person does that?"

Tom's smile slid sideways. "It was a great concert, though. Everyone loved it. You were amazing."

He was trying to cheer her up, but she didn't want that. "I don't feel like getting a drink after all. I'm too mad."

Tom's smile widened, as if he wasn't reading her mood. He thought she was teasing. "What if I ask real nicely? I'll even make a donation."

"Tom! I said no." Couldn't he see she was upset? She turned back to Davey, dismissing Tom. "Think we should make an announcement?"

Davey looked doubtful. "Nobody's gonna pay twice."

"Hey, Sass," Tom tried, but she ignored him. "Sassy?"

She felt him push a folded piece of paper into her hand, and she jerked away when she realized it was a cheque. "I don't want your money."

"Just take it, Sass," Davey said, nudging her.

"What? No! I don't want to go for a drink, and I don't want your money. You can't just step in and solve things like a businessman would. This is about more than that, Tom. Get it?"

"You don't want my donation because I can afford to give it?"

"I don't want it."

Tom's smile fell. "There she is," he said tightly. "That spoiled brat I remember from the jail. I just wanted to help."

"Yeah? Well, I don't want your help."

"Sassy," Davey murmured behind her.

She thrust the cheque back at Tom, but Davey snatched it from her fingers. "Sorry, man," he said, hovering between the two of them. "Thanks. This is awesome."

"Stop it, Davey," she hissed. "Give it back."

He held it behind his back. "Don't be stupid, Sass."

"Stupid's a great word for this," Tom growled. "You've heard of the proverbial gift horse, Sassy? Well, here I am. Give the cheque to the Red Cross or tear it up. I don't care. I'm leaving."

He turned and wound swiftly between the revellers, striding toward the entrance without a backward glance.

"I'm such an idiot," she muttered, her eyes on his receding back. What a fool she was.

"Uh, Sass, I kind of agree."

She scowled. "Shut up, Davey. I thought he and I were clicking, you know? Obviously, I was wrong. I should have known."

Davey sighed. "What you should have done is taken his donation and thanked him for it. For Marion. At least it would be something after this disaster." He unfolded the cheque, and she watched his eyes widen.

"What?" she asked grudgingly.

He flipped it over, toward her. "Eight hundred and fifty dollars, Sass. Made out to the Canadian Red Cross. Sorry, but your answer should have been 'Thanks.' Looks to me like this came straight from his heart."

thirty-five
MARION

☙

The plane's door opened, and a rush of steamy air flooded in, a hot, physical pressure against Marion's body. She was immediately bathed in perspiration and apprehensive about moving. Not Daniel. He was eager to get going. He grabbed her pack along with his own and held out his hand.

"Welcome to Vietnam, Marion. Next stop, Saigon."

They stepped onto the disembarking ramps then the tarmac. The pavement under her boots was so hot it was sticky, and it threatened to seep through the leather soles.

Daniel spread his arms wide and inhaled. "Ah, the sweet stink of jet fuel and burning jungle."

They made it through customs, despite unenthusiastic officials questioning every little thing. They stood by as the officers dug through their luggage, and Marion blushed as they sorted through her underthings.

"What are they looking for?" she whispered.

"Explosive devices."

At last, the bags were closed up again. She was about to ask what was next when another man appeared.

"Please come this way." He led them outside to a white van, clearly marked with the Red Cross symbol on the side. "Fast, please."

In the distance, Marion heard the hammering of a machine gun. She knew the sound from television, but now it was alarmingly real. She didn't need to be told twice. She practically leapt into the back seat of the van.

"Air-conditioning!" she exclaimed, momentarily forgetting the dangers outside.

"Hang on tight," Daniel warned as the driver gunned the engine and tore out of the lot.

The van ploughed through deep holes in the road, eventually passing through a decimated village.

"They saw some heavy fighting here," Daniel noted.

She scanned the devastated area, shocked by the sight. Broken buildings surrounded them, riddled by bullet holes. A child huddled in the doorway of a ruined building, his eyes huge in a skeletal face. Reflexively, she drew away from the window as a man stalked by, cradling a machine gun.

Downtown Saigon, when they finally reached it, was chaotic. It was also completely different from what had come before. The buildings were clean and modern, and the people walked unafraid, breathing air thick with diesel. Boulevards were bordered by well-tended flower beds, and throngs of people moved along wide sidewalks, selling wares, carrying packages, or cooking food. She spotted a line of children trailing behind a pair of nuns, twisting around garbage, beggars, and food stalls, laughing like any other children on a sunny afternoon. As if there was no war at all.

"This is unexpected," she said.

Daniel was observing over her shoulder. "They call this the Paris of the East. Wherever they put us up, it'll be nice."

"Here is hotel," the driver said at last, pulling up in front of a large, white, European-style building. "Is very good."

He helped them unload, then she followed Daniel into the hotel. It was a shock to Marion's system, walking into elegant, vintage French decor, which had carried over from the earlier French occupation. At the reception desk, the clerk handed Daniel two keys.

"We invite you to enjoy the dining room on our roof tonight," the clerk at the desk said. "You cannot get a more exquisite meal anywhere in the country. Tonight's dinner is a gift from the hotel, to thank you for coming to Vietnam."

"Oh, thank you, but I don't know," Marion sighed with regret. "I really need to sleep."

"Understandable; however, it would be a terrible shame if you were to miss this, mademoiselle. You are travelling with the Red Cross, and I can guarantee that there will be nothing like this where you are headed."

Upstairs, Marion slid her key into the lock and sighed with delight when she saw the luxury within. The room was relatively small, but the furnishings were elegant. Not that it mattered. She just planned to sleep.

"It's lovely, Daniel. Oh, uh, thank you. You can put the bag there. I'll deal with it later."

"Remember, there's no rush," he told her, setting it on the floor beside a huge armoire. "Sleep all night if you want. They'll be here to pick us up around noon."

"What about dinner? Do you think we'll make it?"

"Tell you what. First one awake knocks on the other one's door."

Almost giddy with exhaustion, she gave him a sheepish smile. "I may sleep right through your knock."

"That's all right. I'll save you some if I can."

The bed promised oblivion. She kicked off her boots and sank happily into the crisp white sheets without getting undressed, having no idea and not caring when she might wake up. When she awoke after a few hours, it took a moment for her to recall where she was, then she flung the covers back and got to her feet, feeling refreshed and bubbling with curiosity. Marion Hart was in Saigon, Vietnam.

Moving quickly and hoping she hadn't missed Daniel's knock, she washed up then pulled a simple dress and shoes from her suitcase. She stopped in front of the mirror, checking her hair and makeup, and wondered for the hundredth time what she was doing there. She didn't even know what time it was, either here or in Toronto. What would she be doing right now at home, assuming it was sometime after work? Probably sitting on the couch with Chester, reading one of Sassy's books. Maybe Sassy was sitting with him now instead. She'd been very happy to welcome the cat to her apartment, and he had seemed satisfied as well. The two had always gotten along well.

There was a knock on her door, and Marion's heart jumped. Daniel waited in the hallway, dressed plainly in brown trousers and a white shirt. He'd cleaned up and slicked his hair back.

"Good. You're awake. Ready?"

"You're just in time," she said. "I'm famished."

They stepped into the hallway, and she locked her door behind her. When she turned, he was standing with his hands in his pockets, smiling down at her.

"We've never had dinner together before," he said.

"This is definitely the farthest I have ever gone for a date."

He opened his elbow with invitation, and she slipped her arm through, failing to contain her wide grin as they made their way to the restaurant. The opulence of the room was beyond anything she could have imagined, and she smiled with thanks as the maître d' slid in her chair.

"This is incredible," she said, taking everything in. "I'm so glad he recommended we come for dinner."

Daniel nodded, leaning back in his chair. He looked completely relaxed. For a moment, she couldn't look away. How far he had come from that furious, trapped animal, shackled to his bed in that tiny hospital cell. On the day he'd rescued Sassy from Big John, she had been concerned by how dirty and withdrawn he was. Today, he was strong and alive, almost youthful in his contentment.

"You look so happy," she marvelled.

"How could I be anything but? For the longest time I thought my life was over. Now look at me." His gaze was direct enough to melt her. "I have everything I want."

Heat rushed up her neck, and she fumbled for the menu. "Lobster thermidor!" she cried, changing the subject as fast as she could. "I've never had lobster!"

"I used to fish for lobster." He shuddered. "I do not miss the Atlantic. In that water, you freeze before you get a chance to drown."

"That's awful."

"You should get the lobster. Get whatever you want, Marion. Like the man said, we're not going to see food like this for a long time."

"Do you want to get some wine?"

His brow lifted. "Why not? A bottle of white, to go with your lobster?"

Her nerves began to calm while she was eating her salad. "I am still stunned that I'm here. And that you're with me."

"Here in Vietnam? You're living life in a big way, Doc."

"A lot of it is because of you."

He grinned again. "Not true."

"Yes, it is."

He took a sip of his wine, studying her. "So now that we're here, I want something from you."

A thrill raced through her. "What's that?"

"You got to ask me questions before, but I never got a turn. A lot of the time, we talked about what scared me. I want to know what scares you, Marion Hart."

"Oh, I don't know if I want to talk about that."

"It's only fair. Besides, how am I supposed to protect you if I don't know what to watch for?"

"Okay," she said reluctantly, "but let's order first."

The lobster thermidor, the wine, and the need for more sleep lulled her into a state of deep contentment, and Marion let herself relax into the moment. So she told him about the day on the lake when she'd almost drowned.

"I was just a kid, and I shouldn't have been out there. I guess most people would have been smart and taken swimming lessons after that. I did the opposite. I decided never to go near water again in my life. Shortsighted, I guess, and stubborn."

"Got it. No swimming for you."

They talked comfortably through dinner, getting to know a bit about who they were before they'd met, but the conversation inevitably returned to the war.

"Do you think you'll see your unit out here?"

His face fell slightly. "I doubt it. Tex is gone." His nostrils flared with the memory. "I know that for sure. Joey is MIA, but I don't know anything about the others. It's been months, so they would have sent in replacements. Young kids."

"You're all younger than I am." She tilted her head. "But I know the war aged you. The adrenaline. The risks. You were close to death so many times."

"They say you're never so alive as when you're looking death in the eye," he said softly. "I must have been pretty damn close. I looked it in the eye, and it took mine."

At noon the next day, they were back in the van, bumping along cratered roads. The view kept changing the closer they got to Camp Bao Thinh, where they would learn where she and Daniel were to be stationed. When they arrived, the feel of the place was more military, with sentries standing outside buildings, and high defensive walls topped with razor wire.

Every one of Marion's muscles was so stiff when they finally parked and got out of the van, she had to force herself not to gasp.

Daniel pointed at a sign nearby. "See that? Skull and crossbones? Indicates a possible minefield. Remember that."

"Got it. Why are they moving a mirror under our van?"

"In case the Vietcong attached explosives to the undercarriage."

Her jaw dropped. "Of our van?"

"If there's anything there, they'd set it off remotely once it arrived. They'd want it to happen where it could do the most damage. Like here," he said, matter-of-fact. He gestured toward a small group of Vietnamese men in suits and military uniforms standing by a building. "Looks like those are the people we're meeting with."

She followed him toward the men, who were saying something like "Gam un! Gam un!"

"*Không có gì*," Daniel replied, startling her.

"What's that? What's 'com koy ay'?" she asked.

"They're thanking us for coming, so I just said, 'You're welcome.' Lucky you. You wanted a bodyguard, and I threw in a translator for free."

Marion had brought a little book to help her translate, but since the Vietnamese alphabet was nothing like the English one, she had been at a loss for how to handle conversations. She had assumed—or, rather, *hoped* that people at the hospital would understand her needs once she got there, but Daniel's knowledge made everything much simpler. Some of the officials, she discovered, were fairly fluent in English as well. One of them ushered them toward a map on the wall.

"Dr. Hart," he said, looking reluctant, "I am very sorry. Because you are a woman, I wanted to send you to a hospital in Saigon. Here." He tapped the map near the southernmost tip of South Vietnam, then he slid his pointer up, up, up. "But we had an accident happen to a surgeon in Quảng Nam, and they need urgent help in Da Nang. In I Corps."

Daniel stepped up, shaking his head. "*Quá nguy hiểm.*"

"Nig yem?" Marion asked.

"I don't want them to send you that far north. I Corps is the divider between North and South. The Vietcong are strong there. The closer you get to the border, the worse things get."

"Excuse me," the man said, bowing to Daniel. "Is modern, up-to-date surgical hospital. You are safe with marines."

"Marines?" He stood a little straighter, towering over the official. "Which battalion?"

"Number one is at I Corps."

Marion stared at him. "That's your battalion."

Daniel grinned. "It sure is. This trip keeps getting better."

"How do we get to this place, this I Corps?" she asked.

"In the morning we'll fly to Hue, then a chopper will take us to Da Nang." He laughed at her stricken expression. "Sorry. I neglected to say there's a lot of flying in this journey."

"You did."

"Beats walking. Oh, I also forgot to tell you that Da Nang's nickname is Rocket City, because they're always under attack. Now you see why I didn't want you stationed up there? But the First Battalion will be there. We'll be all right."

She stared at the map, trying to squeeze all her doubts into a box in her brain so she could lock it away. She was here now, so she was going to have to deal with whatever came at her. No one had said this would be fun. No one had promised it would be safe. No one had guaranteed anything at all.

"I can do this. I can handle a chopper," she said to herself. She turned to Daniel. "Can I handle a chopper?"

"Marion, you busted out of your safe life, and you flew halfway around the world to a war zone. Honestly, I never expected you'd do any of it. If this was two weeks ago, I'd never take you up there. But it's today. You are in Vietnam. This is a different world, and so far, you're handling it great." He gave her a smile that held her deep inside. "Yeah. You can handle it, Marion. I'll be right beside you."

thirty-six
SASSY

⁕

Mornings were not Sassy's best time of day. And this morning, well, she felt sick even thinking of getting out of bed and going to work. She slammed her hand onto the alarm clock, shutting it off, then she groaned. With effort, she sat up, but the room spun. She had to wait for it to stop before she got up and staggered to her bathroom.

"Idiot," she hissed at her reflection, grabbing her toothbrush.

Last night had been incredible, then devastating. Thinking the worst about Tom had almost broken her. God, she had blathered on like a crazy woman, snapping at him and working herself into a lather. All because Tom wanted to give her a gift.

"Idiot," she mumbled again through toothpaste.

Davey had promised to bring the cheque to the Red Cross first thing in the morning, which was good. She wasn't sure she could hand it over without feeling mortified at her behaviour. She'd left Chez Monique then trudged home, missing Marion. She could have used a boost from her friend. Instead, she had a shot of vodka. And another. It dulled the pain but didn't take away her embarrassment.

Now she threw back a couple of aspirin, dressed, and headed to the office, her stomach curdling the whole way. When she entered, Tom glared across the room at her through eyes as dark as coal. She strode straight to his desk, chin lifted, and peered down her nose at him. Best to get this over with.

"Am I fired?" she demanded.

"No. Do you quit?"

"No." She swallowed her pride in a big gulp. "I owe you an apology. I feel like garbage for what I said. Worse than garbage. I have no excuse, but—"

"There's no excuse, no."

She bristled. "I'm trying to apologize. Back off. It doesn't come easy to me."

He folded his arms.

"I was upset," she blustered. "I didn't know what I was saying. I—"

"Thought you said there was no excuse."

She drooped, and to her horror, her chin quivered. *Don't cry!* "What am I supposed to do?"

He peered closely at her. "Are you hungover?"

She looked at the floor.

"We are not going to discuss this during business hours," he said tightly.

"Then can I buy you lunch? Today?"

She could swear she heard Miss Sloane's big clock ticking behind her while he considered her invitation. At last he nodded decisively, then he dropped his gaze to his work and waved her off with one hand.

It was impossible to concentrate on her work. Mostly she shuffled papers around on her desk, trying to look busy. At noon, he reached for his coat. She watched him grab hers as well, and he carried it to her desk.

"Where do you want to go?"

"I know a place. Can you drive us?"

He nodded. "If it's not too far."

"Sweet little Mexican joint called 'The Peasants Larder.' Carlton Street, one block west of Parliament."

"Near the CBC building," he muttered. "I've driven past it."

She sat quietly in his car as he drove, unsure if he wanted her to talk or not.

"Here it is. Just park right there."

"Why this place?" he asked as they got out.

"A friend of mine suggested it, and I've been meaning to try it. The owners used to live in New York, and they designed this place after a restaurant there called 'Serendipity Three.' She told me it's very eclectic."

"And the food?"

"Her words to me were 'I hope you like it spicy.'"

The decor was adorable. Walnut-stained barn board covered the walls, and no two chairs were the same. Everything was mismatched, as if it had all been picked up at antique sales. The tables looked hand built.

Sassy loved it immediately. The place was half full, and everyone was talking and laughing loudly. A harried-looking waitress arrived right away to take their orders, and Sassy asked about the piano across the room.

"You should've come last night," she said. "Oscar Peterson was here. Oh yeah. This place is always jumping with big names. You've heard of Anne Murray? The Canadian Brass?" She bit her pencil. "A couple of weeks ago we had that guy . . . a skater. He won the Canadian Junior Championships. What's his name? Gosh. I—Toller something. Cranston? Anyway, the owner's deal is that if you entertain, you get your meal free."

Tom looked at Sassy. "Is that how you're going to pay our bill?"

"I can't. It's a short lunch and my boss would kill me if I was late getting back." She smiled up at the waitress. "But I will definitely keep that in mind for next time."

She left, and Sassy braced herself. "So. First, I'm really sorry. Second, thank you for your donation. Third, I'm an idiot."

"Not usually," he replied, but she saw it in his eyes. She'd hurt him.

"Well, I was last night. I was overwhelmed, I guess. The concert and all that emotion, the money being stolen . . ." She exhaled, her shoulders dropping. "It's not just that. It's everything. I feel so stupid these days. I miss Marion and I miss my dad, and I have no idea where Joey is. I can't think straight. I feel so alone sometimes, but I'm supposed to be a grown-up. I'm so embarrassed. Forgive me? Please?"

He tilted his head, considering. "No more temper tantrums?"

"I can't promise. I'm a Libra." She paused. "Tom, I know this has been hard for you, too. I barely gave it a thought because I'm so naturally self-ish—" She hesitated, hoping he'd correct her, but he didn't. "But the truth is, I know my dad was important to you."

"He was. He was more like a dad to me than my own."

She hadn't realized that. "I'm so sorry."

"I was glad you called me. You know. When it happened."

She blinked at him, surprised. "Of course I called you. You're important to him. And to me. Besides, who else would pick up the phone at that hour?"

He dropped his gaze to the wooden tabletop, scarred by knives and forks over the years.

"And the cheque," she said softly. "Thank you. That was a lot of money. You didn't have to do that. Why did you?"

"I want to help."

"But that's a lot."

He shrugged, lifting the collar of his black jacket. "It's important to you, so it's important to me. Especially if it can help to find your brother some-how. I know what it's like to lose someone."

This was new. Tom didn't talk about himself much. Probably because she was always the one doing the talking.

"Who did you lose?" she asked softly.

"I told you my parents died years ago, but also my two brothers and a cousin. All three of those were in the last war. I was fourteen when they left, so I was too young to go. They never found my oldest brother's body, and that's really stuck with me. Somewhere in France, I was told. I can almost picture the other two, since I know where they're buried, but all I can imagine of Jeff are his bones in the mud somewhere. I hate the idea of anyone being left behind, dead or alive."

It was probably inappropriate, thinking of him this way while he was sharing an important story in his life, but Sassy couldn't help herself. He was striking, she thought with a kind of wonderment. His black hair was messed just a little, his icy-blue eyes even more pronounced because of the dark rings beneath them. Was he not sleeping? She didn't think he was sick, but then again, she hadn't had as much time for him lately. The hardness was gone from his face now, his earnest expression winning out over the hurt. He was, she saw clearly, much more handsome than Sean Connery.

Sassy wanted Tom more than she'd ever wanted any man in her life.

"I didn't mean to hurt you," she said softly.

He rubbed his hand hard across his mouth. "You throw me off balance, Sassy. You make me want to scream, and other times I sit back and listen to you laugh, even if I don't know what's funny. It's like nothing I've ever heard before, that laugh." He huffed out his nose. "I wasn't trying to just 'fix everything.' I hated seeing you so upset, and I wanted to see that smile."

She dropped her chin. "I know. I'm sorry. I might have gone a little far."

"You might have."

She rolled up her white napkin and waved it like a flag. "Truce?"

He leaned back, holding her gaze. "Look. The truth is, I want you to find your brother. And I want the Red Cross to have money to spend on saving those poor fools down there. But mostly, Sassy, I want you to be happy."

thirty-seven
MARION

❧

Marion sat on the hard leather seat of the UH-1 Iroquois, wind shoving through the open door and whistling past her ears. She gripped her seat until her knuckles cramped, riding the sky as the helicopter angled one way then the other, curving over rice patties and mud-brown rivers, navigating the tangled, impenetrable chaos of the jungle. As they soared over tiny villages, Marion was painfully aware that some might shelter guns, even grenade launchers. When the helicopter angled sharply, she saw their clear, black shadow skimming over the jungle.

She was too scared to scream. Until a week ago, she'd never even stepped into an airplane, and now she flew two thousand feet in the air, deafened by the hum and *thumpthumpthump* of a Huey—God! She'd watched these helicopters on TV! In front of her, three men in camouflage sat on either side of the cabin's open doors, their legs hanging over the edges, machine guns slung over their laps. In addition, a door gunner stood on either side, each manning an M60 machine gun. Long belts of cartridges spilled onto the floor at their feet. Attached to the outside of the Huey, just behind her and thankfully out of her view, was a pair of anti-tank missiles. Just in case, Daniel had said.

He sat on her left, craning over her shoulder to see what she saw, absently adjusting his eye patch. He pointed at something, but she couldn't hear what he said over the drubbing of the chopper blades and the hammering of her pulse. She turned to ask, her eyes streaming tears from the wind, and her helmet bumped his chin. Without a hint of a smile, he pressed down on it, keeping it secure. She recalled the intimate feel of his fingers on her skin as he'd fastened her helmet under her chin before takeoff.

"Nothing's gonna mess with that brain. Or that face," he'd said, his tone earnest. "Never take that off."

"Yes, Major," she'd said, wanting to make him smile. She had been so afraid, standing by the rumbling helicopter. She needed to hear that reassurance again, the promise that, yes, he would take care of her. A reminder that this was more than a job or duty to both of them. This was him and her.

He didn't smile, but he held her gaze, and she got what she needed.

Strands of her hair had escaped her braid and her metal helmet, and she swiped them out of her face. Dr. Marion Hart, known for her conservative suits and shoes, her perfectly styled, tight roll, and her punctuality, was now buzzing thousands of feet over Vietnam in camo, her hair like a fright wig under a tin can.

A sudden *boom!* to the west, and she felt Daniel shift with her, seeking out the source. Grey smoke ballooned in the distance, then again nearby, but that's all she could see. Daniel was a statue beside her, his hard expression unchanging. The Huey's shadow skimmed over the green of the trees below, and the copilot twisted backward, yelling something at them and gesturing beyond the open door. She saw his mouth move, but she couldn't make out anything over the noise. Daniel could. He was nodding. He stuck out his fist, thumb up, then he brought his mouth to her ear.

"Almost there. Hold tight."

He was shouting, and yet his voice still sounded far away. She wondered if the chopper noise could be harming her hearing long-term, then she rolled her eyes internally. Worrying about her hearing? That should be her last concern.

He pointed out the open door. "Do you see the old temple out there?"

She squinted, but she didn't see anything that looked like a temple. She shook her head.

"It's just broken walls now. I was here when they blew it up. I hate seeing history erased."

He was trying to calm her, she thought. Talking about history when all that mattered to her was the present. "Yes, I think I see it now."

Without warning, the helicopter angled sharply, and Marion's stomach rolled with it. The men at the open doors hugged their weapons tighter, their legs stretching out with the Huey's momentum. The door gunners were alert, fingers on the triggers. Then one fired, blasting seven hundred rounds per minute into the sky, and the other one started up, shooting at something Marion couldn't see. The guns' vibrations thundered in her chest, and the gunners' bodies shook with the weapons' motion, moving in a blur. Marion tried not to hyperventilate, tried not to sob with panic.

"What's happening?" she shouted, gripping Daniel's arm. "What's—"

She screamed and ducked as bullets *pinged!* and ricocheted inside the chopper, then she grunted when Daniel's arm slammed across her middle like a steel belt. One of the men on the side fell back, clutching his leg, and someone dragged him inside so another soldier could take his place. Then she heard a different sound, a kind of snap then crack, and the helicopter's windshield became riddled with holes and fissures. The pilot was yelling into the microphone attached to his helmet when suddenly he slumped, and his head rolled sideways. Marion gawked in horror as the copilot took over, battling the controls and calling for help.

"We'll be all right," Daniel shouted, but she didn't believe him.

A jolt knocked her forward, then the chopper lost control, turning on its own axis as it spiralled from the sky. The green of the jungle awaited them, the shapes and shadows giving way to individual leaves and branches. Far too close and coming closer.

"Hang on!" Daniel yelled, but she was already braced, hugging her knees, holding her breath, praying as hard as she could. *Please God, please God, please—*

thirty-eight
MARION

❧

Can't move. Can't move. Trapped...

"Marion!"

That voice. It sounded like it was coming from far away and through a pillow. Hands were shoving her, moving her. She smelled smoke. An unfamiliar sense of urgency bloomed.

"Marion! Open your eyes!"

She did. Daniel loomed over her, his hands clenched on her biceps. Fresh blood painted the scarred side of his face, and his helmet was gone. Hers was, too, she realized dazedly.

"Are you hurt?"

She blinked at him, confused. Then she remembered the helicopter, free-falling to the earth while she screamed and prayed.

"Are you hurt, Marion?"

She did a mental inventory of her body. She tasted iron, but felt no specific pain. She must have bitten her tongue when they crashed. She had no idea. "I don't think so."

"Can you move?"

She sat up, toppled back, then roused herself again, noting she was about twenty feet away from the crash site. The burning chopper was on its side, smoking amid a shattered stand of trees. Its tail was missing. She counted half a dozen soldiers standing at a distance from it, guns on their shoulders, eyes on their scopes as they scouted the trees.

"We gotta go," he said quietly.

"How did I get over here?"

"I carried you," he said, holding out his hand. "Let's go."

But where? Everything looked the same. Beyond the throbbing in her ears, she heard gunfire. The American soldiers fired back and yelled directions at each other.

Daniel helped her stand, then he pointed. "Do you remember that old temple you saw? The broken wall? It's that way. No matter what happens, I want you to go toward it. You have that compass they gave you in your pack? Good. Pull it out and follow it."

A new panic seized her. "What about you? I can't go without you."

"I will be right behind you."

"How far is it?"

He shrugged. "Just keep running."

The gunfire was louder now, coming from both sides. "Come with me," she begged.

His expression hardened. "Go. Be as quiet as you can. Don't stop." He gave her a gentle push. "I'll be there in a minute. We can't let these guys follow us."

She stumbled forward then turned to see what was happening. Daniel had an M16 in his hands and was striding purposefully toward the soldiers. Where had he gotten *that* from?

He glanced back. "Go!" he shouted, then fresh gunfire burst from the trees, and he began running toward the other men, shooting.

Marion wiped away her tears with a blood-smeared hand, studied her compass, then, going against every impulse, ran away from Daniel. Toward the broken wall at the top of the hill. Or at least she hoped that's where she was headed. So often she had marvelled at the soldiers on television, navigating the impossible sameness of the jungle. Now she floundered in the midst of the tangled trees and vines, the knotted roots, all of it seething with Vietnam's impenetrable heat, and it was so much worse than she'd imagined. There was no straight path to navigate, only obstructions made blurry by the sweat rolling into her eyes. Branches scraped her, clawed at her, and her rattled brain played tricks, forcing her to study everything on the ground and in the air. Daniel had said the Vietcong became part of the jungle itself, they knew it so well. She never should have read that *National Geographic* article about Vietnam, with its venomous vipers and cobras, malarial mosquitoes, battalions of angry weaver ants, and even killer plants, like heartbreak grass. Tigers, elephants, and crocodiles could be anywhere. Not to mention booby traps and the tunnels Daniel had told her about, all of them rigged. The enemy could be anywhere.

She saw nothing, but she imagined a thousand threats watched her.

Out of breath and slick with sweat, she paused to search the space behind her. Daniel was nowhere in sight. Terrible thoughts filled her brain, but she knew not to call out for him and reveal her position. Except she couldn't help wondering: What if he never came? The possibility caught in her throat. She had no time to panic, let alone cry, she reminded herself. She'd come this far. Staying put would only get her killed. When she'd caught her breath, she faced forward again and continued along the nonexistent path, following the tiny, quivering needle of her compass.

After what felt like an eternity of trudging through the jungle, Marion heard a familiar sound and froze. Men's voices. Hardly breathing, she homed in on the sound, and dread curled like a serpent in her stomach. That was not English. With the dense foliage blocking everything, it was difficult to tell where the men were. She took a few very slow, very cautious steps then stopped again, trying to get a feel for where they might be. *There*. Closer now. But in which direction? With no other options, she walked on, checking the compass every few steps. The worst possible thing would be to get lost out here.

No, she thought. There were probably much worse things, but she didn't want to think about those.

A movement among the trees about twenty feet to her left caught her eye. Vibrating with fear, she squatted and counted two darkly clad Vietnamese men—no, there were more. Three more walked behind them, talking softly. They were headed directly toward her, so close they would step on her soon if she didn't move. So she crawled, studying the ground, fearing the jaws of a predator by her hands or a mouth of a gun at her head at any moment. When she thought she might be out of their sight even a little, she stood, hunching low, and picked up as much speed as she could.

They hadn't seen her, but that couldn't last. She gasped with surprise when the canopy of trees magically opened up ahead, and sunlight beamed down on a wide, swiftly flowing, brown river. There would be nowhere to hide once she got there, but she couldn't stop. She scanned the shoreline, seeking a bridge, but there was nothing. Downriver, she spied a sort of path extending out into the water, made up of different-sized stones. Maybe it was shallow there. She headed toward it, because her only hope was to cross the river before they saw her.

A shout cut through the air, and her heart pounded. They'd spotted her; she heard their boots stomping through the forest floor behind her. At the sound of a gunshot, she sprang from the trees like a flushed rabbit, blind with terror. Another shot cracked, and bark blasted off a tree beside her head. Two more shots were fired as she sprinted to the water's edge. If she could cross it before they caught her, maybe she could run downstream and hide. She neared the rough bridge of stones then splashed into the river toward it, feeling warm water rush against her legs. When she reached the rocks, the path was slick with algae, but she kept running, arms outstretched to help her balance, holding her breath as more shouts and gunshots followed.

All of a sudden, the river bottom was gone, and Marion dropped without warning. Her boots were caught and bound by weeds, her body bashed against rocks she couldn't see, and the current swept her steadily downstream. When she finally got purchase, she braced her boots on the bottom then kicked so she shot straight up, gasping for air. Bullets skimmed past her head, plopping into the water, and she remembered Daniel's story that day: *I heard bullets hitting the grass around me. Like sharp whispers.* He had jumped into the water to escape them, but it wasn't deep enough for him to swim, so he had to get out.

Marion's river was plenty deep. But she couldn't swim.

The enemy was on the shore now, lined up five in a row. She paddled madly to keep her head above the surface of the water, and the men kept shooting and laughing, as if it was a sport and she was target practice. She heaved for breath, but the current snatched at her, dragging her under again. She kicked and splashed, reaching for the sunlight, but the glow of the corona kept getting farther away. She was wearing down. She shoved off the bottom again, and as she reached the surface, she felt a searing pain hit the top of her arm. In a daze, she noticed blood filling the brown water, turning it a deep burgundy. She began to sink again, feeling heavy and bone-tired.

A burst of machine-gun fire jerked her out of her stupor, and she sought the surface again. In a brief moment above the water, she saw two of the Vietnamese men crumple to the ground.

"Marion!"

"Daniel!" she wanted to yell, but she was battling too hard to breathe for any sound to come out. He stood on the shore she had just fled, staring at her while keeping an eye on the enemy at the same time. She wanted to tell him she was shot, but she was so, so tired. She wanted to tell him she thought she might be in love with him. She wanted to weep, but she had nothing left.

He fired again, and the remaining three men dove under the brush. They shot back, but Daniel held them in place while he yelled at her.

"Marion! Swim back to me, dammit! Don't you give up!" He was cut off by gunshots. He returned fire before turning back to her. "Swim, Marion! Swim! Please, Marion! I need you!"

In those three words, Marion found a kernel of strength. Holding her breath for as long as she could, she kicked and splashed toward the shore, hauling herself through the water until her arms screamed with the effort. The battle continued on land, but she couldn't waste time looking to see what was happening. Her focus was on a large boulder ahead, which offered an anchor. She tried to time her arrival at the rock with the speed of the current, but when she finally reached it, her hand slipped. With a cry, she went under again.

Then she felt him there. His hands gripped her under her arms, dragged her up and out of the water, then held her tight against his chest.

I'm alive.

She was too tired to open her eyes. Too tired to thank him, but he didn't seem to notice. She lay limply in his arms as he carried her to a safe place, where he pressed down on her gunshot wound. He pulled a bandage from his pack and applied a field dressing, assuring her the wound was minor, but by then, shock had set in. She began to shake. Daniel was her blanket, keeping her safe and alive and warm.

"You did it," he murmured into her ear. "You swam, Marion. You defeated the river."

She moaned, unable to articulate any thoughts. Then she felt him press against the top of her head, and she realized, *He kissed me*.

"Daniel," she whispered, her eyes still closed. Maybe she was dreaming. If she was, she wanted to hang on to it a little longer.

"I'm here, Marion," he said. "I got you."

She felt her control give way, and she clenched her jaw, trying to hold back the rush of tears she knew was coming. That's when his fingers went to her cheek, softly caressing her wet skin.

"Don't cry, Marion," he said. "You made it."

She opened her eyes at last, and he was gazing right at her, his expression tender. It felt like the most natural thing in the world when he leaned in and kissed her. She closed her eyes again, offering an invitation for both of them. His lips touched hers, and she answered, finally letting everything she'd been feeling for him rise to the surface.

"Thank you," she whispered against his mouth.

"Never thank me, Marion. Please."

"You saved my life."

"You saved mine, too," he told her, his arms tightening around her. "Rough first day, huh? We can rest here a few more minutes, but then we gotta go."

thirty-nine
SASSY

S assy was getting used to her father being gone, but the office still felt strange without him. His door was open all the time, not closed. His desk, which was normally a shining example of efficiency, cleared of paper at the end of every day, was piled high with boxes and files.

They both felt it, she knew. Tom was in there now, wearing a brown-checked, short-sleeved shirt and jeans, and she watched him from her desk, giving herself a little treat by admiring him from behind. When he turned, she was quick to look away and appear busy with something.

"At least he was organized," Tom said, not appearing to have noticed. "You and I should be able to sort through these fairly smoothly. I want to spread everything out on his desk so we can pick through them. Can you come help me?"

Sassy was also dressed casually, in light blue flare pants and a loose white blouse, her hair pulled back in a ponytail. She stepped into her father's office, and her gaze dropped to a box on the floor, mostly filled with crumpled paper and old files.

"I can take that out," she offered, but he moved in front of her.

"No, no. I'll get that later."

She frowned. "It's just garbage. It's not too heavy for me. Look."

Before he could argue, she lifted the box then recoiled when she discovered what he hadn't wanted her to see. Two empty whisky bottles. She hated finding these ugly reminders of her father. She only wanted to remember the good man he'd been before all this.

She sighed. "I didn't know he was drinking in here. I thought it was just at home, when he was alone."

"I guess there was a lot we didn't know. His door was closed a lot at the end," he reminded her. "I'm sorry, Sassy. I was hoping you wouldn't see that."

"I know. You tried. I'm too stubborn for my own good, but you already knew that."

Her father had left a lot of files behind, but it was simple enough to sort through them. One pile for open cases, the other for completed ones. They set the finished ones aside then began to read.

"You have a lot of work ahead of you. There are some here that he hadn't touched for weeks," she noted. "Maybe a follow-up?"

"Good idea," he said, carrying another box to the table. "Make a list with dates and details so you can prioritize."

She nodded. "I'll make it easy for you to follow."

She brought out a clean sheet of paper and began writing down what he'd need. When she finished, she glanced up and realized he was studying her, looking thoughtful.

"What if you make another list for you to look after?"

"I'm sorry?"

"I know you're a sworn Marxist and all, but you've been doing a great job of faking it at capitalism lately. What would you think of having some of your own accounts? I'll be with you the whole way for anything you need. And of course, you'd keep all your commissions."

"Selling houses? Oh, I don't know what I'm doing. I only do what you and Dad tell me to do."

"Not true. You've been doing your own research behind the scenes just because it's interesting to you. Your attention to detail is bad."

She dropped her hands at her sides. "*Bad?*"

He wrinkled his nose and dug more files out of the latest box. "Isn't that what kids say now? 'Bad' is good. That's what I meant, anyway. I'm just saying, when I ask you about an account, you already have the details in your head. We have different strengths, and you're only just starting to figure yours out, but you're a natural. You're way ahead of me in a lot of ways. Why not give it a shot?"

How could she say no to him? About anything? "You'll help me?"

"Anything you need. Think about it, Sassy. Down the road, you and I might be partners."

Oh, she had thought about that a lot, but those thoughts had nothing to do with business. She studied the stack of files. "You really think I can do it?"

"I do."

"Right on. One at a time." She glanced behind Tom, at all the books and the few photographs on her father's handsome bookshelves. Stepping closer, she took down the framed medal and skimmed her thumbs over the glass. "I used to think this meant something."

He was observing her closely. "It does. Just not what you thought it meant. He still fought over there, and he still pulled Mr. Moore out of the way when he was injured. I think of it, in a way, kind of like my brothers. I have no idea what they did over there, and I never will, but they will always be heroes to me."

His words put a smile on her face that stayed there while she continued sorting. "Are you going to move into this office?"

He shot her a careful glance. "I don't think so. If I do, it won't be for a long time. It's still his. What do you think?"

She nodded, pleased. He was right. It would have been too soon.

"What's this?" Tom muttered, pulling a small, black leather book from the box. He flipped it open, then his eyes widened. "It looks like a journal of sorts."

"Then close it! You can't read someone else's diary."

"No, no. Not like that. This is a business journal." He turned more pages, working his way to the back. "This is amazing. No wonder his desk was always spotless. All his thoughts were in here. See? He wrote them down as he went and crossed them off when they were done." He kept going, and his smile began to fade. "This is dated about two months ago, and there are a lot of things he didn't cross off."

"I can start with those, if you think I should," she said, waiting for her turn to hold the book. It was a piece of her father, no matter if it was all about real estate. She wanted to hold it.

"Yeah, but . . ." He was distracted, looking through all the entries. "I don't know if you want to see this, Sassy."

"Why not?"

"He's writing about other things in here as well." He kept reading. "Even his writing has changed. He . . . Gosh. He was so hard on himself."

"Let me see."

"Wait. There's a list here with your name on it."

She grabbed the book from his hands, and right away she saw what he meant about the handwriting. It was in the same black ink as the rest of the entries, but the letters were messy.

"Oh, Tom," she said, reading the title of the list and fighting tears. "This is so sad. All he had to do was talk to me."

Things to tell Susan

1. Tell Susan I love her.

2. Tell Susan Rita couldn't get enough of her smile, and I couldn't get enough of Rita's expression every time she held our daughter. Tell her about Rita. How she could sing, how her favourite colour was red, how she loved to listen to the rain, even if it meant she dragged me outside and we got soaked. I didn't mind.

3. Tell Susan she is much smarter than she thinks she is. Her socialist attitude makes me crazy, but she sure can make a point. Even if it is wrong. If she tried, she could carry on her grandpa's legacy. Just because Joey won't doesn't mean she can't. She doesn't need to protest for women's rights. She just needs to stand up for herself. She's smarter than at least half the men I know.

4. *Tell Susan I miss her now that she's at the apartment. Tell her that I snuck in to amateur night at that coffeehouse after a friend of hers phoned me to let me know about it. Nice boy. Hippy.*

5. *Tell Susan her stubbornness is an asset. She just has to learn to temper it and use it to her advantage.*

6. *Tell Susan that when this war is over, I'm going to take Joey and her to Italy, and tell them about that day.*

7.

She read the list twice. Once out loud, once to herself. It was just as hard to read it the second time.

"What do you think number seven would have been?"

"Tell Susan she should give Tom a break and let him take her out for dinner."

She laughed and slapped the book closed. "What?"

"Hmm. Maybe he wouldn't have written that. Not sure."

"Tom, are you trying to ask me on a date? Here and now? This is hardly the place or the time, do you think?"

He shrugged. "I'm never good on timing. And every time I want to ask you out, something goes wrong. So I'm just doing it."

She was speechless, briefly. "I see. Well, if this is going to be a business dinner, the food has to be good." She lifted her chin, watching the little curl on the side of his smile. "If it's a personal dinner, it has to be delicious."

He nodded. "I hope you like the best steak in the city. It's personal."

forty
MARION

❧

After the race, the river, the gunshot, then the kiss—never mind the helicopter crash—Marion was too weak to walk on her own, so Daniel wrapped her good arm around his shoulder, letting her lean against him. After a moment, he found a secluded space and set her gently in the grass, always keeping watch.

"We'll stay here until you're ready," he promised, adjusting the gun where it lay across his lap.

"I didn't know you had a gun with you."

"I had a pistol, which we cleared through Customs because of the Red Cross. This one? I took it off Charlie after he shot down the chopper. He owed me."

The air between them was still with a new awareness. As much as she longed for another kiss, she was glad of the distance. Her gaze lingered on his lips, then she looked away. She couldn't afford to get distracted. Not here.

The other men from the helicopter eventually caught up, following the sound of gunfire. One was a medic, and he went straight over to examine Marion's shoulder wound. She could tell it was only a graze, once he unwrapped Daniel's bandage. The bullet had whizzed by, leaving a deep scrape, but that was quickly put to rights.

She marvelled at the soldier's expediency. "I imagine you do this a lot," she said.

He was young—weren't they all?—with dark hair and a faint moustache. "In my sleep, ma'am."

"What can you tell me about the hospital in Da Nang?"

"Which one? There's a surgical, a medical, and an obstetrics hospital there." She hadn't known that. "Surgical. That's where I'm assigned."

"Surgical is called the Provincial Hospital. It's a great place for black-market goods. Fresh fruit, coffee, flashlights, bug spray, rum, and huge crates of clothing marked 'Not for Sale,' donated by the United Church of Canada. The whole city is a little nuts, to be honest."

Daniel agreed. "The traffic is wild. I can't understand how people aren't killed there on an hourly basis."

A man who appeared to be in charge stood and announced that it was time to move on. He'd arranged a rendezvous where a truck would pick them up, then they'd go straight to Da Nang. The very idea of walking through the jungle then driving to a place nicknamed Rocket City shook Marion's fragile courage.

"I can't do this," she whispered to Daniel as they walked.

He didn't laugh, didn't scold. "I wish I had a dollar for every time I said that."

When at last they climbed into the back of the truck, she could only do it with his help. Holding back tears of panic and exhaustion, she finally laid her head down in his lap and fell asleep.

"We're here," she heard sometime later. He was leaning over her, peering into her face. "Time to wake up, Doc."

The truck's tires crunched over gravelly sand toward a large cement building with yellow stucco walls and orange roof tiles. A large khaki canvas tent stood nearby.

"That's orthopaedics," the medic explained. "Up there is the emergency entrance, and there's a heliport behind that can take in two or three medevacs at a time."

"What's that?" she asked, pointing past the hospital. Small outbuildings stood at the base of a giant cement water tower.

"Laundry and storage facilities." He pointed. "Those are the bathhouses and lavatories. If there's a power failure, they're run by a diesel engine."

She saw hydro poles stretching across the grounds to the transformer station. "Can't the Vietcong sabotage those wires? They're completely exposed."

"Yes, ma'am," the medic said. "Happens all the time."

At last they pulled up to the door of the surgical hospital, and a small flock of nurses greeted Marion at the door. The other soldiers left, but Daniel stuck by her side.

"I don't think they'll let you stay when I'm operating," she said.

"I'm going to be with you whenever it's allowed."

She still wasn't sure how that would work, but she was comforted.

The nurses led Marion and Daniel to the *chef d'administration*, a tall, blond Frenchman who was all business. "*Bonjour, Docteur et Majeure.* Might I suggest, Majeure, that you go with my assistant now? You can speak with the guards outside the hospital while I give Dr. Hart a brief introduction of *l'hôpital*. The guards will answer questions and show you the areas that will concern you."

Daniel checked with Marion, and she gave him a look meant to reassure him. She watched him go, immediately feeling lost, but the chef didn't appear to notice.

"Before we begin, I have spoken with other foreign medical experts, and they all concur with what I am about to say to you, so I hope you will not feel affronted."

"Please," she said, hoping she would remember everything. She still didn't feel fully conscious.

"You can operate the way you are used to doing, but that will not encourage comradery, which you will need. Our best advice is that you incorporate civilian Vietnamese surgeons whenever possible, and share your expertise with the intern staff. They will have different solutions from what you know; however, you must remember that you are in their country. Constructive and useful criticism is welcome, but in the face of emergencies, which you will see on an ongoing basis, it is best to be calm, polite, and open with these local doctors. Remain patient and positive. *Comprenez?*"

"I do."

"Have you any questions?"

A thousand, Marion thought. "Where will I sleep? I saw there's construction going on by the hospital."

"Yes. A walled compound for staff and visiting surgeons. Unfortunately, that is incomplete. We will show you to your accommodations after our tour here."

Learning the compound hadn't been built yet did nothing to instill confidence. "What is the schedule?"

"The general day shift begins at nine o'clock in the morning; we have a three-hour hiatus at noon; then the OR will close at five p.m. Of course nursing staff and anaesthetists will be here prior to that, and we expect surgeons to be scrubbed and ready to go before eight o'clock."

"A hiatus?"

"Of course. A siesta, as they call it. But we also have night-duty surgeons and interns."

"I see."

"Come and I will introduce you to the hospital," he said, and she followed him toward a number of interconnected buildings. "*Attention.* Watch your step."

Marion hadn't expected much from the Provincial Hospital in Da Nang, but right away she saw she should have anticipated worse. The first ward they encountered stopped her in her tracks. Bandaged bodies were everywhere, lying, sitting, crammed into every corner. More than one patient lay in each of the tightly packed cots.

"What is going on here?"

"We are, of course, always overcrowded. But everyone is cared for."

She couldn't stop staring, taking in the filth and the faces. "How overcrowded are you?"

"This hospital has five hundred beds. At the moment, we have approximately fifteen hundred patients."

Holding her breath against the reek of the sick, wounded, and dying, she followed the chef through a labyrinth of wards, slightly panicked at the thought of navigating them by herself. The stench lessened within the wards, since every window was wide open, but that created its own problems. There was no glass, no screens or shutters, which explained why every surface was covered in a fine film of sand, blown in by helicopters landing or taking off. Partway down the hallway, Marion slapped her hand over her nose, repulsed by a solid stink coming from open toilets. Houseflies hovered and landed, and she swatted a couple out of her face.

"The children's ward," the chef announced, appearing not to notice the flies. He indicated the next room, and Marion felt her knees weaken. So many parents and relatives had come to take care of the little ones that the crowding was even worse, resulting in up to five youngsters on one cot.

"Can't the parents go home? To make more room?"

He appeared confused by the question. "Who would prepare their meals and bathe them?" He gestured toward a row of large sinks. "Here is where they wash up."

She sniffed and tried not to gag. "Why do I smell smoke?"

"Cooking fires. They're all around the compound."

"What about all the flies? Can't you do anything about them?"

"Dr. Hart, do you recall what I first said about working with local doctors and not always following the same rules set out in your country? It is possible to learn valuable lessons from other cultures, especially in a place like this. These flies serve a purpose. They may be annoying, but they are especially beneficial to patients with gangrene, pressure ulcers, and napalm burns. They land on the wounds, lay their eggs, and maggots will soon emerge. Maggots, I'm certain you know, consume only dead tissue. Healthy tissue is left behind, ready for skin grafting or whatever is needed."

She'd read about that but never seen it in practice. She peered closer at one child who lay facedown, his buttocks and back covered in what appeared to be napalm burns. Tiny white worms moved among the wounds, doing their job. Regardless of how hard they worked, Marion couldn't help shuddering and quickly moved on.

"Here, you can see, is one of the operating rooms."

A man lay on a bed, his leg shattered. Above him, his surgeon hunched in concentration. Blood pooled on the floor, but the nurses were too busy to mop.

"What do they do for blood transfusions?" Marion asked, unsure she wanted to know the answer. Her mind kept going back to the maggots.

"We have supplies, but the U.S. Naval Hospital will send more over. It's not always fresh, but three-week-old blood is better than none at all, wouldn't you say?" They stood in the doorway a moment, and he pointed out the array of shining silver instruments standing by for use. "We have everything you might need. I understand you are here as a senior medical student, so you will be mostly with the interns, working alongside surgeons doing suturing, debriding entry and exit wounds, and anything else the surgeon requires." He nodded, satisfied. "You are on the schedule for tomorrow morning at eight. Any more questions?"

forty-one
SASSY

Sassy got out of Tom's car and stood on the sidewalk, gazing up at the white-brick building with its black shutters and small burgundy awning. A hanging sign above welcomed them to Barberian's Steak House, Est. 1959.

"I've seen this place so many times, and I've always wondered what it was like inside."

"I've only been once," Tom admitted, opening the front door for her. "With my parents, almost ten years ago. It was their forty-fifth wedding anniversary. Harry Barberian was a friend of my dad's. Now, there's a man who knows how to cook. I think you're gonna like this."

She inhaled as they walked in, and her mouth watered with the promise of perfectly grilled beef, fresh fried onions, baked potatoes, and garlic. Caesar salad, maybe? She smiled up at Tom, pleased with herself. She'd told him a date demanded delicious food, and he had delivered. She had rewarded him by looking fabulous, and he couldn't keep his eyes off her.

She'd bought a pretty dress for the occasion, mindful of Marion's three Cs: *Keep it classy, comfortable, and complementary.* Knowing it would match her eyes perfectly, Sassy had chosen an emerald-green dress with black polka dots, cap sleeves, and a matching belt, cut just above her knees. Earlier that afternoon, she'd rolled up her long chestnut hair then teased out every curl and tied half of it back so the big curls crowded around her shoulders. She decided to have a little fun with her makeup, too. Except for at the fundraising concert, Tom had mostly seen her face au naturel, so she picked up a copy of *Vogue* to copy the latest style. She started with white eyeshadow, brushed all the way to the edge of her eyebrows, then she blended a line of brown around the little dip that outlined her eye, since she'd read that made women's eyes look deeper set and bigger. She painted a careful black line at the base of her top and bottom lashes, extending into a gentle cat's eye, then she stuck on a set of false eyelashes she'd picked up at Eaton's. Lots of mascara to bind it all together, a smack of lipstick, and she was, well, she was spectacular, if she did say so herself.

The maître d' showed them to a corner table with a perfectly white tablecloth and a little candle burning in the centre. The silverware practically sparkled, picking up the candlelight. As Tom pushed in her chair, she smiled up at him from under her lashes. Gosh, he was handsome.

"I'm so glad you don't dress like that every day," he said, shocking her.

"What? You don't like it?"

That little curl at the side of his mouth lifted. "I'd never get any work done."

Reassured, she laid her napkin on her lap. That's how she felt about him, too. Despite all the time they'd spent together, she wasn't the least bit tired of him. He was reading her better, too, knowing when to give and take when it came to her temper, and she was settling down, adjusting to proper behaviour in the workplace and out.

Settling down. She gazed across the table at him, wondering. She'd sworn she'd never get married. But that was a long time ago, before she'd grown up. Before he'd come along.

"I know you like white wine," Tom said, "but this place has the greatest wine cellar, and considering it's a steak house—"

"Red it is," she said, beaming up at the waiter. "You pick, Tom."

After the bottle arrived and the wine was poured into the glasses, Tom lifted his and looked directly at her.

"Here's to you," he said. "The most beautiful woman in the world."

They both took a sip, never looking away.

"And you look dashing." She tipped her head to the side and eyed him coyly. "I have a question. Aren't I a little young for you? I mean, you're, like . . . old."

"I like the immaturity," he said, straight-faced. "Keeps me young."

Trying to hide her smile, she sipped her wine and appreciated the flavours playing on her tongue.

"What do you think?"

"It's very good. I don't know red very well. Tell me what I'm supposed to taste."

"It's a pinot noir. Great with steak. Can you taste a little sweetness? A little cherry or raspberry?"

"Hmm. I think so." She tasted it again. "And there's something kind of . . . earthy?"

"Excellent palate, Sassy. I'm impressed."

They placed their orders—both of them medium rare—then sat back and regarded each other.

"What should we talk about?" she asked.

"Lots going on. Depends where we want to start."

"Marion's in Vietnam," she said, pulling an expression of disbelief. "Seems like a good starting point."

They spoke of many things over dinner, and though there were moments where they both paused to reflect, most of the night was filled with engaging conversation and building with a growing intimacy. When dinner was done, he wiped the corners of his mouth with his napkin.

"Let's talk houses," Tom said, sitting back in his chair. He was relaxed from the wine and the meal, his gaze soft with satisfaction.

Sassy sat back as well. "Ah. Business talk. What about them?"

"Tell me about the market right now. I love listening to how your mind works."

She glowed with the compliment. "Let's see. The average home price in this city is about twenty-four thousand dollars, and it's going up. I know you recently sold a three-storey in Moore Park for forty-two thousand. Congratulations."

He smiled and sipped, enjoying their second bottle. "You noticed. The buyers are in their early forties. They've moved around a lot, and they wanted something bigger this time. Their last place was in Cabbagetown. What do you think of the choice?"

"Dad always said the biggest consideration when you're buying a home is the neighbourhood. I'd say this was a step up for them. Lots of room for grandchildren." She felt a little tug on her heart and dropped her chin. "I think I'm going to keep Dad's house," she said softly. "It needs to be there for Joey when he's back."

"I think that's a practical move." He grinned. "Did you hear that? I just called you practical."

She laughed. "But . . . oh, you're going to think I'm silly."

"Probably. Try me."

She exhaled. "I don't want to leave my apartment. I love it there. I love everyone on my floor, pretty much," she mused. "How can I leave the Romanos, the Levins, the Moores? I can't imagine not having them around whenever I need a cup of sugar or a new plant, or just company. And what am I supposed to do about Marion? I can't live miles away from her. Then there's Mr. Snoop, the guy who always has to see who's coming out of the elevator. I definitely need him in my life."

"Another thing I remember your dad saying was that you should never make a major decision, like buying a house, when you're emotional. It's like buying groceries when you're hungry. You can easily make the wrong decision. You don't have to rush, Sassy. Take your time." He paused. "I do hope you won't quit working just because you're independently wealthy now. Travel around the world, hit all the coolest spots, never come back . . ."

"I'm not going to quit. I'm going to let you teach me, and I'm going to teach you, too."

His smile warmed. "Yeah? I bet you have a lot to teach."

"Practical, remember?"

"I do. My practical Sassy."

Mine.

"Besides," she said, folding her napkin and setting it aside. "I don't think I want to travel around the world. Not yet, anyway, and not by myself. Maybe someday, I'll do it with you."

forty-two
MARION

❧

M arion loved the panic of a hospital emergency room. She loved when people ran to her, bleeding and broken, having no idea what to do. There was no feeling in the world she liked better than being the one who could turn chaos into logic. Pandemonium into efficiency.

But not here. This place seethed with so much turmoil, so much madness, it was like the river where she'd almost drowned. She couldn't catch her breath. She couldn't focus. She watched the orderlies rolling gurneys in or helping the wounded hobble onto a cot, and for the first time in her life, she found herself rattled by the sight of blood. Sure, she was out of practice, but it was more than that. It was the sheer volume of need here. The all-consuming, inescapable tragedy of war.

Her first surgery in Vietnam was a compound femoral fracture. She had done similar procedures in the efficient, sanitary Toronto hospital, but this felt nothing like that. She was assigned to the debriding, but the sheer extent of the damage was shocking. She could not fall back on what she knew would help, because despite this hospital being funded by Canada, they didn't have what she needed. Once the femur was put back together, they needed to extend the muscles, ensuring they maintained length. At home, they did that by using a pulley system with weights. Here, they used sandbags. And at one point, she had three patients in the same bed, all hooked up to the same sandbags.

Later that first morning, a young man ran in, shouting something at her in Vietnamese. When he saw her confusion, he switched to French. "*Venez vite! Maintenant!*" A nurse, the anaesthetist, and Marion ran outside and found an older man lying unconcious on the ground outside. His head was bruised and bleeding, his blood pressure was elevated, and his right pupil was dilated. But it was the swelling over his right temporal area that demanded attention. Even without an X-ray, she was fairly sure it was a skull fracture with a subdural hematoma. As they rushed him inside, the anaesthetist slid in a nasotracheal tube to help him breathe, then the nurse shaved the side of his head with an old, albeit clean, straight razor. Just in time, the surgeon arrived and cut an incision down to the man's skull. He drilled into the bone, and they were rewarded with a spurt of dark blood as the area decompressed. The surgery continued for two more hours at least, and at the end the medical team were feeling cautiously optimistic.

"Keep the nursing staff away from the dressings. This is vital," the surgeon told her. "They will want to change them, but in a case like this, it increases the chance of an infection."

With the revolving shifts, it was impossible to know which nurse might come next to change the dressings. Marion went to one of the interns who spoke passable English, had him translate a phrase for her, then she wrote it on the patient's head bandage.

"*Khong thai bang*," it said. DON'T CHANGE THE BANDAGE.

When the obstetrics doctor was busy elsewhere, Marion successfully delivered a baby through caesarean section. Hours later, another labouring woman arrived, her belly sliced apart by shrapnel. When Marion finally brought her baby into the world, the child was dead. The grieving mother passed away shortly after.

There was *so much*. One after another, patients were rolled into the operating room, barely giving Marion time to change her gloves.

"Say-ow-toy," she said over and over to the blank, pleading faces around her. Daniel had taught her the phrase. *Sẽ ổn thôi*. Or sometimes in French. *Ça va aller*. "It's going to be okay."

Marion's last surgery of the day was on a five-year-old boy, struck in the face by a grenade. Somehow he had kept his eyes, but his jaw had been torn apart, and it took hours to clear enough of the damage to figure out how to rebuild.

When she emerged from the building an hour past the end of her shift, Daniel was waiting for her at the hospital's exit. She felt his troubled examination as he led the way to the dining hall, and when she almost collapsed from exhaustion, he braced her elbow. He told her to sit, then he brought her food. Afterward, he led her back to their separate apartments, and he sat on the side of her bed when she asked him to stay a little while.

"Daniel," she whispered, feeling ashamed. "I don't think I can do this."

He waited.

"It's so much more than I imagined. It's too much." Tears rushed up, hot and urgent. "The children— How can men blow up children? How can they slaughter pregnant women, leaving dead fetuses behind?" She stared at her hands and watched them shake. The cuffs of her shirt were brown with so many strangers' dried blood. "I can't do this. I'm not who I thought I was."

"Who did you think you were, Marion?" he asked. "Superman? Someone who could fly out here and save everyone? Maybe end the war?"

She looked at him, tears streaming down her face. "I just wanted to help. I never thought—"

"Then you didn't think at all." His gaze hardened. "Tell me you didn't watch the news, but I won't believe you. You watched hours and weeks and months of American boys humping through the heat, getting blown up. What did you see after that? Did you see any of this?" He held out his hands, palms up. "It's so convenient at home. We don't know the soldiers, we don't know the enemy, and we don't know any of the children who are being killed. We flip off the TV and go to bed, but we don't see what happens after."

She looked away, ashamed. "I didn't . . ."

"No, really. Who did you think you were, Marion?"

She covered her face, sobbing. "I'm nobody. I don't belong here."

How could she have even contemplated this? She should be in Toronto, drinking wine with Sassy. Hoping some of her patients would come to the community health centre. Maybe one of those would have been Daniel.

Maybe he would have come in, smiled at her, and everything would have been all right.

Instead, she was in a war zone, and after only one day, she was defeated.

Daniel took her hand in his, and his thumb slid over her knuckles. She felt the comfort he offered, stirring the butterflies in her stomach. "Wrong again. You are so far from nobody. You're the bravest woman I know. You did something no one ever thought you'd do. Not even you."

She searched his expression, wanting so badly to believe him. If she could, maybe she could believe in herself again.

"You came because you knew you could make a difference. Nobody can do what you do. My grandpa used to say there are always bumps in the road, but you keep driving anyway. I'm named after him, you know. I'm Little Danny back home." He held his other hand against his chest. "Imagine me being called 'little' anything."

She sighed deeply and managed a small smile.

"You can do this, Marion. This was day one. That's always the hardest. Now you know what you're up against, it'll be better. Never easier, but a little bit predictable."

She snorted. "What about any of this is predictable?"

"You can predict it will be all over the place. Every day different. Every day bringing challenges."

"I wish that made me feel better, Daniel. You're trying so hard. But you're wrong. I'm not made for this. I shouldn't have come. I can't even handle the heat. Look at me. I'm disgusting."

He brought the back of her hand to his lips, stilling her heart. "You're not disgusting. You're amazing." His expression was calm, his breathing steady, like she'd taught him. "I heard people talking. You saved a bunch of lives today. Including a little boy's."

She nodded. That was true. Why was it so easy to focus on what went wrong instead of what went right?

"You know what you need?" he asked.

She was afraid to guess.

"You need a shower. And sleep. And my protection."

The tears came again, but this time from relief. "Yes," she said weakly. "A shower. Sleep. And you."

He leaned in and kissed her lightly on the brow. "I'll see you in the morning, Marion. A brand-new day. You get to live that adventure you wondered about. Not many people are brave enough to try that, you know. Don't worry. If you falter, I'll be right there behind you."

forty-three
SASSY

❧

Work was improving by the day for Sassy. Her first attempt to speak with a couple about selling their house had somehow turned into both a sale and a purchase, and she watched in awe as the reverse domino effect took place. The work that had initially appeared as a tangled mess in her mind was quickly shaping up into straight lines that she could easily navigate. Tom observed, giving her encouragement and more cases to follow up on, but mostly he let her do her thing.

"Your dad was right. You're a natural."

She grinned. "You might be right."

On her walk home from the bus one day, she saw two men sleeping in an alley, and what had once frightened her now made her sad. They wore old fatigues, and she couldn't help thinking of Daniel. From him, she had learned that these men were not bad people. Just lost. From Marion, she had learned that she had the ability to help them somehow.

The next morning, she stopped in at Eaton's and bought a half dozen blankets, which she handed out to shivering men she passed. They stared at her in amazement then asked if she had any money to spare. The day after that, she went to Jack's Variety Store and pulled together bags of things she thought the men might need. Food, toothbrushes, soap. Wool caps and hand-knitted mittens. When she told Esther what she was doing, she and Jack loaded Sassy up with bags of food. She had to phone Tom to come and drive her, because she couldn't carry it all.

"But there's so many of them," she said as he drove. "I'll never be able to make a dent. I want to do more."

He eyed her. "You have a good heart, Sass, but keep in mind what Marion told you. Some of those men should still be in the hospital, medicated. I know how much you care, but keep a safe distance. You never know."

That night, she rode the elevator upstairs then stepped into the hallway. Mr. Snoop's door clicked open, then closed, and Sassy had a thought. She rapped her knuckle against his door.

"Hello?"

There was no response, but she thought she could hear him breathing on the other side of the door.

"You don't have to come out, but I want you to know that if you need anything, you can ask anyone on this floor for help. We're all good people."

Still no sound from the other side, but she hadn't expected any. She slid a Jersey Milk bar under his door before walking on, and that brought a smile to her lips. But down the hall, when she reached Marion's apartment, she hesitated, missing her friend. What a strange situation they were in. Marion was in Vietnam, where no one had ever imagined her being. No one had any real illusions that Marion might find Joey, despite that being the spark that had set all this in motion, but Marion had gone anyway. She was doing all she could to help. Marion, like her father, was a hero.

Sassy turned her key and opened her door, still thinking of her friend. She smiled at Chester, meandering toward her with his tail up like a flagpole. She'd agreed to keep the cat as long as Marion needed, and honestly, Chester was a good roommate. He helped keep the loneliness at bay. And when he purred, contentment rolling deep within him, it was impossible not to feel comforted. Out of habit, she turned on the television then went to the kitchen to make dinner for both her and Chester. While he ate, she carried her plate to the dining table and was about to bite into the sandwich when an awful thought struck her.

What was she doing for anyone beside herself? Sure, she'd helped out a dozen or so men with blankets and food, but Marion had flown halfway across the world, using her skills to save lives. Daniel was helping in his own way, supporting and protecting Marion. Davey had pulled together a fundraiser for the Red Cross, and Tom had made a huge donation.

Chester jumped onto the couch and pressed his sweet face to hers. Even the cat was helping in his own way. He sat beside her and returned her gaze.

"What can I do?" she asked. He promptly lifted his back leg over his head so he could clean himself. She rolled her eyes. "That's no help, Chester."

It was cold outside, but she wrapped a blanket around her body and stepped onto her balcony. The streets had been mostly cleared of snow after the latest blizzard, and the road below shimmered under the streetlamps. A man and woman shuffled past the building, wrapped in coats and hats and boots, scarves hiding their faces. A couple of cars swished past, and Sassy lifted her gaze to take in the city. Miles and miles and miles of streets and buildings, thousands and thousands of people. Over in that direction was her father's big, red-stone house. She smiled, remembering all the nooks and crannies where she and Joey had played hide-and-seek. She remembered her father's closet, where she'd feared the entire world had forgotten her until Joey found her. She thought about the expansive lawn where they'd run in the summer, and the little hut the two of them had built together in the trees. With a flicker of memory, she recalled carrying books to the little hideout and finding peace in the quiet.

And a seed of an idea began to grow.

When she got to work the next morning, Sassy began making notes. She had a few things she wanted to check and confirm, but the more she read, the more confident she felt. What she needed now was to get the advice of an expert.

Tom's door was open, his back to her as he went through his filing cabinet. "Hey," she said.

"Hey yourself," he said, turning to face her.

He was wearing a white dress shirt and navy trousers, his black shoes spit polished, which told her that he had a meeting later. His hair was a little less perfect these days, and she thought he might be growing it longer on purpose. She liked it that way.

"Where's Betty?"

"She wasn't feeling well, so I told her to stay home and get better."

"Probably a cold," Sassy said. "Everyone on the bus was coughing today. Um, Tom, I have an idea I want to run past you."

He slid the filing cabinet drawer closed. "This sounds serious. Let's go to lunch."

She felt a flush of pleasure at the idea, which was a little strange. They were always together these days, either working or talking about work, and yet the idea still excited her.

"I thought you'd never ask."

"Far out." He glanced at his watch. "It's eleven. Maybe in a half hour?"

After five minutes had passed, she stood in front of his desk. "I can't find my watch. Is a half hour up yet?"

He laughed. "We can pretend it is," he said, grabbing his coat and reaching for hers, where it hung by the front door. "Ever been to the Senator? Oldest restaurant in the city."

"Outta sight," she said with a smile.

It was an old two-storey building, with the restaurant on the main floor. Booths and a long counter ran down one wall, where a couple of men sat, reading newspapers.

"Tommy!" A man with dark hair and a wide smile walked toward them from the back of the restaurant.

"Cecil," Tom replied, shaking his hand. "Sassy, this is my good friend Cecil Djambazis, the manager here. Cecil, this is Sassy Rankin—sorry, Susan Rankin."

Cecil leaned back slightly, as if he was examining her. "No. This can't be Jim's little girl. The last time I saw you, you were only this high. You and your little brother." His expression faltered as his memory returned. "I'm very sorry to hear about your dad. It's a great loss to the community. I considered him a good friend."

Sassy thanked him with a quiet smile.

"Yeah. You and your brother. What's his name again?"

"Joey," she said.

"Yeah! Joey. I remember now. Well, you sure did grow up nice. Good to meet you again, Susan."

"You can call me Sassy."

He grinned. "Is that right. What would your dad say about that?"

"He didn't think much of the nickname, but he agreed that I earned it."

Cecil threw back his head and laughed. "Come with me. Let's find you two a booth. Something to drink?"

"Coca-Cola," Sassy said, settling at a table, and Tom ordered the same. Keeping it simple, they ordered two club sandwiches.

"So." Tom sat back, looking curious. "This idea of yours. Let's hear it."

Cecil came around the corner, tray in hand. "Coca-Cola for the lady," he announced, "and one for the ugly guy."

The sandwiches arrived right away, and she took a few bites, delaying the conversation. What she wanted to propose to Tom was pretty innovative, she thought, but what if he thought it was ridiculous? She didn't want him to see her as a fool.

"Don't keep me in suspense, Sass," Tom prodded gently.

She nodded, but her mouth was full.

"You done any thinking on the job offer?" he tried again. "You gonna stay and work with me?"

She lifted one eyebrow. "You're offering me the job I already have?"

"I'd offer you the moon if you wanted it, Sassy."

Her cheeks warmed, and she was just as coy in her reply. "I will remember that."

"You called this meeting, Sassy. What's the topic?"

She cleared her throat. "Did I tell you that Marion was a psychiatrist at the Ontario Hospital?"

"A few times. I'm looking forward to getting to know her when she's back."

"You'll like her. Anyway, we've had some great conversations about the hospital and about when they shut it down. I used to think that was a good idea," Sassy said. "But I learned a lot from Marion. Just like she said was going to happen, a lot of the former patients are now living on the street." She'd decided not to tell him about how she'd first met Daniel, huddled on the icy sidewalk. "Here you and I are, gentrifying the city while these patients, people who are mentally ill, have nowhere to live and are freezing outside. What do you think about that?"

"It's obviously a problem," he said solemnly. "And it's going to get worse. Canada's economy is booming. Over the past four years, our GNP has grown almost ten per cent every year, and investment is rising in nonresidential construction and manufacturing, among other things."

He was smart, and she knew he tracked the markets, which she was starting to get curious about.

"Why's it going to get worse if we're doing so well?"

"Immigration has a lot to do with it. Twenty years ago, the country's population was just over fourteen million. Now we're at twenty million, and still growing, and most of those people live in cities. There's no way, even with the Affordable Housing Act, that the government can keep up the pace of building enough houses to hold them all."

She took another bite of her sandwich, appreciating the thick layer of mayonnaise. Just the way she liked it. She noticed that Tom had finished his sandwich before she started her second half.

"I've thought a lot about Joey lately, obviously, and that's made me think more about Vietnam, which I hate doing."

He leaned back in his chair, taking her topic change in stride. "Hard not to."

"They said the war would end years ago, but North Vietnam is more disciplined than anyone expected."

"That's true."

"Someday, it has to end. Someone will win, but both sides will ultimately lose. So many dead men, not to mention all the women and children. And when it's over, survivors will return to Canada and the States. Tens of thousands will come back. Where will they go?" She bit her lip, keeping her emotions in check. If she started getting weepy, she'd never finish what she wanted to say. "They'll be dumped on the street, and no one will care."

His pale eyes watched hers, shining with sympathy. "People will care."

"My friend Davey works with TADP. Do you know them? They help out the draft dodgers, finding them homes and jobs. I admire those men who refused to fight. I really do. I still think Joey's an idiot for going, but everyone has a right to fight for what they believe in." She dabbed under her nose with a napkin, refusing to cry. "The trouble is, when the men come back from the war, they will discover a lot of the homes have been taken by men who did *not* fight." She caught her breath. "I'm sorry, Tom. It will be so hard for them. They need a place they can go."

"There's no need to apologize. You're right about all of it."

"I wonder about Joey, too. If he comes back, will he be the same man he was?" She took a quick breath. "Ugh. This is not what I wanted to talk about, Tom, but I can't help it. I want my brother back, but I don't know who he will be when he gets here. And I don't know who I will be when he needs me. I feel utterly useless."

"There's nothing useless about you, Sassy. You're smart and creative and compassionate. You have so much love in your heart, and that's what Joey will need. You are capable of so much. When the time is right, you'll know exactly what to do." His gaze lowered to her plate. "Are you going to finish that?"

She shook her head, so he reached across for the rest of the sandwich.

She studied him while he took a bite. Under the table, she crossed her fingers, hoping that her suggestion wasn't nuts. "Well, I have an idea."

He grinned. "I had a feeling you did. I'm all ears."

"After the Great Depression, a lot of people couldn't afford their big homes, so they sold them and moved farther north. Many of the houses they left were turned into rooming houses. Some have up to eight small rooms, with a common kitchen and washrooms."

She was glad to see the appreciation in his expression. "Sure, but these days people are buying them back and reverting them to single-family homes. More of that gentrification you like to complain about."

"Well, what if Rankin Real Estate could slow that down a bit? What if we could buy a couple of those big places and find a way to make them into rooming homes for returning soldiers and former patients who have nothing?"

He chewed on his bottom lip a moment, considering. "That's a big deal, Sassy. A lot of people take advantage of those situations. Without rules, landlords can take the vulnerable tenants' money for themselves and leave them to their own devices. The living conditions fall apart, nobody's watching for safety or anything else, and the people there basically have no rights. That's a pretty slippery slope."

"But what if—and I know nothing about this, so stop me if it's crazy—what if these houses were run properly, like a charity? What if we aligned with the community health centres that Marion told me about and maybe ask the government for funding and whatever else we need? Maybe we could join up with TADP and use their resources, even. I'm sure some of Marion's fellow doctors would donate time. Who knows? With help, some of the people living there might eventually be able to run the places, then they could start to make money for themselves."

He lifted one eyebrow. "You've thought this out."

"Only a little. I wanted to check with you first. Can we afford something like that?"

He exhaled, his blue eyes fixed on her. "Your dad and I were working on some expensive plans for strip malls and a couple of low-rises. You know he was part owner of your apartment building on Isabella, don't you?"

Now it was her turn to stare. "I did not."

"Now you do. As his heir, you are part owner of that building. You and I would have to do a lot of investigating, but we could consider selling that portion to put toward an investment like this if we needed to."

"So you think it could work?"

"It would not be a moneymaker, Sassy. You know that."

"I have enough money," she said, though she still didn't have the final tally from the lawyer. "What's the point of having money if you can't do something good with it?"

His gaze sharpened with interest. She'd seen that look a few times, like when her father had suggested something and dared him to take a risk. It was a look of respect, she realized, and she sat taller, recognizing that. He believed in her idea. He believed in her.

"Let's go back to the office," he said thoughtfully. "I want to show you some charts. But first, I have a question. Where's that spoiled brat I bailed out of jail? She never could have cooked this up."

"She grew up," Sassy replied.

forty-four
MARION

After two weeks in Da Nang, with its endless casualties, ferocious heat, and nearby explosions that shook the building and caused the lights to flicker, Marion's work inside the hospital was getting better. Not easier, but better. Thanks to ten straight hours—sometimes longer—of thinking and working on her feet, she slept pretty well. The work was rewarding, heartbreaking, and grueling, but she was acclimating to it.

At the end of every day, Daniel met her outside the hospital and walked her to dinner. He took his bodyguard role as seriously as he could, considering he wasn't able to be with her when she was operating or tending to patients. He had been quick to contact the U.S. military base by telephone when he arrived, and after they approved his credentials, he was issued weapons, which he slung over his shoulder, hung at his belt, and shoved into a leather holster on his hip. He was physically larger than the men in the Vietnamese Security Forces, so once they got to know him, he became a sort of guard for the entire hospital.

Sometimes he wandered into the nearby jungle to "hunt." Marion was aware that what he meant by that was "recon," and she hated the thought of it.

"I'm not going far, and it's just me," he said. "I can sit in the trees for hours without moving if I need to." When she still wasn't reassured, he scowled. "You want me to just sit here? I'm not made for that, Marion."

She knew that, but still. She thought about mentioning his missing eye and reduced vision, but she knew that would annoy him, not dissuade him.

Then one day, he wasn't there.

Marion stood at the exit to the hospital for an hour after her shift was over, fighting panic when he didn't appear. It was dusk when she stopped to ask two members of the Vietnamese Security Forces if they'd seen him, but they only pointed vaguely toward the trees. By then, the sun was quickly sinking. She couldn't stay put any longer, and she had no time to eat. She walked quickly to the VPVN compound then dove into her room and locked the door.

Daniel was not there in the morning to walk her to the hospital. When she arrived on her own, she went directly to the Security Forces again. They had nothing to tell her, other than to say there had been no local reports of conflicts. If Daniel was out there, they said, he was not fighting.

That did nothing to calm her. All day she was distracted, and once she was reprimanded by the surgeon for not paying attention. When the day was done, she went in search of the chef. He didn't like the idea that she was now without a bodyguard, and he promised to look into it and report back. When the day was done, he sent one of his men to safely accompany her to the compound. In the brief snatches of sleep she caught, she dreamed of him out in the jungle, wounded and alone.

The next morning, she knocked on Daniel's door, hoping, but there was no answer. Jaw set, she marched the few blocks to the hospital and was met by the chef. He waved her into his office and sat her down. His tight expression sent her pulse rocketing.

He closed the door behind her. "*Mes hommes ont trouvé le major.*" She caught her breath, forcing herself to stay quiet, but tears of relief burned. *He's alive!*

"Ah. Pardon! Major Neumann has been seen, but he will not come. He says to tell you he is all right, but *il a beaucoup à faire. Je m'excuse.* He has much to do." He frowned. "He says to my man that he has found American prisoners."

Marion's jaw dropped. "Where? Where is he?"

"About *deux kilomètres à l'ouest.* He found a small camp." Again he frowned.

"This is the first time we are learning of this place. Only one hour away. That is too close to the hospital. We are sending Security Forces out today."

"I want to go with them."

His face twisted with astonishment, then his eyes crinkled as if he might laugh. "You? *Non, non, non.* You are not going out there. You are *un docteur, pas un soldier.* You are needed *ici.* Out there? You are dead."

But Marion could no longer focus on her patients. All morning she was distracted. She needed to get to Daniel somehow, though the idea seemed impossible. When she couldn't stand it any longer, she lied to her boss for the first time in her life, telling the surgeon she was too sick to work. With everything going on around them, he had no time to question her, so he simply called for another intern to take her spot. Determined, she trotted out of the hospital and went in search of the Special Forces. A couple of them stood nearby, arms crossed, their faces painted with green camouflage. As she got closer to them, they exchanged uneasy glances. It made her wonder if they'd been waiting for her.

"You cannot come with us," the first informed her, hugging an M16 to his side.

"All right," she bluffed. "Just point the way to the camp, then. I will get there on my own. It's okay. I have a compass."

The second one glared. "You work. You not come to camp."

"I am coming. I am a doctor. I need to make sure no one is wounded."

Indecision was clear in the first guard's furrowed brow. After a moment, he faced Marion again, and she sensed his reluctance. With that came a rush of adrenaline. She was going to get her way. Just like Sassy would have.

"You not talk, not make a sound. You do what I say. When you are killed, is not my fault."

If, she wanted to exclaim. *You mean* if *I am killed.* Instead, she nodded. "My fault. I understand. When can we go?"

Both men glanced at the door to the hospital then at each other. They said something back and forth in Vietnamese then shrugged. The first man approached Marion and fastened a leather belt around her waist, then he held up a pistol.

"You know this?"

Her mind flew back to Daniel's lessons, and how she'd giggled self-consciously, insisting she'd never need to use it.

"Yes, I know this," she told the guard.

He slid the pistol into a holster on her belt. "Is loaded."

For some reason, seeing it hanging on her hip frightened her, so she draped the bottom of her khaki shirt over the top. The second man opened a tin he'd taken from his pocket, revealing a dark green paste, which he smeared over her face. It smelled rank, and she instantly wanted to scratch, but she kept her hands where they were.

"We go," the first man said. "Me is Bao. He is Ky. Is four more coming, too. You is not making noise."

The deeper they went in the jungle, the more petrified she became. After a while, she feared he might turn on her for being noisy, with her thundering heartbeat and chattering teeth. She had no right to be out here, traipsing silently through the trees behind Bao and the other five, doing "recon." Careful of roots snagging her feet and branches scratching her arms, she scanned the thick canopy of leaves overhead, always searching for threats. If they were ambushed, Daniel had said, she would never see the light of day again.

It took about an hour of stealthy hiking before she finally heard a man's voice. Bao made a downward movement with his hand, and everyone, including Marion, dropped. The voice was clearly Vietnamese, and it seemed unconcerned about possibly being heard. Bao, Ky, and the others crouched near her, listening hard.

"No good," Bao told her quietly. "Too many prisoners."

"Is Major Neumann a prisoner?"

"Not major," he reported.

"How many?" she whispered.

He shook his head then said something to Ky, who stayed where he was while Bao moved closer to the camp. He returned quickly.

"Three sick men in hut," he said.

The image made Marion temporarily forget about Daniel. "I need to help. I need to see how sick they are."

"Is much sick. You fix later."

A dog barked, making her jump.

"Stay," Bao said to her, as if she was the dog itself. Then he and the others moved swiftly forward and vanished into the trees.

It happened again, a frenzied string of barks that set off her internal alarm, and one of the men in the camp shouted at the animal to be quiet. If the dog was some kind of alarm system for the camp, the men weren't minding him. Unable to sit still another moment, Marion glided through the brush in the direction Bao and Ky had gone. To her dismay, they were no longer there. She was alone.

She crouched, shaking so hard the plants around her quivered, acutely aware that her life depended upon staying as still as possible. *Be calm*, she ordered herself. *Inhale. Exhale. 1-2-3, 3-2-1.* The least she could do was not pass out and become a liability. But it took a while to get to the point where her pulse was regular.

Beyond the tall grasses in front of her, something moved. A brown shadow travelling within a forest of green, like the smooth passing of a deer. She stared at the spot, willing herself not to blink while she waited for more, but the shadow was gone. Without a breeze, nothing in the surrounding forest moved. Had it been her imagination? She trained her eyes on the cleared area straight ahead, and she spotted the large, shabbily built hut Bao had mentioned. It stood at one corner of the compound, listing slightly, its dark wood boards partly eaten by humidity. She saw no movement near it, so she scanned the larger area, and her startled gaze landed on three Vietnamese men leaning against a wagon near the other side of the camp, smoking and talking among themselves. How many others were here?

A swish in the grass, and Marion fell back with a gasp. She almost laughed, weak with relief when Bao crouched beside her, glowering. He was clearly unimpressed with how close she had snuck.

"Not my fault. You remember."

She nodded, but he saw the question in her expression.

"I am not seeing major. I see six, maybe seven Vietcong." He grinned, a slash of white against his painted face. "They not seeing us. You have gun?"

She tapped the pistol at her hip, hidden under the tail of her shirt. Then he was off.

She watched him disappear again, wondering what he had seen inside of the hut. She should have brought medical supplies, but she hadn't been thinking ahead. Annoyed with herself, she flapped at her ear when an insect buzzed close, then she jerked away from a spider, spread out in the middle of its web near her elbow. It was a giant, brilliant blue, four inches from top to bottom. She had no idea if it was dangerous, but she wasn't about to test it. She shuffled away, more aware than ever of how alien she was to this land.

There was a shout from the camp, and she forgot about the spider. A rattling of gunfire jerked the three men at the wagon to life, and they sprinted toward the sound. More gunfire followed, and an enemy fighter fell. One of the Security Forces men from the hospital emerged from the trees, shooting, then two more. They disappeared again, and gunfire erupted deeper in the forest, not too far from where Marion hid. She guessed that some of the Vietcong were fleeing in the trees, and she hunched even lower.

Movement by the hut caught her attention. When she could distinguish its shape, her heart jumped in her chest. *Daniel.* He had reached the structure and was crouched at one side. It looked like he was busy with some sort of latch. How she wished she had binoculars. Then there was a shout, and he dove into the jungle, dodging bullets. Two men followed him, and she stared in agony, waiting to see who came out. *There.* Daniel materialized at the edge of the trees, twenty feet from the place where the prisoners were being kept, and as he crept toward the hut again she recognized the effortless brown shadow she'd seen before. The two men who had followed him into the trees were nowhere to be seen. She scoured the tree line, but she was certain they had not come out. Daniel snaked forward, his attention entirely on the small black hut.

Then Marion spotted one of the Vietcong slinking out of the trees, creeping up on Daniel. When Daniel didn't alter his steady stride, she realized he couldn't see the enemy, who was rushing up on Daniel's blind side. He was far too close, and as she watched in horror, the enemy lifted his gun to fire.

"Three!" she screamed, jumping up without thinking. "Three, Daniel! Three o'clock!"

He turned on a dime and shot the attacker, then spun around to stare at her, disbelief written all over his face. That's when she spotted another enemy fighter approaching him from behind.

She pointed. "Three o'clock again!"

He took care of that one as well, then he sprinted toward the hut, shooting her another incredulous look as he ran. Elated, she hopped on her toes and bit her fist to keep from cheering. Then she felt a sharp poke of metal in her back.

"*Đừng di chuyển*," a man growled.

She needed no translation. Marion put her hands in the air and didn't move until she felt the muzzle of his gun shoving her forward. As she stumbled through the undergrowth into the clearing ahead, terror lodged in her chest. She felt exposed, and very much alone. Where was Daniel? Where were the others? She was shaking so badly she couldn't control her hands. Her captor did not appear to notice when she dropped them to her sides. Once he had her in the open, he kept yelling, but not at her. She didn't know what to do, so she just stood there, hyperventilating, as he prodded her from behind.

"American!" he shouted.

"No!" she cried. She knew what would happen next. Daniel would come for her. He would sacrifice himself. He had already made that clear. One of them was going to die today, she realized. Maybe both.

But Daniel did not appear.

"American!" her captor roared again, and the gun shifted roughly to the back of her head, knocking her a step sideways.

Daniel immediately stepped out of the shadows.

"*Không có súng!*" the man shouted. Daniel dropped his gun, raised his hands, and linked them behind his head. Never looking away from her, he slowly walked toward them.

"It's all right, Marion," he said calmly, and she feared she might dissolve, hearing the strength of that voice again. One of his hands lifted slightly above his head and made a fist. *Freeze*, she remembered, but she couldn't stop shaking.

"I'm sorry, Daniel," she whimpered. "I'm so, so sorry."

"It's my fault. I shouldn't have left you." He glared at the Vietcong soldier. "*Rời xa cô ấy.*"

The soldier chuckled. "*Không*, American. *Bạn sẽ chết.*"

She didn't care what they were saying. None of this was real. It wasn't happening. Somehow she had fallen into one of Daniel's nightmares, shivering in the sweltering heat of Vietnam, unable to move. It would pass soon, she told herself. She just needed to wake up.

But this was no dream. This was the end.

She took a long, deep breath, willing her pulse to slow so she could think. This couldn't be the end. There had to be a way.

The man behind her shouted something, and one of his men answered the call. He jogged directly to Daniel, who stopped on command, then he shoved the mouth of his pistol against Daniel's temple. Daniel lifted his chin and looked at her, and in his expression she saw the most terrible regret.

"I'm sorry, Marion. You're the most incredible woman I've ever met. I wish we had more time."

Beside him, the enemy was laughing through a mouth of broken teeth, saying something to the man behind her. He was laughing as well. Marion was staring at the small black gun at Daniel's head, seeking clarity, and in that moment, it came to her. *Someone's gonna get killed*, Daniel had said long ago. *You don't want it to be you. They die or you do. Every man in every war understands that.*

Daniel's gaze had been locked on hers the whole time, and now she dropped her eyes, urging him to follow. She needed him to notice the slight, careful motion of her hand.

As cautiously as she could, Marion slipped her right hand under her shirt bottom. When she came into contact with the gun's metal handle, she twisted her wrist and wrapped her fingers around it. *It's loaded*, Bao had said. With almost no movement, Marion slid the gun from its holster then rotated the pistol toward her own body, on its way to finding that of the enemy behind her. Her hand curled securely around the handle while her thumb located the safety, and she clicked it off. *They die or you do.*

She met Daniel's gaze again and saw the apprehension in his expression. She also saw the tiniest of nods. He knew what to do.

The man beside Daniel stepped back, extending his arm, making room for the blast that would blow Daniel's head off. Behind her, the other man was laughing, egging him on. They were too confident for their own good.

Marion fired.

forty-five
SASSY

❧

Sassy sat across from Tom at his desk, feeling smug. She could definitely afford to buy the house she wanted. Now she needed to know the next step.

"You said to write down what I want to do," she said, ripping open her Cracker Jack box and pouring a bunch into her hand. "Here it is. What's next?"

"Hold on," he said carefully, sliding her binder toward him. "You don't want to pull the trigger until you're positive. The worst thing would be to make a mistake and let everyone know you're not experienced."

"You look it over," she said, popping caramel popcorn into her mouth, "but I'm pretty sure I'm positive."

"You can't be 'pretty sure you're positive.' Not with something this big. You either are, or you're not." He leaned over her notes, frowning in concentration as he flipped from one page to another. He placed his finger on one column. "Is this number . . . Oh, I see. So you're comparing last year's sales."

He nodded as he read, interested, but not noticeably impressed, which was disappointing. She had wanted him to be astounded by her excellent grasp of the business. So she pulled out the file she'd been working on all morning and opened it flat on the table.

"I was looking at this house in the Annex." She set a map in front of him detailing the buildings from Bedford to Spadina and from Bloor to Dupont

Street. "A recent sale was fifty-three thousand, but that buyer was purchasing the building to knock it down and build a low-rise. I would want to renovate. Looking at this floor plan, I believe we could have eight rooms in this one house." She pulled out another sheet. "And this is a list of the contacts I plan to make with the community health centres."

He leaned over the new pages, nodding as he read.

"What do you think?"

"Sassy, this is really good. You've covered a lot. But considering the scale of what you're thinking, I need more. I need a full business plan and proposal. I'll give you an outline of what I mean. You'll have to do the work, though."

"Naturally." She set her notes aside and started out on a fresh piece of paper. "What do I need to do?"

"This is going to take time, Sassy. It's not a one-afternoon-of-research kind of project." He looked meaningfully at the Cracker Jack box. "Are you sharing?"

"Help yourself. I have another box at my desk."

He might inhale sandwiches like an animal, but he was more careful with his snack food. He poured out a few kernels, set them on his desk, then ate them one by one, careful not to get his fingers sticky.

"All right. Business plan. Some of these elements you've seen in smaller projects, but working on a plan this size is going to teach you way more."

"I'm ready."

"I hope so." He stuck up one finger. "Think of it as if you're writing a book. Chapter by chapter, but it all ties together in much straighter lines."

"And it will have a happy ending."

"That's the plan. So let's start with the overall plan and costs. Show me current comparable prices per square foot, like what you've done here but on a wider scale. Break down what you want to do. The term you should use is 'affordable housing.' Oh, and write a note to yourself: you'll need to find out about rezoning, since this will not be a private home after what you want to do."

Sassy wrote down everything he said, and in her mind the assignment took on the shape of a tree. The first branch was for the initial cost, and each little twig growing off it was a subtopic for her to research, like finding comparable buildings' prices and recent sales, factoring in renovation costs with added fees for inspections, and even incidentals like hydro and electricity. With that done, she could begin to put together a timeline.

Another branch was for additional funding. With her inheritance and her unexpected share of the Isabella Street building, she might be able to buy one of these houses flat out, but how would other costs be covered?

"The next section of your business plan is where you explain why the government should consider helping out. Outline how this project would support underprivileged people—veterans, in particular, if that's what you want—by providing undermarket rental housing. Look into how to create a nonprofit company to keep your taxes low. Talk about the need for volunteers, in order to keep labour costs minimal. Maybe even create a rough schedule for them so it can be visualized. I like your idea of including a network of like-minded groups, like Marion's colleagues. From there, you can build in other potential benefactors, charitable groups, et cetera. The entire project needs to demonstrate efficiency. Help them see that their money will be well spent. A positive return on their investment."

He shook more candied popcorn into her hand, then his, then he unwrapped the prize. A little blue plastic horse. He pushed it toward her, unimpressed.

"We'll be operating on a loss in the beginning."

"Okay." She chewed on the end of her pen, trying to take it all in, but she kept getting distracted. She picked up the little blue horse, galloped it over to Tom's hand, and bumped him with it. "You're awfully smart for a hunk."

"Huh?"

"All those looks and a brain as well."

He rolled his eyes. "Focus, Sassy. Now you have to talk about your tenants," he continued, his brows drawn together. "How would it work for the people living in the building? Talk about what you envision for everything inside, including number of bedrooms, bathrooms, kitchens. Would they be independent apartments or will the facilities be shared? Will the rooms be furnished? What else will be in the buildings? You'll have to consider a minimum rent, probably."

She'd been wondering about that. "How do I figure that out?"

"Just like everything else. Ask around. Look at similar systems. You aren't the first to be interested in rooming houses."

She stood up, hugging her file against her. "I think I get it."

"Keep in mind that at the beginning of the whole thing, you want to outline your purpose. You're going to be great at that. Put your heart into it, but stay practical. Your introduction has to be memorable. Especially since you will be performing it live in front of council."

"I'll be *what*?"

"That's why your pitch has to be perfect. We'll work on it together until it is."

That wasn't something she'd considered, but she felt confident she could carry that part of it off. Too bad she couldn't bring her guitar.

"Thanks for everything, Tom. I'm jazzed about this."

He grinned. "It's a great idea in theory, Sassy. If you can get this going, there's no reason the government wouldn't be interested in helping."

She researched the process, and that involved calls and letters to the city as well as other central groups like the Toronto Real Estate Board and the Ontario Association of Real Estate Boards. Through them, she learned about past successes and failures. The more information she collected, the more she wanted to know. Every dotted *i* and crossed *t* brought satisfaction, and when she thought of it that way, she hummed the Rolling Stones song like a soundtrack.

After a week of intense work, Sassy returned to Tom's desk and set her organized notes in front of him, stapled neatly together. On the front cover, in her neatest, steadiest hand, she had written:

MARION'S PLACE
A WELCOME HOME

"Marion," he said softly, approving. "Nice touch."

"I see this project as more than just providing homes. It's more than that. It's responding to what Marion showed me. Despite my initial belief that closing the institutions and bringing those people into the public view was the right thing for everyone, I now understand. Without the guidance and treatment Marion and others provide, many of them are lost. And the public, who wanted them freed, now regards them as trash, since they are forced to sleep in parks and alleys. Marion told me months ago that she believes the result of closing the institutions will eventually make everything much worse. So this project is my humble contribution to slowing that down."

"I like it. You can also look at it as a personal victory for you. By investing in a good old house like this, you are basically delaying gentrification." He laid his hand on the cover. "Can I look?"

Her palms were damp, but she kept her expression neutral. She wanted so badly to impress him. "Please do."

She folded her arms, emulating her father without meaning to. She'd been working hard on the project, and she was was feeling good about what she'd learned. But she'd also thrown in something big that he wouldn't expect. She couldn't wait to see his reaction.

"I went a little deeper than you asked," she said. "Instead of comparing this building to another, I compared it to six others. I did the research on all of them, so that's laid out there in the beginning, in those columns."

He opened her booklet to the table of contents, and after he read through it, he smiled.

"Sassy. This is . . ."

"I know," she said, grinning madly. "Far out, right?"

He turned to the first section and gave a low whistle, scanning the columns she'd mentioned.

"This is the chart, and I was right. The building I initially chose was the best one. See the number of units versus cost outlay?"

"I sure do."

"But what you don't know is that I found something better."

"Oh? Lay it on me."

"I don't have to worry about purchasing costs."

He looked confused, then he studied her pages. After a beat, he stared back at her. "Your father's home?"

"It's my home now."

"But Sassy, this house is your birthright. Do you really want it to become a rooming house?"

"That's exactly what I want. Read on."

She watched his expression as he took it all in, finally seeing on his face the expression she'd wanted. It said, *Oh yeah, Sassy. This is boss.*

He asked a few questions, and she wrote down notes for herself, then he closed the report. "This is so good, Sassy. And knowing you, when you present it in person, you'll win over every single person in that room. Your dad was right. You'll be better than either of us if you keep this up. Will you still let me work here when you take over?"

She grinned, feeling more than just a little proud of herself, and more than a little crazy about Tom. She wanted him to look at her that way—and more—forever.

"Depends on how you behave, mister."

"Guess what? You win a prize." He reached into his desk drawer and pulled out a red Pez dispenser with a Snow White head on top. "Here you go."

She popped the little head up and crunched on a pink candy. "What do I get if there's even more to the plan? Because there is."

A dark eyebrow lifted. "Hmm. Depends on what it is. Good plans, of course, are worth more."

She handed him another sheet of paper. "Future plans."

"What?"

"I've worked out what we could do if all goes well. We can potentially buy another in two years or so. Maybe more than one." She held up a finger. "But! If it doesn't work, I still own the building. It's in a prime location. We'll make a profit no matter what."

"So good, Sassy. You win the grand prize."

"Which is?"

Those blue eyes sparkled. "Dinner tonight?"

Now was the time. She felt it. She lowered her lids to half-mast and her voice to a purr. "With drinks at my place to follow."

He felt it, too. She saw the blue in his eyes deepen to black, and she was lost. Sean Connery had nothing on this man. The heat coming from his gaze melted her insides.

"I'll bring Pixy Stix," he said smoothly. "What flavour?"

"Surprise me."

forty-six
MARION

It happened in the blink of an eye. Marion pulled the trigger, and the Vietcong behind her was obliterated. At the same moment, Daniel stepped out of the other pistol's path, twisted it from the man's grip, and turned it on him instead.

The crack of her gun had been deafening, and she'd fallen to her knees with shock. She started to look back, to see what she'd done, but Daniel gathered her in his arms and held her against his body.

"Don't look, Marion. Hang on to me instead."

She felt the energy coming off him in waves, his own fear dissipating as he held her safe. She burrowed into the fibres of his shirt, unable to get close enough, aware of her own ridiculous whimper, her relentless plea for him to *forgive me, forgive me*, even though she knew she had done the right thing.

"It's all over, Marion. You saved our lives," he murmured, and she soaked in his voice like medicine, craving more. If she could open her veins and pour him into her bloodstream, she would.

He tightened his arms around her. "You're all right, Marion. You're okay. I will hold you as long as you need."

Then he twitched slightly, and she became aware that he'd heard something she had not. Like a little girl hiding beneath the covers, she stayed hidden in his shirt, unsure if she could handle any more. She held her breath, listening, and heard male voices beyond them, speaking Vietnamese.

Daniel lowered his lips to her ear. "They're with us. It's okay. You're safe."

She drew back and looked past him. Some of Bao's men were walking through the open space, nearing the hut.

"Marion," Daniel said. "I have something to tell you."

She met his gaze, shocked to see that he was smiling through the grime on his face. He put one palm on each side of her face so she saw nothing but him.

"Joey's in the hut with two others."

Her jaw dropped. "Joey? *Our* Joey?"

"Yeah. Our Joey." His expression was beautiful. "Ky's with them. They need food and medicine. I think they've been stuck in there for weeks." He leaned in and kissed her lips. "Let's take them home."

Daniel entered the hut first, and she heard the smile in his voice. "Oohrah, boys," he said. "Cavalry's here."

When Marion entered, all three prisoners were sitting on the floor with their backs against the wall, eyes wide. They were skeletal and filthy, and Marion smelled decomposition in the air. A wound gone bad. When she got closer, she saw lice moving in their tangled, greasy hair. One man had lost two front teeth.

None of it mattered; she knew Joey immediately. She dropped to her knees beside him.

"Joey!" she cried. "Oh, Joey."

He looked baffled. "Do I know you?"

She laughed and sniffed back tears. "No, you don't know me. But Sassy says hello."

Hearing his sister's name, Joey's face underwent the most sublime transition, from the emptiness of resignation to a shining, incredulous hope.

"Sassy," he whispered.

"You'll see her soon," she told him gently. The sad news about his father was for another time and the siblings could handle that between them. Today was a celebration. Joey was saved. All of them were.

Boots clomped into the hut behind her, but Marion wasn't afraid.

Daniel stood like the shield he'd promised, watching and keeping her safe.

"Doctor is here?" she heard from behind him.

"Bao!" she said, grinning over her shoulder at him. "Look! I didn't die!"

He laughed. "Good you not dead."

"I need medicine, Bao. I need clean water and bandages. Food? Can you find food?"

Moments later he returned with Ky, their arms full of cloth and bowls. From somewhere in the enemy's camp they dug up a pot of rice, still warm, along with dried fish, and even a can of condensed milk. While Marion cleaned wounds, the men dug grubby fingers into the food and smeared whatever they could find into their mouths. Daniel, finally convinced everything was under control, sat with them.

"This is Hal," he told Marion. "Hal. Slow down. You got rice all over your face, dummy."

Hal was the one with the missing front teeth, so when he laughed, his tongue stuck out a little. He stuck it out farther, seeking out the rice in question. "Better not waste it."

"That's Stu," Daniel said, indicating the man lying on his back nearby, clearly the weakest of the three. "And you already know Joey."

"Welcome to our little p-piece of heaven," Hal said.

He had a heavy stutter, but that didn't slow him down. Energized by the food, he kept talking, going off on tangents Marion couldn't follow, but always coming back to his buddies. His brothers.

"Where's Chip?" Daniel eventually asked.

Joey flinched beside him then reached for a canteen of water. "Don't ask."

Hal's eyes went dark. "Ch-Ch-Chip messed up. Tried to run, b-but Charlie cut off his head." He pointed toward the door. "Left the rest of him in front of the hut for two days, until something dragged it off. N-never saw what happened to his head."

Marion stared at him in shock, but the men seemed to have accepted the horror as part of their lives now.

"I told him not to risk it," Joey said, wiping water from his lips with his sleeve.

"Chip always knew better," Daniel acknowledged. "Sorry to hear it."

Stu exhaled deeply. "Rest in peace, brother."

"He should have waited," Hal said. "G-G-God told me weeks ago that we would go home soon. Joey didn't b-b-believe me." He guffawed. "God said he was sending an angel. I never expected it'd be you, D-Danny."

"I heard the First Battalion was in the area," Daniel said, "but I wasn't sure who might still be in it. And I had no idea you'd been locked up."

"He never forgot any of you," Marion told them, recalling the stories Daniel had told her in his hospital room. Hal was from Ohio, she remembered. He farmed cattle with his dad, the only boy of four siblings. Stu was smaller than the others and rapidly losing what remained of his hair. He was from Seattle. Planned to be a lawyer.

And Joey. Sassy's sweet Joey, with those beautiful green eyes, just like his sister's, dreaming of baseball.

Bao radioed the hospital, and everything Marion requested was delivered within the next hour or so. When they were stable enough, the three men were brought back to the surgical hospital in Da Nang. Stu needed to be carried most of the way, and the other two took frequent breaks to rest, but Hal never stopped talking. Now that it had sunk in that they were truly free, Joey's eyes were bright with relief, looking so much like his sister it took Marion's breath away.

In the hospital, their bodies received much-needed fluid and medicine, and their heads rested on soft pillows. Marion and Daniel returned to the VPVN compound, and Marion finally collapsed into her own cot, dead tired, though she knew she would not sleep for a while. The psychiatrist in her wanted to sort through everything, to understand how and why she felt euphoria and dread simultaneously. Why she wanted to cry for days then dance for joy. Then she thought of Sassy, remembering how her friend could live in the moment in such a magical way. Marion wanted that. She took a deep breath then let everything out. Instead of analyzing it all, she decided to just feel it.

Daniel saw the change in her. She knew he did. He tucked her into her bed then left, but in the morning he returned. They went for breakfast, and he waited for her to begin speaking.

"I think I understand you a little better now," she said.

"Me?"

"What happened back there keeps coming back to me, whether I want to relive it or not. I think I'm fine, busy with something else, and suddenly I'm in the dark, experiencing what happened all over again. I'm shaking in the bush, waiting for someone to kill me. I'm feeling that gun against the back of my head. I wonder if that fear will ever go away."

"You'll move away from it," he assured her. "But like I said a long time ago, if you aren't at least a little bit scared, you are putting yourself in danger. Not just in Vietnam."

"I still feel my pistol firing when I killed him." She held up her hands. They were shaking noticeably. "And I can't forget what I saw. It's so real, I still smell the gunpowder, the smoke from when you shot—"

She hung her head, ashamed. She had seen everything: the cool assurance in Daniel's expression, the astonishment in the other man's. The moment when the bullet struck and burst through his back, ending his life. How the dead man had flailed backward, out of time.

Why did it matter so much to her? Why was it stuck in her mind? Because it was Daniel. The contradiction between the gentle affection in his eyes and his detached ability to kill a human being was hard to reconcile.

How could she, when she was in love with him?

"I can't help it, Daniel. I keep seeing what you did. You were so calm."

"So were you, Marion," he said slowly, but there was no judgement in his expression. "You watched me like a cat the whole time you put your gun behind you. You kept me in place. I don't know what I would have done if you hadn't. Probably killed us both. You understand you did the best thing, right?"

She'd been deafened by the shot, which she appreciated later, because she never heard the man's dying sounds. "I . . . I don't know yet."

"This is war, Marion. What you did, it had to be done."

It had to be done. It had been either him or her. Or Daniel. The knot in her throat broke free. "I don't know how to feel," she sobbed.

"You'll get through this," he said, holding her again. "I'll help you, like you did for me."

The rescued prisoners slept solidly for two full days. Between that and falling asleep again, they ate everything they saw. On the third morning, Marion was back to work in the operating rooms. When she walked past the area where the men were staying, she saw Daniel sitting with them. He touched his eye patch self-consciously, and they all laughed at something. It was the sound of brothers.

Marion paused, mesmerized. From where she stood, his shoulders looked smaller, then she realized it wasn't size but rigidity. All this time, just like he had said, he had needed to see his brothers. Now they were together, the survivors, at least. And it was time to bring them home.

A thought struck her. These were American marines. Was it right to bring them to Canada? What did she need to do about that?

On his cot, Stu said something then dropped his chin, and Daniel reached out to pat his back. His brother smiled sheepishly in return, and a rumble of male, self-conscious laughter travelled to her.

Marion would figure out the politics later. Right now, these men needed each other.

She was about to move away from the door when Joey's gaze caught hers. "Thank you," he mouthed.

She smiled, feeling a rush of anticipation. She couldn't wait to bring him to Sassy. To see her best friend in his arms, laughing and crying with him. It was more than she had dared to dream about this voyage.

―――――――

On the night before they were to fly out of Vietnam, the midnight sky sparkled with stars, and for once, the air was clear of explosions, a strangely hollow vacuum without the jagged rhythm of death being shot into it. Daniel led Marion to a quiet spot overlooking the water, then he stood behind her, arms around her waist. She rested her head back on his chest, listening to his heartbeat and blinking at the sky.

"I've never heard it so quiet here," she sighed.

"Any place can be beautiful." He lowered his chin to her shoulder then kissed her cheek. "Hey. I never said thank you."

"What for?"

"You brought me here. It's because of you that my buddies are safe now."

"I'd say we're even. I'd never have come without you."

She felt him shake his head slowly, his chin on her head. "No. This was you, Marion. All you."

The view was striking, the arc of the moon shining on the still surface of the water, framed by the lines and curves of the jungle. It was unexpected, this beauty. She'd gotten so used to blasts and gunfire, screams and death. This was peace, if only for a little while.

"I feel like a different person," she said softly.

"You're still you." She heard the warmth in his voice. And the smile. "But, ah, the stories you can tell. Did you ever imagine you'd get on an airplane, fly to Vietnam, then rescue POWs in the middle of a war zone? And you did all that with a man you hardly knew? Doesn't seem like the cautious, rule-oriented doctor I knew before."

"Who's this man you say I hardly knew?" She turned in the circle of his arms and rested her hands on the insides of his elbows, where the skin was soft. "I know you, Daniel."

They hadn't kissed since the day the helicopter had crashed, which felt like years before. There had never been a time or place where it felt right. But here, under the stars of another world, Marion let herself fall.

"You changed my life," she told him.

She saw her own gratitude in his gaze, and she relished the slow beat of his pulse under her. He swallowed, always watching her, and she lifted her chin, waiting for what she knew he would bring. His kiss was soft at first, but not brief. He was feeling her there, tasting her, joining with her in the most exquisite sensation she had ever felt. When he drew back, it was as if he gazed into her soul, and she held it open for him. He belonged there, and she belonged with him.

forty-seven
SASSY

❧

Sassy hung up the telephone, shock vibrating through her. Never, *never* could she have imagined she would hear what she'd just heard.

We're coming home! Marion had said, then Sassy heard her voice crack. *We'll be there in two days, Sassy, and*—For a brief moment Sassy wondered if the call had been dropped. It was from such a far distance away. A world away. Then Sassy heard Marion catch her breath.

Are you crying, Marion? Why are you crying? Are you all right?

Sassy! Oh, Sassy. You won't believe what happened. Oh, God, I can't wait to see you.

Sassy's heart stopped. *What? What are you talking about? Are you all right?*

She held her breath, waiting on edge. Then . . . *We found him, Sassy! We found Joey! We're bringing him home.*

Then they both were sobbing, and Marion was saying something about how expensive the phone call was, and the next thing Sassy knew, her phone receiver was back on its cradle, and her whole body was trembling. She wanted to reach over and smother Tom with the news, but he had finally managed to crawl out of bed, take a shower, then head out to buy them something to eat. All she could do was wait for him to return, but she was afraid she'd burst before then. She sat on the couch beside Chester, then she linked her hands on her lap to keep them still. It felt like forever before she finally heard the front door rattle with her key.

"Tom!" she cried, tears starting up again. Chester flew off the couch and disappeared. "Tom! Come here!"

He stepped into the room, arms full. "You beckoned? Hey! What's with the crying? I was gone for, like, ten minutes."

She laughed through more tears. "They found Joey," she cried. "Joey's coming home. He'll be here in two days."

"What?" Tom dropped the two bags he was carrying and ran to the couch, throwing his arms around her. "That is incredible. How did you find out?"

"Marion called me from Vietnam! She just called me! Can you believe it?" She drew back to look at him eye to eye. "I'm freaking out. Joey's safe! He's coming home! This is beyond my wildest dreams. I thought . . . I didn't think I would ever see him again."

Then Tom was kissing her, and she was swept away by the news and his passion. She never wanted it to stop, and when he began to draw away, she pulled him back for more. His eyes were shining when they finally parted.

"You make me crazy," he murmured, kissing her again.

"Ditto," she put in. "We're both nuts. Don't tell Marion I used that word."

He held her gaze a moment longer, stealing her ability to think. Then he grinned, looking so young it made her laugh.

"Let's celebrate," he said, standing. "I brought dinner."

She watched him grab the bags he'd left at the door then pour everything out. A flood of M&M's, Cracker Jack, Starburst, Life Savers, Aero bars, and whatever else he'd been able to find rolled over the cherry-red couch. He knew her so well.

"I think this might be the best day of my life," she said, laughing with more tears.

"Oh, and this." He presented her with a bottle of champagne, cold and wet with condensation. "I thought we might—"

"Grab two glasses, then follow me," she purred. "I know where we should drink that."

The champagne led them to her bedroom, and the candy became dessert after the main course. When he held out a second Cracker Jack box, she held up her hands.

"Stop! I'm going to die of too much sugar."

He peered into the box. "Only two pieces left and the prize."

"You take the popcorn. Give me the prize."

He did, then he rested back against the headboard, hands linked behind his head. When he moved, the sheet slipped off his chest and pooled around his hips, and she felt a passing sympathy for Davey. His body had nothing on Tom's. Then she realized he was observing her the same way.

"What are you looking at?" she teased, tearing into the little prize packet.

"You, Sassy. I could look at you the rest of my life."

Heaven swirled inside her, mixed with all the candy. What a day. Joey was coming home, Marion was coming home, and Tom . . . she was pretty sure he loved her.

Did she deserve to be this happy?

That perfect, black, James Bond eyebrow lifted. His eyes were on the Cracker Jack prize now. "What did you get?"

She recalled the envelope in her fingers and finished opening it, then she pinched the sides together so she could peer inside. At first, she frowned, unsure of what she was looking at. She hadn't seen anything sparkly inside a Cracker Jack box before. Then she knew, and she couldn't breathe. Slowly, she pulled out the little gold ring and blinked at its diamond.

Sassy had decided long ago that she would never get married. She didn't need anyone else, she knew, and she valued her freedom too much to share it. The only way she would ever marry anyone, she'd promised herself, was if they loved each other as fully and as perfectly as her parents had loved each other. She looked at the ring, letting its glittering promise reach for her heart, then she lifted her gaze to Tom's.

His face tightened. Something new simmered in his eyes. Doubt?

She took a deep breath, then she handed him back the ring.

Defeat crept into his expression. "No?"

She'd always enjoyed teasing him, pushing just far enough to get him riled up so they could spar. But not today. She couldn't let him hurt like that.

"You have to ask the right way," she told him primly, holding her emotions tight.

Instantly, light filled his eyes, and he rolled off the bed, dragging the sheet with him. She rushed to the side, laughing with delight as he dropped onto one knee.

"Marry me, Sassy. Please be my wife."

She held out her hand, but he didn't move.

"Well?" she asked.

He held the ring between his thumb and finger. That little curl at the side of his mouth lifted roguishly. "It's your turn. If you want this, you can't just stick your finger out. You have to answer the right way. Let's try this again. Will you marry me, Sassy Rankin?"

Love whooshed from her toes to her lips, and she shared all that she had with him. "Yes, Tom Duncan. Make a respectable woman out of me."

forty-eight
MARION

❦

Hal, Stu, and Joey sat in the row behind Daniel and Marion, still gaunt but clean and happy. Marion watched all three like a hawk, on hand for any physical or mental doctoring, and wondered how they could possibly process everything. After months of unimaginable combat and survival in the jungle then weeks of abuse and starvation in a rotted old hut in the deep of Vietnam, they'd collapsed in a frantic but effective hospital in Da Nang. Now they sat on upholstered seats in an airplane and nodded every time a stewardess asked if they'd like something to eat or drink. They wore brave expressions, laughed when it was called for, but Marion feared it was too much.

Once they were buckled in and the Boeing 737 rolled noisily down the runway, the men's nervous laughter and vulgar comments—which Daniel had happily joined in on—quickly died down. She couldn't see their faces from where she sat, but from the tension in the air, Marion sensed a cautious, collective breath being held. Then they were flying, the familiar swoop in her belly easier to manage now than it had been two months ago.

That's when she heard a quiet sob. It came from the aisle, where Hal sat. Reflexively, she started to rise, but Daniel's hand lowered onto hers and held her in place.

"They need this," he murmured. "They're getting used to the idea that it's over."

Shortly after, she peeked behind and saw the men were asleep, leaning against each other. Daniel, too, had a calmness in his expression that she hadn't seen before. An acceptance, she realized. An understanding that what he had lived and breathed and needed so badly was now in the past, though it would always haunt his present. They both knew that.

There was vulnerability as well. He, too, was getting used to the idea.

"How are you feeling, Marion?" he asked, curling his fingers around hers. "You just had the adventure of a lifetime."

"I was just about to ask you the same question."

"I beat you to it. What's on your mind?"

"Not much right now," she admitted. "I'm glad we're going home."

"Are you sorry you went?"

"Not on your life!"

He laughed. "No? Helicopter crash, near drowning, being a hostage, et cetera, et cetera . . ."

"I'm not saying it was a restful vacation." She smiled softly, remembering. "But no, I couldn't possibly be sorry. Before all this, I couldn't even read mystery novels without leaving all the lights on. And now . . . well, once I recover, maybe I'll try something else. Not Vietnam, but . . ."

She exhaled, picturing the hospital ward with five patients piled on one cot. The stink of cooking fires mingling with the reek of bandages in need of changing. The inconceivable composure she had seen, the stoic determination on parents' faces as they held their mutilated babies. They were used to that life. They expected it.

"We were lucky," Daniel murmured, reading her mind. "The hospital didn't get bombed while we were there."

She nodded. "I feel . . . I feel like I just spent a lifetime on another planet. I feel like landing in Toronto is going to feel odd."

A stewardess was slowly making her way down the aisle. Her orange dress was cut well above her knees, accessorized with a striped belt and a silver pin on her collar in the shape of airplane wings. Her thick black hair had been back-combed into a loose beehive, and her makeup would have made Raquel Welch proud. When she paused at their row, Marion took in the young woman's tall black boots and wondered how comfortable they were. Maybe she'd get herself a pair when she got home. Sassy could take her shopping for something . . . new.

The stewardess leaned down so her face was in Daniel's, her false eyelashes blinking slowly. "May I offer you a drink, sir? A martini, perhaps?"

He glanced at Marion, who shrugged then nodded. She hadn't had a martini in a couple of years, but it sounded like exactly what she wanted.

"My lady would like a martini, please, and I'll have a beer." The stewardess took a step down the aisle, but he stopped her. "Oh, and don't wake the men behind me. They need their sleep. I'm sure they'll order something real strong when they wake up."

When the drinks arrived. Marion tasted hers and approved. She'd forgotten the nice, dry bite of a gin martini. Beside her, Daniel let out a satisfied sigh.

"Cold beer. What a miracle."

One of the men snored quietly behind them, and it was a comforting sound.

"What are you going to do when you get back?" Marion asked.

"I've been trying not to think about that," he admitted, taking a long gulp that just about finished the bottle. "I gotta find a place to live. I thought I might try to get the four of us into a place together. Might be good for all of us, you know, so we can talk about things."

"Sassy might want Joey with her."

"Joey's a big boy. That'll be up to him."

"Of course." She hesitated. "Are you going to check out the community health centres, do you think?"

He picked at the label on his beer bottle, easing up one corner. "Yeah. I will this time. I think I'll be better able to cope now. Plus these guys will need me to show them it's possible to move on. Can I go to whichever centre you're at?"

"I don't see why not," she said, though she was sure there were rules about friends and family treating patients. She'd figure out what to do about that if the time ever came.

The stewardess breezed by, but he stopped her and held up his bottle. "Another?"

"Certainly, sir," she said, taking the empty one.

Marion took another sip of her martini. "I'm going to take my time on this," she said. "Not interested in getting drunk on a plane."

He grinned. "I'd love to see you get drunk, Marion."

"No, you wouldn't. Ask Sassy. I just get silly."

"Exactly. I'd love to see that."

She wasn't sure if it was the martini or the look in his eye, but a warm shiver ran through her at the thought. "You want to see me get silly?" she dared, gazing up from beneath her lashes.

"Roger that," he said, his expression changing again, becoming more serious. "Marion, do you, I mean, when we're back in the city and all, do you think that we . . ." He hesitated, biting his lower lip briefly. "I'd like to take you to dinner. A real one. You could even have lobster thermidor again, if you want."

For weeks, an awareness had been building deep within Marion, rising through her chest and scaring her just enough that she had pushed it back down. It seemed like too much, then it seemed exactly right, but she'd been too afraid to say anything out loud. Now she searched his gaze, that sense of power rising within her again. Was there any reason why she shouldn't say what was on her mind?

"I have a better idea," she said shyly, shoving through her anxiety. "I'm a pretty good cook. And a good baker as well. How about I make dinner?" She took a deep breath, holding his gaze. Her face was on fire. "Then in the morning I'll whip up some muffins. Or I could make eggs . . ."

The longer he stared, the hotter her face became. Had she just made a huge mistake? Was it too much? She had no idea. Had she ruined everything?

Finally, the corner of his mouth drew up in a careful smile. "Are you sure?"

She swallowed, holding his gaze. "Doctor's orders."

forty-nine
SASSY

❧

"Calm down, Sass. You've got everything organized. You have nothing to worry about."

"What are you talking about?" Sassy snapped. "Everything has to be perfect."

Tom wrapped his big, warm hands around her upper arms and forced her onto one of the airport waiting room's hard plastic chairs. They'd arrived an hour before the plane was expected, which she was aware was way too early, but he hadn't balked. He simply accepted her craziness and went along with it.

To a point.

"Everything *is* perfect," he said, purposefully calm.

"But where is everyone?"

"You told them seven o'clock. It's only six thirty."

"Do you have the banner?"

He held up the long paper flag they'd made the night before. "Right here."

She regarded it with concern. "You folded it. Is it going to look all right?"

"Sassy, we scotch-taped eight pieces of paper together so it all fit. We *had* to fold it. It'll look fantastic." He sank into the chair beside her. "Know what, though? Joey won't even notice it. He'll be so happy to see you, nothing else will matter."

Her chin quivered. "Joey's coming home."

He hugged her tight. "Maybe he can be my best man."

Smart man. He'd known he could distract her from tears with that. "You're gonna like him, Tom. He's kind of like me, but weirder. He's got even more energy. I don't know how he will be now, but . . . Think you'll like him?"

"I know I will." He glanced over her shoulder. "Hey, look who's here!"

She jumped up. "Who? Oh! Everyone came together! My gosh!"

She was shocked to see that Mrs. Moore had managed to talk Mr. Moore into a wheelchair for the occasion, and even more surprising, he was wearing an army uniform, just like the one in her father's photograph. And there were the Levins and the Romanos—and they'd brought someone else she didn't know, who was also in uniform. She was curious, but too happy to question anything. They'd explain, she knew.

She left Tom in her wake as she rushed to the group, swallowing tears. "Thank you all for coming! This means so much to me!"

Hank Moore nodded with approval. "Good for you, Sassy. Your dad would be proud."

Mr. Romano cleared his throat in a meaningful way, then he and the rest of the neighbours gathered around the man she didn't know, who appeared to be about the same age as the others. He was small and lean, and he looked more than a little uncomfortable in a uniform that was too large, but he stood still as stone. The only thing that moved were his eyes. He wore thick round glasses that made them look huge, and they darted constantly from side to side, as if he sought escape.

"Sassy, we want to introduce you to someone," Mr. Romano said.

The stranger lifted his chin and looked directly at Sassy. His face, she saw, had been cut and slashed into multiple scars across his brow, through his cheek, and disappearing into his chin.

"Hello," she said carefully.

"This is Dickie Roy of the Black Watch of Canada," Mr. Romano said. "He was a member of one of the world's most elite sniper units."

"Nice to meet you, Mr. Roy," she said, but she didn't step any closer. Something about the man made her nervous.

Mr. Roy did not smile. Considering all his scars, she wondered if he still could.

"I'm here for your brother and the other men," he said sharply, but he didn't sound angry. His expression was set, though his eyes continued to scan the airport waiting room. He was constantly scouting. Fully aware of his surroundings at all times. "The men and women serving in Vietnam deserve respect and gratitude. I'm here for them."

"Thank you," she said, still confused.

Mrs. Levin came to her side. When she looked at Mr. Roy, her expression was one of deepest respect.

"Sassy," she said quietly, "Mr. Roy is one of our neighbours. He wanted to join us today."

Sassy frowned, feeling a little stupid. She'd thought she knew everyone on the floor.

Mrs. Romano slid in on Sassy's other side, keeping her back to the others so they could speak in private. "We don't know what he did in the past, but your father sent Mr. Roy to Isabella Street and has been paying his rent for the past twenty years. This is the first time many of us have spoken with him."

"I don't remember ever seeing him," Sassy whispered.

"No, you wouldn't." Mrs. Romano exchanged a glance with Mrs. Levin. "But you've seen where he lives. It's the door across from the elevator that opens and closes every time you walk by."

Sassy's jaw dropped. *Mr. Snoop.*

Mrs. Levin's expression was sad. "His only son went to Vietnam. He came home a year or so ago, but he struggled." Her brow creased. "He took his own life back in December."

"Oh no!" Sassy stepped toward him.

Mrs. Romano took her arm. "Move slowly, Sassy. He is easily alarmed."

"I'm very sorry to hear what happened to your son," Sassy said, and paused briefly the old sniper's eyes. He stared at her, showing no emotion whatsoever, then he blinked and broke the spell.

"Thank you. He deserved respect, just like these boys."

"Yes, he did," Sassy said, her heart breaking for both him and his son. He could have been Joey. He could have been Daniel.

Hank Moore glanced up. "Is Marcus coming?"

She had worried about that. "I left a message with his wife, but they live pretty far away, and—"

"Mr. and Mrs. Hart!" Tom exclaimed behind her. He strode past, holding out his hand. "And you must be Marion's sister, Pat."

"Thank you so much for coming!" Sassy said again, flustered. Marion would be so surprised. "I know this was an inconvenience—"

"Nonsense," Mr. Hart said, and Sassy saw a glimpse of Marion in his smile. "We're glad you let us know when she'd be home." He walked past her, toward the others, then stopped short. "Dickie? My God. Is that you?"

"Marcus."

Sassy spotted a tiny crack in the sniper's composure, and it almost broke her. The hint of a smile. A vague glossiness in his sharp eyes. A sign that he had once been a young man, and a friend.

"It's good to see you," Mr. Roy said, sounding slightly hoarse.

Beside her, Mrs. Levin clutched Mrs. Romano's arm. Sassy caught them both valiantly sucking back sobs.

Sassy had called only one other family, but she'd known they wouldn't be able to come. Daniel's parents were practically on the other side of the country. Still, she thought they should know what was happening with their son, so she had looked them up and phoned. She had ended up talking with Daniel's mother, Grace, for a long time. She'd have loved to meet her in person. At least she could tell Daniel that she'd tried.

A garbled announcement came over the public address system, and Tom pointed toward a window. "The plane's here."

fifty

MARION

✦

"We made it," Daniel said, smiling broadly. As the plane rolled to a stop at the terminal, he stood and faced his three friends. "Welcome home, boys."

Marion had thought the trip would wear her down so much that she wouldn't have anything left for celebrating their arrival, but she was wrong. Hearing the men's eagerness, she couldn't wait to disembark and get back to real life. But first, she was dying to rush through the airport, dragging Joey with her, then present him to Sassy. Sassy had promised she and Tom would be there to pick them up, and Marion couldn't wait to see the reunion. She missed her friend with an urgency, and she had to make a conscious effort not to push people out of her way as the four of them went for luggage. Joey, Stu, and Hal didn't have much, but they weren't about to leave Daniel. While he watched for bags, the other three stood off to the side, exhausted but in high spirits.

Marion stayed beside Daniel and willed her courage back into place. It had been hours since they had discussed their plans. "So . . . I think I know where you're sleeping tonight. Am I right in thinking . . . ?"

Daniel's expression sent a thrill through her. "I was hoping you hadn't changed your mind."

"I didn't," she said, pushing through the nerves. "Now I have another question. I'm sure Sassy will bring Joey to her apartment tonight, but what about the other two? There's no room in my apartment."

"Yeah, I was thinking about that. I really don't know."

"Maybe I can pay for a hotel room for a night or two, and we can try to figure out things while that's happening."

He looked surprised. "You'd do that?"

"I flew to Vietnam for these guys. I'm not going to just dump them."

His smile faltered. "What are you going to tell Joey? You know. About his dad."

"It's not up to me," she said. "I have to leave it to Sassy. If she wants my help, I'll be there, of course."

He looked away, pretending to search for the bags, but she saw his pained expression.

"What's the matter?"

"After everything Joey's been through, now he's gonna find out about his dad. And you know what he'll think? That it was his fault."

"Yes. I thought about that. So many layers to work through. But you and I managed."

He let the reality of that sink in, then he bent his head and kissed her. "You saved my life," he reminded her.

"You saved your own life. I was just there to offer assistance." She raised an eyebrow. "On the other hand, you actually *did* save my life when you dragged me out of that river."

"Oh yeah? What about your sharpshooting?"

"We'll have to call that one a draw, since we saved each other that day." She drew him back for another kiss. "All I know is that you saved my life, but more than that, you changed it."

He slid his mouth to her ear, making her shiver. "Let's call that one a draw, too."

The bags arrived, so they went to collect the other three men. They had been cornered by a group of young men. Daniel and Marion rushed over, seeing Joey's face dark with anger.

"You got no right to say that," he seethed, pushing his face into one of the hippy's faces. "Freaking dove. What have you done to—"

"Baby killer!" one man hissed, and Daniel stepped in, ready to defend. The others might be weakened by where they'd been, but Daniel was healthy and strong, and his presence changed the attackers' mood. They stepped back, and Daniel moved with them, creating space.

"Get outta here. You have no idea what you're dealing with."

"Sure we do," one tried. "Bunch of cowards. Killing innocent people, raping women, destroying homes . . ."

"We were sent to do a job, and we did it," Daniel informed them, steely-eyed. "We offered our lives for yours, and that's what you get out of it?" He scanned the young man up and down, curling his lip with disgust. "We did our job," he repeated. "Looking at you, I doubt you know what a job is."

Marion glanced at the others, who looked ready to jump on the hippies and make this a very real situation. She had no doubt they would, given the opportunity.

"Daniel," she murmured for only him to hear.

He huffed violently, but he got her message. "Let's go home, boys." He hiked both their bags over one shoulder and shoved through the hippies. Stu and Hal followed quietly, but Joey stood his ground. As Daniel had done, he went almost nose to nose with one of the men.

"You wanna know what a coward is?" Joey growled through clenched teeth. He shoved him back a few steps, rolling his sleeves up as he went. "Look in the goddamn mirror."

Marion swooped in and took Joey's hand, leading him out of reach. "Let's go see Sassy."

He was hot with anger, but he let her lead him out of the jungle, a little calmer with every step.

"That won't be the last of it," Daniel told his friends. "People don't like us much."

"B-but we're vets," Hal said. "We're supposed to be heroes."

Daniel nodded. "No heroes in this war, my friend. Everybody here hates the Vietnam War, and we're the face of it. I've been spat on, shoved, cursed . . ." He held Joey's gaze. "But you gotta hold back the demons, Joey. The police will lock you up, vet or not. It's not worth it."

"That's FUBAR, man," Joey muttered. "Guy's begging for it. I'll take them all."

"You'll learn," Daniel said. "It's a war here, too. Just different. Over here, we're the enemy."

They continued down the echoing corridor without a word, until Marion gave them a grin. "At least you're all home. Let's figure that out first."

"Joey!" Sassy's shout shattered the quiet, and Marion saw her struggling against a security guard, needing to get past. "Joey!"

All the anger dropped from Joey's face, and he ran. "Sass!"

By the time Marion reached them, they were hugging each other, crying and laughing, oblivious to the rest of the world. Sassy's sheer joy over seeing her brother again filled Marion's heart to overflowing. After a moment, she left her brother's arms and hugged Marion, still crying.

"I missed you!" she exclaimed. "Oh, we have so much wine to drink to go with your stories. Those short little postcards you sent only whet my appetite." She snuck a glance behind Marion, and when she looked back, she was batting her eyelashes. "Tom and I . . . Gah! I have so much to tell you! But not here. Come on. So many people want to say hello."

Taking their hands, Sassy dragged Marion and Joey toward the waiting room and a familiar-looking crowd of people. Tom stood at the back, holding up a handwritten banner that said *Welcome home!* and Marion laughed out loud.

"Mrs. Levin? Mr. Romano?" She took in the group of friends. "I can't believe you're all here! This is such a wonderful surprise!"

"It's everyone from Isabella, see?" Sassy leaned in conspiratorially. "Even that guy with the scars. I'll tell you all about him later."

"I can't believe you did all this," Marion said, hugging Sassy again.

"This is just the beginning. Mrs. Romano wants everyone to come for dinner tonight." She winked. "We'll see. I have something else up my sleeve."

"What are you—"

"Dad?"

Marion stepped back, startled by Daniel's exclamation. A man and a woman had appeared at the side of the group, and right away Marion knew the man was his father. The resemblance was unmistakable. She saw the split second when his father took in the eye patch, but he was quick to recover.

"Dad? What are you . . . Mom?" His voice cracked. "How did—"

"Daniel!" his mother cried, rushing to him. Daniel buried his face in her hair, holding her tight, then he looked up, his eye glassy with emotion as his father approached.

"Welcome home, son," he said.

The love in his parents' gaze was so intense, Marion had to look away. She faced Sassy instead, tears welling up in her eyes. "What did you do? He hasn't seen his parents since he shipped out. He's been afraid to call them."

"Yeah, his mom told me he probably felt that way. She's cool, Marion. She totally wanted to come, but I didn't think they'd make it. Flights aren't cheap. This is out of sight, meeting them in person."

"Marion?" Daniel took her arm and faced her toward his parents. "I'd like you to meet my parents, Adam and Grace Neumann. They flew in from Halifax. Mom, Dad, this is Marion Hart." He met her gaze, and she blushed, wondering what he was about to say. "She was my doctor. Now she's the love of my life."

"I'm very happy to meet you both," she said, "You have a wonderful son."

His mother, Grace, was beautiful, with pitch-black hair and eyes like her son's. She gave Marion a warm embrace. "It's wonderful to meet you, Marion. I hear you did some heroic things over there. You'll have to tell us all about it."

"I think a few family nights will have to be arranged before you fly back. Mrs. Neumann, these are my parents, Marcus and Cindy Hart, and my sister, Pat."

Sassy seemed glued to Joey's side. "Your face is going to hurt tomorrow," Marion teased. "So much smiling."

"I can't believe you brought him back. That's some kinda miracle," Sassy replied.

Tom gave Sassy a nudge. "Time?"

"Yeah. I think so."

Marion grinned, seeing Tom take her friend's hand, then Sassy caught her attention again. She looked like she was ready to burst. "Everyone, may I have your attention, please?"

fifty-one
SASSY

❦

Four cars drove from the airport toward downtown Toronto, and Sassy kept twisting in her seat, checking that everyone was still behind them. Tom's car was full, with Joey, Marion, Daniel, and her. The Levins and Romanos had come together, and they were driving Mr. Roy. The Moores had their own vehicle, which was tight with the wheelchair. Daniel's parents had a rental car, and they offered to drive Stu and Hal to Sassy's secret destination.

"What's with the mystery?" Joey asked. "Come on, Sass. I'm tired."

"I know!" she said with a little squeal. "But you're gonna love this."

"It's a fair question," Marion said. "Where are we going?"

"Nope," Sassy replied.

Joey groaned. "At least turn up the radio."

"'Jumpin' Jack Flash,'" Tom said, in case Joey hadn't heard it before. "Rolling Stones' latest."

"Yeah. We got all the music out there," Joey said. "But it sounds different here."

Sensing Sassy's eyes on him, Tom slipped his hand onto her thigh and gave her an encouraging squeeze. Ever since he'd slid that ring onto her finger, she'd felt like a different person. Her dad had been so right in his journal:

she didn't have to protest for women's rights. All she had to do was believe in herself and stay on track. And she'd chosen the track Tom was on.

"Oh! I almost forgot." She grabbed the bag at her feet and dug out the treats she'd brought. "I have a Hershey's bar, Peanut M&M's, Mini Eggs, some Lay's—"

"Oh my God, Sass," Joey exclaimed, then she heard him laugh for the first time. She felt a sharp pain in her heart, registering its new sound. Laughter no longer rolled from his belly like a baby's. It sounded weak and unsure. But it was laughter. It was freedom. He shoved his open hands into the front-seat area. "You have Doritos?"

It felt like forever before they pulled up in front of the old red-stone house. Tom parked in the circular driveway, then everyone climbed out.

Joey stood a while, gazing up at what had been his bedroom window. "I wondered if I'd ever see this place again," he admitted.

"Don't go in yet," Sassy said. "We have to wait for everyone to park. Here they come."

"The house is the surprise?" Joey asked dryly.

"Well, kind of," she said, praying he wouldn't ask about their dad. Not yet. "But there's a bit more to it."

Joey rolled his eyes. "Please tell me you didn't plan a surprise party. I hate those."

"I promise we did not plan a surprise party." She winked at Tom, who went on ahead, stopping at the front door.

"All right. Now that everyone's here, I have an announcement to make." She held out her arm. "This is the house where Joey and I grew up. Yeah, it's huge. I know. Way too big for just us. So we've done something about it. For the past few weeks, Tom and I have been working really hard on putting together something that will hopefully help a few people, particularly vets like you guys," she said, looking at Hal and Stu, then Joey. Her brother was looking confused.

Her gaze went to Marion, who was holding Daniel's hand. "Marion taught me a lot, but one thing really got me, and that was the question of where men returning from the war would live. Most don't have money, and a lot of vets aren't ready to face real life yet. There are rooming houses around the city, but many have problems, like overcrowding. And no one really has any qualifications to help the men if they need help."

Marion shifted, regarding her closely. Sassy took another breath, eager to get to the good part.

"I've always been a spoiled brat, like Tom says," she told everyone. "I've been selfish without even thinking about it."

Joey chuckled, his dark brow lifted with sarcasm. "Really? I had no idea."

"Anyway," she said, narrowing her eyes at him, "things, hopefully, have changed." She held her breath as she walked to the front door then stopped beside Tom. "I'd like to welcome you all to a very special place," she said, shoving through the knot in her throat.

Tom held a shallow box in his hand, tied with a red bow. Right on cue, he opened it and displayed the plaque they had etched onto a brass rectangle, two feet wide, one foot tall.

"This is now 'Marion's Welcome Home,'" Tom announced.

"What?" Marion exclaimed. Nobody moved.

"Yes!" Sassy cried, hopping on her toes. "You're the inspiration, Marion."

Tom put a gentle arm around Sassy's shoulders, but he couldn't keep her feet on the ground. "Sassy has worked really hard on transforming this building into a place that will be called home by eight returning veterans who have nowhere else to go."

Sassy's attention was caught by one of the men they'd brought back—was his name Hal? He dropped his head, and she heard him sniff. When he raised a hand to wipe away tears, Sassy shot Tom a look of panic.

He nodded. "It's okay, Sass. It's a big deal." He looked back at the group. "We are in negotiations to create more Welcome Homes at the moment. Possibly two more by the end of the year. The one thing Sassy's lousy at is being patient. She wants it all when she wants it, and that's pretty much this minute."

She gave him a dramatic shrug, but she wasn't the least bit sorry. "There's more to it, and I'll explain as we go, but I wanted to let you know that you're not off the hook, Marion." She glanced fleetingly at Daniel, then back at her best friend. "Remember I told you this is for some of the men who aren't quite ready to return to this world after everything they've been through? Well, you're going to help me along the way, but you're not the only one."

She pulled open the front door, and Marion's jaw dropped. "Paul? What are you doing here?"

"Hey, Marion. I'll be volunteering here at least once a week, and some others have agreed to come on, too," he told her with his usual confident smile.

"This is Dr. Paul McKenny," Tom explained to the others. "He is one of Marion's colleagues from the Ontario Hospital. He and others will be providing counselling services for the residents." He glanced fondly at Sassy. "We even have a cook. Sassy's thought of everything."

"I want to see this place!" Mr. Romano declared. "Enough standing around. My old back is killing me."

"Who's this cook?" Mrs. Levin asked, walking inside. "You know we want to help out, too, yes?"

Joey stood back and frowned at her as the others went inside, and Sassy fought the lump in her chest. She knew what was coming.

"I don't get it, Sass. Dad gave you the okay on this? Where is he, anyway? Didn't want to come see me?"

She waited until she, Joey, and Marion were the only ones still, then she held Joey's gaze. "Something happened." She swallowed hard. "Dad passed away in February."

Joey paled. "He . . . what?"

"I'm sorry, Joey. I didn't know how to find you and tell you. It happened so fast. But this house . . . he would have wanted this."

He stared at her, disbelief clear in his glittering eyes. "But how? What happened?"

"Come inside. Please, Joey. I'll tell you more after."

He was still staring at her in shock, rooted in place.

"I understand what you're feeling, Joey," she said softly. "I promise, when we're alone, I will tell you everything, but not now. This isn't the time. Please, let's go inside. Your room is still yours, but I also have rooms for your . . . brothers. A safe place to be."

He looked dazed, but he kept ahold of her hand as they went into the house. She could hear exclamations coming from down the hall as Tom started the tour.

Then it was only Sassy and Marion, and her friend was regarding her with the most beautiful expression.

"I wanted to help," Sassy said simply. "And I ended up making myself feel great."

"For the record," Marion said, wiping tears from her cheeks, "you were never selfish. You are probably the most giving person I've ever met."

"What do you think of the plaque?" The sign was still at the front door, on the stoop. Tom had leaned it against the wall. "We wanted to put it by the door, but the tradesmen couldn't get here in time. We'll put it up this week."

"'Marion's Welcome Home.'" Her friend sighed, then she opened her arms and squeezed Sassy tight. "I am truly honoured, my friend."

"I wish my dad could see this."

They both stood back and looked past the trees and gardens, beyond the big front door with its shining brass knob, then up to the windows, where the setting sun still sparkled.

"Oh, Sassy," Marion said softly. "He sees you. And he is so, so proud of you."

a note to readers

When I began writing this book, I had very little idea of its direction, but I knew three things. I knew I wanted to explore the 1960s: the counterculture, music, fashion, drugs, free love, politics, and protests. I knew I wanted to learn about Canada's part in the Vietnam War, which is rarely discussed in popular culture because Canada was not officially "in" the war. And I knew how the novel would begin: with two girls who had nothing in common, except the place where they lived.

Then, of course, there had to be a boy. Maybe two. What if they, too, were completely different? Four almost polar-opposite characters who must come together in the end. Well, I thought, what if one of those men was part of the third generation of the Baker family? The timing for that was just right. If you are a reader of my books, did you spot Daniel's parentage and background from *Tides of Honour* and *Come from Away*? Knowing what we know of his family's military background, I knew he had to be a fighter.

The 1960s, with all its cultural changes, was a time for Canada to rethink our identity as a country. We saw ourselves as the freethinking, liberated offspring of the stiff-upper-lip British mentality, but we were also the impressionable and curious younger sibling of the U.S., heavily influenced by the landslide of protest music that hit the charts that decade. We wanted the freedom those singer-songwriters were talking about, but we weren't ready to get into the violent, radical protests fought in the U.S. and in London.

I began my research in Toronto, where I grew up. The first thing I learned was that regardless of the fact that Canada officially chose not to fight in the Vietnam War, approximately 40,000 Canadians (the numbers are unclear) obscured their nationality and sometimes their age to enlist with the American troops to fight in Vietnam. Why would any of them choose to go to war? Was it a craving for adventure? A family tradition? A determination to fight communism on any front? According to the Canadian Vietnam Veterans Memorial Association, at least 173 Canadian soldiers died or were MIA. One 2024 CBC article stated, "To put that number in perspective, 158 Canadian soldiers were killed during the mission in Afghanistan."

The names of every one of those lost Canadians has been inscribed on the Vietnam Veterans Memorial in Washington, D.C.

In contrast, the government of Canada never formally acknowledged the Canadians killed or MIA in Vietnam because, officially, they were part of the American forces. Canadian Vietnam veteran, the late Ron Parkes, from Winnipeg, was the cofounder and eventual president of the Canadian Vietnam Veterans Association. He said they were ignored or forgotten for years.

"When I came back and brought up the subject, it was always 'Who cares? We weren't there. We weren't in it,'" he said in a 2015 CBC interview. "When I went down to the Royal Canadian Legion, they wouldn't accept us, our service." One of his most meaningful quotes (for me) was, "I don't know if what we did was right or wrong, but I'm proud of my service." For more from Ron Parkes and others, I highly recommend watching the documentary by Nick Vergados and White Tower Films, *Honor and Remember: The Canadians Who Fought in the Vietnam War*. The link is included in the source list on page 406.

It wasn't until 1994 that the Royal Canadian Legion officially recognized Canadian Vietnam veterans for regular membership. The following year, a group of American veterans privately funded "The North Wall," a memorial in Windsor, Ontario. It's a moving and welcome sign of respect, but 1995 was far too late for tens of thousands of men and women to understand that they were appreciated, and that their service mattered. A 2013 study revealed that 271,000 vets still suffered from war-zone related PTSD.

This year marks the thirtieth anniversary of that monument's creation, and Canadians who served (as well as their families) are invited by the

Canadian Vietnam Veterans Memorial Association to a special ceremony in Windsor on July 6, 2025.

While the Canadians who fought in Vietnam went unrecognized for so long, we were far less ignorant of the approximately 40,000 American "war resisters" or "draft dodgers" who sought and found shelter here between 1966 and 1972. In 1965, the Toronto-based Student Union for Peace Action's Anti-Draft Programme published a widely distributed fact sheet suggesting to Americans an alternative to serving in the U.S. military: *Want to come to Canada instead? Let us answer your questions* was the basic offer (paraphrased). The response in Vancouver, Montreal, and then Toronto was so positive they created the TADP (Toronto Anti-Draft Programme), cofounded by a twenty-year-old American Vietnam War resister living in Toronto named Mark Satin. "By 1968 we were receiving one hundred letters and seventeen visitors a day," Satin wrote. The organization helped with immigration counselling, jobs, legal help—even for the more serious crime of desertion—and basic supplies. They had an emergency loan fund and two hostels. In addition, over two hundred Torontonians volunteered to temporarily house the arriving resisters.

Draft dodgers/war resisters are not deserters. Author John Boyko, who wrote *The Devil Trick: How Canada Fought the Vietnam War*, explained in an interview that "draft dodgers were those who decided that their number was coming up, they were about to be drafted and to be drafted was to go to the war. They had not yet put on the uniform. Deserters, however, were people who had either enlisted or [had] been drafted and were about to go to Vietnam."

Deserters have never been pardoned by the government. Over sixty years later, if they choose to return to their home country, they could still be arrested.

The war resisters crossed our border at different locations. Some settled in cities, some kept moving farther north. Most came from middle-class backgrounds, and very few were "active political radicals," but they brought with them the "American" counterculture and rebellious attitudes, including protests, massive music festivals, and cannabis grow-ops.

Evidently, the Americans liked it here. In 1977, U.S. president Jimmy Carter offered to pardon the draft dodgers, but nearly half of them stayed in Canada despite that.

While I was in the process of writing *On Isabella Street*, I was promoting *The Secret Keeper* at book events and would often gave a brief outline of what I was working on. Readers were interested in the Vietnam aspect, but when I brought up the topic of deinstitutionalization, hands shot up. That surprised me; people are generally more intrigued by major events, like a war, rather than by ongoing processes or movements.

Deinstitutionalization, the release of institutionalized individuals from psychiatric institutions and the transfer of their care to community health centres, mostly occurred between the late 1960s and the 1980s (I condensed the timeline for this book for creative purposes), and its repercussions are visible today. Deinstitutionalization was a worldwide movement that included care standards from ten European countries and the World Health Organization. The Saskatchewan Association for Community Living (SACL) was created in 1955, and it became the first Canadian step toward deinstitutionalization.

The Toronto Lunatic Asylum, 1868
William Notman, The Toronto Library Archives

Up until 1949, these mental hospitals were reviled as "bedlam," "Snake pits," and "houses of horror" (American Psychiatric Association, 1949; Deutsch, 1948; Ward, 1946), hiding vulnerable people away so the public would not see. The concept of "freeing" the patients seemed laudable in light of the rampant and horrifyingly true stories of patient abuse and neglect in those early mental institutions.

If that was all there was to the story, deinstitutionalization would have been a done deal with no more conversation required around it. But by the mid-1960s, medications and modes of therapy were vastly improved from the old days.

Many patients benefitted greatly from deinstitutionalization and successfully returned to society. Those with manageable psychiatric issues who had supportive families and friends willing to help by overseeing the patient's day-to-day care, meals, medicines (if necessary), and appointments were able to move on.

But consider the patients whose psychiatric issues were unmanageable unless they were under a doctor's care, properly medicated and observed. Not all of these patients were dangerous, but some were. Many found themselves unable to meet the most basic requirements of self-care. Released into the "wild," with no shelter and no idea how to get food, many turned to crime, even if they didn't realize they were doing it. Others would live a miserable life with no home and no steady care.

What happened to all these people after they'd been shown the door? In Toronto, the Ontario Hospital (now the Centre for Addiction and Mental Health) and the Lakeshore Psychiatric Hospital closed at the same time. The Ontario Hospital was demolished in 1976, and the Lakeshore Psychiatric Hospital was parceled out to different groups, including Humber College. Where did all those patients go? Homeless shelters did not appear until the 1980s; however, there were rooming houses—large family homes that had been renovated to accommodate groups of people who could not afford to pay for a meal, let alone rent.

After the two psychiatric institutions in Toronto closed, the local neighbourhood (Parkdale in Toronto) became the largest gathering place of psychiatric homeless people in Canada. I spoke with Victor Willis, executive director of PARC (Parkdale Activity-Recreation Centre) and he offered a bleak response to my question. Yes, there were rooming houses, but there no rules or regulations governing them until the 1970s to1980s. No one watched over the welfare of these vulnerable people. According to Victor, many self-serving landlords basically took all of the tenants' money, put five or so people in a room, and left them to care for themselves. It's no surprise that many preferred homelessness to those living conditions.

After thirty years of disputes over rooming houses of ill repute and illegal bachelor apartments, the Parkdale Pilot Project (PPP) was created, which offered Parkdale landlords an opportunity to regularize and legalize their buildings. Electric outlets and fire alarms were finally checked, maintenance done. By the time the programme ended around 2018, eighty buildings had been legalized.

Not all of the rooming houses and bachelor apartments participated in the PPP, and not everyone was willing to follow the same guidelines. As a result, rooming houses were made illegal across two-thirds of Toronto. They are also banned in Scarborough, North York, and East York, which has resulted in fewer safe places for the vulnerable in our society to live.

Homelessness, or "houselessness" as it is referred to today, increased greatly after deinstitutionalization. Not all these people had mental illnesses; however, an April 2024 University of Calgary study published by Dr. Dallas Seitz, MD, PhD, a psychiatrist and clinician-researcher at the Cumming School of Medicine, quantified the connection between homelessness and mental health disorders.

> We found 66 to 75 per cent of people who are experiencing homelessness have an underlying mental health condition. We have always known that mental health disorders are overrepresented among people experiencing homelessness, but we didn't have a clear understanding of how many people are affected.

My original idea for this book—where the two main characters live on the same floor as each other, in the same building, but on the surface have little else in common—brought me to 105 Isabella Street.

I wanted the location to be downtown, within a half hour of everything the girls would need, and 105 Isabella Street was one of the earlier high-rise apartment buildings in Toronto. Plus, I've driven past the old building so many times growing up, it just felt right.

When I was visiting Toronto in June 2024, I took advantage of a gorgeous day and walked from my downtown hotel to Isabella Street to see the building in person after decades of my being away. I asked at the building's office if I could speak with someone about its history and was disappointed that they said no—until a friendly resident came out to the lobby and changed all that. Community leader and spokesperson Phil Parsons has lived at 105 "forever," and he took me under his wing for the next two hours, walking me all over the Village area from Jarvis to Church, between Hayden and Wellesley, sharing so many wonderful tidbits I couldn't write them down fast enough. Our tour began on the corner of Isabella and Jarvis at a beautiful red stone and brick heritage house from 1875. In 1941, the building was the national headquarters for the YWCA, and in 1988 it was renovated to become Casey House, Canada's first stand-alone treatment facility for people living with HIV/AIDS, and Ontario's first freestanding hospice. Since then, it has become more of a specialty hospital, working with people living with and at risk for HIV.

The tour continued past old brick homes and apartment buildings along Isabella Street, many of which are slowly but surely being rebuilt to join the jungle of condominiums that is now downtown Toronto. Phil taught me about "renovictions," which are now happening at 105 as well as many other places. Basically, it's Sassy's dreaded gentrification, but on a massive scale.

Just a hop, skip, and a jump from Isabella Street is the neighbourhood of Yorkville, Canada's version of New York's trendy Greenwich Village. Back in the day, Yorkville was made up of about twenty-five city blocks of good times, and over thirty venues offering live music. The area was a magnet for anyone looking for a "counterculture lifestyle." Before they were international recording stars, Canadian artists like Gordon Lightfoot, Neil Young, Joni Mitchell, Buffy Sainte-Marie, Leonard Cohen, and Murray McLauchlan frequented the hottest spots, like the Riverboat Coffee House, the Penny Farthing, the Purple Onion, and yes, Chez Monique.

Outside the Riverboat Coffee House in Yorkville, Toronto, 1968
Courtesy of B. C. Fiedler

In general, the middle-aged, upwardly mobile residents of Toronto weren't fans of what Yorkville had become. They called its denizens drug addicts and vagrants, which, to be fair, wasn't entirely wrong. Yorkville's youth, and especially those who rejected the old-school idea of working for money, depended partly on a group called "the Diggers" to provide them with food and shelter. In an effort to change public opinion about the Yorkville crowd, the Diggers put together the love-in at Queen's Park on May 22, 1967, where Sassy met Davey. Over 5,000 people attended and enjoyed some great entertainment, including a performance by Buffy Sainte-Marie.

An unfortunate result of the love-in was that Yorkville became even more popular, creating traffic gridlock in the area. The Diggers suggested that the Toronto City Council should consider turning the area into a pedestrian mall, closing it to motor vehicles, but the city denied the request. In response, the Diggers staged a sit-in on Yorkville Avenue. At 3:00 a.m. on August 20, 1967, three hundred Yorkville residents sat peacefully in the middle of Yorkville Avenue and blocked all traffic. Twenty-five hundred people observed, creating more congestion. Still protesting the denial of their request to turn Yorkville into a place for pedestrians only, 150 hippies came out three nights later and staged a sleep-in in front of city hall.

The street closures never happened despite their peaceful protests.

Buffy Sainte-Marie sings at the peaceful love-in at Queen's Park in 1967
Bill Dampier, Courtesy of the Toronto Telegram, *Clara Thomas Archives and Special Collections, York University*

Writing historical fiction is more than writing about history. It's writing about human lives caught up in that history. I love riding that roller coaster with my characters. It's what got me into writing in the first place: imagining myself somewhere else, as someone else, in another time.

From the beginning, I knew Marion needed to go to Vietnam with Daniel. But how? First, there was the question of changing her medical specialty from emergency medicine to psychiatry, which I thought was a stretch—until I remembered my uncle, a surgeon, had done pretty much the same thing before I was born. After making an unfortunate mistake in an operating theatre, he suffered a breakdown and was treated in a facility for a while. Psychiatry helped him immensely—to the point that he eventually became a psychiatrist. So it's a bit of a twist, but it's based on reality. Oh, and that illness Marion had that derailed her chosen specialty? That was based on something I went through in 1999. Like Marion, I was fortunate to leave the hospital alive, and I've never forgotten that.

———————

Now let's address the probability of Dr. Marion Hart, psychiatrist, being approved to go on that mission: extremely low. When I was about halfway through writing the book, I woke up one morning in a complete panic because my psyche had suddenly declared there were no Canadian doctors in Vietnam. But my psyche was wrong! I discovered a fantastic book, *Into the Dragon's Jaws* by Dr. Garry L. Willard, a former member of VPVN (Volunteer Physicians in Viet Nam), who is still practicing surgery at Brampton Civic Hospital. Dr. Willard was generous enough to read sections of my book (which he liked!), and when I asked him about Marion's qualifications, he said that it was possible that she had gone, even at her stage of medicine. His words: "I know that your main character is female, but I never met a female surgeon over there, ever. That does not mean that they did not exist. I met many women who as VPVNs were medical internists, anaesthetists, and paediatricians. (So why not a female surgeon?)"

John Boyko's book *The Devil's Trick* goes into depth about the experiences of Montreal nurse and hospital administrator Claire Culhane. Hearing that there were Canadian-built and Canadian-staffed hospitals in Vietnam, she went to help. Once there, she realized that not only were the conditions horrific, there was an inconceivable lack of basic medicines and tools, like generators.

Even worse, she learned that the reasons those Canadian hospitals were overflowing with patients was because they had often been wounded by Canadian-supplied weapons.

"It was everything from guidance systems to boots to the green berets that were worn by the marines and also involved napalm. And it also involved Agent Orange. They were manufactured in Canada and sent to Vietnam," Boyko was quoted. "About $375 million a year of weaponry was being manufactured in Canada and sold to the Pentagon for use in Vietnam.

Equivalent in today's dollars, that would be about $2 billion of arms sales that were going directly to the Vietnamese and South Vietnamese for use in the war."

As Sassy's father said, "War is good for business."

Ms. Culhane returned to Canada after six months, disgusted by what she had seen in Vietnam. She wrote to Prime Minister Pierre Elliott Trudeau for twenty months, requesting a meeting and demanding an end to Canadian arms sales to the U.S. On Christmas Eve 1969, she and a small group of anti-war protestors held a candlelight vigil at Parliament Hill, waiting to speak with the prime minister. Determined to see him, they camped in the freezing cold for nineteen days and nights, but PM Trudeau claimed he did not have time to meet with them. He did, however, sit with John Lennon and Yoko Ono while the protestors shivered outside. There is a CBC link to a video of Claire speaking with a reporter about that protest on page 407.

Also built by Canada was the Bell CH-118 Iroquois helicopter, otherwise known as a Huey due to its original designation as HU-1. About 7,000 Hueys were deployed to Vietnam. According to *Air & Space/Smithsonian* magazine, "Between 1966 and 1971, one Army helicopter was lost for every 7.9 sorties—564 pilots, 1,155 crewmen and 682 passengers were killed in accidents alone. More Hueys were downed in Vietnam than any other type of aircraft."

———

Alongside Sassy, Marion, the Levins, the Romanos, and the Moores, one mystery man lived on the fifth floor of 105 Isabella Street. Not even I knew who he was for a long time, so quiet, so quick to open and close 509's door. It wasn't until close to the end that Dickie Roy finally revealed himself to me, and I was so proud of him.

Late in my research, I came across another piece of Canadian World War II history that I'd never heard of: the story of Canada's Black Watch snipers. That's when it all came together for me. No wonder Dickie was so wary.

Following D-Day, 320 men from Canada's Black Watch regiment made their way to Verrières Ridge to push the Germans out of position. In one of Canada's worst defeats in the war, the Black Watch was ambushed, and all but twenty of those men were killed, wounded, or taken prisoner. According to a wonderful documentary on YouTube, the story doesn't end there. A small group of these men volunteered to join the scout platoon. They became snipers, stealthy hunters whose job it was to clear the scene before the rest of the men arrived. As the narrator in the film said, "We didn't fight on the front lines. We fought in front of them." Dickie Roy is a fictional member of that platoon, and part of my little battalion on the fifth floor of 105 Isabella Street.

sources

BOOKS

Belshaw, John Douglas. *Canadian History: Post-Confederation.* BC Open Text-book Collection, 2016.

Boyko, John. *The Devil's Trick: How Canada Fought the Vietnam War.* Toronto, ON: Knopf Canada, 2021.

Willard, Dr. Garry L. *Into the Dragon's Jaws: A Canadian Combat Surgeon in the Vietnam War.* Victoria, BC: Tellwell Talent, 2021.

ARTICLES and VIDEOS

ISABELLA STREET

Micallef, Shawn. "An Ode to the Midcentury Toronto Apartment." *Toronto Star,* May 26, 2018. https://www.thestar.com/opinion/star-columnists /an-ode-to-the-mid-century-toronto-apartment/article_477128ca-5c1b-5c94 -aeec-08a05f508daf.html.

TORONTO

"This Is What Toronto Streets Looked Like in the 1960s." *blogTO,* July 1, 2022. https://www.blogto.com/city/2016/11/the_cluttered_beauty_of_toronto _streets_in_the_1960s/.

TORONTO ANTI-DRAFT PROGRAMME

Satin, Mark (in Consultation with Some Others from That Era). "Toronto Anti-Draft Programme: Where the Guys Who Said 'No!' Came for Help." *Radical Middle Newsletter,* 2014. https://www.radicalmiddle.com/tadp .htm.

YORKVILLE

Allison-Cassin, Stacy, and Michael Primiani, Michael. "Yorkville and the Folk Revival in Toronto: Yorkville and the Coffee Houses." *Folk Music and Yorkville Coffeehouses*, April 28, 2017. https://scalar.usc.edu/works/music toronto/yorkville-and-the-coffee-houses-1.

Bloom, Alexander. "Review: [Untitled]." *The American Historical Review*, 118, no. 1 (February 2013): 170–71. Reviewed Work: Henderson, Stuart. *Making the Scene: Yorkville and Hip Toronto in the 1960s*. Oxford University Press, 2013.

Crisolago, Mike. "When We Walked a Magic Street: Remembering Toronto's Summer of Love." Everything Zoomer, August 13, 2020. https://www .everythingzoomer.com/arts-entertainment/2020/08/13/toronto-summer -of-love/.

Cross, Alan. "Looking Back on Toronto's Yorkville Scene of the 1960s." *A Journal of Musical Things*, November 9, 2017. https://www.ajournalof musicalthings.com/looking-back-torontos-yorkville-scene-1960s/.

Guest contributor. "What Yorkville Was Like in the 1960s." *blogTO*, July 31, 2022. https://www.blogto.com/city/2016/08/what_yorkville_was_like_in _the_1960s/.

"Riverboat Coffee House." B.C. Fieldler Management, n.d. http://theriver boat.ca/.

"The Riverboat." Sounds Like Toronto, 2020. https://soundsliketoronto.ca/en /stories/venues/the-riverboat#canadian-legends.

Schabas, Jake. "Throwback Thursday: Yorkville and the Death of Toronto's First Scene." *Spacing*, June 25, 2009. https://spacing.ca/toronto/2009/06 /25/throwback-thursday-yorkville-and-the-death-of-torontos-first-scene/.

VIETNAM

Boyko, John. "Historian Examines Neglected Truth Behind Canada's Role in Vietnam War." Clare Culhane interview. CBC Radio, October 7, 2021. https://www.cbc.ca/radio/ideas/historian-examines-neglected-truth-be hind-canada-s-role-in-vietnam-war-1.6203086.

"Canadian Vietnam Veterans Memorial Association." 2010. http://www.cana diansinvietnam.com/.

Corday, Chris. "Lost to History: The Canadians Who Fought in Vietnam." CBC, November 10, 2015. https://www.cbc.ca/news/canada/british -columbia/lost-to-history-the-canadians-who-fought-in-vietnam-1.3304440.

Goldsworthy, Ryan. "The Canadian Way: The Case of Canadian Vietnam War Veterans." *Canadian Military Journal* 15, no. 3 (Summer 2015): 48–52. http://www.journal.forces.gc.ca/vol15/no3/eng/PDF/CMJ153Ep48.pdf.

White Tower Films. "Honor and Remember." June 5, 2020. https://vimeo. com/426430910.

POWs/MIAs

Lewis, Adrian R. "Vietnam War POWs and MIAs." *Encyclopedia Britannica* April 28, 2016. https://www.britannica.com/topic/Vietnam-War-POWs -and-MIAs-2051428.

SUICIDE NUMBERS

Bullman T.A., et al. "Suicide Risk Among US Veterans with Military Service During the Vietnam War." *JAMA Netw Open*, December 28, 2023. https:// jamanetwork.com/journals/jamanetworkopen/fullarticle/2813418.

VIETNAM VET MEMORIES

Mabe, G. Mike. "Memoirs of Vietnam." Veterans History Project, American Folklife Center, Library of Congress, 2006–2008. https://www.loc.gov /resource/afc2001001.93323.pm0001001/?sp=2&st=image.

STORIES OF VETS COMING HOME

Greene, Bob "Vietnam Vets Recall Their Homecomings—Often Pain- fully." *Dessert News*, February 14, 1989. https://www.deseret.com/19 89/2/4/18800994/vietnam-vets-recall-their-homecomings-often-painfully.

U.S. CONSCRIPTION

"Vietnam War: Annual Number of U.S. Military Personnel Conscripted 1964– 1973." Statista, September 2, 2024. https://www.statista.com/statistics /1336037/vietnam-war-us-military-draft/.

GARRY L. WILLARD

Evans, Tyler. "Doctor Pens Book About Life as Combat Surgeon in Vietnam." *Barrie Today*, October 6, 2021. https://www.barrietoday.com/local-news /doctor-pens-book-about-life-as-combat-surgeon-in-vietnam-4482951.

COMBAT MEDIC

Lavendar, Natasha. "What It Was Really Like as a Medic in the Vietnam War." *Grunge*, January 23, 2023. https://www.grunge.com/321306/what-it-was -really-like-as-a-medic-in-the-vietnam-war.

PTSD/ILLNESSES POST-VIETNAM

Abdullah, Aisha. "Disturbing Long-Term Health Impacts from the Vietnam War." *Medical News*, April 20, 2023. https://medical-news.org/disturbing -long-term-health-impacts-from-the-vietnam-war/46407/.

"History of PTSD and Trauma Diagnoses: Vietnam Wars Years 1955– 1975." Trauma Dissociation. http://traumadissociation.com/ptsd/history -of-post-traumatic-stress-disorder.html#vietnam

CANADIAN PEACEKEEPERS IN VIETNAM

Moore, Erin. "An Impossible Peace." CBC, November 10, 2023. https:// www.cbc.ca/newsinteractives/features/canadians-vietnam-war-remem brance-day.

AGENT ORANGE CBC

Forestell, Harry. "Agent Orange Continues to Haunt Lives of U.S. Veterans Trained in New Brunswick." CBC, July 17, 2023. https://www.cbc.ca /news/canada/new-brunswick/agent-orange-us-gagetown-1.6906995.

HELICOPTERS

"Still Hovering: Ex-Door Gunner's Vietnam Memories Never Far Away." *Pacific Citizen*, November 9, 2018. https://www.pacificcitizen.org/still-hovering -ex-door-gunners-vietnam-memories-never-far-away/.

Skaarup, Harold A. "Canadian Warplanes 7: Bell CH-118 Iroquois Helicopter." Military History Books, 2024. https://www.silverhawkauthor.com /post.canadian-warplanes-7-bell-ch-118-iroquois-helicopter.

BLACK WATCH SNIPERS

History Hit. "The Harrowing Story of an Elite Allied Sniper Unit | The Black Watch Snipers." YouTube, June 25, 2023. https://www.youtube.com /watch?v=iWCrKatprzU

ABOUT EARLY INSTITUTION

Davies, M., et al. "After the Asylum in Canada: Surviving Deinstitutionalisation and Revising History." In *Deinstitutionalisation and After: Mental Health in Historical Perspective*, edited by D. Kritsotaki, V. Long, and M. Smith. Palgrave Macmillan, 2016. https://doi.org/10.1007/978-3 -319-45360-6_4.

"How an Insane Asylum Shaped this Toronto Neighbourhood." Housecreep, https://www.housecreep.com/lists/how-an-insane-asylum-shaped-this -toronto-neighbourhood.

Seeman, Mary. "The 1960s in North American Psychiatry." *Hektoen International: A Journal of Medical Humanities*, n.d. https://hekint.org/2017/11 /16/1960s-north-american-psychiatry/.

MARION'S FAVOURITE PROF

Muldoon, Maureen. "A 1960s Course in Medical Ethics in a Canadian Medical School." *Canadian Journal of Practical Philosophy* 9 (2023). https://ojs. uwindsor.ca/index.php/cjpp/article/view/8148/5549.

DEINSTITUTIONALIZATION: WHY DID IT HAPPEN—3 REASONS

Yohanna, Daniel, MD. "Deinstitutionalization of People with Mental Illness: Causes and Consequences." *AMA Journal of Ethics,* October 15, 2013. https://journalofethics.ama-assn.org/article/deinstitutionalization-people -mental-illness-causes-and-consequences/2013-10.

1950s

Seeman, Mary V., MD. "TPH: History and Memories of the Toronto Psychiatric Hospital, 1925–1966." *American Journal of Psychiatry*, September 1, 2000. https://ajp.psychiatryonline.org/doi/10.1176/appi.ajp.157.9.1537-a.

TALES FROM THE 1850s

Raible, Chris. "999 Queen Street West: The Toronto Asylum Scandal." *Canada's History*, January 24, 2016. https://www.canadashistory.ca/explore/science-technology/999-queen-street-west-the-toronto-asylum-scandal.

ABOUT NEW ATTITUDES RE: INSTITUTION

Bradbeer, Janice. "Once Upon a City: Changing Minds About Mental Illness." *The Toronto Star*, May 25, 2017. https://www.thestar.com/news/gta/once-upon-a-city-changing-minds-about-mental-illness/article_2c55ec1f-1eb7-5289-96c9-026b45f4bac7.html

Centre for Mental Health and Addition. "History of Queen Street Site." https://www.camh.ca/en/driving-change/building-the-mental-health-facility-of-the-future/history-of-queen-street-site.

MY SPOTIFY LIST

https://open.spotify.com/playlist/6fJkiJCIh59MOmqxLAp592?si=f2253d3cbaad49c2

Readers Group Guide
ON ISABELLA STREET

How well do you think the author conveys the time period (i.e., do you think she remained true to the events, social structures, and political events of the time period)? Is this an era that you knew about before you read this book, or did you learn a lot from this narrative?

Is it difficult to keep our own, modern-day experiences from influencing the reading of a historical fiction tale like *On Isabella Street*? Can we imagine what life was really like for the characters within the context of their time period and not our own?

On Isabella Street tells the story of two women from very different backgrounds, with Marion coming from fairly humble beginnings, while Sassy had a more privileged upbringing. How do you think their upbringings contributed to their unique personalities? What similarities and differences did you notice between the two characters? Which woman's story resonated with you the most?

How do Sassy and Marion change, grow, or evolve throughout the course of the story? Do you think they do so for better or worse? What events (if any) would you say trigger these changes?

Relationships are at the core of *On Isabella Street*. What did you make of the friendship between the two female main characters? How does their friendship compare to their romantic relationships in this narrative?

In what ways do the girls challenge each other's points of view? Do you think one of them has a greater impact on the other, or do they equally impact each other's lives? How do you think their lives would be different if they'd never met?

Discuss the author's treatment of social issues such as deinstitutionalization, social housing, and homelessness in this narrative. Did the novel impact your understanding or perception of these issues? What did you think of the fact that Marion didn't really speak up against deinstitutionalization until it was too late? Did you find this to be a cowardly act, or did you understand where she was coming from?

Daniel is a significant character in this novel, and yet, he doesn't narrate his own perspective. Discuss the impact of his limited presence on the page, and the role he plays in Marion's life and understanding of the world.

What did you make of Sassy's relationship with Davey, and Davey himself as a character? How does their relationship compare to her relationship with Tom? What do you think her life would have been like had she ended up with Davey?

Discuss the different reasons the men in this novel had for either joining the war or becoming a "resistor." What did you think of their reasons for either enlisting or refusing to? Do you know anyone who has fought in a war and come back home with issues like Daniel and Marcus Hart?

What do you make of the intergenerational tensions in this novel (e.g., between Sassy and her father; between the older, more conservative generation as opposed to the "hippy" generation; etc.)? Do you think these tensions only apply to this specific time period, or are they still relevant in the present? What generation would you classify Marion as being a part of?

Discuss the character of Jim Rankin. What do you make of the secret he had been keeping for most of his adult life? Did you find him to be a sympathetic character? What did you think of the agreement he and Marcus struck with regard to keeping their secret? How do you think it was for those men to keep their secret for so long, especially from their families?

What role do novels have in our understanding of history? Did *On Isabella Street* change your perception of the Vietnam War? What about your perception of the changing 1960s culture?

What did you make of the confrontation between Daniel, Joey, Stu, and Hal, and the group of young men at the airport who call them "baby killers" and "cowards," which is representative of the kind of reception many veterans faced upon their return from the Vietnam War? How did you think this treatment might have affected the veterans in both the long and short term?

Take turns reading your favourite passage/excerpt out loud to the group. What did you like about this passage specifically? How does this particular passage relate to the story as a whole? Does it reveal anything important about any of the characters or illuminate certain aspects of the story?

Compare this book to other works of historical fiction your group has read. Is it similar to any of them? Did you like it more or less than other books you've read?

Were you satisfied with Sassy and Joey's reunion at the end of this novel? How do you imagine their relationship evolved after the novel ended?

What do you think happens with Sassy and Marion, and their respective romantic relationships with Tom and Daniel, after the ending?

What did you like or dislike about the book that hasn't been discussed already? Were you glad you read this book? Would you recommend it to a friend? Do you want to read more works by this author?

Finally, who cried—or at least got a little choked up—while reading this book? Which scene(s) moved you the most? Which character's story resonated most with you? Did the book move you, inspire you, haunt you? What will you remember most about *On Isabella Street*?

acknowledgements

W hen I began writing this book, I knew the basic points I wanted to cover: counterculture, music, fashion, drugs, free love, politics, protests—there were so many, I wasn't sure how they might connect.

Then I decided I wanted to write about everything I mentioned above plus the Canadians who served in the Vietnam War. The "Unknown Veterans," as they are known today. But when I went on tour to launch *The Secret Keeper*, readers reacted to a different aspect of what I was saying, so the story changed its focus. Or rather, the focus grew.

Deinstitutionalization. There's a word I had never heard before, and one that I had to practice saying out loud a few times, to be honest. What did it mean? Why did it happen?

One reason for deinstitutionalization was to end the horrible conditions that had been going on at psychiatric facilities, or mental institutions, before 1967. I started reading up on nonfiction horror stories about those places, based on medical journals, and my eyes were opened. The first person I need to mention here is the late Canadian psychiatrist Dr. Mary V. Seeman. I ran across a couple of her published pieces a while back while looking for information about changes in psychiatry over the years. Initially, I was intrigued by her 1969 review of an article entitled "Recollections of a Patient at TPH: Snakepit" by Dr. Peter Keefe, University of Toronto, and when I reached out to him, he was surprised (but pleased) to learn of it! I wrote to Dr. Seeman after that, wondering if I could use her articles as a base for writing about Marion's studies, and she happily agreed. As professor emerita of the Department of Psychiatry at the University of Toronto, her work deepened the world's understanding of schizophrenia. I was sad to learn recently that she died in April 2024 at the age of eighty-nine.

When I am researching, I can be a bit of a pest, I'm sure. I need to thank the amazing Jackie Edwards, archivist at the Centre for Addictions and Mental Health (CAMH), who not only answered every question I sent—from how many patients did each doctor treat to how PTSD was regarded in 1969, and lots more—she sent me maps and diagrams and charts and books without hesitation, and she was always quick and friendly when I sent yet another email. I appreciate your patience and your generosity so much, Jackie!

In June 2024, I spent a week or so in Toronto, and I decided to go see 105 Isabella Street in real life. In the main office, I asked to speak with someone about the history of the building. Not thirty seconds later, I was approached by a fascinating tenant of the building named Phil Parsons, "an out and proud resident of the Church and Wellesley neighbourhood for over thirty years," currently retired from the Canadian House of Commons, where he was assistant to two former federal ministers and one member of Parliament. When I told him what I was looking for, Phil generously gave me more than two informative hours of his time, including a walking tour of 105 Isabella, the surrounding buildings, and the Village, as well as facts about the area's history and future. My meeting with him sparked the story I am presently working on for spring of 2026.

Wanting to understand housing post-deinstitutionalization as well as post–Vietnam War, I spoke with a very interesting man named Victor Willis, executive director of PARC (Parkdale Activity-Recreation Centre), "a community where people rebuild their lives." From him I learned about early rooming houses, the lack of rules and regs that destroyed many lives, and more. His information helped make "Marion's Welcome Home" a realistic possibility.

Now I want to thank someone I regard as a true hero: Dr. Garry L. Willard, the real-life Canadian combat surgeon upon whose story I based Marion's adventures in Vietnam. After graduating from Queen's University, Garry and his classmate Ken (Brad) Bradley shipped to Saigon then Da Nang as VPVNs (Volunteer Physicians to Viet Nam), connected with the U.S. Marines. In his incredible book, *Into the Dragon's Jaws*, he talks about everything he experienced in the middle of such a horrific war, and we learn about some of the unsung Canadian heroes who deserve to be recognized. Garry and I had a terrific phone call as well as a bunch of emails back and forth, and he agreed to read my Vietnam sections of my book to make sure I hadn't messed anything up. Then he mailed me a hardcover copy of his massive book, and it's incredible! I'd only ever seen it as an e-book. Thank you, Garry! This will get a place of honour on my shelves!

One of the most fun parts of my job is speaking with experts in their own fields, passionate about getting the facts straight. Thank you to Robert Lubinski, archivist at the Halton County Radial Railway, who helped me navigate the changing transportation system in Toronto at the time. The detail he gave me was incredible! And what about all that candy Sassy was munching on? Ann Brogley, a member of the Cracker Jack Collectors Association (CJCA), helped me find out about the surprises inside Cracker Jack boxes. Remember those? She also told me that her husband was a marine in the Vietnam War, and I would like to acknowledge him here.

She will be surprised, I think, to see this note, but thank you to my lifelong friend Cori Ashley—who was born twelve hours before I was, making her half a day wiser. When I was working on details about Toronto in the 1960s, Cori told me about her friend Roshelle, whose parents, Jack and Esther Weisbroad, owned Jack's Variety Store, which was located on Yonge Street, south of Isabella Street. During the Second World War, Jack had laboured in a Siberian camp, where he wore his boots continuously for eight months because it was so cold. Esther was imprisoned in Poland and bore the hateful Nazi tattoo on her arm until she died at almost one hundred years of age. Incredibly, Jack made it to 103.

As an added thank you to Cori for so much she's given me in my life, I included her parents' quirky, welcoming restaurant, the Peasant's Larder, which was in Cabbagetown. I remember going there one night with my dad before a Maple Leaf game. When Cori's dad told us he was making the world's hottest hot sauce on a dare that night, I had to have a teeny taste—and I couldn't feel my mouth for the next two hours. Cori is an internationally acclaimed composer and producer, and she recently founded the empowering and hugely successful "Super Me!" Program (www.super meprograms.com). Look her up!

Ten years ago (2015), Simon & Schuster Canada published my first book with them: *Tides of Honour*, and they have never given me less than their best. The company's cast of characters may change from time to time, but they are always so generous with me, and more like family than colleagues. I'm excited to be working with S&S Canada's new and celebrated president, Nicole Winstanley, and I cannot wait to meet her in person next time I am in Toronto. I miss my dear friend and brilliant former editor, Sarah St. Pierre, but I adore my new editor, Adrienne Kerr (senior editor). She and I make a great team—wait until you see what we have in store for you next! And wow, just WOW to cover designer extraordinaire Jessica Boudreau, who keeps hitting it out of the park for me.

Nothing happens with books without the support of booksellers everywhere, and getting my books onto their shelves is the job of the sales team, including Shara Alexa (director of sales, National Accounts) who I finally got to meet on my last visit. And how do you hear about the books (besides my shameless promoting)? Well, I'm not sure anyone in publishing works harder than the resourceful people in marketing and PR. My #1 for years has been Mackenzie Croft (associate marketer and incredible friend) and Alyssa Boyden (publicist and the most patient driver I've ever met when faced with Toronto traffic). Oh, and a personal thank you to Hunter Sleeth (friendliest admin ever) for spoiling me with so many books!

I love visiting booksellers. Last year I was flabbergasted to be featured as Indigo's Author of the Month for May, and then I had the best time travelling from independent bookstore to independent bookstore, having a blast with the book-loving folks at Analog (Lethbridge), Owls Nest (Calgary), Café Books (Canmore), Daisy Chain and Audrey's (Edmonton), Blue Heron (Uxbridge), the Alice Munro Festival in Clinton . . . and libraries! The world's gift to readers! I spoke to wonderful crowds in Grimsby, Cambridge, Kitchener, and more. I cannot wait to hear what they think of *On Isabella Street* because I want to go visit again!

Back in 2010, I met the very first literary agent to show any interest in my writing, Mr. Jacques de Spoelberch. Through his experience and expertise, he helped me navigate this wild and crazy publishing world for over a decade. I am forever grateful for his guidance. Last fall, I made an exciting change in my career by becoming a client of the Transatlantic Literary Agency and starting out fresh with my new and fabulous agent, Carolyn Forde. I've been writing hard for a few years now, and it's easy to slow down when you *ahem* reach a certain age, but Carolyn has lit a fire under me, and now I have so many ideas it's hard to contain them all. So keep tuned for lots more!

My readers: ah, I love and value you so much! My favourite line after someone reads one of my books is always "I never knew about that!," and I am keen to bring you more and more of those moments. Thank you for all your support, with buying and recommending my books, coming to see me at events . . . I am so grateful for your enthusiasm!

Everyone who knows me, knows my family is my world and my biggest support. I couldn't do what I do without their encouragement. My other half, Dwayne, helps me navigate plots, then he reads my completed books out loud to me every time they publish—and despite knowing everything about the story, we both still cry at the endings. He has always believed in me and in my dreams, and I never would have done any of this without his support. So, after you finish reading one of my books, please make sure to close the cover then say a quiet "Thanks, Dwayne" before you tuck it into your shelves.